QUINCAS BORBA

QUINCAS BORBA

A Novel by
JOAQUIM MARIA MACHADO DE ASSIS

Translated from the Portuguese by
GREGORY RABASSA

WITH AN INTRODUCTION BY DAVID T. HABERLY

AND AN AFTERWORD BY CELSO FAVARETTO

Oxford University Press
New York   Oxford

Oxford University Press

Oxford   New York
Athens   Auckland   Bangkok   Bogotá   Buenos Aires   Calcutta
Cape Town   Chennai   Dar es Salaam   Delhi   Florence   Hong Kong   Istanbul
Karachi   Kuala Lumpur   Madrid   Melbourne   Mexico City   Mumbai
Nairobi   Paris   São Paulo   Singapore   Taipei   Tokyo   Toronto   Warsaw
and associated companies in
Berlin   Ibadan

Copyright © 1998 by Oxford University Press

First published by Oxford University Press, Inc., 1998

First issued as an Oxford University Press paperback, 1999

Oxford is a registered trademark of Oxford University Press

Library of Congress Cataloging-in-Publication Data
[Quincas Borba. English]
Quincas Borba / a novel by Joaquim Maria Machado de Assis :
translated by Gregory Rabassa : with an introduction by David T.
Haberly : and an afterword by Celso Favaretto.
p.   cm. — (Library of Latin America)
Includes bibliographical references.
ISBN 0-19-510681-4
ISBN 0-19-510682-2 (Pbk.)
I. Rabassa, Gregory.   II. Title.   III. Series.
PQ9697.M18Q513   1998
869.3—dc21   97-27706

1 3 5 7 9 10 8 6 4 2

Printed in the United States of America

Contents

Series Editors'
General Introduction

The Library of Latin America series makes available in translation major nineteenth-century authors whose work has been neglected in the English-speaking world. The titles for the translations from the Spanish and Portuguese were suggested by an editorial committee that included Jean Franco (general editor responsible for works in Spanish), Richard Graham (series editor responsible for works in Portuguese), Tulio Halperín Donghi (at the University of California, Berkeley), Iván Jaksic (at the University of Notre Dame), Naomi Lindstrom (at the University of Texas at Austin), Francine Masiello (at the University of California, Berkeley), and Eduardo Lozano of the Library at the University of Pittsburgh. The late Antonio Cornejo Polar of the University of California, Berkeley, was also one of the founding members of the committee. The translations have been funded thanks to the generosity of the Lampadia Foundation and the Andrew W. Mellon Foundation.

During the period of national formation between 1810 and into the early years of the twentieth century, the new nations of Latin America fashioned their identities, drew up constitutions, engaged in bitter struggles over territory, and debated questions of education, government, ethnicity, and culture. This was a unique period unlike the process of nation formation in Europe and one which should be more familiar than it is to students of comparative politics, history, and literature.

The image of the nation was envisioned by the lettered classes—a minority in countries in which indigenous, mestizo, black, or mulatto peasants and slaves predominated—although there were also alternative nationalisms at the grassroots level. The cultural elite were well educated in European thought and letters, but as statesmen, journalists, poets, and academics, they confronted the problem of the racial and linguistic heterogeneity of the continent and the difficulties of integrating the population into a modern nation-state. Some of the writers whose works will be translated in the Library of Latin America series played leading roles in politics. Fray Servando Teresa de Mier, a friar who translated Rousseau's *The Social Contract* and was one of the most colorful characters of the independence period, was faced with imprisonment and expulsion from Mexico for his heterodox beliefs; on his return, after independence, he was elected to the congress. Domingo Faustino Sarmiento, exiled from his native Argentina under the presidency of Rosas, wrote *Facundo: Civilización y barbarie*, a stinging denunciation of that government. He returned after Rosas' overthrow and was elected president in 1868. Andrés Bello was born in Venezuela, lived in London where he published poetry during the independence period, settled in Chile where he founded the University, wrote his grammar of the Spanish language, and drew up the country's legal code.

These post-independence intelligentsia were not simply dreaming castles in the air, but vitally contributed to the founding of nations and the shaping of culture. The advantage of hindsight may make us aware of problems they themselves did not foresee, but this should not affect our assessment of their truly astonishing energies and achievements. It is still surprising that the writing of Andrés Bello, who contributed fundamental works to so many different fields, has never been translated into English. Although there is a recent translation of Sarmiento's celebrated *Facundo*, there is no translation of his memoirs, *Recuerdos de provincia (Provincial Recollections)*. The predominance of memoirs in the Library of Latin America series is no accident—many of these offer entertaining insights into a vast and complex continent. Nor have we neglected the novel. The series includes new translations of the outstanding Brazilian writer Joaquim Maria Machado de Assis' work, including *Dom Casmurro* and *The Posthumous Memoirs of Brás Cubas*. There is no reason why other novels and writers who are not so well known outside Latin America—the Peruvian novelist Clorinda Matto de Turner's *Aves sin nido*, Nataniel Aguirre's *Juan de la Rosa*, José de Alencar's *Iracema*, Juana Manuela Gorriti's short stories—should not be read with as much interest as the political novels of Anthony Trollope.

A series on nineteenth-century Latin America cannot, however, be limited to literary genres such as the novel, the poem, and the short story. The literature of independent Latin America was eclectic and strongly influenced by the periodical press newly liberated from scrutiny by colonial authorities and the Inquisition. Newspapers were miscellanies of fiction, essays, poems, and translations from all manner of European writing. The novels written on the eve of Mexican Independence by José Joaquín Fernández de Lizardi included disquisitions on secular education and law, and denunciations of the evils of gaming and idleness. Other works, such as a well-known poem by Andrés Bello, "Ode to Tropical Agriculture," and novels such as *Amalia* by José Mármol and the Bolivian Nataniel Aguirre's *Juan de la Rosa*, were openly partisan. By the end of the century, sophisticated scholars were beginning to address the history of their countries, as did João Capistrano de Abreu in his *Capítulos de história colonial*.

It is often in memoirs such as those by Fray Servando Teresa de Mier or Sarmiento that we find the descriptions of everyday life that in Europe were incorporated into the realist novel. Latin American literature at this time was seen largely as a pedagogical tool, a "light" alternative to speeches, sermons, and philosophical tracts—though, in fact, especially in the early part of the century, even the readership for novels was quite small because of the high rate of illiteracy. Nevertheless, the vigorous orally transmitted culture of the gaucho and the urban underclasses became the linguistic repertoire of some of the most interesting nineteenth-century writers—most notably José Hernández, author of the "gauchesque" poem "Martín Fierro," which enjoyed an unparalleled popularity. But for many writers the task was not to appropriate popular language but to civilize, and their literary works were strongly influenced by the high style of political oratory.

The editorial committee has not attempted to limit its selection to the better-known writers such as Machado de Assis; it has also selected many works that have never appeared in translation or writers whose work has not been translated recently. The series now makes these works available to the English-speaking public.

Because of the preferences of funding organizations, the series initially focuses on writing from Brazil, the Southern Cone, the Andean region, and Mexico. Each of our editions will have an introduction that places the work in its appropriate context and includes explanatory notes.

We owe special thanks to Robert Glynn of the Lampadia Foundation, whose initiative gave the project a jump start, and to Richard Ekman of the Andrew W. Mellon Foundation, which also generously supported the project. We also thank the Rockefeller Foundation for funding the 1996 symposium "Culture and Nation in Iberoamerica," organized by the editorial board of the Library of Latin America. We received substantial institutional support and personal encouragement from the Institute of Latin American Studies of the University of Texas at Austin. The support of Edward Barry of Oxford University Press has been crucial, as has the advice and help of Ellen Chodosh of Oxford University Press. The first volumes of the series were published after the untimely death, on July 3, 1997, of Maria C. Bulle, who, as an associate of the Lampadia Foundation, supported the idea from its beginning.

—*Jean Franco*
—*Richard Graham*

Introduction

Joaquim Maria de Machado de Assis (1839–1908) is the greatest nineteenth-century novelist of Latin America and one of the most remarkable literary talents to appear in the Americas as a whole. His most important fictions are complex and highly original texts that were carefully and deviously designed to be open to multiple interpretation. As Antônio Cândido noted in 1970, Machado's major texts are so rich in potential meanings that successive generations of critics have found in these works "their own obsessions, their own ideas of what must be expressed."[1]

Machado's major novels, including *Quincas Borba* (1891), often strike English-speaking readers as at once comfortably familiar and disquietingly alien. We recognize the narrative voice, discursive, descriptive, and often intrusive, as one we have encountered in British and French novels of the eighteenth and nineteenth centuries. Machado, despite his relative isolation in a nation on the fringes of nineteenth-century Western culture, immersed himself in the European fictional tradition; Laurence Sterne was Machado's favorite novelist and one of his primary models, but echoes of a great many other novelists can be found everywhere in his texts. In the case of *Quincas Borba*, for example,

Sofia owes a great deal to Emma Bovary. Because we are familiar with at least some of the European novels Machado relied upon to create his own fictions, we recognize both some of his basic plot elements—the quest for a socially suitable spouse and even, perhaps, a happy marriage; the struggle to move upwards in society or, at the very least, to hold on to status and respectability. Moreover, Machado's characters play out their dramas surrounded by carefully described artifacts, almost all imported from Europe. Beyond this, Machado's various narrators constantly refer to both major and minor figures from the whole sweep of European cultural history, reflecting the profound and remarkable knowledge of Classical and Renaissance literature of a self-educated Brazilian who never traveled more than a few hundred miles from Rio de Janeiro.

At the same time, there are many elements in Machado's texts that fall considerably outside both the European cultural tradition and our own experiences and expectations as readers of eighteenth- and nineteenth-century European fiction. To suggest but a few examples, the stars Machado's characters contemplate, in moments of passion or despair, are the constellations of the Southern Hemisphere. In *Quincas Borba*, Sofia tends her roses—but outside the walls of her garden lies Brazilian nature in all its lush exoticism, a nature that has survived intact, in at least a few areas of the city, despite the nineteenth-century urbanization of Rio de Janeiro. Machado's novels deal at some length with the politics and personalities of the Brazilian Empire, an Empire about which most English-speaking readers know very little. And while Cristiano Palha assures Rubião, in the first chapters of *Quincas Borba*, that Rio de Janeiro is fast becoming a South American Paris or London, it is impossible to read this novel without realizing that imperial Brazilian society, despite its architectural imitations and imported European artifacts, was very different indeed from that of nineteenth-century France or England. Many of the most striking differences do not appear overtly in the text, largely because Machado and his readers took them so much for granted; those differences—the oppressive heat, the tropical diseases, the filth and squalor of much of the city, the omnipresent poverty, the African origins of the great majority of Rio's population—can better be seen in contemporary photographs and in the narratives and drawings of European and North American visitors. But one absolutely essential difference does appear in *Quincas Borba*, and is here described more openly and in greater detail than in any of Machado's other novels: while Rubião takes Cristiano Palha's advice and hires European servants, hidden behind the kitchen door is Rubião's black slave—symbolic of the hundreds of thousands of black slaves who served imperial Brazil until the abolition of slavery in 1888.

The alien quality of Machado's fiction, however, extends beyond these differences in setting and social context into the nature of the text itself, as the novelist alters or ignores the ground rules of nineteenth-century European Realism. The stars are not simply a different set of heavenly bodies; they look back down at Machado's characters and, sometimes, comment upon those characters. The European roses in Sofia's garden converse with each other, discussing her character and actions. A major character in *Quincas Borba* is a dog of the same name, who may or may not be the reincarnation of a philosopher named Quincas Borba. The erudite narrator of the novel occasionally inverts or even perverts his references to the European classics, transforming them in bizarre ways; for example, a quote from *Hamlet* ("There are more things on heaven and Earth, Horatio, than are dreamt of in your philosophy") appears in several whimsical and almost incomprehensible variations. The voice of that narrator, moreover, is often extreme, referring to the novel's characters—and to us, his readers—with sarcasm and patronizing condescension. A good many of the very brief chapters into which the narrator's text is divided do not appear to be directly related to the action; the narrator uses some of those chapters to reflect at some length upon the nature of his text, upon his defects as a narrator and our defects as readers, upon the problems inherent in any attempt to portray reality. Above all, careful readers of *Quincas Borba* come to realize that the novel's third-person omniscient narrator is, like all of the narrators of Machado's greatest novels, utterly unreliable.

Readers wishing to approach *Quincas Borba* entirely on its own terms, fully experiencing the text within the context of their own reactions—and, quoting Antônio Cândido again, "their own obsessions"—should stop here and go directly to Machado's novel; Celso Favaretto's Afterword and the rest of this Foreword can be read later. Those, on the other hand, who wish to first find out a bit more about the novel's social and historical context, about its structure, and about a few possible interpretations of the text should read on—but should also be aware that any discussion of the novel necessarily gives away large chunks of the plot and that, further, in Machado's fictional universe any attempt to construct a single interpretation of any phenomenon is *prima facie* evidence of mental instability.

*   *   *

QUINCAS BORBA WAS SERIALIZED in a women's magazine, *A Estação*, between 1886 and 1891, but was considerably revised before its final publication in 1891.[2] We can only guess at what contemporary Brazilian readers made of the text, for one of the curiosities of Machado's career is that his major novels, which sold very well and established his reputation as Brazil's greatest writer, were almost never reviewed. Two phrases in one review of *Quincas Borba*, by Tristão de Alencar Araripe Júnior, nonetheless suggest that at least a few of Machado's readers did read the novel in ways not dissimilar from modern interpretations of the text. Araripe Júnior, first, posed a basic question about Rubião, the novel's central figure: "Can anyone say," he asked, "that this character is not Brazil?" Secondly, Araripe Júnior described Rubião as "the stalking-horse for the rage of a philosopher hiding in the bushes."[3]

Let us turn first to the idea, suggested by Araripe's rhetorical question, of *Quincas Borba* as allegory. A modern critic, John Gledson, has argued that Rubião is an allegorical representation of Pedro II, ruler of Brazil from 1831 to 1889.[4] There is certainly considerable evidence within the text to support this view. For example, Rubião's full name, Pedro Rubião de Alvarenga, is very close to the Emperor's given name, Pedro de Alcântara. Rubião first meets the Palhas on the Pedro Segundo Railway, and his later fantasies that he is Napoleon III of France draw heavily upon real or imagined details of life in the Brazilian Court and can be read as a carefully oblique attack on Pedro II's pretensions to imperial status.

I would argue, however, that Machado's allegory extends beyond the person of the Emperor to include the Empire itself. Machado interrupted the serialization of *Quincas Borba* several times, most significantly between July and November of 1889; the Empire fell on November 15 of that year. Machado appears to have realized that Pedro II's rule was coming to an end and used these interruptions to make substantive changes in the text, changes that refocused the novel ever more closely on the Empire and allowed him to express, in carefully ambiguous ways, his central perception of that Empire: it was a shared national illusion, a vast and complex fictionalization of reality. I would argue, in addition, that Machado came to this view of the Empire as a fiction in the late 1870s and that this perception fundamentally shaped the great novels he produced after 1879.

Machado, of course, was fundamentally right about the Empire. It was in many ways a fiction held together by its central character, Pedro II; the Emperor—a highly intelligent and learned man who impressed and charmed all those he met on his frequent trips abroad—was the "mysterious Prospero" who transformed Brazil into "a sublime masquerade" (*Quincas Borba*, Chapter LXXXII). The Empire's title, chosen to emphasize the country's physical size, was part of this masquerade, suggesting that Brazil's rulers were more important than European kings and queens. Brazil was governed, in theory, by a parliamentary democracy modeled on that of Victorian England; as Machado's description of Brazilian politics in *Quincas Borba* suggests, however, personal and regional alliances were far more important than ideology, and the elections—in which only a minuscule percentage of the population was eligible to participate—were overwhelmingly fraudulent.

This sense of the fictive nature of the Empire liberated Machado the novelist. His earlier fictional texts provide clear evidence of his struggle to deal with the novel as a genre and with the larger question of what he called "ideas out of place," that is, ideas Brazilians imported from Europe but which had absolutely nothing to do with Brazil's reality. Deeply embedded within the plot structures of most of the nineteenth-century European novels he had read were social patterns—true love leading to marriage, upward mobility, the rise of the middle classes, for example—that were utterly alien to a society in which virtually all upper-class marriages were arranged and characterized by its rigidly immobile and hierarchical structure, without anything approaching a European bourgeoisie. After 1879, therefore, Machado stopped trying to be realistic in his plots and descriptions; he recognized that he was describing an apparent reality that was itself fundamentally fictional. Courtship and marriage were reduced to subplots acted out by relatively minor characters, and the central focus of his three greatest novels, including *Quincas Borba*, became adultery—symbolic, perhaps, of a society unfaithful to its own reality. These accounts of real or potential infidelity are presented by unreliable (that is, unfaithful) first-person and third-person narrators who refer repeatedly to the difficulties of textualizing reality and even question, in one way or another, the very existence of an objective reality.

All of these elements can be found in *Quincas Borba*, particularly in the sections which deal with Rubião's increasing inability to separate reality and fantasy and his consequent descent into madness. One of the first indications that fantasy is replacing reality—in Rubião's mind as in Machado's vision of the Empire—comes in Chapter LXXXI. Planning his wedding (although he does not yet, of course, have a bride), Rubião recalls the Emperor's magnificent coach and the lesser but still splendid vehicles that followed that coach in royal processions; he would be happy to settle for one of the latter as his wedding coach, but the setting becomes increasingly imperial as he envisions the rest of the ceremony and the reception. This wedding fantasy is linked, by the Emperor's carriage, to Rubião's dream in Chapter CIX, the formal beginning of his vision of himself as Napoleon III. From that point on, Rubião's fantasies become ever more specific and more destructive. At the same time, Machado carefully sets up a series of interlocking emblems of imperial pretension. The mad Rubião believes that he is Napoleon III, ruler of France's Second Empire (1852–1870). Louis Napoleon, Napoleon I's nephew, called himself Napoleon III, but he was surely a second-rate imitation of his glorious uncle, a real Emperor. The last link in this chain, implicitly, is Pedro II, ruler of a fictive Second Empire in the Americas.

Rubião's circular journey, like the text itself, begins and ends in the town of Barbacena, in the province of Minas Gerais. Despite his desperate efforts to adapt to life in Rio de Janeiro and his consequent madness, Rubião's ultimate loyalty is to the real Brazil of the interior. Machado, however, chose Barbacena for specific and important reasons. In Chapter LXXXII, Rubião's wedding dreams lead him to fantasies of titled nobility, and he selects a title for himself: the Marquis of Barbacena. However, another nobleman associated with Barbacena already existed in Brazilian history—the Viscount of Barbacena, colonial governor of the Province of Minas Gerais who, in 1789, smashed the potential conspiracy against Portuguese rule that is known as the "Inconfidência Mineira." The accused leader of the conspiracy, the shadowy figure known as Tiradentes, was hanged and quartered in Rio in 1792. The official historiography of the Empire attributed Brazilian independence in 1822 entirely to the Portuguese royal family, but a popular mythology developed around the Inconfidência and around Tiradentes. When Rubião returns to Barbacena, he wanders endlessly up and down Tiradentes Street, symbolically searching both for his own past and for the nation's true history. Machado suggests, finally, that the crown of imperial Brazil, like the crown Rubião so carefully and lovingly places on his head at the end of the novel, is not real; it is not even a literary allusion (in this case, to the barber's basin Don Quixote fantasizes as Mambrino's helmet). Rather, the essence of the Empire—the world in which Machado spent most of his life—is its absolute, irreducible nothingness.

The bitter intensity of this symbolic negation of the Empire leads us back to Araripe Júnior's other perception about *Quincas*

Borba: his description of Rubião as "the stalking-horse for the rage of a philosopher hiding in the bushes." Rage is, clearly, not too strong a term for Machado's attitude toward the Empire. It is more difficult to ascertain the source of this virulent hostility. After all, Machado's is one of the real success stories of imperial Brazil; his books sold well, a high-ranking government job provided financial security, and the Emperor rewarded him with membership in the elite Order of the Rose. Nonetheless, one very plausible explanation of the novelist's rage can be found in Chapters XLIII through XLVIII, one of the defining moments of *Quincas Borba*.

Rubião has just left a party at the Palhas' house after quite violently declaring his love for Sofia, the wife of his host; this declaration is, in fact, the only forceful and fully conscious action Rubião ever takes. Other guests, Major Siqueira and his spinster daughter, Dona Tonica, do not witness the declaration, but they clearly understand what has taken place. Tonica goes home, bitter that one more potential suitor has fallen in love with another woman, and fantasizes about attacking Sofia—strangling her, ripping out her heart. Tonica represses this violence and turns to tears, but the narrator tells us that, just for an instant, "a tiny thread of Caligula," the monstrous Roman emperor, ran through her soul.

At the same time, Rubião walks down the hill to the center of town, debating what to do next: Should he be loyal to his friend Palha, or should he continue to pursue Sofia? Several horse-drawn cabs are waiting for passengers, and Rubião finds it hard to choose among them—an indecision that reflects his internal debate about his relationship with the Palhas. As the drivers call out to Rubião, Chapter XLVI restates one of Machado's convictions: powers greater than ourselves, if they in fact exist, care nothing about our existence and our actions and can provide neither help nor guidance.

As Chapter XLVII begins, Rubião does not consciously choose a cab; he simply gets into the closest one. As he tries to avoid thinking about the choice he must make regarding Sofia, he suddenly remembers an incident from his youth. During a previous visit to Rio de Janeiro many years before, he came across a mob watching the execution of a black slave. While such scenes were commonplace in Rio in the nineteenth century, this is virtually the only description of a slave execution in Brazilian literature of the period; it is shocking today, but must have absolutely appalled Machado's readers in its unexpected revelation of the darkest side of the nation's life.

Rubião had been alternately attracted and repulsed by the spectacle of the slave execution; he tried to leave, but his feet could not decide in which direction to move. The narrator overtly links Rubião's past indecision to his uncertainty about which cab to pick and which path to choose with Sofia, and compares Rubião—the friend and disciple of Quincas Borba, a mad philosopher who declared himself the reincarnation of Saint Augustine—to Saint Alypius, Augustine's closest friend and disciple; Alypius's weakness, as Augustine describes it in the *Confessions,* was his love of bloody spectacles.[5] Rubião stayed to watch the execution, but then fainted; he appears to lose consciousness in the present as well, suddenly awakened from his memories by the cab driver, who loudly praises his horse and insists that horses—and dogs—are almost human. This observation leads Rubião to embrace the possibility of the transmigration of souls: the soul of the philosopher Quincas Borba may now reside in the body of Quincas Borba the dog. Rubião is so obsessed with this possibility that he forgets to tell the cab driver where he lives.

These chapters reveal a great deal about Machado's view of the world in which he lived; that view, inevitably, was conditioned by the rage he must have felt, as a descendent of African slaves on his father's side, at the continuation and omnipresence of slavery in Brazil. The impulse to violence, first, exists in even the meekest and gentlest humans; moral societies restrain that violence and channel it into acceptable outlets. Imperial Brazil, however, like Caligula's Roman Empire of bloodthirsty circus entertainments, is founded upon the violence of slavery and depends upon that violence for its very existence. The fundamental immorality of Brazilian society, moreover, forces even its most decent citizens to confront painful and morally destructive choices. Educated Brazilians found themselves secretly embarrassed and offended by slavery but unprepared to accept the social and economic consequences of its abolition.

The political system of the Empire that Machado describes and satirizes throughout this novel could not offer a solution, primarily because Pedro II was unable to resolve the dilemma in his own mind, at least until the late 1880s. Pedro II, whose illustrious foreign friends implored him to abolish slavery, declared that he was personally opposed to the institution; at the same time, however, he was afraid that to end it would destroy both Brazil's economy and his family's rule. The first small step towards abolition, the timid and tentative "Law of the Free Womb," freeing newborn slaves once they reached the age of twenty-one, was enacted in 1871—the year in which much of the action of *Quincas Borba* takes place. As he wrote the novel in the 1880s, Machado was very much aware that the 1871 law had failed to accomplish even its minimal, temporizing aims.[6] The nation's inability to confront and resolve the issue had ensured the survival of the institution for another seventeen years and had revealed fundamental flaws in the Empire itself. The bifurcation and consequent inertia Rubião experienced at the slave execution parallel his inability, in the novel's present, to choose between morality and his desire for Sofia; this bifurcation will slowly deepen into schizophrenia and lead inevitably to Rubião's destruction. In the same way, the fall of the Empire—its glory reduced to the nothingness of a nonexistent crown—can be traced back to the divisive and destructive issue of slavery, an issue that made painfully clear the abyss between image and reality that was, for Machado, the essence of imperial Brazil.

Araripe Júnior's reading of *Quincas Borba* not only perceived Machado's rage, but also described the novelist as "a philosopher hiding in the bushes," that is, a philosopher who is not prepared to express his ideas openly and whose text is at least potentially a trap for the unwary. This seems, at first glance, a strange characterization; the third-person narrator of *Quincas Borba* talks openly, repeatedly, and at considerable length about philosophy.

Furthermore, that narrator tells us that he is the creator of the *Posthumous Memoirs of Brás Cubas*, Machado's 1881 novel in which the character of Quincas Borba the philosopher first appeared. We quite naturally presume, therefore, that the narrator and Machado de Assis are one and the same. We also presume, on the basis of our experience with various forms of narration, that an omniscient third-person narrator is a reliable guide to the characters and events described in the text.

The narrator, however, is not Machado de Assis but one of the novelist's fictional creations. The charm and self-assurance of this chatty, irreverent, and sophisticated man-about-town both propel the narrative and guarantee its validity. The discourse and social attitudes of the narrator are very much those of the imperial elite; the philosophy the narrator expounds, while clearly a pastiche, nonetheless represents much of educated Brazilian thinking in the late nineteenth century, particularly in its justification of social and economic privilege.

Quincas Borba the philosopher first propounded the theory of Humanitism in Machado's *Posthumous Memoirs of Brás Cubas*, but gives his friend and disciple Rubião a more detailed explanation in the first chapters of *Quincas Borba*. The narrator later restates the theory through a parable of his own, the story of the poor woman's hut and the rich man's cigar (Chapter CXVII), and clearly implies that his entire narrative demonstrates the validity of Quincas Borba's vision. Humanitism is an exaggerated fusion of Auguste Comte's Positivism—with its belief in the inevitability of progress and the goodness of all things—and the application of theories of natural selection to the study of human society that is generally referred to as Social Darwinism. As the narrator constructs his text, we as readers are supposed to see Humanitism validated by the success of the winners (Palha and Carlos Maria in particular) and the failure of the losers (Major Siqueira, Dona Tonica, and, of course, Rubião, the most unfit character of all). Like Rubião, we are supposed to realize, by the last chapters of the text, that the winners do indeed get—and richly deserve—the potatoes. The Positivist component of Humanitism, moreover, preaches that Rubião's destruction, like the death of Quincas Borba's grandmother, is natural and inevitable and that we are not supposed to feel either pity or sorrow at the outcome of the text.

Machado clearly did not accept the imported philosophies upon which Humanitism is based, but he chose to satirize their ideas rather than attack them directly. Machado, however, went beyond pastiche, using the structure of his text to demolish these rationalizations of injustice. The key here is the character of Machado's narrator, since the validity of the text—and the validity of the philosophy that narrator insists is exemplified in his narrative—depend upon our willingness to believe him.

The narrator, first, while enormously self-confident, is also extremely self-conscious about his enterprise. He addresses us directly, eager for our full attention and understanding, and frequently comments—both directly and through what can best be described as authorly parables—on the act of writing. He discusses his own text and his decision to use numbers rather than long titles for his chapters (CXII–CXIV); he contemplates the difference between events and written descriptions of those events in Camacho's account of Rubião's rescue of Deolindo (LXVII); he satirizes the editors and typographers upon whom writers, alas, depend (Chapters CXI and CXIX).

Beyond this, the narrator constantly warns us, in an increasingly patronizing way, about the dangers of misreading; these warnings are issued to us directly or through *exempla*, such as Rubião's misreading of the note that accompanies the strawberries. At the same time, the narrator's discourse contains elements that appear to contradict his messages about the importance of accuracy and clarity. He does not seem able, for example, to decide who we are and how he will treat us; he addresses us as female and as male, as singular and as plural, with both grammatical formality and familiarity. His discourse jumps from detailed descriptions to self-indulgent flights of fancy, from seriousness to sarcasm. Some of his explanations of character and of events seem entirely reasonable; others strike us as odd and incomplete.

The narrator's full betrayal of our trust occurs in the section that begins with Chapter LXIX and runs until Chapter CVI. We have already been presented with one possible adulterous relationship, that between the central female character in the text, Sofia, and Rubião. We believe, on the basis of what appears to be reasonable evidence, that Sofia is at least potentially unfaithful to her husband, but we have come to realize—if Rubião has not—that the affair is not going to take place. In this new section, the presumably omniscient narrator carefully and persuasively presents us with bits and pieces of quite plausible evidence which lead both us and Rubião to conclude that an adulterous relationship between Sofia and Carlos Maria has very probably been consummated. In Chapter CVI, however, the narrator condescendingly describes the reader as "disoriented" and a "wretch," responsible, along with Rubião, for slandering two upstanding characters. Rubião believed because he misread and misinterpreted the unopened circular and the coachman's tale; we are also dismissed as bad readers, since the narrator declares that the truth would have been evident, "had you read slowly." The narrator, who has dealt a stacked deck to Rubião and to us, then gloatingly points out just how cleverly and effectively he misled us.[7]

As we come to realize that only one act of infidelity occurs in the text—the narrator's betrayal of our trust—we cease to believe in the narrator *and* in the philosophy he is propounding. The narrator goes on to accuse us of being the sort of readers who need detailed chapter titles so that we can understand what is happening, or who claim to have read the text when we have only skimmed the titles (Chapter CXIII). Furthermore, the narrator increasingly ignores Rubião, with whom we have come to identify. We catch only an occasional glimpse of Rubião as he spirals downward to insanity and penury; the narrator, like Rubião's faithless friends in Rio de Janeiro, is eager to move on to other, more interesting topics. Our frustration turns to shock in the final chapters of the novel; nothing in the text, we feel, has prepared us for the unexpected and miserable deaths of Rubião and Quincas Borba the dog—deaths to which the narrator insultingly suggests we may react with laughter.

Araripe Júnior was correct, then, in his perception that Machado was manipulating us, as readers, through his text; he was also correct in implying that Machado had his own philosophy—a philosophy very different from Humanitism. That philosophy, moreover, while expressed through the text of *Quincas Borba*, transcends the particular—the details of nineteenth-century Brazilian life and society upon which this introduction has necessarily focused. Rubião, despite some positive qualities and the affection Machado leads us to feel for him, is very much an antihero; *Quincas Borba* can usefully be read as an antinovel through which Machado sought to express a skepticism so absolute and universal that it approaches an antiphilosophy.

Unlike Quincas Borba the philosopher, Machado did not reject the existence of evil in the world; unlike Saint Augustine, the emblem of Quincas Borba's final insanity, Machado did not believe that any external force—other than the pitiless and unknowable operations of blind chance—controls our lives for good or evil. As suggested by the constantly shifting quote from *Hamlet*, for Machado all of reality lies beyond human philosophizing. Machado's friend José Veríssimo described him, in a 1908 eulogy, as a Pyrrhonian—a believer in an extreme form of philosophical skepticism which holds that the truth is utterly unknowable and that for every possible theory of existence one can find an equally plausible but antithetical theory.[8] The only coherent position is to suspend belief—"When in doubt, abstain," as Teófilo tries to put it in Chapter CXIX.

Any approach to reality other than pure skepticism is, for Machado, a denial of that reality and, implicitly, a form of insanity. Quincas Borba's Humanitism, beyond its justification of the social order, represents a failed attempt to deny the ultimate reality of human existence, the inevitability of death; as the doctor points out to Rubião in Chapter IV, "philosophy is one thing and dying is another." Machado's skepticism, however, extends beyond philosophical explanations of reality. Any belief around which an individual organizes his or her life can easily become a destructive obsession—Camacho's politics, Palha's capitalism,

Sofia's longing to be adored are just a few examples. And while Rubião never quite comprehends Quincas Borba's grand theories, he has his own *philosophia*—here not the love of knowledge, but an obsession with Sofia the woman—that likewise leads to madness and to death.

The most fundamental denial of reality, for Machado, is the belief that an unknowable reality which is based upon blind chance can somehow be ordered and thereby understood. Human consciousness nonetheless seeks order, endeavoring to create structures that are essentially mathematical: time is circular and repetitive, and the events it measures are therefore predictable; events, like numbers, can be sequenced into an order in which the past prepares the future; individuals and circumstances can be described and understood, particularly when they are viewed as replicating or mirroring other individuals and circumstances.

The ultimate example of this human quest for order is the created, knowable reality of the literary text. The singularity of *Quincas Borba* lies in its denial of the validity of the text as a version of reality; we are betrayed by the narrator in large measure because he so carefully sets up doublings that we instinctively want to accept: the real Machado and the narrator of *Quincas Borba*; Quincas Borba and Rubião; Rubião and Napoleon III; Quincas Borba the philosopher and Quincas Borba the dog; the Rubião-Sofia relationship and the Sofia–Carlos Maria relationship.

Through the narrator's betrayal, moreover, Machado betrays our expectations as readers and demands the unexpected of us. He presents us with the "tatters of reality" his narrator has stitched together into an ordered sequence, but the narrator's evident unreliability invalidates that order and forces us to create our own reality from those tatters. A unitary explanation of events, imposed by a narrator or an author, gives way to chaos—a potentially infinite number of possible readers and of possible readings. And, finally, each of those readings may fail to capture an ultimately unknowable reality, since our human vision of our own lives, of the lives of others, of the world in which we live, is vague, fragmentary, and formless—just a bit more complex, perhaps, than "the ideas of a dog, a jumble of ideas" (Chapter XXVIII).

—*David T. Haberly*

NOTES

1. Antônio Cândido, *Vários Escritos* (São Paulo: Duas Cidades, 1970), p. 18.

2. The chronology of the serialized version and the meaning of some of the changes are discussed by John Gledson, *Machado de Assis: Ficção e História* (Rio de Janeiro: Paz e Terra, 1986) and by J. C. Kinnear, "Machado de Assis: To Believe or Not To Believe," *Modern Language Review*, 71 (1976), 54–65.

3. "Idéias e Sandices do Ignaro Rubião," first published on Feb. 5, 1893, in the *Gazeta de Notícias* (Rio de Janeiro); in Araripe's *Obra Crítica*, II (Rio de Janeiro, MEC, 1960), 309.

4. John Gledson, *Machado de Assis: Ficção e História* and *The Deceptive Realism of Machado de Assis* (Liverpool: Francis Cairns, 1984). For more general discussions of Machado's attitude towards the Empire, see Raymundo Faoro, *Machado de Assis: A Pirâmide e o Trapézio* (São Paulo: Editora Nacional, 1976), and Roberto Schwarz, *Ao Vencedor as Batatas* (São Paulo: Duas Cidades, 1977).

5. Agustine's *Confessions*, Book Six, chapters 7–9.

6. For a discussion of Machado and the slavery question, see Gledson, *Deceptive Realism*, pp. 123–30.

7. A more detailed analysis of the narrator's betrayal can be found in Kinnear, "Machado de Assis."

8. José Raimundo Maia Neto traces the influence of this form of skepticism in several of Machado's novels in *Machado de Assis, the Brazilian Pyrrhonian* (West Lafayette, Ind.: Purdue University Press, 1994).

QUINCAS BORBA

Prologue to the Third Edition

The second edition of this work sold out faster than the first. Here it is in the third with no changes except for certain typographical corrections, such as they were, and so few that even if they had been left in they would not have altered the meaning.

An illustrious friend and confrère insisted that I follow this book up with another. "Along with *The Posthumous Memoirs of Brás Cubas*, from which this is derived, you should make a trilogy, and the Sofia from *Quincas Borba* will have the third part all to herself." For some time I thought that it might be possible, but as I reread these pages now I say no. Sofia is here completely. To have continued her would have been repeating her, and that repetition would be a sin. I think this is how some have found fault with this and a few other books that I've gone about putting together, over time, in the silence of my life. There were voices, generous and strong, that defended me then; I've already thanked them in private and now I do so cordially and publicly.

—*Machado de Assis, 1899*

I

Rubião was staring at the cove—it was eight o'clock in the morning. Anyone who'd seen him with his thumbs stuck in the belt of his dressing gown at the window of a mansion in Botafogo would have thought he was admiring that stretch of calm water, but in reality I can tell you he was thinking about something else. He was comparing the past to the present. What was he a year ago? A teacher. What is he now? A capitalist. He looks at himself, at his slippers (slippers from Tunis that his new friend Cristiano Palha had given him), at the house, at the garden, at the cove, at the hills, and at the sky, and everything, from slippers to sky, everything gives off the same feeling of property.

"See how God writes straight with crooked lines," he thinks. "If my sister Piedade had married Quincas Borba it would have left me with only a collateral hope. She didn't marry him. They both died, and here I am with everything, so what looked like misfortune . . ."

W hat a gulf there is between the spirit and the heart! The ex-teacher's spirit, bothered by those thoughts, changed course, looked for a different subject, a canoe passing by. His heart, however, let itself go on beating with joy. What difference did it make if there was a canoe or a canoeist or that Rubião's wide-open eyes followed him? It, the heart, goes along saying that since sister Piedade had to die, it was good that she hadn't married. There might have been a son or a daughter . . . "What a fine canoe!" So much the better! "The way it follows the man's paddle!" What's certain is that they're in heaven!

A servant brought him coffee. Rubião picked up the cup and while he was putting in the sugar he was surreptitiously looking at the tray, which was silver work. Silver, gold, they were the metals he loved with all his heart. He didn't like bronze, but his friend Palha told him that it was valuable and that explained the pair of figures here in the living room, a Mephistopheles and a Faust. If he had to choose, however, he would choose the tray—a masterpiece of silver work, of delicate and perfect execution. The servant was waiting, stiff and serious. He was Spanish, and it had only been after some resistance that Rubião accepted him from the hands of Cristiano, no matter how much he argued that he was used to his blacks from Minas Gerais and didn't want any foreign languages in his house. His friend Palha insisted, pointing out the necessity of having white servants. Rubião gave in regretfully. His good manservant, whom he wished to keep in the parlor as a touch of the provinces, couldn't even stay in the kitchen, where a Frenchman, Jean, reigned. The slave was downgraded to other duties.

"Is Quincas Borba getting impatient?" Rubião asked, drinking his last sip of coffee and casting a last glance at the tray.

"Me parece que sí."

"I'll be right there and set him loose."

He didn't go. He allowed himself to stay there for a while, gazing at the furniture. Looking at the small English prints that hung on the wall over the two bronzes, Rubião thought about the beautiful Sofia, Palha's wife, took a few steps and went over to sit down on the ottoman in the center of the room, staring off into the distance . . .

"It was she who recommended those two small pictures to me when the three of us were out shopping. She was so pretty! But what I like best about her are her shoulders, which I saw at the colonel's ball. What shoulders! They looked like wax, so smooth, so white! Her arms, too, oh, her arms! So well shaped!"

Rubião sighed, crossed his legs and tapped the tassels of his robe against his knees. He felt that he wasn't entirely happy, but he also felt that complete happiness wasn't far off. He reconstructed in his head some mannerisms, some looks, some unexplained swaying of the body which had to mean that she loved him and that she loved him a great deal. He wasn't old. He was going on forty-one and, quite frankly, he looked younger. That observation was accompanied by a gesture. He ran his hand over his chin, shaved every day, something he hadn't done before out of frugality and because there was no need. A simple teacher! He wore sideburns (later on he let his full beard grow)—so soft that it was a pleasure to run his fingers through them . . . And in that way he was remembering the first meeting, at the Vassouras station, where Sofia and her husband were getting on the train, into the same car on which he was coming from Minas. It was there that he discovered that set of luxuriant eyes that seemed to be repeating the exhortation of the prophet: Come unto the waters all ye who thirst. He didn't have any ideas in response to that invitation, it's true. He had the inheritance on his mind, the will, the inventory, things that must be explained first in order to understand the present and the future. Let's leave Rubião in his parlor in Botafogo, tapping the tassels of his robe against his knees and thinking about the beautiful Sofia. Come with me,

7

reader. Let's have a look at him months earlier by the bed of Quincas Borba.

I V

This Quincas Borba, in case you have done me the favor of reading *The Posthumous Memoirs of Brás Cubas*, is that very same castaway from existence who appeared there, a beggar, an unexpected heir, and the inventor of a philosophy. Here you have him in Barbacena now. No sooner had he arrived than he fell in love with a widow, a lady of middle-class station and with scarce means of livelihood, but so bashful that the sighs of her lover found no echo. Her name was Maria da Piedade. A brother of hers, who is the Rubião here present, did everything possible to get them married. Piedade resisted and pleurisy carried her off.

It was that little novelistic bit that brought the two men together. Could Rubião have known that our Quincas Borba carried that little grain of lunacy that a doctor thought he found in him? Certainly not. He took him to be a strange man. It's true, however, that the little grain hadn't left Quincas Borba's brain—neither before nor after the malady that slowly devoured him. Quincas Borba had some relatives there in Barbacena, all dead now in 1867. The last was the uncle who left him heir to his goods. Rubião was left as the philosopher's only friend. At that time Rubião was running a school for children, which he closed in order to care for the sick man. Before being a school teacher, he'd tried his hand at some enterprises that went under.

His job as nurse lasted more than five months, closer to six. Rubião's care was superb. It was patient, smiling, multiple, listening to the doctor's orders, administering medicine at the prescribed time, taking the patient out for a walk, never forgetting anything, neither the management of the house nor the reading of newspapers as soon as they arrived from the capital or from Ouro Preto.

"You're a good man, Rubião," Quincas Borba would sigh.

"That's a fine thing to say! As if you were a bad one!"

The doctor's considered opinion was that Quincas Borba's illness would slowly follow its path. One day our Rubião, seeing the doctor to the street door, asked him what was the real state of his friend's health. He heard that he was done for, completely done for, but he should be cheered up. Why make death all the worse by letting him know the truth . . . ?

"None of that, no," Rubião put in. "For him dying is an easy matter. You've never read a book he wrote years ago, I can't remember, some kind of philosophy . . ."

"No. But philosophy is one thing and dying is another. Goodbye."

V

Rubião had a rival for Quincas Borba's heart—a dog, a handsome dog, medium-sized, lead-colored with black markings. Quincas Borba took him everywhere. They slept in the same room. In the morning it was the dog who would awaken his master by climbing onto the bed, where they would exchange their first greetings. One of the master's eccentricities was to give it his own name, but he explained that it was for two reasons, one doctrinal, the other personal.

"Since Humanitas, according to my doctrine, is the principle of life and is present everywhere, it also exists in the dog, so, therefore, he can have a human name, be it Christian or Muslim . . ."

"Fine, but why don't you give him the name Bernardo?" Rubião asked, thinking of a political rival in the region.

"That brings us to the personal reason. If I should die first, as I presume I shall, I will survive in the name of my dog. It makes you laugh, doesn't it?"

Rubião made a negative gesture.

"Well, you should be laughing, my dear fellow, because immortality is my lot or my spot or whatever name you can come up with for it. I will live in perpetuity through my great book. Those who can't read, however, will call the dog Quincas Borba and . . ."

The dog, hearing his name, ran to the bed. Quincas Borba, touched, looked at Quincas Borba.

"My poor friend! My good friend! My only friend!"

"Only?"

"Pardon me, you are, too, I know that quite well and I thank you very much. But you've got to forgive a sick man everything. Maybe my delirium is starting. Let me see the mirror."

Rubião gave him the mirror. For a few seconds the sick man studied the thin face, the feverish eyes that revealed the suburbs of death, towards which he was walking with a slow but certain step. Afterwards, with a pale and ironic smile:

"Everything on the outside there corresponds to what I feel inside here. I'm going to die, my dear Rubião . . . Don't wag your finger, I'm going to die. And what is dying, for you to look so horrified?"

"I know, I know, you have your philosophy . . . But let's talk about dinner, what will it be today?"

Quincas Borba sat on the bed letting his legs hang down and their extraordinary thinness could be imagined through his trouser legs.

"What is it? What do you want?" Rubião came over.

"Nothing," the sick man replied, smiling. "Philosophy! You use such disdain when you say that to me! Say it again, go ahead, I want to hear it again. Philosophy!"

"But it wasn't disdain . . . Am I capable of disdaining philosophy? All I'm saying is that you can believe that death isn't anything because you've got your reasons, your principles . . ."

Quincas Borba searched for his slippers with his feet. Rubião pushed them over to him. He put them on and began to walk to stretch his legs. He petted the dog and lighted a cigarette. Rubião tried to dress him and brought him a morning coat, a vest, a dressing gown, a cape, whatever he could find. Quincas Borba rejected them with a gesture. He had a different look now. His eyes, turning inward, saw his own brain thinking. Af-

ter several steps he stopped for a few seconds in front of Rubião.

V I

"In order for you to understand what life and death are, it's
enough to tell you how my grandmother died."
"What was it like?"
"Have a seat."
Rubião obeyed, trying to look as interested as possible while
Quincas Borba kept walking about.
"It was in Rio de Janeiro," he began, "in front of the Imperial
Chapel, which was called the Royal Chapel then, on a day of
great celebration. My grandmother came out, crossed the churchyard in order to get to the sedan chair that was waiting for her
on the Largo do Paço. People were thick as ants. The masses
wanted to see the entrance of the great ladies in all their finery.
At the moment when my grandmother was coming out of the
churchyard to go to her sedan chair, a short distance away, it so
happened that one of the animals hitched to a carriage was
spooked. The animal took off, the other one followed suit, confusion, tumult. My grandmother fell, and the mules and the carriage both ran over her. She was lifted up and carried into a
pharmacy on the Rua Direita. A blood-letter arrived, but it was
too late, her head was split open, a leg and a shoulder were
broken, there was blood all over. She died minutes later."
"What a real tragedy," Rubião said.
"No."
"No?"
"Listen to the rest of it. This is how it all happened. The
owner of the carriage was in the churchyard, and he was hungry,
very hungry, because it was late and he'd had an early breakfast
and hadn't eaten very much. From there he was able to signal
his coachman. The latter whipped the mules in order to go pick

up his master. The carriage ran into an obstacle halfway there and knocked it down. That obstacle was my grandmother. The first act of that series of acts was a movement of self-preservation: Humanitas was hungry. If instead of my grandmother it had been a rat or a dog, it's certain my grandmother wouldn't have died, but the basic fact would remain the same: Humanitas needs to eat. If instead of a rat or a dog it had been a poet, Byron or Gonçalves Dias, the case would have been different in the sense that it would have furnished material for a great many obituaries, but the basic fact would endure. The universe still wouldn't stop because it would be missing some poems that died, nipped in the bud, in the head of a famous or obscure man, but Humanitas (and that's what matters above all), Humanitas needs to eat."

Rubião listened with his soul in his eyes, as they say, sincerely wanting to understand, but he couldn't grasp the necessity that his friend attributed to the death of his grandmother. Certainly the owner of the carriage, no matter how late he got home, wouldn't die of hunger, while the good lady really died, and forever more. He explained those doubts to him as best he could and ended up asking him:

"And what is this Humanitas?"

"Humanitas is the beginning. But no, I won't say anything, you're not capable of understanding this, my dear Rubião. Let's talk about something else."

"Whatever you say."

Quincas Borba, who hadn't stopped pacing, stopped for a few seconds.

"Would you like to be my disciple?"

"I would."

"Good. It won't take you long to understand my philosophy. On the day when you've penetrated it completely, ah!, on that day you'll have the greatest pleasure of your life, because there's no wine as intoxicating as the truth. Believe me, Humanitism is the pinnacle of all things, and I, who formulated it, am the greatest man in the world. Look, do you see how my good Quincas Borba is looking at me? It's not he, it's Humanitas . . ."

"But what is this Humanitas?"

"Humanitas is the first principle. All things have a certain hidden and identical substance in them, a principle that's sin-

gular, universal, eternal, common, indivisible, and indestructible—
or, to use the language of the great Camões:

> A truth there is that moves in things,
> Living in the visible and the invisible.

"Well, that substance or truth, the indestructible principle is
what Humanitas is. That's what I call it, because it sums up the
universe and the universe is man. Understand?"

"Not too much, but even so, how is it that your grandmother's
death . . ."

"There's no such thing as death. The meeting of two expan-
sions, or the expansion of two forms, can lead to the suppression
of one of them, but, strictly speaking, there's no such thing as
death. There's life, because the suppression of one is the condition for the survival of the other, and destruction doesn't touch
the universal and common principle. From that we have the pre-
serving and beneficial character of war. Imagine a field of potatoes and two starving tribes. There are only enough potatoes to
feed one of the tribes, who in that way will get the strength to
cross the mountain and reach the other slope, where there are
potatoes in abundance. But, if the two tribes peacefully divide
up the potatoes from the field, they won't derive sufficient nourishment and will die of starvation. Peace, in this case, is destruction; war is preservation. One of the tribes will exterminate the
other and collect the spoils. This explains the joy of victory, an-
thems, cheers, public recompense, and all the other results of
warlike action. If the nature of war were different, those dem-
onstrations would never take place, for the real reason that man
only commemorates and loves what he finds pleasant and advantageous, and for the reasonable motive that no person can can-
onize an action that actually destroys him. To the conquered,
hate or compassion; to the victor, the potatoes."

"But what about the point of view of those exterminated?"

"Nobody's exterminated. The phenomenon disappears, but the
substance is the same. Haven't you ever seen boiling water? You
must recall that the bubbles keep on being made and unmade
and everything stays the same in the same water. Individuals are
those transitory bubbles."

"Well, the opinion of the bubble . . ."

"A bubble has no opinion. Does anything seem sadder than those terrible epidemics that devastate some point on the globe? And, yet, that supposed evil is a benefit, not only because it eliminates weak organisms, incapable of resistance, but because it leads to observation, to the discovery of the drug that will cure it. Hygiene is the offspring of century-old putrescences. We owe it to millions of cases of corruption and infection. Nothing is lost, everything is gained. I repeat, the bubbles stay in the water. Do you see this book? It's *Don Quixote*. If I were to destroy my copy I wouldn't eliminate the work, which goes on eternally in surviving copies and editions yet to come. Eternal and beautiful, beautifully eternal, like this divine and supradivine world."

VII

Quincas Borba fell silent out of exhaustion and sat down panting. Rubião hastened to help him, bringing some water and asking him to lie down and rest, but the sick man, after a moment, replied that it was nothing. He was out of practice in making speeches, that's what it was. And, having Rubião move himself back so he could face him without effort, he undertook a brilliant description of the world and its wonders. He mingled his own ideas with those of others, images of all sorts, idyllic and epic, to such a degree that Rubião wondered how it was that a man who was going to die at any moment could deal so gallantly with those matters.

"Come, rest a little."

Quincas Borba reflected:

"No, I'm going for a walk."

"Not now, you're too tired."

"Bah! It's passed."

He stood up and laid his hands paternally on Rubião's shoulders.

"Are you my friend?"

"What a question!"

"Answer me."

"As much as or more than this animal here," Rubião replied in a burst of tenderness.

Quincas Borba squeezed his hands:

"Good."

VIII

The next day Quincas Borba woke up with a resolve to go to Rio de Janeiro. He would be back after a month. He had certain business to attend to . . . Rubião was flabbergasted. What about his illness, and the doctor? The patient replied that the doctor was a charlatan and that illness needed to be distracted, just like health. Illness and health were two pits of the same fruit, two states of Humanitas.

"I'm going on some personal matters," the sick man ended, saying, "and in addition to that I've got a plan that's so sublime that not even you will be able to understand it. You have to pardon my frankness, but I prefer being frank with you, more than with any other person."

Rubião was positive that with time this project would pass like so many others, but he was mistaken. It so happened that the patient seemed to be getting better. He didn't go to bed, he went out, he wrote. At the end of a week he had the notary sent for.

"The notary?" his friend repeated.

"Yes, I want to draw up my will. Or we can both go to him . . ."

The three of them went, because the dog wouldn't let his master leave without accompanying him. Quincas Borba drew up his will with the usual formalities and returned home tranquilly. Rubião felt his heart pounding violently.

"Naturally I'm not going to let you go to the capital alone," he said to his friend.

"No, it's not necessary. Besides, Quincas Borba's not going, and I don't trust him with anyone but you. I'm leaving the house just the way it is. I'll be back a month from now. I'm going tomorrow. I don't want him to sense my leaving. Take care of him, Rubião."

"Yes, I'll take care of him."

"You swear?"

"By the light that guides me. Do you think I'm a child?"

"Give him his milk at the proper time, his meals as usual, and his baths. And when you take him out for a walk see that he doesn't run off. No. It's best that he doesn't go out . . . doesn't go out . . ."

"Rest assured."

Quincas Borba was weeping for the other Quincas Borba. He didn't want to see the dog when he left. He was really crying, tears of madness or affection, whichever they were, he was leaving them behind on the good soil of Minas like the last sweat of a dark soul ready to fall into the abyss.

IX

Hours later Rubião had a horrible thought. People might think that he himself had pushed his friend into taking the trip in order to kill him quicker and come into possession of his legacy, if he really was included in his will. He felt remorse. Why hadn't he made every effort to hold him back. He could see Quincas Borba's corpse, pale, stinking, staring up at him with a vengeful look. He resolved that in case the trip took a fatal turn he would renounce the legacy.

For his part, the dog spent his time sniffing about, whining, trying to run away. He couldn't sleep restfully. He would get up many times at night, run through the house, and return to his corner. In the morning Rubião would call him to his bed, and the dog would come happily. He imagined that it was his own master. He would then see that it wasn't, but he would accept the petting and return it, as if Rubião were going to take him to his friend or bring his friend there. Besides, he'd taken a liking to him, and he was the bridge linking him to his previous existence. He didn't eat for the first few days. He was bothered more by thirst. Rubião managed to get him to drink milk. It was his only nourishment for some time. Later on he would pass the hours in silence, sad, rolled up into a ball or with his body stretched out and his head between his paws.

When the doctor returned he was astounded at his patient's temerity. They should have tried to stop him. It was certain death.

"Certain?"

"Sooner or later. Did he take that dog with him?"

"No, sir, he's with me. He asked me to take care of him and he cried. You should have seen him. I thought he'd never stop. The truth is," Rubião then said as a defense of the sick man, "the truth is that the dog deserves his master's esteem. He's just like a person."

The doctor took off his broad-brimmed straw hat to adjust the band, then he smiled. "A person? So he's just like a person, eh?" Rubião repeated it and then explained. He wasn't a person like other persons, but he had touches of feeling, even intelligence. Look, he was going to tell him a . . .

"No, old man, not now, later, later, I've got to go see a patient with erysipelas . . . If any letters come from him and they're not private, I'd like to see them, hear? And give my regards to the dog," he concluded as he left.

Some people began to make fun of Rubião and the strange duty of guarding a dog when the dog should be guarding him. The mockery began, the nicknames. Look how the teacher had ended up! Sentry for a dog! Rubião was afraid of public opinion. It did, in fact, look ridiculous to him. He would avoid other people's eyes, look at the dog with annoyance, curse him, curse life. If it weren't for the hope of a legacy, small as it might be. It was impossible that Quincas Borba wouldn't leave him some remembrance.

X

Seven weeks later this letter postmarked Rio de Janeiro arrived in Barbacena, all in Quincas Borba's handwriting:

My dear friend,

You must be puzzled by my silence. I have not written you because of some very special reasons, etc. I shall return soon, but I wish to pass on to you right now a private matter, most private.

Who am I, Rubião? Saint Augustine. I know that you'll smile at that because you're an ignoramus, Rubião. Our intimacy allows me to use a crueler word, but I make you this concession, which is the last. Ignoramus!

Listen, ignoramus. I'm Saint Augustine. I discovered that the day before yesterday. Listen and be quiet. Everything in our lives coincides. The saint and I have spent a portion of our time in pleasures and heresy, because I consider heresy everything that isn't my doctrine of Humanitas. We've both stolen things, he, as a boy, some pears in Carthage, I, a young man already, a watch from my friend Brás Cubas. Our mothers were religious and virtuous. In short, he thought as I do that everything that exists is good and he demonstrates why in Chapter XVI, Book VII, of his *Confessions*, with the difference that for him evil is a deviation of the will, a natural illusion of a backward century, a concession to error on Augustine's part, since evil doesn't even exist, and only his first affirmation is true. All things are good, *omnia bona*, and goodbye.

Goodbye, ignoramus. Don't tell anyone what I have just entrusted to you if you don't want to lose your ears. Be silent, be on guard, and thank your good fortune for having a great man like me for a friend, even if you don't understand me. You will understand me. As soon as I return to Barbacena I'm going to give you, in simple, explicit terms, suitable for the understanding of a jackass, the true notions of a great man. Goodbye. Remember me to my poor Quincas Borba. Don't forget to give him milk, milk and baths. Goodbye, goodbye . . . Yours from the bottom of my heart,

QUINCAS BORBA

Rubião could barely hold the paper in his hands. After a few seconds he sensed that it might be one of his friend's japes, and he reread the letter. But the second reading confirmed his first impression. There was no doubt about it, he was crazy. Poor Quincas Borba! So his odd ways, his frequent changes of mood, his meaningless drive, his disproportionate acts of tenderness were nothing but the foretoken of the total ruin of his brain. He was dying before he died. So good! So jolly! He had his impertinences, to be sure, but they were explained by his illness. Rubião wiped his eyes, moist with feeling. Then the thought of the possible legacy came to him, and he was all the more afflicted as he was shown what a good friend he was going to lose.

He tried to read the letter one more time still, slowly now, analyzing the words, breaking them up to catch the meaning better and really to discover if it was the banter of a philosopher. That way of disconcerting a person by playing was well known, but everything else confirmed the suspicions of disaster. Almost at the end now, he stopped, his heart pierced. Might it not be that with the insanity of the testator proven the will would be null and void and the inheritance lost? Rubião had a dizzy spell. He still had the open letter in his hands when he saw the doctor appear in search of news of his patient. The postman had told him that a letter had arrived. Was that it?

"This is it, but . . ."

"Is it some private message . . . ?"

"Precisely, it has a private message, very private. Personal matters. May I?"

Saying that Rubião put the letter in his pocket. The doctor left. He breathed deeply. He'd escaped the danger of making public such a dangerous document by which it would be possible to prove Quincas Borba's mental condition. Minutes later he was sorry, he should have turned over the letter, he felt remorse, he thought about sending it to the doctor's house. He called a slave, but when he came Rubião had already changed his mind again. He thought it would be imprudent. The sick man would soon be back—in a few days—he would ask about the letter, would accuse him of being indiscreet, a snitch . . . Easy remorse, which didn't last long.

"I don't want anything," he told the slave. And he thought about the legacy once more. He estimated the figure. Less than ten *contos*, no. He would buy a plot of land, a house, he would grow this or that, or he would mine for gold. The worst was that if it was less, five *contos* ... Five? That wasn't much, but in any case it might not go beyond that. Let it be five, it was less but better less than nothing. Five *contos* ... It would be worse if the will were found null and void. All right, then, five *contos*!

X I

At the beginning of the following week when he received the newspapers from the capital (Quincas Borba's subscriptions still), Rubião read this item in one of them:

Mr. Joaquim Borba dos Santos has died after enduring his illness philosophically. He was a man of great learning, and he wore himself out doing battle against that yellow, withered pessimism that will yet reach us here one day. It is the *mal du siècle*. His last words were that pain was an illusion and that Pangloss was not as dotty as Voltaire indicated ... He was already delirious. He leaves many possessions. His will is in Barbacena.

XII

"His suffering is over," Rubião sighed.

Immediately after, taking another look at the news item he saw that it spoke of a man of merit, appreciation, to whom a philosophical controversy was attributed. No mention of dementia. On the contrary, at the end it said he was delirious during his final moments, the effect of his illness. So much the better! Rubião read the letter again and the hypothesis of a jape seemed likely once again. He knew that he had a sense of humor. He was surely poking fun at him. He went to Saint Augustine in the same way as he might have gone to Saint Ambrose or Saint Hillary, and he wrote an enigmatic letter in order to confuse him until he could return and have a good laugh over his success. Poor friend! He was sane—sane and dead. Yes, now he no longer suffered. Seeing the dog, he sighed:

"Poor Quincas Borba! If you only knew that your master was dead . . ."

Then he said to himself, "Now that my obligation is over, I'm going to turn him over to my friend Angélica."

XIII

The news spread through the town; the vicar, the druggist, the doctor all sent to find out if it was true. The postman, who'd read about it in the papers, came in person to bring Rubião a letter that had come for him in the pouch. It could have been from the deceased although the handwriting of the sender was different.

"So the man finally gave up the ghost, eh?" he said as Rubião opened the letter and ran his eyes down to the signature, where he read *Brás Cubas*. It was just a note:

"My poor friend Quincas Borba died yesterday in my home,

where he had appeared a while back, filthy and in tatters, the effects of his illness. Before dying he asked me to write you and give you this news personally along with many thanks. The rest will be done according to legal procedures."

The thanks made the teacher turn pale, but the legal procedures brought his blood back. Rubião folded the letter without saying anything. The postman spoke of different things and then left. Rubião ordered a slave to take the dog to his dear friend Angélica, telling her that since she liked animals, here was another one, that she should treat him well because he was used to good treatment, and, finally, that the dog's name was the same as that of his master, dead now, Quincas Borba.

XIV

When the will was read, Rubião almost keeled over. You can guess why. He was named sole heir of the testator. Not five, not ten, not twenty *contos*, but everything, his whole estate, with the possessions specified: houses in the capital, one in Barbacena, slaves, bonds, stocks in the Bank of Brazil and other institutions, jewelry, coins, books—everything, in short, passed into Rubião's hands directly, without any legacies to other people, without any charitable donation, without any debts. There was only one condition in the will, that the heir was to keep with him his poor dog, Quincas Borba, a name he had given it out of the great affection he felt for it. It demanded that the said Rubião treat the dog as if it were the testator himself, without skimping in any way for its needs, protecting it from annoyances, flight, robbery, or death that people might wish upon it out of evil. In short, to treat it as if it were not a dog but a human being. Item, the condition is imposed that when the dog dies it is to be given decent burial in its own plot, which will be covered with flowers and sweet-smelling plants, and, furthermore, he was to disinter the bones of said dog after the suitable period and gather them together in a casket of fine wood, to be placed in the most honored place in the house.

X V

Such was the clause. Rubião found it natural enough since he'd only had thoughts for the inheritance. He'd imagined just a legacy, and out of the will all of the possessions had come his way. He had trouble believing it. He had to have his hand shaken many times, strongly—the strength of congratulations—in order not to imagine that it was a lie.

"Yes, sir, you scored a goal," the owner of the pharmacy that had supplied Quincas Borba's medicines said to him.

Heir was a lot, but sole . . . That word puffed up the cheeks of the inheritance. Heir to everything, not a teaspoon left out. And how much would it all amount to? he was thinking. Houses, bonds, stocks, slaves, clothing, chinaware, a few paintings that he had in the capital, because he was a man of good taste, he had a fine knowledge of artistic things. And books? He must have had a lot of books because he was always quoting from them. But what could the figure for all of it be? A hundred *contos*? Maybe two hundred. It was possible that three hundred wouldn't be a surprise. Three hundred *contos!* Three hundred! And Rubião had an urge to dance in the street. Then he calmed down. If it was two hundred or even a hundred it was a dream that the Good Lord was giving him, but it was a long dream, one that would never end.

The remembrance of the dog managed to take hold in the whirlwind of the thoughts that were going through our man's head. Rubião found the clause natural enough but unnecessary because he and the dog were two friends, and nothing was more certain than that they should stay together to remember the third friend, the deceased, the author of the happiness of both. There were, of course, a few strange items in the clause, the bit about the casket, and he didn't know what else, but they would all be fulfilled unless the sky fell in . . . No, with God's help, he added. Good dog! Fine dog!

Rubião was not forgetting the many times he'd tried to get rich in enterprises that had died in bloom. He considered himself at that time a poor unfortunate, an unlucky person, when the truth was that a person with God's help caught more worms than the early bird. So it wasn't impossible to become rich, since he was now rich.

"What's impossible?" he exclaimed aloud. "It's impossible for God to sin. God doesn't hold out on someone he's made a promise to."

He went along like that, up and down the streets of the town, without heading home, without any plan, with his blood pounding in his head. Suddenly this grave problem arose: whether he should go live in Rio de Janeiro or stay in Barbacena. He felt the urge to stay, to shine where he'd been in the shadows, to get one up on the people who'd paid scant attention to him before, mostly the ones who'd laughed at his friendship with Quincas Borba. But immediately after came the image of Rio de Janeiro, which he knew, with its enchantment, movement, theaters everywhere, pretty girls dressed in the latest French fashions. He decided it was better. He would come back up to his hometown many, many times.

X V I

"Quincas Borba! Quincas Borba! Hey!" he shouted as he went into the house.

No dog to be seen. Only then did he remember having sent him to Angélica. He ran to the woman's house, which was quite distant. Along the way all kinds of ugly ideas came to him, some extraordinary. One ugly idea was that the dog had run away. Another extraordinary one was that some enemy, aware of the clause and the gift, had gone to deal with the woman, stolen the dog, and hidden or killed it. In that case the inheritance . . . A cloud passed over his eyes. Then he began to see more clearly.

"I'm not familiar with legal matters," he thought, "but it seems to me that I'm not involved. The clause supposes the dog to be alive or at home. But if he runs away or dies there's no reason to invent a dog. Therefore the original intent . . . But my enemies are capable of chicanery. If the clause isn't fulfilled . . ."

Here our friend's brow and the palms of his hands became damp. Another cloud came over his eyes. And his heart was beating rapidly, rapidly. The clause was beginning to seem outlandish to him. Rubião grasped at his saints, promised masses, ten masses . . . But there was the woman's house. Rubião picked up his pace. He saw someone, was it she? It was, it was she, leaning against the door and laughing.

"What kind of a figure is that you're cutting, old friend? Have you gone crazy, waving your arms around?"

XVII

"Where's the dog, friend?" Rubião asked, apparently indifferent but very pale.

"Come in and have a seat," she answered. "What dog?"

"What dog?" Rubião replied, getting paler and paler. "The one I sent you. Don't you remember that I sent you a dog to keep for a few days, for some rest, to see if . . . In short, a dearly-loved animal. It's not mine. I came here to . . . But don't you remember?"

"Ah! Don't talk to me about that creature!" she answered, pouring out the words.

She was small, she would tremble over anything, and when she was excited the veins on her neck stood out. She repeated that he shouldn't talk to her about the creature.

"But what's he done to you, old friend?"

"What's he done to me? What could he do to me, the poor animal? He won't eat anything, he won't drink, he cries just like a person, and all he does is go around looking for a way to run off."

Rubião gave a sigh of relief. She went on talking about her annoyance with the dog. He was anxious, he wanted to see him.

"He's in the back there, in the large pen. He's all by himself so the others won't bother him. But have you come for him? That's not what they told me. I seemed to hear that he was for me, a present."

"I'd give you five or six if I could," Rubião answered. "But I can't this one. I'm only taking care of him. But let's drop it, I promise you a son of his, the message was garbled."

Rubião went with her. The woman, instead of leading him, was walking alongside. There was the dog in the pen, lying down at some distance from a bowl of food. Dogs and birds were leaping about on all sides out there. On one side there was a hen coop, farther on pigs, beyond that a cow, lying down, dreamy, with two hens next to it pecking at its belly and pulling off lice.

"Look at my peacock!" the woman said.

But Rubião only had eyes for Quincas Borba, who was sniffing impatiently and who leaped up on him as soon as a black boy opened the gate of the pen. It was a delirious scene. The dog was repaying Rubião's pats by barking, leaping, licking his hands.

"Good heavens! What a friendship!"

"You can't imagine, old friend. Goodbye, I promise you a son of his."

XVIII

Rubião and the dog, when they entered the house, sensed, heard the person and the voice of their departed friend. While the dog sniffed about everywhere, Rubião went to sit in the chair where he'd been when Quincas Borba referred to the death of his grandmother with scientific explanations. The memory brought back the philosopher's arguments, albeit confused and frayed. For the first time he gave careful consideration to the allegory of the starving tribes, and he understood the conclusion: "To the victor, the potatoes!" He clearly heard the dead man's voice expounding the situation of the tribes, the fight, and the reason for the fight, the extermination of one and the victory of the other, and he murmured in a low voice:

"To the victor, the potatoes!"

So simple! So clear! He looked at his worn drill pants and his patched waistcoat, and he noted that up until a short time before he'd been, in a manner of speaking, someone exterminated, a burst bubble, but not now, now he was a victor. There was no doubt about it, the potatoes had been made for the tribe that eliminates the other in order to get over the mountain and reach the potatoes on the other side. His case precisely. He was going to go down from Barbacena to dig up and eat the potatoes in the capital. He had to be hard and implacable, he was powerful and strong. And leaping up, all excited, he raised his arms, exclaiming:

"To the victor, the potatoes!"

He liked the formula, found it ingenious, compendious, and eloquent in addition to being profound and true. He imagined the potatoes in their various shapes; he classified them as to taste, aspect, nutritive power; he stuffed himself in advance at the banquet of life. It was time to have done with the poor, dry roots that only deceived the stomach, the sad meal of so many long years. Now full, solid, perpetual eating until the day he died, and dying on silk cushions, which is better than on rags. And he went back to the affirmation of being hard and implacable and to the formula from the allegory. He got to composing in his head a seal for his use with this motto: TO THE VICTOR, THE POTATOES.

He forgot about the seal, but the formula lived on in Rubião's spirit for a few days: "To the victor, the potatoes!" He wouldn't have understood it before the will. On the contrary, we saw that he'd considered it obscure and in need of an explanation. It's so true that the landscape depends on the point of view and the best way to appreciate a whip is to have its handle in your hand.

XIX

We mustn't forget to mention that Rubião took it upon himself to have a mass sung for the soul of the deceased, even though he knew or sensed that Quincas Borba hadn't been a Catholic. He didn't say anything nasty about priests nor did he discredit Catholic doctrine, but he never spoke of the Church or its servants. On the other hand, his worship of Humanitas made his heir suspect that this was the testator's religion. Nonetheless, he had a mass sung, considering that it wasn't following the wishes of the dead man, but a prayer for the living. He further considered that it would be scandalous in the town if he, named as heir by the deceased, neglected to give his protector the prayers that are not denied the most miserable and avaricious people in the world.

If some people didn't appear, in order not to be part of Rubião's glory, many did come—and not riffraff—who saw the true grief of the former schoolteacher.

XX

As soon as the preliminary motions for the liquidation of the inheritance were under way, Rubião made ready to go to Rio de Janeiro, where he would settle as soon as it was all over. There were things to do in both places, but things promised to move along swiftly.

XXI

At the station in Vassouras, Sofia and her husband, Cristiano de Almeida e Palha, got on the train. He was a healthy young man of thirty-two, and she was between twenty-seven and twenty-eight. They sat down on the two seats opposite Rubião and arranged the baskets and packages of souvenirs they were bringing from Vassouras, where they'd gone to spend a week. They buttoned up their dusters and exchanged a few words in low voices.

After the train started up Palha noticed Rubião, whose face, among so many frowning or bored people, was the only one that was calm and satisfied. Cristiano was the first to start a conversation, telling him that railroad trips were boring, to which Rubião replied that they were. For someone used to muleback, he added, the train was boring and uninteresting. One couldn't deny, however, that it was progress.

"Of course," Palha agreed. "Great progress."

"Are you a farmer?"

"No, sir."

"Do you live in the town?"

"Vassouras? No. We came to spend a week here. I live in the capital itself. I haven't got any wish to be a farmer, although I consider it a good and honorable occupation."

From farming they passed on to cattle, slavery, and politics. Cristiano Palha cursed the government, which had inserted remarks concerning servile property in the Emperor's annual Speech from the Throne. But, to his great surprise, Rubião didn't leap to indignation. It was Rubião's plan to sell the slaves the testator had left him, except for a houseboy. If he lost anything, the rest of the inheritance would cover it. Besides, the Speech from the Throne, which he'd also read, ordered that current property be respected. What did he care about future slaves, since he wasn't going to buy any? The houseboy would be freed as soon as he came into possession of his goods. Palha dropped it and went on to politics, the chambers of parliament, the war with Paraguay, all general matters to which Rubião paid attention, more or less. Sofia was barely listening. She only moved her eyes, which she knew were pretty, focusing them now on her husband, now on the one he was speaking to.

"Are you going to stay in the capital, or are you going back to Barbacena?" Palha asked after twenty minutes of conversation.

"My desire is to stay, and I'm going to stay," Rubião replied. "I'm tired of the provinces. I want to enjoy life. I might even go to Europe, but I'm not sure yet."

Palha's eyes lighted up instantly.

"You're doing the wise thing. I'd do the same if I could. Right now I can't. You've probably been there before, haven't you?"

"I never have. That's why I got the idea when I left Barbacena. Not right now. People have got to get the melancholy out of their systems. I still don't know when it'll be, but I'm going . . ."

"You're right. They say there are a lot of splendid things there. It's not surprising, they're older than we are, but we'll catch up. And there are things in which we're just as good as they are, even better. Our capital, I'm not saying it can compare with Paris or London, but it's beautiful, you'll see . . ."

"I've already seen."

"Already?"

"Many years ago."

"You'll find it better. There's been a lot of rapid progress. Then, when you go to Europe . . ."

"Have you ever been to Europe, ma'am?" Rubião interrupted, addressing Sofia.

"No, sir."

"I forgot to introduce you to my wife," Cristiano hastened to say. Rubião bowed respectfully and, turning to the husband, smiling:

"But aren't you going to introduce yourself to me?"

Palha smiled too, realizing that neither of them knew the other's name, and he was quick to give his.

"Cristiano de Almeida e Palha."

"Pedro Rubião de Alvarenga, but Rubião is what everybody calls me."

The exchange of names relaxed them a little. Sofia didn't join in the conversation, however. She loosened the reins of her eyes, which she let follow their own desires. Rubião was talking, smiling, and he was listening attentively to Palha's words, thankful for the friendship of a young man he'd never seen before. He even got to suggest that maybe they could go to Europe together.

"Oh, I won't be able to go during these first years," Palha replied.

"I'm not saying right away either. I won't be going so soon. The desire I had when I left Barbacena was just a desire, with no time in mind. I'll go, no doubt about that, but later on, God willing."

"Ah! I, too, when I say a few years from now also add God willing, because He might decide something else. Who knows, maybe a few months from now? Divine Providence decides what is best."

The expression that accompanied those words was one of conviction and piety, but neither did Sofia see it (she was looking at her feet), nor did Rubião himself hear those last words. Our friend was dying to tell the reasons for his coming to the capital. He had a mouth full of secrets, ready to release them into the ear of his traveling companion—and only because of a trace of scruples, flimsy now, did he still hold them back. But why hold them back if it wasn't a crime and would be a public matter?

"First I've got take care of the inventory of a will," he finally murmured.

"Your father's?"

"No, a friend's. A great friend who remembered to make me his sole heir."

"Ah!"

"Sole heir. You might believe that there are friends in this world, but few like that one. He was made of gold. And what a mind! Such intelligence! Such learning! He was ill during his last days, and an occasional impertinence came out of that, a few whims. You understand, don't you? Rich and sick, no family, he naturally had demands ... But pure gold, fourteen-carat-gold, the kind that when it's assayed is immediately recognized. We were friends, and he didn't say anything to me. The day came when he died, his will was opened, and I found myself with everything. That's the truth. Sole heir! You see, there isn't a single legacy in the will for anyone else. He didn't have any relatives either. The only relative he would have had would have been me if he'd got to marry a sister of mine who died, poor thing! I was just a friend, but he knew how to be a friend, don't you think?"

"Most certainly," Palha agreed.

The latter's eyes were no longer gleaming, they were reflecting deeply. Rubião had entered a thick wood where all the birds of fortune were singing to him. He was expansive, talking about the inheritance. He confessed that he still didn't know the full amount, but he could estimate from a distance . . .

"It's best not to estimate at all," Cristiano put in. "Could it be less than a hundred *contos?*"

"Hah!"

"Since it's above that, it's best to wait in silence. And, something else . . ."

"I don't think it can be less than three hundred . . ."

"Something else. Don't repeat your situation to strangers. I thank you for the trust you've shown in me, but don't expose yourself to the first person you meet. Discretion and accommodating faces don't always go together."

XXII

When they reached the station in the capital, they took leave of one another in an almost familiar way. Palha offered him their house in Santa Teresa. The ex-teacher was going to the União Inn and they promised to visit each other.

XXIII

The next day Rubião was anxious to be with his newfound friend from the train, and he decided to go to Santa Teresa that afternoon. But it was Palha himself who looked him up first that morning. He was coming by to pay his respects, to see if Rubião was all right there or would prefer his house, which was up on the heights. Rubião didn't accept the offer of the house, but he did accept that of a lawyer, a relative of Palha's by marriage whom the latter considered one of the best in spite of his being rather young.

"You better take advantage of him before he gets to where he charges for his fame."

Rubião took Palha to lunch and went with him to the lawyer's office in spite of the protests of the dog, who wanted to go, too. Everything was arranged.

"Come dine with me tonight in Santa Teresa," Palha said on leaving. "There's no reason to hesitate. I'll expect you there," he concluded as he went on his way.

XXIV

Rubião was perplexed because of Sofia. He didn't know how to behave with ladies. Luckily he remembered the promise he'd made to himself to be strong and implacable. He went to dinner. A blessed decision! Where would he have found hours like those? Sofia was much better at home than on the train. There she'd been wearing a cape, even though she had her eyes uncovered; here she had her eyes and her body in plain view, elegantly clad in a cambric dress, showing her hands, which were pretty, and the beginning of an arm. In addition, here she was the lady of the house, she spoke more, outdid herself in kindnesses. Rubião went back down half in a daze.

XXV

He dined there many times. He was timid and bashful. Frequency lessened the impressions of the first days. But he always carried hidden, barely hidden, a certain private fire that he was unable to extinguish. While the inventory was going on and, principally, the challenge to the will made by someone who alleged that Quincas Borba was unfit to make a will because of manifest dementia, our Rubião was distracted. But the challenge was defeated, and the inventory went rapidly along to its conclusion. Palha celebrated the event with a dinner in which the three were joined by the lawyer, the notary, and the clerk. That day Sofia had the most beautiful eyes in the world.

XXVI

It was as if she'd bought them in some mysterious craftsman's workshop, Rubião thought as he went down the hill. I've never seen them as they were today.

This was followed by his move to the house in Botafogo, part of his inheritance. It was necessary to furnish it, and here his friend Palha was of great help to Rubião once more, guiding him with his taste, his knowledge, accompanying him to shops and auctions. Sometimes, as we already know, the three of them would go, because there are things, Sofia would graciously say, that only a woman can choose well. Rubião accepted with thanks and made the purchases drag on as long as possible, making consultations for no reason, inventing needs, everything, just so he could keep the young woman beside him. She let herself stay, talking, explaining, demonstrating.

XXVII

All of that was going through Rubião's head now after coffee, in the same place where we'd left him sitting, looking far away, very far away. He continued rapping with the tassels of his dressing gown. Finally he remembered to go see Quincas Borba and turn him loose. It was his daily chore. He got up and went to the garden in the rear.

XXVIII

"But what a sin is this that pursues me?" he thought as he walked. "She's married, she gets along with her husband, her husband's my friend, he trusts me, completely . . . What are these temptations?"

He stopped and the temptations stopped too. He, a lay Saint Anthony, was different from the anchorite in that he liked the devil's suggestions once they grew insistent. Out of that came an alternative monologue:

"She's so pretty! And she seems to like me so much! If that isn't liking, I don't know what liking is. She shakes my hand with such pleasure, such warmth . . . I can't keep away, even if they let me, I'm the one who can't resist."

Quincas Borba heard his steps and began to bark. Rubião hastened to turn him loose. It was turning himself loose from that persecution for a few moments.

"Quincas Borba!" he shouted, opening the door.

The dog tore outside. What joy! What enthusiasm! What leaps around his master! He comes to lick his hand out of contentment, but Rubião cuffs him, which hurts. He draws back a little, sad, with his tail between his legs. Then his master snaps his fingers, and there he is again, back with the same joy.

"Easy! Easy!"

Quincas Borba follows him through the garden, goes around the house, sometimes walking, sometimes leaping. He savors his freedom but doesn't lose sight of his master. Here he sniffs, there he cocks an ear, over there he goes after a flea on his belly, but with a leap he recovers the space and the time lost and once again dogs the heels of his master. It appears that Rubião isn't thinking about anything now other than walking back and forth, only to make him walk too and make up for the time he was tied up. When Rubião halts, he looks up, waiting. The master's thinking about him, naturally. It's some plan, they'll go out together or something just as pleasant. He never thinks of the possibility of a kick or a whack. He has a feeling of trust and a very short memory for blows. On the other hand, petting makes a deep and fixed impression on him, no matter how casual it might have been. He likes being loved. He's happy believing that he is.

Life there isn't completely good or completely bad. There's a black boy who bathes him every day in cold water, a devilish custom that he can't get used to. Jean the cook likes the dog; the Spanish servant doesn't like him at all. Rubião spends a lot of time away from the house but doesn't treat him poorly, and he allows him inside, lets him stay with him at lunch and dinner, accompany him in the parlor or the study. Sometimes he plays with him, makes him leap. If visitors of some importance arrive, he has him taken away or brought downstairs, and since he always resists, the Spaniard leads him quite carefully at first, but gets his revenge soon after, dragging him by an ear or a leg, flinging him and cutting him off from all communication with the house.

"*Perro del infierno!*"

Bruised, separated from his friend, Quincas Borba then goes to lie down in a corner and remains there for a long time, silent. He moves about a little until he finds a final position and closes his eyes. He doesn't sleep; he's gathering ideas, combining them, remembering. The vague figure of his dead friend might pass in the distance, far off, in bits and pieces, then it mingles with that of his present friend, and they seem to be one single person. Then other ideas . . .

But there are a lot of ideas now—there are too many ideas. In any case, they're the ideas of a dog, a jumble of ideas—even less than a jumble, the reader is probably explaining to himself. But the truth is that the eye that opens from time to time to stare into space so expressively seems to be translating something that's glowing there inside, deep inside there behind something else that I don't know how to define, how to express a canine part that isn't the tail or the ears. Poor human tongue!

Finally he dozes off. Then the images of life play in him in a dream, vague, recent, a scrap here, a patch there. When he awakens, he's forgotten the bad things. He has an expression that I'll say could be melancholy, at the risk of annoying the reader. One can speak of a landscape as being melancholy, but the same thing can't be said of a dog. The reason can't be any other than the fact that the melancholy of the landscape is in ourselves, while to attribute it to a dog is to place it outside of ourselves. Whatever it might be, it's something that's not the joy of a while before. But let there be a whistle from the cook or a signal from his master, and it all vanishes, the eyes shine, pleasure lifts up his muzzle, and his legs fly so fast that they look like wings.

XXIX

Rubião spent the rest of the morning happily. It was Sunday. Two friends had come to have lunch with him, a young man of twenty-four who was nibbling at the first items of his mother's possessions that had been handed down, and a man of forty-four or forty-six who no longer had anything to nibble on. Carlos Maria was the name of the first, Freitas that of the second. Rubião liked both of them but in different ways. It wasn't just age that linked him closer to Freitas, it was also the man's nature. Freitas praised everything, greeted every dish and every wine with a special delicate phrase, and he would leave there with his pockets full of cigars, thus proving that he preferred that brand over all others. They'd been introduced in a certain shop on the Rua Municipal, where they dined together once. They'd told him Freitas' story there, his good and bad luck, but they didn't go into details. Rubião had turned up his nose. Freitas was some castaway whose acquaintance wouldn't bring him any personal pleasure or public esteem, of course, but Freitas soon softened that first impression. He was lively, interesting, a good storyteller, as jolly as a man with an income of fifty *contos*. Since Rubião had mentioned his pretty roses, Freitas asked permission to go see them. He was crazy about flowers. A few days later he appeared there, saying that he was coming to see the beautiful roses, just for a few minutes, if it wasn't inconvenient, if Rubião didn't have something to do. The latter, on the contrary, was pleased to see that the man hadn't forgotten their conversation, and he came down into the garden where the man had been waiting and went to show him the roses. Freitas found them admirable. He examined them so carefully that it was necessary to pull him away from one rosebed to take him to another. He knew the names of all of them, and he went along mentioning species that Rubião didn't have and didn't know—mentioning and describing, like this and like that, this size (indicating it by making a circle with his thumb and forefinger), and then he would name some people who owned good specimens. But Rubião's bushes were of the best species. This one, for example, was rare, and that one too, etc. The gardener was listening to him in awe. When everything had been examined, Rubião said:

"Come have something to drink. What would you like?"

Freitas was happy with anything. When they got inside, he found the house nicely furnished. He examined the bronzes, the paintings, the furniture, he looked out at the sea.

"Yes, sir!" he said. "You live like a prince."

Rubião smiled. Prince, even as a comparison, was a word that had a nice sound to it. The Spanish servant came with the silver tray holding various liqueurs and some goblets, and it was a good moment for Rubião. He himself offered Freitas this or that liqueur. He finally recommended one that they'd told him was the best of all its type on the market. Freitas smiled in disbelief.

"Maybe it was to raise the price," he said.

He took the first sip, savored it slowly, then a second, then a third. Finally, amazed, he confessed that it was a beauty. Where had he bought it? Rubião replied that a friend, the owner of a large wine shop, had given him a bottle of it as a present. He, however, had liked it so much that he'd ordered three dozen. It didn't take long for their relationship to grow close. And Freitas came to have lunch or dinner there many times—more times even than he wanted to or could—because it's hard to resist a man who's so accommodating, so fond of seeing friendly faces.

X X X

Rubião once asked him:
    "Tell me, Mr. Freitas, if I got it into my head to go to Europe, would you be able to come along?"

"No."

"Why not?"

"Because I'm a free friend, and it might happen that we'd start off disagreeing about the itinerary."

"Well, I'm sorry, because you're a jolly sort."

"You're mistaken, sir. I wear this smiling mask, but I'm a sad person. I'm an architect of ruins. I would go first to see the ruins of Athens, then to the theater to see *The Poor Man of the Ruins*, a weepy drama. Later on to bankruptcy court, where ruined men are found . . ."

And Rubião laughed. He liked Freitas' expansive and frank ways.

XXXI

Do you want the reverse of this, curious reader? Take a look at the other guest at lunch, Carlos Maria. If the first one has "expansive and frank" ways—in a laudatory sense—it's quite clear that this man has just the opposite kind. So it won't be difficult at all for you to see him enter the parlor, slow, cold, and superior, to be introduced to Freitas and look away. Freitas, who had already cursed him cordially because of his lateness (it's almost noon), treats him now with great courtesy, with friendly greetings.

You can also see for yourself that our Rubião, if he likes Freitas better, holds the other in higher esteem. Rubião waited for Carlos Maria until now and would have waited for him until tomorrow. Carlos Maria is the one who doesn't hold either Freitas or Rubião in high esteem. Take a good look at him! He's an elegant young man with large, placid eyes, very much in control of himself and even more in control of others. He looks beyond things, he doesn't have a jovial laugh but a mocking one. Now, as he sits down at the table, picks up his utensils, opens his napkin, it can be seen in everything that he's doing the host a great favor—perhaps two—that of eating his food and that of not calling him a fool.

And, in spite of the disparity of personalities, the lunch was merry. Freitas was devouring his food, with a pause now and then, of course—and confessing to himself that the lunch, if the man had come at the appointed time (eleven o'clock) might not have tasted so good. Now he was sailing into the first mouthfuls that heightened his castaway's hunger. After some ten minutes he was able to start talking, full of laughter, expanding with gestures and looks, stringing together a whole series of sharp witticisms and picaresque anecdotes. Carlos Maria listened to most of them with a serious look in order to humiliate him, to such a point that Rubião, who really found Freitas amusing, no longer dared to laugh. Toward the end of the lunch Carlos Maria loosened up a little, grew expansive and made reference to other people's amorous adventures. Freitas, in order to flatter him, asked him to tell about one or two of his own. Carlos Maria burst out laughing.

"What role do you want me to play?" he asked.

Freitas explained. It wasn't a discourse, but deeds, he was asking him for deeds, nothing untoward or anything left to the imagination.

"Are you comfortable living here in Botafogo?" Carlos Maria interrupted, addressing the host.

Freitas, cut off, bit his lip and cursed the young man a second time. He leaned back in his chair, taut, serious, looking at a picture on the wall. Rubião answered that he was quite comfortable, that the beach was beautiful.

"It's a pretty view, but I was never able to stand the stench there is here on certain occasions," Carlos Maria said. "What do you think?" he went on, turning to Freitas.

Freitas straightened up and said everything he thought, that they could both be right. But he insisted that the beach, in spite of everything, was magnificent. He went on without any ill humor or annoyance. He even did Carlos Maria the favor of calling his attention to a small piece of fruit that had become stuck to the tip of his mustache.

They reached the end. It had been a little over an hour. Rubião, silent, was mentally recomposing the lunch, dish by dish, he looked with pleasure at the glasses and the remains of the wine there, the scattered crumbs, the final appearance of the table just before coffee. From time to time he would glance at the servant's jacket. He managed to catch Carlos Maria's face in flagrant pleasure as he was taking the first puffs on one of the cigars that Rubião had asked to be distributed. At that point the servant entered with a small basket covered with a cambric handkerchief and a letter that had just been delivered.

XXXII

"Who sent this?" Rubião asked.

"Dona Sofia."

Rubião didn't recognize the handwriting. It was the first time she'd written him. What could it be? His commotion was visible on his face and his fingers. While he was opening the letter, Freitas, in a familiar way, uncovered the basket: they were strawberries. Rubião's hand trembled as he read these lines:

> I'm sending you these bits of fruit for lunch, if they arrive in time. And by order of Cristiano you're invited to come and dine with us tonight without fail. Your true friend,
>
> SOFIA

"What kind of fruit is it?" Rubião asked, folding the letter.

"Strawberries."

"They arrived late. Strawberries?" he repeated without knowing what he was saying.

"You don't have to blush, my dear friend," Freitas told him, laughing, as soon as the servant left. "These things happen to people in love . . ."

"People in love?" Rubião repeated, really blushing. "But you can read the letter, look . . ."

He was going to show it but withdrew it and put it in his pocket. He was beside himself, half confused and half happy. Carlos Maria took delight in telling him that he couldn't hide it, that the little gift was from some sweetheart. And there was no reason to scold him, love was a universal law. If it was some married lady, he praised his discretion . . .

"But for the love of God!" the host interrupted.

"A widow? It's the same thing," Carlos Maria went on. "Discretion there is still worthy. The greater sin, after the sin, is the publication of the sin. If I were a legislator, I would propose that all men convicted of indiscretion in these matters be burned at the stake. And they would go to the flames like prisoners of the Inquisition with the difference that instead of sackcloth they would wear a cape of parrot feathers . . ."

Freitas couldn't contain his laughter and pounded on the table as a way of applause. Rubião, half skewered, hastened to say that it wasn't either a married woman or a widow . . .

"A single woman, then?" the young man replied. "A wedding on its way? Well, it's about time. Betrothal strawberries," he continued, picking some up with his fingers. "They smell of a maiden's chamber and a priest's Latin."

Rubião didn't know what else to say. Finally he went back to the beginning and explained. They were from the wife of a close friend. Carlos Maria winked. Freitas put in his word saying that now, yes sir, it was all explained. But that at first the mystery, the arrangement of the basket, the look of the strawberries themselves—adulterous strawberries, he said, laughing—all those things gave the matter an immoral and sinful look. But it turned out all right in the end.

They drank their coffee in silence. Then they went into the parlor. Rubião outdid himself in courtesies, but he was worried. After a few minutes he was content with the first supposition of his two guests: that of an adulterous love affair. He even thought that he'd defended himself too heatedly. Since he hadn't mentioned anybody's name, he could have confessed that it really was an intimate affair. But it also might have happened that the very heat of his denial might have left doubts in the minds of the two, some suspicion . . . At this he smiled, consoled.

Carlos Maria consulted his watch. It was two o'clock. He was leaving. Rubião thanked him warmly, obsequiously, and asked him to come back again. They could spend some Sundays like that in good friendly conversation.

"I second the motion!" Freitas shouted, coming over.

He had half a dozen cigars in his pocket, and as he left he whispered into Rubião's ear:

"These are the usual souvenirs. Six delightful days. A delight every day."

"Take some more."

"No, I'll come back for them another time."

Rubião accompanied them to the iron gate. Quincas Borba, as soon as he heard voices, ran out from the back of the garden to greet them, especially his master. He paid particular attention to Carlos Maria, tried to lick his hand. The young man drew back with repugnance. Rubião gave the dog a kick, which made him yelp and run away. Finally they all said goodbye.

"Which way are you going?" Carlos Maria asked Freitas.

Freitas calculated that he would be going to visit someone in the direction of São Clemente and wanted to accompany him.

"I'm going to the end of the beach," he said.

"I'm going back," the other replied.

XXXIII

Rubião watched them leave, came back in, went into the parlor and read Sofia's note again. Every word on that unexpected page was a mystery, the signature a capitulation. Only *Sofia*, no other family or married name. *Your true friend* was obviously a metaphor. As for the first words, *I'm sending you these bits of fruit for lunch* breathed the innocence of a good and generous soul. Rubião saw, felt, touched everything with only the force of instinct and gave in, kissing the paper—I'm not saying it right, kissing the name, the name given at the baptismal font, repeated by her mother, handed over to her husband as part of the moral document of marriage, and now stolen away from all those origins and ownerships to be sent to him at the bottom of a piece of paper . . . Sofia! Sofia! Sofia!

XXXIV

"Why did you come so late?" Sofia asked him as soon as he appeared at the garden gate in Santa Teresa.

"After lunch, which lasted until two o'clock, I was working on some papers. But it's not all that late," Rubião went on, looking at his watch, "it's only four-thirty."

"It's always late for friends," Sofia replied with a look of censure.

Rubião got hold of himself but not in time to withdraw his hand. Facing him, on an iron bench alongside the house, were four silent ladies eying him curiously. They were Sofia's guests, who were awaiting the arrival of the capitalist Rubião. Sofia brought him over to be introduced. Three of them were married, one was single, or more than single. She was thirty-nine, with a pair of dark eyes that were weary from waiting. She was the daughter of a Major Siqueira, who appeared in the garden a few moments later.

"Our friend Palha has spoken about you, sir," the major said after being introduced to Rubião. "I can vouch that he's your very good friend. He told me that chance brought you together. Those are generally the best friendships. When I was thirty-something, a little before becoming a major, I made a friend, my best friend in those days, whom I met by chance like that in Bernardes' pharmacy. His nickname was *Johnny Spats*. I think he wore them when he was young, between 1801 and 1812, and the nickname happened to stick. The pharmacy was on the Rua de São José, corner of Misericórdia . . . *Johnny Spats* . . . You know, it was a way of making his ankles look bigger . . . Bernardes was his name, João Alves Bernardes . . . He owned the pharmacy on the Rua de São José. He would stay there long hours in the afternoon, into the night. People went around with their capes and their big walking sticks. Some carried lanterns. Not me. I only wore my cape . . . He went around in a cape, Bernardes— João Alves Bernardes was his full name. He was from Maricá but he grew up here in Rio de Janeiro . . . *Johnny Spats* was his nickname. They said he went around in spats when he was young, and it seems he was one of the dandies of the city. I never forgot: *Johnny Spats* . . . He went around in a cape . . ."

Rubião's soul was flailing its arms under that torrent of words, but it was up a blind alley with no way out on any side. Walls all around. No open door, no hallway, and the rain kept falling. If he could have looked at the young ladies he would have seen, at least, that he was the object of the curiosity of all of them, most of all the major's daughter, Dona Tonica. But he couldn't. He was listening, and the major was raining cats and dogs. It was Palha who brought him an umbrella. Sofia had gone to tell her husband that Rubião had just arrived. Palha was in the garden in no time and greeted his friend, telling him he was late. The major, who was explaining the druggist's nickname one more time, abandoned his prey and went over to the young ladies. Then he went outside.

X X X V

The married ladies were pretty. Even the single one couldn't have been ugly when she was twenty-five. But Sofia stood out among all of them.

That's probably not all that our friend was feeling, but it was a good part of it. She was of that breed of women whom time, like a slow sculptor, doesn't finish immediately but goes on perfecting all along its passage. Slow sculptures like that are miraculous. Sofia was bordering on twenty-eight. She was more beautiful than at twenty-seven. It was to be imagined that the sculptor would only give the final touches at the age of thirty, unless he wished to prolong the work for two or three more years.

Her eyes, for example, are no longer the same ones they were on the train when our Rubião was talking to Palha, and they were underscoring the conversation . . . They seemed darker now, and they weren't underscoring anything. They were setting type themselves in bold, clear letters, and it wasn't a line or two but whole chapters. Her mouth seems livelier. Shoulders, hands, arms are better, and she makes them even better by means of well-chosen postures and gestures. There was one feature that the lady could never tolerate—something that Rubião himself found detracted from the rest of her face at first—her heavy eyebrows—even they, without having been diminished in any way, give the whole a very special look.

She wears clothes well. Her waist and bodice are drawn in by a chestnut corselet of fine wool, a simple piece, and she's wearing two genuine pearls on her ears—a gracious gift that our Rubião had made to Palha at Easter.

The beautiful lady is the daughter of an old civil servant. At the age of twenty she married this Cristiano de Almeida e Palha, an idler on city squares, who was twenty-five at the time. The husband made money. He was skillful, active, and had a nose for business and circumstances. In 1864, in spite of being new in the business, he guessed—there's no other term for it—he guessed that there would be bank failures.

"We've got something here, for better or for worse. It's held together by a thread. The slightest cry of alarm will carry it all off."

The bad part was that he spent everything he earned and more. He was attracted to the good life: frequent gatherings, expensive clothing and jewels for his wife, household furnishings, usually of the latest style or invention—all carried off present and future profits. Except for meals he was frugal with himself. He went to the theater quite often without enjoying it and to balls where he didn't have a good time—but he went not so much for himself as to show off his wife's eyes, her eyes and her breasts. He had that one touch of vanity. He would have his wife wear low-cut gowns whenever he could and even where he shouldn't in order to show others his personal good fortune. In that way he was a kind of King Candules,* more personal on one side, more public on the other.

Now let us do justice to our lady. At first she gave in to her husband's wishes under protest, but such was the admiration received and since habit accustoms people to circumstances, it reached the stage where she ended up enjoying being seen, seen often for the enjoyment of others. Let's not make her more of a saint than she is, nor less. For the demands of vanity her eyes were sufficient. They were laughing, restless, inviting, only in-

---

* King of Lydia in the seventh century B.C. According to Herodotus, Candules was so proud of his wife's beauty that he forced a courtier, Gyges, to see her nude. The queen caught Gyges spying on her and compelled him to kill her husband, marry her, and become king. [Ed.]

viting. They could be compared to the light of a guest house with no accomodations. The lamp made everybody stop, it was beautiful in its color and in the originality of its emblems. People would stop, look, and go on their way. Why open the windows wide? She opened them finally, but the door, if we can call her heart a door, was closed tight and bolted.

X X X V I

" God, she's beautiful! I feel capable of causing a scandal!" Rubião was thinking that night by the window with his back to the outside, looking at Sofia, who was looking at him.

A lady was singing. The three husbands from out of town who were there on a visit interrupted their card game and came into the parlor for a few moments. The singer was the wife of one of them. Palha, who was accompanying her on the piano, didn't see the mutual looks between his wife and the capitalist. I don't know if all the other people were in the same situation. One of them, I do know, was watching them: Dona Tonica, the major's daughter.

"God, she's beautiful! I feel capable of causing a scandal!" Rubião kept thinking, leaning against the window with his back to the outside, his eyes lost on the pretty woman who was looking back at him.

XXXVII

It must be understood that Dona Tonica was watching the mutual contemplation of the pair. Ever since Rubião had arrived, she did nothing but attempt to attract him. Her poor thirty-nine-year-old eyes, eyes with no partners in the world, ready now to slip into the weariness of despair, had a few sparks left. Rolling them about once and several times, putting a tender expression on them, was her long-held stock in trade. It was no problem for her to aim them at the capitalist.

Her heart, half-disillusioned, got worked up once more. Something was telling her that heaven had destined this rich man from Minas Gerais to solve her marriage problem. Rich was more than she was asking for. She wasn't asking for riches, she was only asking for a husband. None of her campaigns had been made with any pecuniary considerations. In recent times they'd been getting lower, and lower, and lower. The last had been waged against a poor student . . . But, who knows, could it be that heaven had meant her precisely for a rich man? Dona Tonica had faith in her patron saint, Our Lady of the Immaculate Conception, and she attacked the fortress with great skill and valor.

"All the others are married," she thought.

It didn't take her long to notice that Rubião's eyes and those of Sofia were aimed at each other. She noted, however, that Sofia's looks were less frequent and lingered less, a phenomenon that seemed explainable by the natural caution called for by the situation. It could be that they were in love . . . That suspicion pained her, but desire and hope told her that a man, after one or more affairs, could very well arrive at marriage. The question was to catch him. The perspective of marrying and having a family could well end up doing away with any other inclination on his part, if there was such.

With that she redoubled her efforts. All her charms were called into action, and they obeyed, even though faded. Gestures with her fan, opening her lips, eyes askance, walking back and forth to make a good display of the elegance of her body and her narrow waist, everything was put to use. It was the old formula in action. None of it had brought her anything up till then, but that's how the lottery works: a ticket comes along that makes up for all the previous losses.

Now, however, at night, on the occasion of the singing and the piano, Dona Tonica caught them taken with each other. She had no more doubts. They weren't apparently casual, brief looks, as up till that point, it was contemplation that shut out everything else in the room. Dona Tonica could hear the croak of the old raven of despair. Quoth the raven: NEVERMORE.

Even so she continued the battle. She managed to get Rubião to come and sit beside her for a few minutes, and she tried to say pretty things, phrases she'd got from novels, others that the melancholy of her situation itself inspired in her. Rubião listened and replied, but he got restless when Sofia left the room and was no less so when she returned. At one time the distraction was too much. Dona Tonica was confessing that she'd like to see Minas very much, especially Barbacena. What was the climate like?

"The climate," he repeated mechanically.

He was looking at Sofia, who was standing with her back to him, talking to the two seated ladies. Rubião admired her figure once more, her sculptured torso, narrow below, broad above as it emerged from her ample hips the way a large bouquet comes out of a vase. Her head, he was able to tell himself then, was like a single, straight magnolia thrusting up in the center of the bouquet. That was what Rubião was looking at when Dona Tonica asked him about the climate in Barbacena, and he repeated her word without even giving it the same interrogative tone.

XXXVIII

Rubião was resolute. Never had Sofia's soul seemed to be inviting his so insistently to fly off to those clandestine lands from which people generally return old and weary. Some don't return. Others stop halfway there. A great number never get beyond the edge of the roof.

XXXIX

The moon was magnificent. Up there on the heights, between the sky and the flatland below, even the least audacious soul was capable of going against an enemy army and destroying it. One is not permitted to say how he would behave with a friendly army like this one. They were in the garden. Sofia had put her arm on his so they could go look at the moon. She'd invited Dona Tonica, but the poor lady answered that her leg had gone to sleep, that she'd be along shortly, but she didn't come.

The two of them remained silent for some time. The other people could be seen through the open windows chatting and even the men, who'd finished their game of cards. The garden was small but the human voice has a wide range, and they were able to recite poetry without being heard.

Rubião remembered an old comparison, a very old one he'd picked up from some ten-line stanza back in 1850 or thereabouts or from some page of prose from all ages. He called Sofia's eyes the stars of the earth and the stars the eyes of heaven. All of that in a low, tremulous voice.

Sofia was astonished. She suddenly straightened up her body, which had been weighing on Rubião's arm until then. She was so accustomed to the man's bashfulness . . . Stars? Eyes? She wanted to tell him to stop teasing her, but she didn't know how to put a response together without rejecting a conviction that was also hers or encouraging him to continue on. A long silence was the result.

"With one difference," Rubião continued. "The stars are not even as beautiful as your eyes, and I really don't know what they are. God, who put them up so high, did so because they can't be seen close up without losing much of their beauty . . . But not your eyes. They're right here beside me, large, luminous, more luminous than the sky . . ."

Loquacious, daring, Rubião seemed like a completely different person. He didn't stop there. He went on talking a great deal, but always within the same circle of ideas. He didn't have too many, and the situation, in spite of the man's sudden transformation, tended more to hedge them in rather than to inspire new ones in him. Sofia was the one who didn't know what to do. She'd been holding a little dove, tame and quiet, in her arms, and it was turning into a hawk on her—a grasping and voracious hawk.

It was necessary to reply, to make him stop, to tell him that he was going where she didn't want to go, and all that without making him angry, without driving him away . . . Sofia was searching for something. She couldn't find it because she was running up against the problem, insoluble for her, of whether it was better to show that she understood or that she didn't understand. At this point she remembered her own gestures, her soft words, her special attentions. She couldn't ignore the meaning of the man's compliments. But to confess that she understood and not to order him from the house was where the delicate point lay.

X L

Up above the stars seemed to be laughing at that inextricable situation. Let the moon see them! The moon doesn't know how to mock. And poets, who find her nostalgic, must have perceived that in times gone by she'd loved some vagabond star who'd abandoned her after long centuries. Perhaps they're still in love. Her eclipses (forgive my astronomy) might be nothing more than lovers' trysts. The myth of Diana's coming down to meet Endymion might well be true. The coming down isn't what's too much. What's wrong with the pair of them meeting up there in the sky like crickets in the treetops down here? Night, a charitable mother, takes it upon herself to watch over everyone.

After all, the moon is solitary. Solitude makes a person serious. The stars, in a throng, are like girls between the ages of fifteen and twenty, talkative, laughing and talking at the same time about everything and everybody.

I won't deny that they're chaste, but so much the worse— they've probably laughed at what they don't understand... Chaste stars! That's what Othello the terrible and Tristram Shandy the jovial call them. Those extremes in heart and spirit are in agreement on one point: the stars are chaste. And they heard everything (chaste stars!), everything that Rubião's bold mouth was pouring into Sofia's startled soul. The one who'd been bashful for months on end was now (chaste stars!) a libertine no less. You're probably saying that the Devil was at work deceiving the young woman with the two great wings of an archangel that God had put on him. Suddenly he was putting them in his pocket and taking off his hat, revealing the two malignant points sticking out of his forehead. And, laughing that oblique laugh evil people have, he proposed buying not only her soul but her soul and her body... Chaste stars!

X L I

"Let's go in," Sofia murmured.

She tried to pull her arm away, but he held it back forcefully. No. Why go in? They were fine there, quite fine... What could be better? Or was he boring her, perhaps? Sofia hastened to say no, on the contrary, but she had to go attend to her guests... They'd been out there too long!

"It hasn't been ten minutes," Rubião said. "What are ten minutes?"

"But they may have noticed our absence..."

Rubião quivered at that possessive: *our* absence. He found it a beginning of complicity. He agreed that they might have noticed *our* absence. She was right, they should separate. He was only asking for one thing, two things. The first was that she not forget those sublime ten minutes, the second was that every night at ten o'clock she look at the Southern Cross. He would be looking at it too, and the thoughts of both would go to find themselves together there, intimate, in between God and men.

The invitation was poetic, but only the invitation. Rubião was devouring the young lady with eyes of fire and was gripping one of her hands so she wouldn't run away. Neither his eyes nor his gesture had any poetry about them. Sofia was on the point of uttering some harsh word, but she immediately swallowed it as she remembered that Rubião was a good friend of the house. She tried to laugh but couldn't. Then she acted annoyed, then resigned, finally pleading. She begged him on the soul of her mother who should be in heaven . . . Rubião didn't care about heaven or her mother or anything. What was a mother? What was heaven? his face seemed to be saying.

"Ouch, you're breaking my fingers!" the young woman moaned in a low voice.

This was when he began to come to. He relaxed his grip without releasing her fingers.

"Go ahead," he said, "but first . . ."

He leaned over to kiss her hand when a voice a few steps away woke him up completely.

XLII

"Hello there! Admiring the moon? It really is delightful. It's a night made for lovers . . . Yes, delightful . . . It's been a long time since I've seen a night like this . . . Just look down below there, the gaslights . . . Delightful! For lovers . . . Lovers always like the moon. In my time, in Icaraí . . ."

It was Siqueira, the awful major. Rubião didn't know what to say. Sofia, after the first few moments, got hold of herself. She replied that the night really was beautiful. Then she said that Rubião insisted in saying that Rio nights couldn't compare with those in Barbacena, and in line with that he'd told an anecdote by a Father Mendes . . . "It was Mendes, wasn't it?"

"Mendes, yes, Father Mendes," Rubião murmured.

The major had trouble holding back his surprise. He'd seen the two hands together, Rubião's head leaning over, the quick movement of them both when he came into the garden. And out of all that he got a Father Mendes . . . He looked at Sofia, saw she was smiling, tranquil, impenetrable. No fright, no fluster, she spoke so simply that the major thought his eyes had deceived him. But Rubião ruined everything. Annoyed, silent, all he could do was take out his watch to see what time it was, holding it up to his ear as if he thought it wasn't running, then cleaning it with his handkerchief slowly, slowly, without looking at one or the other . . .

"Well, you two have a talk. I'm going to see to the ladies, who shouldn't be left alone. Have the men finished their dreadful card game yet?"

"Just now," the major replied, looking at Sofia curiously. "Just now, and they were asking about this gentleman. That's why I came out, to see if I could find him in the garden. But have you been out here long?"

"We just came out," Sofia said.

Then, patting the major lovingly on the back, she left the garden and went into the house. She didn't go in through the parlor door but through another that opened into the dining room, so that when she reached the parlor from inside it was as if she'd just given orders for tea.

Rubião, coming to, still couldn't find anything to say and yet it was most urgent that he say something. That story about Father Mendes was a good idea. The worst of it was that there was no priest and no anecdote, and he was incapable of inventing anything. It seemed to him sufficient to say this:

"The priest! Mendes! A very amusing person, Father Mendes!"

"I knew him," the major said, smiling. "Father Mendes? I knew him. He died a canon. Was he in Minas a long time?"

"I think he was," the other murmured, horrified.

"He was from here, from Saquarema. He was missing this eye," the major went on, raising his finger to his left eye. "I knew him well, if it's the same one. It might be a different one."

"It might be."

"He died a canon. He was a man of good habits, but he had an eye for pretty girls, the way you look at a masterpiece. Is there any greater master painter than God? This Dona Sofia, for example, he never saw her on the street but what he'd say to me: 'I saw the pretty Mrs. Palha today . . .' He died a canon. He was from Saquarema . . . He really did have good taste . . . Our Palha's wife really is a beauty, beautiful in face and in figure. Although I find her more well put together than pretty . . . What do you think?"

"I think you're right . . ."

"She's a fine person, an excellent lady of the house," the major continued, lighting a cigar.

The light from the match gave the major's face a mocking expression, or something less harsh but no less adverse. Rubião felt a chill run up his spine. Could he have heard? Seen? Guessed? Was he an indiscreet person, a busybody? The man's face didn't clarify that point. In any case, it was safer to believe the worst. Here we have our hero like someone who, after sailing close to shore over the years, finds himself one day in the midst of the high seas. Luckily, fear is also an officer with ideas and it gave him one then: flatter the man. He didn't waste any time in finding him amusing and interesting and telling him that he had a house on Botafogo beach, number such-and-such, that was open to him. It would be a great honor to have him for a friend. He didn't have many friends here: Palha, to whom he owed many favors; Dona Sofia, who was a lady of rare prudence; and three or four other people. He lived alone. He might even be going back to Minas.

"Soon?"

"I can't say soon, but it might not be too long from now. You know, for a person who's lived all his life in a place it's hard to get used to another."

"That depends."

"Yes, that depends . . . But it's the general rule."

"It may be the general rule, but you're going to be the exception. The capital is a devilish place. You catch a passion for it the way you catch a cold. One breath of air and you're lost. Look, I'll bet that within six months you'll be married . . ."

"He didn't see anything," Rubião thought.

And then, merrily:

"It could be, but marriages take place in Minas, too. And there's no lack of priests there."

"Father Mendes is lacking," the major put in, laughing.

Rubião smiled weakly, not knowing whether the major's words were innocent or malicious. The latter was the one who took up the reins of the conversation and steered it onto other matters: the weather, the city, the cabinet, the war and Marshal López.* And just note the contrast in the occasion. That torrential rain, heavier than the one at the beginning, was like a ray of sunshine for our Rubião. Behold his soul flapping the dust off its wings to the heat of the major's endless discourse, injecting a small word here and there if he could and always nodding with applause. And he was thinking once more, "No, he hadn't seen anything."

"Papa! Papa, are you there?" a voice said at the door to the garden.

It was Dona Tonica. She'd come to fetch him so they could leave. Tea was on the table, it was true, but she couldn't stay any longer; she had a headache, she told her father in a low voice. Then she held out her fingers to Rubião. The latter asked her to wait just a few minutes more, the distinguished major . . .

"You're wasting your time," the major interrupted. "She's the one who governs me."

Rubião offered him his hospitality again. He even demanded that they set a date that very week, but the major was quick to say that he couldn't promise a specific day. He would come as soon as it was possible. His life was quite busy. He had duties at the arsenal, a lot of them, and besides that . . .

"Papa! Let's go!"

"I'm coming. See? I can't stop and chat for even a minute. Did you say goodbye already? Where's my hat?"

* Francisco Solano López (1826–1870), dictator of Paraguay during the 1865–1870 war with Brazil, Argentina, and Uruguay. [Ed.]

XLIII

On the way down Dona Tonica went along listening to the remainder of her father's discourse as he changed subjects without changing style—diffuse and digressive. She was listening without understanding. She went along all wrapped up in herself, absorbed, putting the night through the mill again, recomposing the looks between Sofia and Rubião.

They reached their home on the Rua do Senado. The father went to bed, but the daughter didn't lie down right away, sitting up in a small chair beside her dressing table, where she had an image of the Virgin. She wasn't carrying any ideas of peace and innocence. Without having known love, she knew what adultery was, and the persona of Sofia seemed rotten to her. She saw a monster in her now, half-human, half-snake, and she felt that she hated her, that she was capable of getting her revenge by telling her husband everything.

"I'll tell him everything," she was thinking, "either orally or in a letter . . . No, not a letter. I'll tell him everything face-to-face one day."

And imagining the dialogue, she foresaw the man's surprise, then his anger, then his curses, the harsh words that he would address to his wife: miserable wretch, unworthy, vile woman . . . All those names sounded good to the ears of her desire. She was able to bring out her own rage with them. She could only bring her down that way, placing her beneath her husband's feet, since she couldn't do it herself . . . Vile, unworthy, miserable woman . . .

That explosion of inner rage lasted for a long time—close to twenty minutes. But her soul grew tired, and she became herself again. Her imagination couldn't do anything further, and the reality around her caught her sight. She looked about, looked at her old maid's bedroom, artistically arranged—that ingenious art which turns cotton into silk and an old swatch into a ribbon, which decorates, arranges, embellishes the nakedness of things as much as possible, adorns sad walls, beautifies the few modest pieces. And everything there seemed made to receive a loving bridegroom.

Where did I read that an ancient tradition made a virgin in Israel wait for divine conception during a certain night of the year? Wherever it was, let's compare her to this other one, who differs from the first only in that she doesn't have one fixed night but all of them, all, all . . . The wind whistling outside never brought her the hoped-for male, nor did maiden dawn tell her the spot on earth where he lived. It was only waiting, waiting . . .

Now, with her imagination and resentment soothed, she looks and looks again at her lonely bedroom. She remembers her friends from school and family, the closest ones, all married. The last of them married a naval officer at the age of thirty, and that was what made the hopes of her unmarried friend bloom again. She wasn't asking for so much because a cadet's uniform had been the first thing to seduce her eyes at the age of fifteen . . . Where did they go? But that was five years ago. She was thirty-nine and would soon be forty. An old maid of forty. Dona Tonica shuddered. She kept on looking, remembering everything. She stood up suddenly, turned around twice, and threw herself onto the bed weeping . . .

X L I V

You mustn't believe that the pain here was more real than the anger. By themselves they were equal; the effects were what was different. Anger didn't lead anywhere. Humiliation dissolved into legitimate tears. And, nonetheless, that lady still had an urge to strangle Sofia, to trample her, tear out her heart in pieces, telling her to her face the cruel names she'd attributed to her husband . . . All of it was imagined! Believe me, there are tyrants by intention. Who knows? In that lady's soul there was a slight touch of Caligula . . .

XLV

While one is weeping, the other one laughs. It's the law of the world, my fine fellow, it's universal perfection. Nothing but weeping would be monotonous, nothing but laughter would be wearisome. But a proper distribution of tears and polkas, sobs and sarabands ends up by giving the soul of the world the necessary variety, and it becomes the balance of life.

The other one that's laughing is Rubião's soul. Listen to the merry, bright tune with which it goes down the hill, saying the most intimate things to the stars, a kind of rhapsody made of a language that no one ever gave an alphabet to because it's impossible to find a sign to convey the words. Down below the deserted streets seemed full of people to him, the silence a tumult, and leaning out of all the windows were the figures of women, pretty faces and thick eyebrows, all Sofias and one single Sofia. Over and over Rubião thinks he was rash, indiscreet; he remembers that business in the garden, the resistance, the young woman's annoyance, and he begins to repent. Then he has chills, is terrified by the thought that the door might be slammed in his face and relations broken off completely. All because he'd got ahead of things. Yes, he should have waited. It wasn't the right occasion. Visitors, all the lights, what kind of a notion was it to talk about love, carelessly, shamelessly . . . ? He thought she was right. It would have been proper for her to turn him away at once.

"I was crazy!" he said aloud.

He wasn't thinking about the dinner, which was sumptuous, or the wines, which were abundant, or the very electricity of a room in which there were lovely ladies. He was thinking that he'd been crazy, absolutely crazy.

Immediately after, the same soul that was being accused defended itself. It seemed to him that Sofia had encouraged him to do what he did. Her frequent looks, then stares, her manners, her compliments, the honor of having her seat him next to her at the dinner table, paying attention only to him, telling him pleasant things in a melodious voice, what could all that be if not encouragement and solicitation? And the good soul explained the lady's annoyance in the garden afterwards: it was the first time she'd heard such words outside her conjugal relationship, and close to all the people there. She naturally must have trembled a lot, too. He'd opened up so much that he brought it all out. No gradations. He should have gone step by step and never taken her hands with so much force that he annoyed her. In sum, he found himself to have been rude. The fear that the door would be closed on him came back. Then he returned to the consolation of hope, to the analysis of the young lady's actions, to the invention of Father Mendes, a lie of complicity. He also thought of her husband's esteem . . . He shuddered there . . . Her husband's esteem gave him remorse. Not only did he have his trust, but added to that was a certain monetary debt, some three notes Rubião had taken on for him.

"I can't, I mustn't," he was saying to himself. "It's not right to go on. It's also true that I didn't start anything, really. She's the one who's been challenging me for a long time. So let her challenge, then! Yes, I've got to resist her . . . I lent the money almost without being asked because he needed a lot and I owed him favors. The notes, yes, the notes he asked me to sign, but he didn't ask for anything else. I know that he's honest, that he works hard. It's that devil of a woman who did the wrong thing in coming between us with her beautiful eyes and her figure . . . What a figure, God in heaven! Just tonight it was divine. When her arm brushed mine at the table, in spite of my sleeve . . ."

Confused, uncertain, he went along thinking about the loyalty he owed his friend, but his conscience was split in two, one part accusing the other, the other explaining itself, both disoriented . . .

He found himself on the Praça da Constituição. He'd been wandering aimlessly. He thought about going to the theater, but it was too late. Then he headed for the Largo de São Francisco to get a cab and go to Botafogo. He found three of them, whose owners immediately came over to offer their services, mainly praising their horses: a good horse—an excellent animal.

XLVI

The sound of the voices and the vehicles woke up a beggar who was sleeping on the steps of the church. The poor devil sat up, saw what it was, then lay down again, but awake, on his back, his eyes fixed on the sky. The sky was staring back at him, as impassive as he, but without the beggar's wrinkles or his worn shoes or his tatters, a clear, starry, calm, Olympian sky, like the one that presided over Jacob's wedding and Lucretia's suicide. They looked at each other in a kind of judgment game, with a certain air of rival and tranquil majesties, without haughtiness or wretchedness, as if the beggar were saying to the sky:

"Well, you won't be falling on me."

And the sky:

"And you won't be climbing up me."

XLVII

Rubião was not a philosopher. The comparison he made between his cares and those of the ragamuffin only brought a touch of envy to his soul. "That beggar isn't thinking about anything," he said to himself. "In just a little while he'll be asleep, while I . . ."

"Get in, master, it's a fine animal. We'll be there in fifteen minutes."

The two other coachmen were telling him the same thing with almost the same words.

"Come over here, master, and you'll see . . ."

"Look at my little horse . . ."

"Please. It's a thirteen-minute ride. You'll be home in thirteen minutes."

Rubião, still hesitating, got into the cab that was closest at hand and told the driver to go to Botafogo. Then he remembered an old forgotten episode, or it was the episode that unconsciously gave him the solution. One thing or the other. Rubião was directing his thoughts in an attempt to get away from the night's feelings.

It had been a long time ago. He was still quite young, and poor. One day, at eight o'clock in the morning, he left the house, which was on the Rua do Cano (now Sete de Setembro), went onto the Largo de São Francisco de Paula, and from there went down the Rua do Ouvidor. He worried as he walked. He was living at the home of a friend who was beginning to treat him like a three-day guest, and he'd already been a four-week one. They say that the three-day ones stink. Dead people stink a lot earlier than that, at least in hot climates like this . . . What was certain was that our Rubião, simple as the good native of Minas that he was but as wary as someone from São Paulo, went along full of worries, thinking about leaving as soon as possible. It can be believed that from the moment he left the house, went out on to the Largo de São Francisco and down the Rua do Ouvidor to the Rua dos Ourives, he hadn't seen or heard a single thing.

On the corner of the Rua dos Ourives his way was blocked by a crowd of people and a strange procession. A man in judicial robes was reading aloud from a sheet of paper: the sentence. In addition to the judge there were a priest, soldiers, and onlookers. But the principal figures were two black men. One of them, of medium height, thin, had his hands tied, his eyes cast down, bronze-colored skin, and a rope tied around his neck. The end of the rope was in the hands of another black man. This one was looking straight ahead, and his color was uniformly jet black. He was bearing the curiosity of the crowd with poise. When the paper had been read the procession continued on along the Rua dos Ourives. It was coming from the jail and was on its way to the Largo do Moura.

Rubião was naturally affected by it. For a few seconds he was the way he'd been just now about the choice of a cab. Inner forces were offering him their horses, some for him to turn back or to go about his business—others to go along and watch the black man be hanged. It was a rare opportunity to see a hanging! Sir, in twenty minutes it's all over!—Sir, let's go and take care of something else! And our man closed his eyes and let himself go as chance would have it. Chance, instead of leading him down the Rua do Ouvidor to the Rua da Quitanda, turned his path along the Rua dos Ourives behind the procession. He wasn't going along to see the execution, he thought, it was only to watch the prisoner's walk, the face of the executioner, the ritual . . . He didn't want to see the execution. Every so often everything came to a halt, people appeared in doors and windows, and the court officer read the sentence again. Then the procession continued moving with the same solemnity. The onlookers were discussing the crime—a murder in Mata-Porcos. The murderer was known to be a cold-blooded, violent man. The news of those qualities made Rubião feel better. It gave him the strength to look the prisoner in the face without melting into pity. It was no longer the face of crime. Fright hid perversity. Without noticing, he arrived at the execution square. There were quite a few people there already. Along with those arriving they formed a compact mass.

"Let's go back," he said to himself.

The truth is that the prisoner hadn't mounted the steps to the gallows yet. They were in no hurry to kill him. There was still time to run away. And since Rubião was staying, why wasn't he closing his eyes the way a certain Alypius had done at the sight of the wild beasts? It must be noted that Rubião had never heard of that ancient youth. He was unaware that he had not only closed his eyes but had also opened them immediately after, slowly and curiously . . .

There was the prisoner, mounting the gallows. A murmur ran through the crowd. The executioner went to work. It was here that Rubião's right foot made a turn in the direction it had come, obeying a feeling to go back. But the left foot, taken by a contrary feeling, stayed where it was. They fought for a few moments . . . Look at my horse!—See, he's a fine animal!—Don't be bad!—Don't be faint-hearted! Rubião was like that for a few seconds, all that was needed for the fatal moment to arrive. All eyes were fixed on the same spot, the same as his. Rubião couldn't understand what beast was gnawing at his insides or what iron hands were clutching his soul and keeping it there. The fatal instant really was an instant. The prisoner kicked, stiffened; the executioner climbed onto him in an agile and skillful way. A loud noise spread through the crowd. Rubião gave a shout and saw nothing more.

XLVIII

"Your Worship must have seen what a fine little horse I have . . ." Rubião opened his half-closed eyes and saw the coachman who was lightly poking with the tip of his whip in order to rouse the animal. Inside he was annoyed with the man, who'd just brought him out of ancient memories. They weren't pretty, but they were ancient—ancient and curative, because they were giving him an elixir to drink that seemed to have completely cured him of the present. And there was the coachman, tugging at him and waking him up. They were going up the Rua da Lapa, and the horse really was eating up the road, as if it were going downhill.

"This horse feels a great friendship for me," the coachman went on, "unbelievable. I could tell you amazing things. There are people who say that they're all lies of mine, but they're not, no, sir, they're not. Doesn't everybody know that horses and dogs are the animals that like people the most? Dogs, I think, like us even more . . ."

The mention of dogs brought Quincas Borba back into Rubião's memory. He was probably waiting anxiously for him there at home. Rubião wasn't forgetting the conditions of the will. He was fulfilling them to the letter. It must be said that part of the fear of seeing him run away was that of seeing the loss of his possessions. The lawyer's assurances were useless. The latter had told him that there was no clause in the will making it revert to anyone else in case the dog ran away. The estate couldn't leave his hands. What difference would the dog's running away make for him since it would be one less care? Rubião gave the impression of accepting the explanation, but the doubt still remained, the thought of long, drawn-out lawsuits, a variety of judicial opinions concerning one single point, the acts of some envious person or an enemy, and, what summed it all up, the terror of being left without anything. Out of that came the strict confinement, out of that also the remorse of having spent the afternoon and evening without thinking even once about Quincas Borba.

"I'm an ingrate!" he told himself.

He immediately corrected himself. He was an even greater ingrate because he hadn't thought about the other Quincas Borba, who'd left him everything. Then suddenly the thought occurred to him that the two Quincas Borbas might be the same creature through the effect of the dead man's soul entering the body of the dog, not so much to purge his sins as to keep an eye on his owner. It had been a black woman from São João d'El-Rei who'd put that idea of transmigration into his head when he was a child. She'd said that a soul full of sin would enter the body of a beast. She even swore that she'd known a court clerk who'd been turned into an opossum . . .

"Your Worship mustn't forget to tell me where your house is," the coachman suddenly told him.

"Stop."

XLIX

The dog was barking inside the gate, but as soon as Rubião entered, he received him with great joy and, no matter how bothersome it was, Rubião outdid himself with petting. The possibility of the testator's being there gave him the shivers. They went up the stone steps together. They remained there for a few moments in the light of the lamp that Rubião had ordered left on. Rubião was more credulous than believing. He had no reason to attack or defend anything: eternally virgin soil for anything to be planted. Life in the capital had given him a trait, though: among incredulous people he had come to be incredulous . . .

He looked at the dog while he waited for them to open the door. The dog was looking at him in such a way that inside him there the selfsame and deceased Quincas Borba seemed to be present. It was the same meditative look that the philosopher had had when he was examining human motives . . . Another shiver. But the fear, while great, wasn't so great that it tied his hands. Rubião reached them out to the dog's head, scratching his ears and neck.

"Poor Quincas Borba! You like your master, don't you? Rubião is a good friend of Quincas Borba . . ."

And the dog moved his head left and right to facilitate the petting of his two drooping ears. Then he lifted up his jaw so he could be scratched underneath it, and his master obeyed. But then the dog's eyes, half closed with pleasure, took on the look of the philosopher's eyes, in bed, telling him things of which he understood very little or nothing at all . . . Rubião closed his eyes. They opened the door for him. He took leave of the dog but with such petting that it was the same as inviting him in. The Spanish servant took charge of taking him back down.

"Don't hurt him," Rubião ordered.

He didn't hurt him, but just going down was painful enough and the dog-friend whimpered in the garden for a long time. Rubião went in, got undressed, and lay down. Oh, he'd lived through a day full of diverse and contrary sensations, from his morning memories and lunch with his two friends up to that last idea of metempsychosis, passing along the way through the memory of the hanged man and through a declaration of love that wasn't accepted, was barely repulsed, was seemingly suspected by other people . . . He was mixing everything in. His spirit was going back and forth like a rubber ball between the hands of children. All in all, the major feeling was that of love. Rubião was amazed at himself, and he repented. But the repentance was the work of his conscience, while his imagination wouldn't for any price release the image of the beautiful Sofia . . . One, two, three o'clock . . . Sofia far off, the barking of the dog down below . . . Evasive sleep . . . Where had three o'clock gone? Three-thirty . . . Finally, after a great effort, sleep came for him, squeezed out the opium from its poppies, and it took only an instant. Before it was four o'clock, Rubião was asleep.

L

No, my dear lady, that ever so long day isn't over yet. We still don't know what happened between Sofia and Palha after everyone had left. It's even possible that you'll find a better taste here than in the case of the hanged man.

Be patient. It's a matter of going back to Santa Teresa now. The parlor is still lighted by a gas jet. The other lights have been extinguished, and the last one was about to be when Palha ordered the servant to wait inside for a bit. The wife was about to leave the room; the husband held her back. She trembled.

"Our party was quite nice," he said.

"It was."

"Siqueira's a bore, but we've got to be patient. He's a jolly sort. His daughter didn't look too bad. Did you see how Ramos gobbled up everything that was put on his plate? You just watch, someday he's going to swallow his wife."

"His wife?" Sofia asked, smiling.

"She's fat. I admit, but the first one was even fatter, and I don't think she died. He most certainly gobbled her up."

Sofia, reclining on the settee, laughed at her husband's witticisms. They discussed a few more episodes of the afternoon and evening; then Sofia, stroking her husband's hair, said suddenly:

"But you still don't know what the best episode of the evening was."

"Which was it?"

"Guess."

Palha was silent for some time, looking at his wife, trying to guess what had been the best episode of the evening. He couldn't. This one or that one came to mind, but they weren't it. Sofia would shake her head.

"Which was it, then?"

"I don't know. Guess."

"I can't. Come on, tell me."

"Under one condition," she hastened to say. "I don't want any huffing or any row . . ."

Palha grew more serious. Huffing? Row? What the devil could it be? he thought. He wasn't laughing any longer. All he had left were the remains of a forced and resigned smile. He stared hard at her and asked her what it was.

"Do you promise what I asked?"

"All right. What was it?"

"Well, you should know, then, that I heard a declaration of love."

Palha grew pale. He hadn't promised not to grow pale. He loved his wife, as we know, even to the point of showing her off. He couldn't hear that news coldly. Sofia saw his paleness and enjoyed the bad impression she'd made. To savor it all the more she leaned her breast over him, loosened her hair, which had been bothering her a little, gathered the hairpins in a handkerchief, then shook her head, breathed deeply, and grasped her husband's hands as he stood there.

"It's true, you fine fellow, your wife was courted."

"So who was the scoundrel?" he asked, impatient.

"Easy. If this is the way things are going to go, I won't tell. Who was it? You want to know who it was? You've got to hear it calmly. It was Rubião."

"Rubião?"

"I couldn't have imagined such a thing. He always seemed so bashful and respectful to me. It only proves that the habit doesn't make the monk. I've never heard the slightest peep out of all the men who've come here. They look at me, naturally, because I'm not ugly . . . Why are you walking back and forth like that? Stop. I don't want to have to raise my voice . . . Fine, like that . . . Let's get down to cases. He didn't make an out and out declaration to me . . ."

"Oh, no?" her husband put in eagerly.

"No, but it amounted to the same."

And then she told him what had happened in the garden, from the time the two of them had gone out there until the major appeared.

"That's all there was," she concluded, "but it's enough to see that if he didn't say love it was because the word hadn't got to his tongue. But it did get to his hand, which squeezed my fingers . . . That's all, but, even so, it's too much. It's good you're not getting angry, but we've got to shut the door on him—either all at once or little by little. I'd prefer it all at once, but

I'll accept either way. What do you think is the best way to do it?"

Biting his lower lip, Palha continued looking at her like a dunce. He sat down on the settee, silent. He was thinking the matter over. He found it natural that his wife's charms should captivate a man—and Rubião could be that man. But he trusted Rubião so much that the note Sofia had sent him along with the strawberries had been dictated by him. His wife had limited herself to copying it down, signing it, and sending it off. Never, however, had the idea crossed his mind that his friend would make a declaration of love to anybody, much less Sofia, if it really was love. He might have been making a joke between close friends. Rubião would look at her a lot, it was true, and it also seemed that Sofia, on some occasions, would repay those looks with others of her own . . . The concessions of a pretty woman! But, after all, while their eyes stayed like that some flashes might come out of them. One shouldn't be jealous of the optic nerve, the husband was thinking. Sofia got up, went to put the handkerchief with the hairpins on the piano, and took a look in the mirror to see herself with her hair down. When she returned to the settee her husband took her hand, laughing:

"It seems to me that you've got more upset than the case deserves. Comparing a young woman's eyes to the stars and the stars to her eyes, after all, is something that can be done in front of everybody among close friends and in prose or verse in front of the general public. The blame belongs to those pretty eyes of yours. Besides, in spite of what you're telling me, you know that he's just a bumpkin . . ."

"Then the devil's a bumpkin, too, because he didn't seem like anything less than the devil to me. What about his asking me to look at the Southern Cross at a certain time so that our souls could meet?"

"That, yes, that does have the smell of lovemaking about it," Palha agreed. "But you can see that it's the request of a poor innocent soul. That's the way fifteen-year-old girls talk. That's the way boobs talk all the time; poets, too. But he's not a young girl and he's not a poet."

"I don't think so. And what about grabbing my hand to keep me in the garden?"

Palha felt a chill. The idea of the contact of hands and the force taken to hold his wife back was what mortified him most. Frankly, if he could have done so, he was capable of having it out with Rubião and laying his hands on his throat. Other ideas, however, came and dissipated the effect of the first. So that although Sofia had thought she'd upset him, she saw him shrug his shoulders with disdain and respond that it was only a matter of coarse manners after all.

"But after all, Sofia, whatever gave you the idea of inviting him to go have a look at the moon, please tell me?"

"I called Dona Tonica to come with us."

"But once Dona Tonica refused you should have found ways and means not to go into the garden. They're things that can immediately incite a person. You're the one who gave him the opportunity . . ."

Sofia looked at him, contracting her thick eyebrows. She was going to answer, but she remained silent. Palha continued developing the same theme. The blame was hers. She shouldn't have given him the opportunity . . .

"But didn't you tell me yourself that we should treat him with special consideration? I certainly wouldn't have gone into the garden if I could have imagined what was going to happen. But I never expected that a man who was so quiet, so I don't know what, would throw care to the winds and say strange things to me . . ."

"Well, from here on avoid the moon and the garden," her husband said, trying to smile . . .

"But, Cristiano, how do you want me to talk to him the next time he comes here? I'm not up to such a thing. Look, the best thing would be to break off relations."

Palha crossed his legs and began to drum on his shoe. For a few seconds they remained silent. Palha was thinking about the proposal to break off relations, not that he wanted to accept it, but he didn't know how to reply to his wife, who was showing such resentment and was reacting so properly. It was necessary neither to reject nor accept the proposal, but nothing came to mind. He got up, put his hands in his pockets, and, after taking a few steps, stopped, facing Sofia.

"Maybe we're getting all upset over the simple effect of some wine. He's wet behind the ears. A weak head, a little prodding, and he pours out everything he's got inside . . . Yes, I won't deny that you might have given a certain impression, like so many other women. A few days ago he went to a ball in Catete and came back all dazzled by the ladies he'd seen there, one most of all, the widow Mendes . . ."

Sofia interrupted:

"Then why didn't he invite that beauty to look at the Southern Cross?"

"He didn't dine there, naturally, and there wasn't any garden or any moon. What I'm trying to say is that *our friend* wasn't in control of his senses. Maybe right now he's sorry for what he did, ashamed, not knowing how to explain himself or if he'll ever be able to explain anything . . . It's even quite possible that he'll stay away . . ."

"That would be best."

". . . if we don't invite him," Palha finished.

"So why invite him?"

"Sofia," her husband said, sitting down beside her. "I don't want to go into details. I'm only saying that I won't allow anyone to show you a lack of respect . . ."

There was a slight pause. Sofia was looking at him, waiting.

"I won't allow it, and God help the one who does it, and God help you if you let him. You know that I'm made of steel in that respect and that the certainty of your friendship—or, getting right down to it—the love you have for me is what keeps me calm. So nothing has shaken me regarding Rubião. Believe me, Rubião's our friend, I owe him obligations."

"A few presents, a few jewels, boxes at the theater, they're no reason for me to gaze at the Southern Cross with him."

"God grant it were only that!" the opportunist sighed.

"What else?"

"Let's not go into details . . . There are other things . . . We'll talk about them later . . . But rest assured that nothing would make me draw back if you came to tell me about some serious matter. There isn't any. The man's a simpleton."

"No."

"No?"

Sofia got up. She didn't want to go into details either. Her husband took her by the hand. She stood there in silence. Palha, his head resting on the back of the sofa, looked at her smiling, unable to find anything to say. After a few minutes his wife decided it was late, she should have all the lights turned out.

"All right," Palha replied after a brief silence. "I'll write him tomorrow not to set foot here."

He looked at his wife, expecting a refusal. Sofia was frowning and didn't answer anything. Palha repeated his solution, and it might have been that he was sincere that time. His wife then said, with an air of tedium:

"Come on, Cristiano . . . Who's asking you to write any letters? I'm already sorry I brought the matter up. I told you about an act of disrespect and said it was best to break off relations— little by little or all at once."

"But how can relations be cut off all at once?"

"By shutting the door on him, but I didn't say as much. Let it be little by little if you want . . ."

It was a concession. Palha accepted it but immediately grew somber, released his wife's hand with a gesture of desperation. Then, taking her around the waist, he said in a louder voice than he had used until then:

"But, my love, I owe him a lot of money."

Sofia covered his mouth and looked toward the hallway, concerned.

"It's all right," she said. "Let's drop it. I'll keep an eye on his behavior, and I'll try to be colder . . . In that case you're the one who mustn't change, so it won't look as if you knew what had happened. I'll see what I can do."

"You know. Business troubles, mistakes . . . having to plug a hole here, another there . . . damned business! That's why . . . But let's laugh at it, my sweet. It's not worth anything. Just know that I trust you."

"Let's go, it's late."

"Let's go," Palha repeated, kissing her on the cheek.

"I've got an awful headache," she murmured. "I think it's the dew, or this whole story . . . I've got an awful headache."

L I

Bathed, shaved, half-dressed, Palha was reading the newspapers, waiting for breakfast, when he saw his wife come into the study, a little pale.

"Are you feeling worse?"

Sofia answered with a gesture of her lips that was as negative as it was positive. Palha believed that as the day went on the upset would pass. Last night's agitation, dining late . . . Then he asked her to let him finish an article dealing with a certain matter in the market. It was a fight between two merchants that had to do with some loans. One of them had written the day before, and today the other one was replying. A complete reply, he said, as he finished reading. And he explained in detail to his wife the matter of the loans, the mechanism of the operation, the situation of the two adversaries, the rumors on the exchange, all with technical vocabulary. Sofia listened and sighed. But the despotism of the profession admitted neither the sighs of women nor the courtesies of men. Luckily, breakfast was on the table.

Left alone, our friend, who'd only had some broth around two o'clock, went to sit in the garden by the door of the house. Naturally she started thinking again about the episode of the night before. She didn't feel right or wrong, either with God or with the devil. She regretted having told her husband about the episode, and at the same time she was bothered by the attempts at an explanation that he gave her. In the midst of her reflections she distinctly heard the major's words: "Hello there! Appreciating the moon?" as if the leaves had held them and were repeating them now that the breeze had set them in motion. Sofia shuddered. Siquiera was indiscreet—indiscreet in sniffing about and looking into other people's business. Would he be capable of making it public? Sofia now considered herself the object of suspicion or calumny. She made plans. She wouldn't visit anyone. Or she'd go away, to Nova Friburgo or even farther. Her husband's demand to receive Rubião as before was too much. Especially after what had happened. Not wishing to obey or disobey, she considered leaving town, under any pretext.

"It was my fault!" she sighed to herself.

The fault lay in the special attention she'd paid the man: con-
cerns, mementoes, special favors, and, the night before, those
eyes fixed on him for so long. If it hadn't been for that . . . That
was how she was getting lost in multiple reflections. Everything
was bothering her: plants, furniture, a cicada that was singing,
the sound of voices in the street, another of dishes in the house,
the coming and going of the slave girls, and even a poor old
black man across from her house who was having trouble climbing up a section of the hill. The black man's difficulties were
getting on her nerves.

L I I

A t that moment a tall young man passed who greeted her
smiling and languidly. Sofia returned the greeting, somewhat startled by the person and by the act.

"Who is that fellow?" she wondered.

And she went in to ponder where it was she'd met him, because his face really wasn't strange to her, nor his manner, nor
his large placid eyes. Where could she have seen him? She reviewed several houses without hitting the right one. Finally, she
thought, at a certain ball—the month before—at the home of a
lawyer who was celebrating his birthday. That was it. She'd seen
him there. They'd danced a quadrille, a concession on his part,
as he never danced. She remembered hearing many pleasant
words from him concerning a woman's beauty, which, he said,
consisted mainly in her eyes and shoulders. Hers, as we know,
were magnificent. And he spoke about almost no other subject—
shoulders and eyes—he related several anecdotes involving them,
things that had happened to him, some of them interesting, but
he spoke so well! And the subject was so close to her! She was
remembering now that as soon as he'd left her Palha came over,
sat down in the chair beside her, and told her the young man's
name because she hadn't heard too clearly the person who'd

introduced them. It was Carlos Maria—the very same who'd lunched with our Rubião.

"He cuts the finest figure in the room," her husband told her with the pride of having seen him spend so much time with her.

"Among the men," Sofia explained.

"Among the women it's you," he was quick to add, looking at his wife's bosom, then casting his eyes about the room with a look of possession and domination that his wife was already familiar with and which made her feel good.

When she'd finished remembering it all, the young man was probably already well on his way. At least it was an interruption in the series of annoyances that occupied her spirit. She had a pain in her back that had abated for a few moments. It returned immediately, insistent, annoying. Sofia leaned back in the chair and closed her eyes. She wanted to see if she could get some sleep, but she couldn't. Her thoughts were as insistent as the pain and even worse for her. From time to time a quick flutter of wings would break the silence. It was the doves from a neighboring house returning to their loft. Sofia at first opened her eyes, once, twice, then she became accustomed to the sound and left them closed to see if she could sleep. After some time had passed she heard footsteps on the street and raised her head, thinking it was Carlos Maria on his way back. It was the postman, who was bringing her a letter from the country. He handed her the letter. As he left the garden, the postman tripped over the leg of a bench and sprawled on the ground, scattering his letters all over. Sofia couldn't hold back a laugh.

L I I I

You must forgive that laugh. I know quite well that an upset, a bad night, the fear of public opinion, everything is in contrast to that inopportune laugh. But, my dear lady reader, perhaps you've never seen a postman take a fall. The gods of Homer—

and, moreover, they were gods—once had a serious and even furious argument on Olympus. Proud Juno, jealous of the conversation between Thetis and Jupiter about help for Achilles, interrupted the son of Saturn. Jupiter thunders and threatens. His wife trembles with rage. The others moan and sigh. But when Vulcan picks up an urn of nectar and limps over to serve everybody, a great inextinguishable gale of laughter bursts forth on Olympus. Why? My dear lady, you most certainly have never seen a postman take a tumble.

Sometimes he doesn't even have to fall. Other times he doesn't even have to exist. It's enough to imagine him or remember him. The shadow of the shadow of a grotesque memory casts itself over the midst of the most hateful passion, and a smile will sometimes come to the surface of one's face, faint as it may be—a trifle. Let's leave her laughing and reading her letter from the country.

L I V

Two weeks later, while Rubião was at home, Sofia's husband appeared. He was coming to ask what had become of him. Where had he been keeping himself since he hadn't made an appearance? Had he been ill? Or didn't he care about poor people anymore? Rubião was fumbling with words, unable to put a complete sentence together. In the middle of that Palha saw that there was a man in the room looking at the pictures, and he lowered his voice.

"I'm sorry. I didn't see that you had company," he said.

"Sorry for what? He's a friend, just like you. Doctor, this is my friend Cristiano de Almeida e Palha. I think I've mentioned him to you before. This is my friend Dr. Camacho—João de Sousa Camacho. Camacho nodded, spoke two or three phrases, and made ready to leave, but Rubião hurried over, no, sir, he should stay. They were both friends of his, and in a little while the moon would soon light up the beautiful cove of Botafogo.

The moon—the moon again—and that phrase, *I think I've mentioned him to you before*, so stupefied the new arrival that it was impossible for him to speak a single word for some time. It well might be added that the host, too, didn't know what to say. The three of them sat there, Rubião on the couch, Palha and Camacho in chairs facing each other. Camacho, who'd kept his cane in his hand, held it upright between his knees, touching his nose with it and looking at the ceiling. Outside the sound of carts, a troop of horses, and voices. It was seven-thirty in the evening, or closer to eight o'clock. The silence was longer than was proper for the occasion. Neither Rubião nor Palha was aware of it. Camacho was the one who was troubled, and he went to the window and exclaimed to the two of them from there:

"There's the moon coming out!"

Rubião assumed one expression, Palha another, but how different they were! Rubião was ready to be carried off to the window, Palha was ready to grab him by the throat. He relented, less from possibly divulging the adventure than from the memory of the ferocity with which he'd grabbed his wife's hands and pulled her to him. They both held back. Immediately thereupon Rubião, crossing his left leg over his right, turned to Palha and asked him:

"Do you know that I'm going to leave you people?"

L V

The other man had expected anything but that. Hence the amazement into which his rage dissolved; hence, too, a touch of sorrow that the reader least expects. Leave them? He was leaving Rio de Janeiro of course. It was the punishment he was imposing upon himself for his actions in Santa Teresa. He'd become immediately upset and had repented. He didn't have the gall to put in an appearance before his friend's wife. That was Palha's first conclusion, but other hypotheses came to mind. For example, the passion might still persist, and his departure was a way of getting away from the person he loved. It might also be that some marriage plan was involved.

The last hypothesis brought a new element that I don't know what to call to Palha's features. Disappointment? The elegant Garrett could find no other term for such feelings, and, even though it was English, he didn't reject it.* Let disappointment stand. Mingled with the sadness of the separation you mustn't forget the rage that had rumbled softly at first, and there are doubtless many people who will say that this man's soul is a patchwork quilt. It could well be. Moral quilts made of one piece are so rare! The main thing is for the colors not to contradict each other—when they are unable to follow symmetry and regularity. That was the case with our man. He had a mixed-up look at first sight, but with close attention, as opposite as the tones might be, the man's moral unity could be found there.

L V I

But why was Rubião leaving, then? What was the reason? What kind of business was it? The day after the events in Santa Teresa he'd awakened oppressed. He didn't enjoy breakfast. He put on his African slippers without interest, didn't look at the beautiful or simply expensive furniture that filled his house. He could only bear the dog's nuzzling for two minutes. As soon as Rubião greeted him in the room he sent him away. The dog managed to trick the servants and come back into the room, but such was the clout he got on the ear that he didn't repeat his

---

* João Batista de Almeida Garrett (1799–1854), Portuguese romantic poet and dramatist. [Ed.]

nuzzling. He lay down on the floor with his eyes on his friend.

Rubião was repentant, irritated, ashamed. In Chapter X of this book it was written that this man's remorse came easily but didn't last long. What was missing was an explanation of the nature of the actions that could make it of short or long duration. Back there it was a matter of that letter written by the late Quincas Borba, so telling as to the mental state of its author and which he'd concealed from the doctor and which might have been of some use to science or the law. If he'd turned over the letter, he wouldn't have had any remorse and, perhaps, any legacy—the small legacy he was expecting from the sick man at that time. In the present case it was an attempt at adultery. Of course, he'd been sighing a long time before that and had had inner urges, but it was only the young woman's liveliness and the excitement of the moment itself that led him to make the declaration that was rejected. After the vapors of the night had passed, it wasn't just annoyance that he felt but also remorse. Morality is one, sins are several.

Let's skip over everything he was feeling and thinking during those first days. He reached the point of expecting something on Sunday, a note like the one on the previous Sunday—with strawberries or without them. On Monday he was determined to go to Minas and spend a couple of months. He felt the necessity of restoring his soul in the air of Barbacena. He hadn't counted on Dr. Camacho.

"Leave us?" Palha finally asked.

"I plan to. I'm going to Minas."

Camacho, turning away from the window, sat down in the chair where he'd been before.

"What's this about Minas?" he asked, smiling. "Forget about Minas for now. You can go there when it's necessary, and it won't be long before it will be."

Palha was no less surprised by the words of this man than by those of the other. Where had a man with such an air of domination over Rubião come from from? He looked at him. He was a person of average height, narrow face, thin beard, long jaw, big, broad ears. That was all he could take in at a glance. He also saw that his clothing was of good quality, not luxurious, and that he was wearing rather good shoes. He didn't examine his eyes or his smile or his mannerisms. He didn't notice the beginning of baldness or his thin, hairy hands.

LVII

Camacho was a political man. A law graduate of the Faculty of Recife in 1844, he had returned to his native province, where he set himself up in practice. But the law was a pretext. At school already he'd written a political journal, with no definite party in mind but with a lot of ideas picked up here and there. A person who had collected those first fruits of Camacho had put together an index of his principles and aspirations:—*Order through freedom and freedom through order;—Authority cannot abuse the law without hitting itself;—A life of principle is the moral necessity of new nations as well as old nations;—Give me good politics and I will give you good finances* (Baron Louis);—*Let us plunge into the constitutional Jordan;—Make way for the valiant, men of power, and they will be your support—*etc., etc.

In his native province that set of ideas had to give way to others, and the same could be said of his style. He founded a newspaper there, but since local politics was less abstract, Camacho lowered his wings and descended to the level of the appointment of chiefs of police, provincial work projects, fees, a fight with a rival paper, and proper and improper names. The adjectivation called for great precision. Disastrous, prodigal, shameful, perverse were the obligatory terms when he attacked the government, but as soon as there was a change in provincial presidents, he went over to defending it, and the characterizations changed, too: energetic, enlightened, just, faithful to principles, a real glory of an administration, etc., etc. That sniping lasted for three years. At the end of them political passion had come to dominate the young lawyer's soul.

A member of the provincial assembly and immediately after of the Chamber of Deputies, then president of a second-rate province where, by a natural twist of fate, he read in the opposition press all the names he had written in times gone by: disastrous, prodigal, perverse. Camacho had seen times that were great and times that were petty. He was active inside the chamber and out. He orated, wrote, and fought constantly. He ended up coming to reside in the capital of the empire. A deputy because of a compromise between parties, he saw the Marquis of Paraná become head of the government, and he pressed for some appointments, which were granted. But whether it was really true that the Marquis sought his advice and was accustomed to confiding his plans to him, no one could tell for sure, because when it was a matter of his own interest, Camacho had no problem in lying.

What can be believed is that he wanted a cabinet position, and he worked to get it. He attached himself to various groups according to what seemed advantageous. In the chamber he would expatiate at length on administration affairs, put figures together, legislative articles, bits of reports, passages from French authors, although poorly translated. But between the ear of corn and the hand there is the wall the poet speaks of, and no matter how far our man reached out his hand in his desire to pick it, the ear remained on the other side, where other hands, more or less eager or even casual, were picking it.

There is such a thing as a political old bachelor. Camacho was entering that melancholy category where all nuptial dreams evaporate with time. But he didn't have the superior grace to give it up. No one who organized a cabinet dared, even though he may have wished, give him a portfolio. Camacho felt himself sinking. In order to give the appearance of influence, he dealt with the powerful people of the day on familiar terms, spoke in a loud voice about his visits to ministers and other dignitaries of state.

He didn't lack for food. His family was small: wife, a daughter going on eighteen, a godson of nine, and his law practice took care of them. But he had politics in his blood. He didn't read, he didn't pay attention to anything else. He had absolutely no concern for literature, the natural sciences, history, philosophy, or art. Nor did he have any great knowledge of the law. He still retained a few things from school along with subsequent legislation and court procedures. With that he argued in court and earned money.

L V I I I

Some days before, when he went to spend the evening at the home of a counselor, he found Rubião there. They were talking about the conservatives' assumption of power and the dissolution of the chamber. Rubião had attended the session in which the Itaboraí ministry presented the budgets. He was still trembling as he expressed his impressions, describing the chamber, the speakers, the galleries filled to the rafters, José Bonifácio's speech, the motion, the vote . . . That whole narrative was coming out of a simple soul, it was obvious. The wild gestures, the heat of the words carried the eloquence of sincerity. Camacho listened to him attentively. He found a way to get him over to a corner by the window and give him his considered opinion of the situation. Rubião expressed himself with nods or with random words of approval.

"The conservatives won't be in power for long," Camacho told him finally.

"No?"

"No. They don't want war, and they're bound to fall. Read what I had to say in my program in the newspaper."

"What newspaper?"

"We'll talk later."

The next day they had lunch at the Hôtel de la Bourse at Camacho's invitation. The latter told him that some months before he'd founded a newspaper with the sole program of continuing the war at all costs . . . He was very much aware of the dissension among liberals. It seemed to him that the best way to serve his own party was to give it a neutral and nationalist terrain.

"And this is to our benefit now," he concluded, "because the government is leaning toward peace. Tomorrow an angry article of mine is coming out."

Rubião listened to it all, almost without taking his eyes off the other man, eating quickly during the intervals when Camacho himself leaned over his plate. He was pleased to see himself as a political confidant, and, to put it briefly, the idea of getting into a fight that might bring him something in the end, a seat in the chamber, for example, spread its golden wings in our friend's mind. Camacho had nothing more to say. Rubião looked him up the following day and didn't find him in. Now, a short time after he'd arrived, Palha came by to interrupt them.

L I X

"Yes, but I've got to go to Minas," Rubião insisted.
"What for?" Camacho asked.

Palha asked him the same question. Why would he be going to Minas unless it was something that could be taken care of quickly. Or was he already bored with the capital?

"No, I'm not bored, on the contrary . . ."

On the contrary, he liked it very much. But one's homeland—no matter how ugly—a village even—makes people nostalgic—all the more so when we leave as adults. He wanted to see Barbacena. Barbacena was the best place in the world. For a few minutes Rubião was able to remove himself from the presence of the others. He had his homeland inside himself. Ambitions, public vanities, ephemeral pleasures, all gave way to the longing of the man from Minas for his province. Even though his soul might pretend sometimes, and he would listen to the voice of self-interest, now it was the simple soul of a man repentant of pleasures and uncomfortable with his own wealth.

Palha and Camacho looked at each other . . . Oh! That look was like calling cards exchanged between the two consciences. Neither told its secret, but they saw the names on the cards and they greeted each other. Yes, it was necessary to stop Rubião from leaving. Minas might keep him there. They agreed that he could go, but later—a few months later—and Palha might go, too. He'd never been to Minas. It would be an excellent opportunity.

"You?" Rubião asked.

"Yes, me. I've been wanting to go to Minas and São Paulo for a long time. Look, it's been over a year that we've been on the verge of going ... Sofia is a good companion on trips like that. Do you remember when we met on the train ...? We were coming from Vassouras, but the Minas idea has never left us. The three of us will go."

Rubião grabbed at the upcoming elections. But Camacho intervened there, stating that it wasn't necessary, that the serpent had to be crushed right there in the capital. There'd be plenty of time afterward to take care of his nostalgia and receive his rewards. Rubião was agitated on the settee. The reward, no doubt, would be his diploma as deputy. A magnificent vision, an ambition he'd never had when he was just a poor devil ... He was taken by it as it whetted all his appetites for grandeur and glory. He still insisted, however, on a quick trip and, to be exact, I must swear that he did so with no great desire for them to accept his proposal.

The moon was shining brightly by then. The cove, seen through the windows, presented the seductive look that no true native of Rio de Janeiro can believe exists in any other part of the world. Sofia's image passed by in the distance on the slope of the hillside and dissolved in the moonlight. The last tumultuous session of the chamber echoed in Rubião's ears ... Camacho went over to the window and came right back.

"But for how many days?" he asked.

"That I don't know, but not many."

"In any case, we'll talk tomorrow."

Camacho left. Palha stayed on for a few moments more to tell him that it would be strange to return to Minas without their settling accounts ... Rubião interrupted him. Accounts? Who was asking him about accounts?

"It's easy to see that you're not a businessman," Cristiano retorted.

"I'm not, that's true, but accounts are settled whenever they can be. That's how it's been between us. Unless, maybe, do you need some money?"

"No, I don't need any, thank you very much. I've got to put together a transaction, but it will take more time. I came to see you in order not to put an ad in the papers saying 'Missing, a friend, Rubião by name, who has a dog . . .'"

Rubião liked the sally. Palha left, and he accompanied him to the corner of the Rua Marquês de Abrantes. When he said goodbye, he promised to visit him in Santa Teresa before leaving for Minas.

L X

Poor Minas! Rubião walked slowly back thinking about a way not to go there now. And the words of both men went along with him in his head like little goldfish in a glass bowl, back and forth, glimmering: *"The serpent's head had to be crushed right here"*—*"Sofia is a good companion on trips like that."* Poor Minas!

The next day he received a newspaper he'd never seen before, *Atalaia*, the Lookout. Its editorial thrashed the government. The conclusion, however, was extended to all parties and the entire nation: *Let us plunge into the constitutional Jordan.* Rubião found it excellent. He tried to find out where the newspaper was published so he could subscribe. It was on the Rua da Ajuda. He headed right there as soon as he left the house. There he discovered that the editor was Dr. Camacho. He ran to his office.

But along the way, on the same street:

"Deolindo! Deolindo!" a woman's anguished voice screamed at the door of a mattress shop.

Rubião heard the cry, turned, and saw what it was all about. There was a cart coming down the street and a child of three or four crossing. The horses were almost on top of him, hard as the driver tried to rein them in. Rubião threw himself at the horses and pulled the boy to safety. The mother, as she took him from the hands of Rubião, was speechless. She was pale, trembling. Some people began to berate the driver, but a bald man came out and ordered him to be on his way. The driver obeyed. So when the father, who'd been inside the mattress shop, came out the cart had already turned the corner onto São José.

"He would have been killed," the mother said, "If it hadn't been for this gentleman, I don't know what would have become of my poor son."

It was an event on the block. Neighbors came out to see what had happened to the child. On the street small children and urchins were peering in awe. The child only had a scratch on his left shoulder from where he'd fallen.

"It was nothing," Rubião said. "In any case, you shouldn't let the boy out on the street. He's too young."

"Thank you so much," the father put in. "But where's your hat?"

Rubião then noticed that he'd lost his hat. A ragged boy who'd picked it up was waiting by the door of the mattress shop for a chance to return it. Rubião gave him a few coins as a reward, something the boy hadn't thought of when he went to retrieve the hat. He'd only picked it up in order to be a part of and to do something in that glorious moment. He accepted the coins gladly, however. It was, perhaps, his awakening to the mercenary side of human actions.

"But hold on," the mattress maker said, "are you hurt?"

Indeed, our friend's hand was bleeding, a cut on the palm, nothing serious. Only then was he starting to feel it. The child's mother ran to get a basin and a towel in spite of Rubião's saying it was nothing, it wasn't worth the bother. The water arrived. While she was washing his hand, the mattress maker ran to a nearby pharmacy and brought back some arnica. Rubião was healed. He tied the cloth around his hand. The mattress maker's wife brushed off his hat and, when he left, both parents thanked him effusively for having saved their son. The rest of the people in the doorway and on the sidewalk lined up to let him pass.

LXI

"What's that on your hand?" Camacho inquired as soon as Rubião entered the office.

Rubião told him about the incident on the Rua da Ajuda. The lawyer asked him a lot of questions about the child, the parents, the number of the house. But Rubião ran out of answers.

"Don't you even know the little one's name?"

"I heard him called Deolindo. Let's get down to important matters. I've come to subscribe to your newspaper. I received a copy, and I want to contribute to . . ."

Camacho replied that he didn't need subscriptions. As far as subscriptions were concerned, the paper was doing well. What he needed was material to print and develop in the text, to expand it, put in more news, articles, the translation of a novel for the supplement, activity at the port, the marketplace, etc. He had advertisements, as you could see!

"Yes, sir."

"I've got almost all the backing I need. Ten people are enough, and we're already eight, myself and seven others. We need two more. With two more people the backing will be complete."

Camacho tapped the edge of the desk with a pocket knife, silent, watching the other man out of the corner of his eye. Rubião cast his eyes about the room. Not too much furniture, a few briefs on a stool beside the lawyer, shelves with books, Lobão, Pereira e Sousa, Dalloz, *National Ordinances*, a portrait on the wall facing the desk.

"Do you know him?" Camacho asked, pointing to the portrait.

"No, sir."

"You must know him."

"I have no way of knowing who it is. Nunes Machado?"

"No," the ex-deputy replied, putting on a sad look. "I couldn't get a good picture of him. They sell some prints that don't seem too good to me. No, that's the marquis."

"Of Barbacena?"

"No, of Paraná. It's the great marquis, a personal friend of mine. He tried to bring the factions together, and that's how I got to be associated with him. He died too soon. The work couldn't go forward. Today, even if he wanted me, he'd find me on the other side. No! No conciliation. War to the death. We've got to destroy them. Read *Atalaia*, my good comrade-in-arms. You'll receive it at home . . ."

"No, sir."

"Why not?"

Rubião lowered his eyes before Camacho's inquiring nose.

"No, sir. I stand firm. I want to help my friends. Getting the paper free . . ."

"But I just told you that we're doing fine as far as subscriptions are concerned," Camacho replied.

"Yes, sir, but didn't you also say that you still needed two backers?"

"Two, yes. We've got eight."

"How much is the backing?"

"It comes to fifty *contos*, five per person."

"Then I'll come in with five."

Camacho thanked him in the name of ideas. He'd had the intention of asking him to join. It was a right earned through the convictions, the fidelity, the love for public affairs of his new friend. Since he'd joined spontaneously, he begged his forgiveness. He showed him the list of the others. Camacho was the first. He went on about the paper, the material at hand, the subscriptions, and the labors of Hercules . . . He was about to correct himself, but he boldly repeated: the labors of Hercules. He could say that it was just that without faking or lying. Strangling snakes while they're still young. It was becoming an addiction. He enjoyed a good fight, he would die in it, wrapped in the flag . . .

LXII

Rubião left. In the hallway he passed a tall lady dressed in black with a rustle of silks and beads. Going down the stairs he heard Camacho's voice, higher pitched than before: "Oh, baroness!"

He halted on the first step. The lady's silvery voice began to speak her first words; it was a lawsuit. Baroness! And our Rubião went down carefully, softly, so as not to let it seem he'd been eavesdropping. The breeze was putting a delicate, fine aroma into his nostrils, a dizzying sort of thing, the aroma left by her. Baroness! He reached the street door. Parked there he saw a coupé, the footman standing on the sidewalk, the coachman on his perch watching, both in livery . . . What news could there be in all that? None. A titled lady, perfumed and wealthy, bringing suit perhaps to relieve her boredom. But the fact of the matter was that he, Rubião, without knowing why, in spite of his own wealth, felt like the same old teacher from Barbacena . . .

LXIII

On the street he ran into Sofia and an older lady and another young woman. His eyes weren't up to taking a good look at their features. Everything he had was barely enough for Sofia. They chatted awkwardly for scarcely two minutes and went their ways. Rubião stopped and turned around, but the three ladies were going along without looking back. After dinner, to himself:

"Shall I go there tonight?"

He thought about it a lot without getting anywhere. Now yes, now no. He'd found her in a strange mood, but he remembered that she'd smiled—only a little, but she'd smiled. He put the matter up to chance. If the first carriage that passed came from the right, he'd go, if from the left, he wouldn't. And he sat there on the couch in the parlor watching. Right away a tilbury came from the left. It was settled. He wouldn't go to Santa Teresa. But here his conscience reacted. He wanted to follow the strict terms of the proposition: a carriage. A tilbury isn't a carriage. It has to be what's commonly called a carriage, a whole or half calèche, or even a victoria. In a short while, coming from the right, several calèches came along, returning from a funeral. He went.

L X I V

Sofia shook his hand politely with no trace of rancor. The two ladies from her stroll were with her, in indoor clothing. She introduced them: the young one was her cousin, the old one her aunt—that aunt from the country who'd sent the letter Sofia got in the garden from the hands of the postman who'd taken a tumble immediately after. The aunt's name was Dona Maria Augusta. She had a small estate, a few slaves, and some debts that her husband had left her along with nostalgia. The daughter was Maria Benedita—a name that bothered her because it was an old woman's name, she said. But her mother replied that old women had been young ladies and girls once and that names that fit people were the invention of poets and storytellers. Maria Benedita was the name of her grandmother, the goddaughter of Luís de Vasconcelos, the viceroy. What more could she ask?

They told all that to Rubião, and she didn't get annoyed. Sofia, either to settle the matter or for other reasons, added that the ugliest names can become beautiful, it's all according to the person. Maria Benedita was a beautiful name.

"Don't you think so?" she concluded, turning to Rubião.

"Stop teasing, cousin!" Maria Benedita put in, laughing.

We can believe that neither the old lady nor Rubião understood what was being said—the old lady because she was beginning to nod off—Rubião because he was petting a little dog Sofia had been given, small, thin, nimble, rowdy, with dark eyes and a bell on its neck. But since his hostess insisted, he answered yes, not knowing what it was all about. Maria Benedita went tsk-tsk. If the truth be known, she was no beauty. She didn't have fascinating eyes or one of those mouths that whisper something even when silent. She was natural, but without the awkwardness of a country girl. And she had a charm of her own that offset her incongruous attire.

She'd been born in the country, and she liked it there. Their place wasn't too far away, Iguaçú. From time to time she would come to town to spend a few days, but after the first two or so she was already anxious to return home. Her education had been brief: reading, writing, religion, and a little needlework. In more recent times (she was going on nineteen), Sofia had been pushing her to take piano lessons. Her aunt consented and Maria Benedita came to her cousin's and was there for around eighteen days. She couldn't take any more. She missed her mother and returned to the country, to the consternation of her teacher, who'd declared from the very first day that she had great musical talent.

"Oh, no doubt about it! A great talent!"

Maria Benedita laughed when her cousin told her that, and she could never take the man seriously afterward. Sometimes she would break out in laughter in the middle of a lesson. Sofia would frown, as if scolding her, and the poor man wondered what was going on and would explain to himself that it must have been some girlish memory and would go on with the lesson. Neither piano nor French—another gap that Sofia could scarcely excuse. Dona Maria Augusta couldn't understand her niece's consternation. Why French? Her niece told her that it was indispensable for conversation, for shopping, for reading a novel . . .

"I've always been content without any French," the old lady would answer. "And country bumpkins are too. They don't need it any more than blacks do."

One day she added:

"There'll be no lack of prospective husbands because of it. She can get married. I've told her already that she can get married whenever she wants to, that I got married, too. And she can even leave me in the country all alone to die like an old animal . . ."

"Mama!"

"Don't feel sorry. All you need is for a fiancé to appear. When he does, go off with him and leave me behind. Did you see what Maria José did to me? She's living up there in Ceará."

"But her husband's a judge," Sofia argued.

"He could be a crook! As far as I'm concerned it's the same thing. The old lady's left like a rag. Get married, Maria Benedita, get married as soon as you can. I'll die in God's hands. I won't have any children, but I'll have Our Lady, who's everybody's mother. Get married, go on, get married!"

All that bad temper was calculated. What she had in mind was to draw her daughter away from marriage, arouse fright and pity in her, slow her down at least. I don't believe that she revealed that sin to her confessor, or that she came to realize it herself. It was the product of the resentful selfishness of old age. Dona Maria Augusta had been loved deeply. Her mother was crazy about her, her husband loved her with the same intensity until his last day. With both of them dead, all of her filial and matrimonial longings were placed on the heads of her two daughters. One had abandoned her by getting married. Threatened with solitude if the other one also got married, Dona Maria Augusta was doing everything she could to avoid the disaster.

L X V

Rubião's visit was a short one. At nine o'clock he got up discreetly, awaiting some word from Sofia, a request to stay a little longer, a request to wait for her husband, who was on his way, any kind of surprise: *Wait!* But not even that. Sofia held out her hand, which he was barely able to touch. In spite of it all, the young woman had appeared quite natural during the visit, showing no bitterness . . . Of course, she didn't have those long, loquacious looks of before. It even seemed that nothing had happened, neither good nor bad, neither strawberries nor moonlight. Rubião trembled, he couldn't find the words. She'd found all she wanted, and if she had to look at him, she did it directly and calmly.

"Regards to Palha," he murmured, hat and cane in hand.

"Thank you! He had to make a call. I think I hear steps. Maybe it's he."

It wasn't he. It was Carlos Maria. Rubião was startled to see him there, but he immediately thought that the presence of the plantation owner and her daughter probably explained everything. They might even be related.

"I was just leaving when you came in," Rubião told Carlos Maria after he saw him sitting next to Dona Maria Augusta.

"Ah!" the other man answered, looking at Sofia's portrait.

Sofia went to the door to take leave of Rubião. She told him that her husband would be sorry he hadn't been at home, but he'd been obliged to make a call. Business . . . He'd ask to be forgiven.

"Forgiven?" Rubião replied.

It appeared as if he wanted to say something more, but Sofia's handshake and the bow she made were the signal for him to leave. Rubião bowed and crossed the garden, hearing Carlos Maria's voice coming from the parlor.

"I'm going to denounce your husband, my dear lady, he's a man of very bad taste."

Rubião stopped.

"Why?" Sofia asked.

"He's got this portrait in the living room here," Carlos Maria went on. "You're much more beautiful, infinitely more beautiful than the painting. Just make a comparison, ladies."

LXVI

"The natural way in which he says those things!" Rubião thought at home, recalling Carlos Maria's words. "Negating the portrait in order to praise the person! The portrait is obviously a good likeness."

LXVII

In the morning in bed he had a surprise. The first newspaper he opened was *Atalaia*. He read the editorial, a letter to the editor, and a news item. Suddenly he came upon his name.

"What's this?"

It was his very name in print, bold, repeated, nothing less than a report of what had happened on the Rua da Ajuda. After surprise, annoyance. What kind of a devilish idea was that, printing a personal matter told in confidence? He didn't want to read anything. As soon as he saw what it was, he dropped the newspaper onto the floor and picked up another. Unfortunately, he'd lost his calm and he read cursorily, skipped lines, didn't understand others, or he'd find himself at the end of a column without knowing how he'd slipped down to that point.

When he got up, he sat down in an armchair beside the bed and picked up the *Atalaia*. He cast his eyes over the article: it was more than one column. A column and more for such a minor matter! he thought to himself. And with an aim to see how Camacho had filled up the page, he read everything, somewhat hurriedly and annoyed at the adjectives used and the dramatic description of the incident.

"A fine job!" he said aloud. "Who told me to be such a blabbermouth?"

He went into the bathroom, dressed, combed his hair, not forgetting the chitchat in the newspaper, embarrassed at the publication of something he considered unimportant and even more at the exaggeration the writer had given it, as if it were a matter of evaluating something political. At breakfast he picked up the paper again to read other things: government appointments, a murder in Garanhuns, the weather, until his unfortunate eye fell on the item, and this time he read it slowly. Here Rubião confessed that he might very well believe the writer's sincerity. The enthusiasm of the language was explained by the impression the deed had made on him. It was such that it didn't allow him to be more circumspect. Naturally, that's how it was. Rubião remembered going into Camacho's office, the way he spoke, and from there he went back to the act itself. Relaxing in his study he brought back the scene: the boy, the cart, the horses, the cry, the leap he made, carried along by an irresistible impulse—even now he couldn't explain it. It was as if a shadow had passed over his eyes . . . He threw himself onto the child and onto the horses, blind and deaf, without considering the risk to himself . . . And he could have ended up there, under the animals, crushed by the wheels, dead or injured, any kind of injury . . . Could he or couldn't he have? It was impossible to deny that the situation had been serious . . . The proof was that the parents and the neighbors . . .

Rubião interrupted his thoughts to read the item one more time. It was well written, that it was. There were parts he reread with great satisfaction. The devil of a fellow seemed to have witnessed the scene. What narration! What a vivid style! A few points had been added—the confusion of memory—but the addition didn't detract. And didn't he feel a certain pride as he saw his name repeated? "Our friend, our distinguished friend, our brave friend . . ."

At lunch he laughed at himself. He thought he'd been too mortified. After all, why shouldn't the man give his readers a news item that was true, that was interesting, dramatic—and certainly—uncommon? As he left he received some compliments. Freitas called him Saint Vincent de Paul. And our friend smiled, thanked him, played it down, it was nothing . . .

"Nothing?" someone replied. "I'd like to have a lot of nothings like that. Risking your own life to save a child's . . ."

Rubião went along agreeing, listening, smiling. He retold the scene to a few curious people who wanted to hear it from the mouth of the man who'd done it himself. A few listeners replied with deeds of their own—one who'd saved a man, another a girl about to drown in the estuary by the Passeio where she was swimming. There were also unsuccessful suicides because of the intervention of a listener who took the poor man's pistol away and made him swear . . . Every little hidden glory pecked at the shell of the egg and stuck its head out, eyes open, featherless, all around Rubião's maximum glory. There were also envious people, some who didn't even know him except from hearing him being praised aloud. Rubião went to thank Camacho for the item, not without a bit of censure for the abuse of confidence, but gentle censure, out of the corner of his mouth. From there he went to buy some copies of the newspaper for his friends in Barbacena. No other paper carried the item. On the advice of Freitas he had it reprinted in the letters to the editor in the *Jornal do Comércio*, in boldface type.

LXVIII

Maria Benedita finally consented to learn French and piano. For four days her cousin pressed her at every moment and in such an artful way that the girl's mother resolved to hasten their return to the plantation in order to avoid her accepting in the end. The daughter resisted mightily. Her mother's answer was that they were superfluous things, that a young woman from the country had no need for city accomplishments. One evening, however, when Carlos Maria was there, he asked her to play something. Maria Benedita turned beet red. Sofia came to her aid with a lie:

"Don't ask her that. She hasn't played anything since she got here. She says that she only plays for country people now."

"Well, it's all right. We're country people," the young man insisted.

But then he changed the subject to the ball at the Baroness of Piauí's (the same that our friend Rubião had met in Camacho's office), a splendid ball, oh, splendid! The baroness thought highly of him, he said. The following day Maria Benedita declared to her cousin that she was prepared to learn piano and French, fiddle, and even Russian if she wanted to. The difficulty was in winning her mother over. The latter, when she learned of her daughter's decision, put her hands to her head. What French? What piano? She roared no, or she'd cease to be her daughter. She could stay and play and sing and speak Cabinda or the language of the devil himself, who could take them all. Palha was the one who finally persuaded her. He told her that no matter how superfluous those accomplishments might seem to her, they were the minimum embellishments of an education for society.

"But I raised my daughter in the country and for the country," the aunt interrupted.

"For the country? Who knows what children are brought up to be? My father had me destined for the priesthood, which is why I can manage a little Latin. You're not going to live forever, ma'am. Your affairs are all a jumble. It could happen that Maria Benedita will be left destitute . . . I don't mean destitute as long as one of us is alive, but isn't it better to be prepared? It could even reach the point that if there were none of us left, she could earn a good living just by teaching French and piano. Just by knowing those things she'll be in better circumstances. She's pretty, as you were at her age, and she has outstanding moral qualities. She's capable of getting a rich husband. Did you know that I've already got someone in mind, a proper person?"

"Oh, yes? Then is it French, piano, and love-making that she's going to learn?"

"What do you mean, love-making? I'm talking about a secret thought of mine, a plan that I think is just right for her happiness and that of her mother . . . Because I'd . . . Come now, Aunt Augusta!"

Palha seemed a bit mortified that the aunt's tone had gone from harsh to dry. She was still resisting. But that night he gave her some good advice. The state of her affairs along with the possibility of a son-in-law with means overcame other arguments. The best sons-in-law in the country had linked up with other plantations, other prominent families with solid wealth. Two days later they reached a *modus vivendi*. Maria Benedita would stay with her cousin. They would go to the country from time to time, and the aunt would also come to the capital to visit them. Palha went so far as to say that as soon as the state of the market allowed, he would arrange a way to liquidate her holdings and bring her here. But the good lady shook her head at that.

It mustn't be thought that all this was as easy as has been written. In practice, there were obstacles, vexations, longings, rebellions on the part of Maria Benedita. Eighteen days after her mother had gone back to the plantation, she wanted to visit her, and her cousin went with her. They spent a week there. The mother, two months later, came to spend a few days here. Sofia skillfully got her cousin accustomed to the amusements of the city: the theater, visits, walks, gatherings at home, new dresses, pretty hats, jewelry. Maria Benedita was a woman, even though a strange one. She liked things like that but she kept in mind, to herself, that as soon as she felt like it she'd break those ties and go to the country. The country would come to her sometimes in a dream or in wandering thoughts. After the first soirées, when she returned, it wasn't the sensations of the evening that filled her soul, it was a longing for Iguaçú. It became greater at certain times of day when house and street were completely quiet. Then she would fly off to the veranda of the old house where she drank coffee next to her mother. She would think about the slaves, the antique furniture, the pretty slippers sent her by her godfather, a wealthy plantation owner from São João d'El-Rei— and which had been left behind at home there. Sofia wouldn't let her bring them.

The piano and French teachers were men who had a good knowledge of their fields. Sofia was especially fearful about telling them that her cousin was bothered by learning at so late an age, and she asked them never to talk about such a pupil. They promised not to. The piano teacher only mentioned the request to a few colleagues who found it amusing and recounted other anecdotes about their pupils. What was certain was that Maria Benedita was learning with singular ease. She studied hard, almost constantly, to such a point that her cousin herself thought it best to interrupt her:

"Take a rest, my dear!"

"Let me make up for lost time," she answered, smiling.

Then Sofia would invent outings at random in order to make her take a rest. Now to one neighborhood, now to another. On certain streets Maria Benedita wouldn't waste her time. She would read signs in French and ask the meaning of new nouns, which her cousin sometimes couldn't tell her as her vocabulary was limited to matters of clothing, salons, and flirtation.

But it wasn't in those disciplines alone that Maria Benedita was making rapid progress. The person had become adjusted to the milieu much quicker than her natural taste and life in the country would have made one believe. She was already in competition with the other woman, even if there was an effrontery in it and a sort of strange expression that in a way gave color to all the lines and movements of her figure. In spite of that difference, it was certain that she was observed and noticed to such a degree that Sofia, who'd begun by praising her everywhere, didn't disparage her now but would listen in silence when she was being praised. Maria Benedita spoke well—but when she was silent it would go on for a long time. She said they were her "moods." She danced the quadrille lifelessly, which was the perfect way to dance it. She liked to watch the polka and the waltz very much. Sofia, imagining that it was out of fear that her cousin didn't waltz or polka, tried to give her some lessons at home, all by themselves, with her husband at the piano, but her cousin always refused.

"That's still a bit of your country shell," Sofia told her once.

Maria Benedita smiled in such a strange way that the other woman didn't insist. It wasn't a smile of annoyance or of resentment or of disdain. Why disdain? In any case, what's certain is that the smile seemed to come out of the blue. Not the least was the fact that Sofia polkaed and waltzed eagerly, and no one could cling better to her partner's shoulder. Carlos Maria, who rarely danced, would only waltz with Sofia—two or three spins, he would say—Maria Benedita counted them one night: fifteen minutes.

LXIX

The fifteen minutes were counted on Rubião's watch as he stood beside Maria Benedita, and she asked him what time it was at the beginning and the end of the waltz. The girl leaned over herself to take a good look at the minute hand.

"Are you sleepy?" Rubião asked.

Maria Benedita looked at him out of the corner of her eye. She observed his placid face where there was neither malice nor merriment.

"No," she answered. "All I can say is that I'm afraid Cousin Sofia will want to go home early."

"She won't go home early. There's no more excuse for her of climbing up to Santa Teresa since she lives nearby."

In fact they both lived on Flamengo Beach now, and the ball was on the Rua dos Arcos.

It must be pointed out that eight months have passed since the beginning of the previous chapter, and a lot of changes have taken place. Rubião is a partner of Sofia's husband in an import house on the Rua da Alfândega with the name of Palha and Company. It was the business that the latter had come to propose that night in which he found Dr. Camacho at the house in Botafogo. In spite of his being an easy mark, Rubião resisted for some time. It was asking a goodly amount of *contos* from him. He didn't understand business, he had no head for it. Besides, his personal expenses were already quite large. The investment had to be handled to bear interest and with some saving to see if it could recover its early vigor and health. The handling indicated for that aim wasn't clear. Rubião couldn't understand Palha's figures, his estimates of profits, the price lists, customs duties, none of it. But the spoken language made up for the written. Palha spoke of extraordinary things. He advised his friend to take advantage of the occasion and put his money to work, multiply it. If he was afraid, it was different. He, Palha, would arrange matters with John Roberts, who was a partner in the firm of Wilkinson, founded in 1844, whose chief had returned to England and was now a member of Parliament.

Rubião didn't give in right away. He asked for time, five days.

He was freer with himself. But this time the freedom only served to confuse him. He calculated the funds expended, estimated the gap left in the capital left him by the philosopher. Quincas Borba, who was with him in the study, lying on the floor, chanced to lift his head and stare at him. Rubião shuddered. The supposition that the soul of the other Quincas Borba was in that one had never entirely left his mind. This time he noticed a tone of censure in the eyes. He laughed. It was foolishness. A dog couldn't be a man. Without thinking, however, he lowered his hand and scratched the animal's ears in order to win him over.

Following reasons for rejection came others to the contrary. What if the deal showed profit? If it really did multiply what he had? He added to that the fact that the position was respectable and could be advantageous to him in the election when he would stand for parliament like the former head of the house of Wilkinson. Another even stronger reason was the fear of offending Palha, of seeming not to trust him with money when it was certain that a few days earlier he'd received back part of the old debt, and the remainder was to be repaid within two months.

None of these reasons was a pretext for the next. They were sufficient of themselves. Sofia only appeared at the end, not without having been there from the start, a latent, unconscious idea, one of the ultimate causes for the action and the only one that remained disguised. Rubião shook his head to get rid of it and stood up. Sofia (astute lady) withdrew into the man's unconscious, respectful of his moral freedom, and left him to decide for himself that he would enter into a partnership with her husband, with certain safety clauses. That was how the corporation was formed. And that was how Rubião legitimized the frequency of his visits.

"Mr. Rubião," Maria Benedita said after a few seconds of silence, "don't you think my cousin is quite pretty?"

"Without taking anything away from you, yes."

"Pretty and shapely."

Rubião accepted the combination. They both followed the waltzing couple with their eyes as they moved across the salon. Sofia was magnificent. She was wearing a dark blue dress, very low-cut—for the reasons cited in Chapter XXXV. Her bare, full arms, with a tone of clear gold, were in harmony with her shoulders and breasts, just right in the gaslight of the salon. A diadem of artificial pearls, so well made that they matched the natural pearls that adorned her ears, which Rubião had given her one day.

Beside her Carlos Maria didn't come off badly. He was a handsome young man, as we know, and he wore the same placid look he'd had at lunch with Rubião. He didn't have the humble mannerisms or reverent bows of other young men. He bore himself with the grace of a benevolent king. If, however, at first sight he seemed only to be doing that lady a favor, it was no less certain that he went along proud at having by his side the most elegant woman of the evening. The two feelings are not contradictory. Both were based on the adoration the young man had for himself. So for him, Sofia's contact was the reverence of a devotee. He wasn't surprised at anything. If he woke up emperor one day he would only be surprised at how long it had taken for the position to have come his way.

"I'm going to take a little rest," Sofia said.

"Are you tired or . . . bored?" her partner asked.

"Oh, only tired!"

Carlos Maria, regretful at having imagined the other possibility, was quick to eliminate it.

"Yes, I think you're right. Why should you be bored? But I must say that you're capable of making the sacrifice of dancing a little more with me. Five minutes?"

"Five minutes."

"Not even a minute more? For my part, I could dance till eternity."

Sofia lowered her head.

"With you, of course."

Sofia went along with her eyes to the floor, not answering, not agreeing, not thanking him at least. It was probably nothing more than a gallantry, and gallantries customarily received thanks. She'd already heard similar words from him in the past that put her ahead of all women in this world. She'd ceased hearing them for six months—four that he spent in Petrópolis—two in which he didn't appear. Lately he'd begun to frequent the house again, to pay her compliments like that, sometimes in private, sometimes in public. She went along. And they both went on in silence, silence, silence—until he broke it, telling her that the sea in front of her house had been pounding quite strongly the night before.

"Did you pass by?" Sofia asked.

"I was there. I was on my way to Catete. It was already late, and I remember going along Flamengo Beach. The night was clear. I stayed there for about an hour, between the sea and your house. Could I wager that you were not dreaming about me? In any case, I could almost hear your breathing."

Sofia tried to smile. He went on:

"The sea was pounding hard, it's true, but my heart wasn't pounding any less hard—with this difference: the sea is stupid, it beats without knowing why, while my heart knew it was beating for you."

"Oh!" Sofia murmured.

With fright? With indignation? With fear? A lot of questions all at once. I'd wager that the lady herself couldn't answer precisely, such was the commotion the young man's declaration brought on in her. In any case, it wasn't with disbelief. I can only say that the exclamation came out so faint, so muffled, that he barely heard it. For his part, Carlos Maria made a good job of dissembling in full view of the whole room. Neither before, nor during, nor after those words did his face show the slightest upset. It even had the trace of a caustic smile, the smile he used when mocking something. He looked as if he'd just produced an epigram. Nevertheless, more than one woman's eye was peering into Sofia's soul, studying the young lady's somewhat bashful expression and her instantly fallen eyelids.

"I've upset you," he said. "Hide it with your fan."

Sofia began fanning herself mechanically and raised her eyes. She saw that many people were staring at her, and she grew pale. The minutes moved along with the speed of years. The first five and then the second five took a long time. They were on the thirteenth. After that the hands kept pointing to another, and another. Sofia told her partner she wanted to sit down.

"I'll leave you and withdraw."

"No," she said quickly.

Then she added:

"It's a nice ball."

"It is, but I want to take away the best memory of the evening. Any other word I hear now will be like the croak of a frog after the song of a beautiful bird, one of those birds you have at home. Where would you like me to leave you?"

"Beside my cousin."

L X X

Rubião gave up his seat and accompanied Carlos Maria as he crossed the room and went into the anteroom where the coats were kept and some ten men were chatting. Before the young man went into the room, Rubião took him by the arm in a familiar way to ask him something—it didn't matter what—but really to hold him back and try to sound him out. He was beginning to believe possible or real an idea that had been tormenting him for several days. Now that extended conversation, her behavior . . .

Carlos Maria hadn't taken notice of the long passion of the man from Minas. It was guarded, suffering, unable to be confessed to anyone—hoping for the rewards of chance—content with little, with the simple sight of the person, sleeping poorly at night, supplying money for business operations . . . Because he wasn't jealous of her husband. The intimacies of marriage had never aroused hatred against her legitimate spouse in him. And that was how months and months had passed, with no change in feeling or any end of hope. But the possibility of an outside rival had got him all upset. This is where jealousy took a bloody bite out of our friend.

"What is it?" Carlos Maria asked, turning around.

At the same time, he entered the anteroom where the ten men were talking politics, because this ball—I neglected to mention—was being given at Camacho's house in honor of his wife's birthday. When the two of them went in, the conversation was generalized, the subject the same, and everyone was talking at the same time—a swirl of comments, diverse statements . . . One of them, a doctrinaire person, succeeded in dominating the others as they fell silent for moments, smoking.

"They can do anything they like," the doctrinaire man was saying, "but moral punishment is certain. The debts of the parties will be paid with interest down to the last penny and to the last generation. Principles never die. Parties that forget that end up in filth and ignominy."

Another balding man didn't believe in moral punishment and was saying why. But a third mentioned the dismissal of some tax collectors and tempers, dizzy with doctrine, became aroused. The tax collectors had no other faults except their beliefs. And the action couldn't even be defended by the worthiness of their replacements. One of those had an embezzlement on his shoulders, another was the brother-in-law of a certain marquis who'd taken a shot at the chief of police in São José dos Campos . . . And the new lieutenant-colonels? Real jailbirds.

"Are you leaving so soon?" Rubião asked the young man when he saw him take his coat out from among the others.

"Yes, I'm tired. Help me straighten out this sleeve. I'm tired."

"But it's still early. Stay. Our friend Camacho doesn't want the young men to leave. Who's going to dance with the young ladies?"

Carlos Maria replied, smiling, that he wasn't all that fond of dancing. He'd waltzed with Dona Sofia because she's an expert at it. If it weren't for that, not even with her. He was tired. He preferred his bed to an orchestra. And he held out his hand languidly. Rubião shook it, half uncertain.

He didn't know what to think. The act of going, of leaving her at the ball instead of waiting to accompany her to her carriage as on other occasions . . . It could be a deception of his . . . And he was thinking, remembering the night in Santa Teresa when he dared declare his feelings to the young woman, taking her by her delicate hand . . . The major had interrupted them, but why hadn't he repeated it later on? And she didn't treat him badly, nor did her husband notice anything . . . At this point the idea of the possible rival returned. It's true he was leaving because he was tired, but her behavior . . . Rubião went to the door of the salon to take a look at Sofia. Then he went over to a corner of the room, or to the card table, upset, annoyed.

L X X I

At home, as she undid her hair, Sofia spoke of that soirée as an irksome affair. She yawned, her legs ached. Palha disagreed. She was in a bad mood. If her legs ached, it was because she'd danced too much. To which his wife replied that if she hadn't danced she would have died of boredom. And she went on taking out the hairpins, dropping them into a crystal glass. Her hair soon streamed down over her shoulders, which were partly covered by her cambric nightgown. Palha, behind her, said that Carlos Maria waltzed very well. Sofia trembled. She looked at him in the mirror. His face was calm. She agreed that he didn't waltz badly.

"No, ma'am, he waltzes quite well."

"You praise other people because you know that nobody is capable of taking your place. Come on, my proud fellow, I know you too well."

Palha, reaching out his hand and taking her by the chin, made her look at him. Proud of what? Why was he proud?

"Oh," Sofia moaned, "you're hurting me."

Palha kissed her on the shoulder. She smiled, without any annoyance, without any headache, just the opposite of that night in Santa Teresa when she told her husband about Rubião's advances. The hillside must have been unwholesome and the beach healthful.

The next day Sofia woke up early to the sound of the birds trilling in the house as they seemed to be sending her a message from someone. She let herself remain in bed, and she closed her eyes in order to see better.

To see what better? Certainly not the unwholesome hillside.

The beach was something else again. Stationed at the window a half hour later, Sofia was contemplating the waves that were rising and falling at the entrance to the bay. The imaginative lady was wondering if that was the waltz of the waters, and she let herself be carried along on that current without sail or oars. She caught herself looking at the street beside the sea as if seeking a sign of the man who'd been there the night before last, late . . . I can't swear to it, but I think she saw the sign. At least it's certain that she matched what she saw with the text of the conversation:

"The night was clear. I stayed there for about an hour, between the sea and your house. Could I wager that you were not dreaming about me? In any case, I could almost hear your breathing. The sea was pounding hard, it's true, but my heart wasn't pounding any less hard—with this difference: the sea is stupid, it beats without knowing why, while my heart knew it was beating for you."

Sofia had a chill. She tried to forget the text but the text kept on repeating: "The night was clear . . ."

L X X I I

Between two phrases she felt someone's hand on her shoulder. It was her husband who'd just had breakfast and was leaving for downtown. They said goodbye affectionately. Cristiano advised her to look after Maria Benedita, who'd awakened quite upset.

"Up so soon!" Sofia exclaimed.

"When I came down I found her in the dining room already. She woke up with her mania to go back to the country. She'd had a dream . . . I don't know what about . . ."

"Irritable!" Sofia concluded.

And with her light and skillful fingers she straightened her husband's tie, pulled the collar of his morning coat to the front, and they said goodbye again. Palha went downstairs and left. Sofia remained by the window. Before rounding the corner he turned his head and they waved goodbye in the usual way.

LXXIII

"The night was clear. I stayed there for about an hour, between the sea and your house. Could I wager . . ."

When Sofia was able to tear herself away from the window, the clock downstairs was striking nine. Angry, repentant, she swore to herself on her mother's soul that she wouldn't think about an episode like that anymore. She didn't consider it of any value. The mistake had been in letting the young man follow to the end of his boldness. The truth is that in proceeding in that way, she'd avoided a great scandal, because he was capable of accompanying her to her chair and telling her the rest in front of other people. And the rest was being repeated once more in her memory like an insistent musical passage, the same words and the same voice. "The night was clear. I stayed there for about an hour . . ."

LXXIV

While she was repeating the declaration of the night before, Carlos Maria was opening his eyes, stretching his limbs, and, before going in to bathe, dress, and take a horseback ride, he reconstructed the night before. He had that habit. In the successes of the previous day he always found something done, something said, some touch that made him feel good. That was where his spirit lingered. Those were the halts in his route where he dismounted to sip a drink of cool water. If there was no success in any of them—or if they'd only gone against him, even so his feelings weren't disheartening. All he needed was the taste of some word that he himself had said—some gesture he'd made, subjective contemplation, the pleasure of having felt alive—for the day before not to have been a complete loss.

Sofia figured in the day before. It even seemed that she was the main figure in its reconstruction, the façade of the building, broad and magnificent. Carlos Maria savored the whole memory of the evening, but when he remembered his confession of love, he felt both good and bad. It was a compromise, an obstacle, an obligation. And since the benefits made up for the bother, the young man remained between both feelings, without any plan. As he remembered the story he'd told her of having gone to Flamengo Beach the other night, he couldn't hold back a laugh, because it wasn't true. The idea had come to him out of the conversation itself. But he hadn't gone there, nor even thought of doing so. Finally he controlled his laughter and was even sorry. The fact that he had lied gave him a feeling of inferiority, which dampened his spirits. He got to thinking about rectifying what he'd said the next time he was with Sofia, but he realized that the correction was worse than the sonnet, and that there are pretty sonnets that lie.

His spirits quickly rose. In his memory he saw the room, the men, the women, the impatient fans, the offended mustaches, and he stretched out full length in a bath of envy and admiration. The envy of others, let it be well noted. He lacked that terrible feeling. The envy and admiration of others was what was giving him an inner delight even then. The princess of the ball was giving herself to him. That was how he defined Sofia's superiority, even though he was aware of a capital defect—her upbringing. He found that the young woman's polished manners came from adult imitation, after marriage or a little before, which, even so, didn't rise up very much out of the milieu in which she lived.

LXXV

Other women came into play—the ones who preferred him to other men as company and in the contemplation of his person. Was he courting or had he courted all of them? It's not known. For some, of course: it's certain, however, that he took delight in all of them. There were those of proven chastity who enjoyed having him alongside them in order to enjoy the contact of a handsome man without the reality or the danger of sin— like the spectator who takes pleasure in the passions of Othello and leaves the theater with his hands clean of the death of Desdemona.

They all came to surround Carlos Maria's bed, weaving the same garland for him. They weren't all young women in bloom, but distinction took the place of youth. Carlos Maria received them as an ancient god, quiet on his marble, must have received his beautiful devotees and their offerings. In the general hubbub the voices of all could be distinguished—not all at the same time—but by threes and fours.

The last was that of the recent Sofia. He listened to her, still taken with love but without the excitement of the beginning, because the memory of the other ladies, persons of quality, was now reducing the importance of the latest one. Nonetheless, he couldn't deny that she was very attractive and that she waltzed perfectly. Would he get to have strong love for her? At that moment the lie about the beach appeared again. He got out of bed, annoyed.

"What the devil made me say a thing like that?"

Once again he felt the desire to reestablish the truth. And this time more seriously than the last. Lying, he thought, was for lackies and their ilk.

A half hour later he mounted his horse and left his house, which was on the Rua dos Inválidos. Heading for Catete he remembered that Sofia's house was on Flamengo Beach. Nothing more natural than to twist the reins, go down the streets perpendicular to the sea, and pass by the waltzer's door. Find her there at the window, perhaps, see her blush, greet her. All that passed through the young man's head in a few seconds. He got to give a tug on the reins, but his soul—not the horse—reared; it was going after her too fast. He gave another tug on the reins and continued on his ride.

L X X V I

He rode well. Everyone who passed or was in a doorway enjoyed watching the young man's posture, his elegance, the regal calm with which he went along. Carlos Maria—and this was the point where he gave in to the crowd—took in all those expressions of admiration, no matter how insignificant. When it came to adoring him, all men formed part of humanity.

L X X V I I

"Up so soon?" Sofia repeated on seeing her cousin reading the newspapers. Maria Benedita gave a start, but she calmed down immediately. She'd slept poorly and had awakened early. She wasn't up to those late-night revelries, she said, but the other woman replied right away that she would have to get used to it, that life in Rio de Janeiro wasn't the same as in the country, where they went to sleep with the hens and woke up with the roosters. Then she questioned her about her impressions of the ball. Maria Benedita shrugged her shoulders indifferently, but she answered verbally that they were good. The words came out few and faint. Sofia, however, wondered about the fact that she'd danced a lot except for polkas and waltzes. Why hadn't she polkaed and waltzed too? Her cousin gave her a nasty look.

"I don't like to."

"What do you mean you don't like to? You're afraid."

"Afraid?"

"You're not used to it," Sofia explained.

"I don't like to have a man hold my body tight against his and to move along with me like that in sight of other people. It bothers me."

Sofia became serious. She didn't defend her point or continue on with it. She mentioned the country, asked if what Cristiano had said was true, that she wanted to go home. Then the cousin, who was idly thumbing through the newspapers, replied eagerly that she did. She couldn't live away from her mother.

"But why? Haven't you been happy with us?"

Maria Benedita didn't say anything. She ran her eyes over one of the newspapers as if she were looking for some item, biting her lip, hesitant, restless. Sofia insisted on knowing the reason for that sudden change. She took her hands, found them cold.

"You need to get married. I've already got a husband for you."

It was Rubião. Palha wanted it to come to that, marrying his partner to his cousin. Everything would stay in the family, he told his wife. The latter took it upon herself to handle the matter. She was keeping her promise to him now. She had a husband all ready for her.

"Who?" Maria Benedita asked.

"Somebody."

Can you believe it, future generations? Sofia was unable to give out Rubião's name. She'd told her husband once already, had suggested him, and she was faking. Now, when she was really about to suggest him, the name wouldn't leave her lips. Jealousy? It would be singularly strange if this woman, who didn't love the man at all, was unwilling to give him to her cousin as a fiancé, but nature is capable of anything, my dear and respected friends. It contrived Othello's jealousy and that of the Chevalier Desgrieux, and it was capable of contriving this other jealousy in a person who didn't want to release what she didn't want to possess.

"But, who?" Maria Benedita repeated.

"I'll tell you later. Let me arrange things," Sofia answered and changed the subject.

Maria Benedita's expression was different. Her mouth broke

into a smile, a smile of hope and joy. Her eyes were thankful for the promise, and they spoke words that no one could hear or understand, obscure words.

"Likes to waltz. That's what it is."

Who likes to waltz? Probably the other woman. She'd waltzed so much the night before with Carlos Maria himself that she could well have been using the dance as a pretext. Maria Benedita concluded now that that was the very reason, the only one. They talked a lot between numbers, it's true, but, naturally, she was the one they'd been talking about, since her cousin had taken it upon herself to get her married and was only asking her to let her arrange things. Maybe he found her ugly or graceless. Since her cousin wanted to arrange things, however . . . All that was being said by the girl's happy eyes.

LXXVIII

Rubião was the one who hadn't lost his suspicions so easily, just like that. He thought about talking to Carlos Maria, interrogating him, and he went so far as to go to the Rua dos Inválidos the next day three times. Not finding him in, he changed his mind. He cloistered himself for a few days. Major Siqueira pulled him out of his solitude. He came by to let him know that he'd moved to the Rua Dois de Dezembro. He liked our friend's house very much, the furnishings, the luxury, all the details, the gold work, the curtains. He discoursed on that subject at length, recalling antique furniture. He stopped suddenly to tell him that he seemed bored. It was quite natural, something was missing there.

"You're happy, but something's missing here. You need a wife. You should get married. Get married and then tell me if I'm wrong."

Rubião remembered Santa Teresa—that famous night and his talk with Sofia—and he felt a chill run up his spine. But there was no sarcasm in the major's voice. Nor was it driven by interest. His daughter was the same as we'd left her in Chapter XLIII with the difference that she'd turned forty. She immediately started wailing over the years on the morning she passed the mark. She didn't put a ribbon or a rose in her hair. No party. Only a speech by her father at breakfast, recalling her as a child, anecdotes about her mother and her grandmother, a costume at a masked ball, a baptism in 1848, a Colonel Clodomiro's tapeworm, different things all mixed together to pass the time. Dona Tonica was barely listening to him, all wrapped up in herself, gnawing on the crust of her moral solitude as she regretted the latest efforts made in search of a husband. Forty years old. It was time to call a halt.

The major remembered nothing of that now. He was sincere. He felt that Rubião's house lacked a soul. And as he took his leave he repeated:

"Get married, and then tell me if I'm wrong."

L X X I X

And why not? a voice asked after the major had left. Rubião, terrified, looked around. All he could see was the dog, standing and looking at him. It was so absurd to think that the question had come from Quincas Borba there—or, rather, from the other Quincas Borba whose spirit was in his body—that our friend smiled scornfully. But at the same time, he repeated the gesture from Chapter XLIX, reaching out his hand and lovingly scratching the dog's ears and neck—an act that could give satisfaction to the dead man's spirit.

That was how our friend, without an audience, opened up to himself.

L X X X

B ut the voice repeated: "Why not?" Yes, why shouldn't he
get married? he went on thinking. It would put an end to
the passion that was slowly eating at him with no hope or consolation. Besides, it was the gateway to a mystery. Get married,
yes, marry soon and well.

He was by the gate when that idea began to flower. From
there he went inside, going up the stone steps, opening the door,
unaware of anything. As he closed the door, a leap from Quincas
Borba, who'd accompanied him, brought him to. Where had the
major gone? He wanted to go back down and see him, but he
realized in time that he'd just taken him to the street. His legs
had done everything. They were what had carried him along all
by themselves, straight, lucid, without stumbling, so that his head
was left with nothing but the task of thinking. Good old legs!
Friendly legs! Natural crutches for the spirit!

Holy legs! They took him to the couch, slowly stretched out
along with him while his spirit worked on the idea of marriage.
It was a way of freeing himself from Sofia. It could be even more.

Yes, it could also be a way of bringing back to life the unity
he'd lost with the change of milieu and fortune. But this last
consideration wasn't really the product of his spirit or his legs
but was caused by something else, which, like a spider, he
couldn't tell if it was good or bad. What does a spider know
about Mozart? Nothing. But it listens with pleasure to a sonata
by the master. The cat, who has never read Kant, could still be
a metaphysical animal. Marriage might really be the knot that
would tie up his lost unity. Rubião felt scattered. Transitory
friends whom he loved so much, who courted him so much, gave
life the feeling of a journey to him, a trip where language
changed with the cities, Spanish here, Turkish there. Sofia contributed to that state. She could be so diverse herself, now this,
now that, that the days went by with no set accord, no lasting
disenchantment.

Rubião had nothing to do. In order to get through his long
and empty days, he would observe trials, attend sessions of the
Chamber of Deputies, watch battalions on parade, take long

walks, pay unnecessary visits at night or go to the theater without any pleasure. His house was still a good place for his spirit to rest in with its glow of luxury and the dreams that floated in the air.

He'd been doing a lot of reading lately. He read novels, but only the historical ones by Dumas *père* or contemporary ones by Feuillet, the latter with difficulty, as he didn't have a good knowledge of the original language. Those of the former had plenty of translations. He would accept others if he found they had the principal attraction of the first: a noble and royal society. Those scenes of the French court invented by the wonderful Dumas with their adventurous, noble swordsmen, Feuillet's countesses and dukes in elegant greenhouses, all of them with words that were discreet, haughty, or witty, made time gallop along for him. Almost always he would end up dropping the book, his eyes staring into space, thinking. Perhaps some dead old marquis was telling him anecdotes of a different age.

L X X X I

Before thinking about a bride, he thought about marriage. On that day and others he created the matrimonial ceremonies in his head, and the coaches—if there still were such, antique and sumptuous, as he'd seen pictured in books on customs of past times. Oh, big, superb coaches! How he enjoyed going to the gate of the city palace to wait for the Emperor on important holidays and watch the imperial procession, especially His Majesty's coach with its broad dimensions and strong springs, delicate painted panels, and four or five teams of horses driven by a grave and dignified coachman! Others followed, less in grandeur but yet so grand that they were a delight to one's eyes.

One of those others, or even a smaller one, might have served him at his wedding if all society hadn't been brought down to equality by the common coupé. So, in the end, he would ride in a coupé. He pictured it with magnificent upholstery. What kind? Of some unusual fabric that he himself couldn't describe right now, but that would give the vehicle a look it didn't have to start with. A remarkable team. A coachman in a gold uniform. Oh, but of a gold never seen before! Guests of the top rank, generals, diplomats, senators, one or two cabinet ministers, many prominent businessmen. And what about the ladies, the great ladies? Rubião lined them up in his head. He watched them enter as he stood at the top of the palace steps, his eyes lost on the carpet leading down—they were coming through the entrance way, climbing the steps in their small, light satin pumps—only a few at first—then more, and still more. Carriage after carriage . . . There came the Count and Countess of So-and-So, a dashing gentleman and an outstanding lady . . . "My dear friend, here we are," the count would say to him at the top of the stairs. And then the countess: "Mr. Rubião, the reception is splendid . . ."

Suddenly, the Papal Nuncio . . . Yes, he'd forgotten that they would have to be married by the Nuncio. There he would be in his purple stockings of a monsignor and his large Neapolitan eyes in conversation with the Russian ambassador. The crystal and gold chandeliers lighting up the most beautiful throats in the city, some frock coats upright, others curved, listening to the fans that were opening and closing, epaulets, diadems, the orchestra signalling a waltz. Then the black arms, bent, went off seeking the bare arms with gloves to the elbow as the couples went spinning off across the room. Five, seven, ten, twelve, twenty couples. A splendid banquet. Bohemian crystal, Hungarian china, Sèvres glasses, nimble servants in livery with Rubião's initials on their collars.

LXXXII

Those dreams came and went. What mysterious Prospero had transformed a banal island into a sublime masquerade in that way? "Go, Ariel, bring your fellows here for I must bestow upon the eyes of this young couple some variety of mine art." The words would be the same as those in the play, the island was what was different, the island and the masquerade. The former was our friend's own head, the latter wasn't made up of goddesses or poetry but of human beings and salon prose. But it was magnificent. Let us not forget that Shakespeare's Prospero was a Duke of Milan and there, perhaps, you have why he intruded onto our friend's island.

If the truth be known, the brides who appeared at Rubião's side in those nuptial dreams were always titled. The names were the most resonant and natural in our book of peerage. Here is your explanation: a few weeks before, Rubião had picked up a Laemmert almanac, and as he started leafing through it he came upon the chapter on holders of titles. If he knew some of them, he was far from being familiar with all of them. He bought an almanac and read it several times, letting his eyes run down from the marquises to the barons, going back, repeating the beautiful names, learning many by heart. Sometimes he would pick up a pen and a sheet of paper, choose an ancient or modern title, and write it repeatedly, as if he himself were its owner and were signing something:

Marquis of Barbacena

Marquis of Barbacena

Marquis of Barbacena

Marquis of Barbacena

Marquis of Barbacena

Marquis of Barbacena

He went on like that to the bottom of the page, varying his hand, now large, now tiny, tilting backwards, straight up, in all different shapes. When he finished the page, he picked it up and compared the signatures. He put the paper down and was lost in space. From there to the hierarchy of the brides. The worst thing was that they all had Sofia's face—at the very first they might resemble some neighbor woman or the girl he'd greeted that afternoon on the street. They could begin very thin or fat—but it didn't take them long to change their figures, putting on or taking off weight, and above this the face of the beautiful Sofia would gleam with her own restless or quiet eyes. Was there no way to get away from her, even through marriage? Rubião began to think about Palha's dying. It came to him one day as he left her house after hearing her say some pleasant, vague things. His feeling of contentment was great, but he immediately rejected the idea as a terrible omen. Days later, with a change in feeling, he went firmly back to his plans. More than once it was Palha himself who awakened him from those conjugal dreams.

"Are you doing anything tonight?"

"No."

"Here's a ticket to the Teatro Lírico, Box 8, first row on the left."

Rubião would get there early, wait for them, offer Sofia his arm. If she was in a good mood, the night was one of the best in the world. If not, it was a martyrdom, to repeat his own words to the dog one day:

"Yesterday was martyrdom for me, my poor friend."

"Get married, and then tell me if I'm wrong," Quincas Borba barked at him.

"Yes, my poor friend," he answered, picking up the dog's front paws and placing them on his knees. "You're right. You're in need of a good woman friend who can give you the care I can't or don't know how to give you. Quincas Borba, do you still remember our Quincas Borba? My good friend, my great friend, I was his friend, too, two great friends. If he were alive he'd be the best man at my wedding, at least he'd give the toast in honor of the happy couple—and it would be with a cup made of gold and diamonds that I would have made especially for him . . . Great Quincas Borba!"

And Rubião's spirit hovered over the abyss.

LXXXIII

O ne day, since he'd left home early and didn't know where to spend the first hour, he walked to the warehouse. He hadn't been to Flamengo for a week, as Sofia had fallen into one of her periods of indifference. He found Palha in mourning. His wife's aunt, Dona Maria Augusta, had died on her plantation. The news had arrived two days earlier, in the afternoon.

"The mother of that girl?"

"Precisely."

Palha spoke of the dead woman with great exaggeration. Then he spoke of the grief of Maria Benedita, who was suffering greatly. He asked him if he wouldn't go to Flamengo that same evening to help them take her mind off it. Rubião promised to go.

"Go, you'll be doing us a great favor. The poor little thing deserves everything. You can't imagine what a good person she is. A fine upbringing, very strict. And as for the social graces, if she didn't have them as a child, she made up for the lost time amazingly fast. Sofia is her teacher. As the lady of a house? In that respect, my friend, I don't know if you could find such a perfect example at such an age. She's staying with us now. She has a sister, Maria José, married to a judge in Ceará. She also has a godfather in São João d'El-Rei. The dead woman spoke very highly of him. I don't think he'll send for her, but even if he does, I won't give her up. She belongs to us now. Not even for what her godfather might want to leave her in his will would we let her go. She's staying here," he concluded, whisking a speck of dust from Rubião's collar.

Rubião thanked him. Then, as they were in the rear of the office, he looked through the blinds and saw some men in uniform coming into the warehouse. He asked what they were bringing.

"It's some English calico."

"English calico," Rubião repeated indifferently.

"By the way, did you know that the house of Morais & Cunha is paying all of its creditors in full?"

Rubião didn't know anything about it or if the firm existed or if they were its creditors. He listened to the news, answered that he was very glad for them, and made ready to leave. But his partner held him back for a few moments. He was jolly now, as if no one close to him had died. He talked about Maria Benedita again. He intended to get her a good marriage. She wasn't a girl to give in to the gabble of fancy paupers or let herself be carried away by foolish fantasies. She was a discreet girl and deserved a good husband, a serious person.

"Yes, sir," Rubião was saying.

"Look," his partner said softly all of a sudden, "don't be surprised at what I'm going to say to you. I think you're the one who should marry her."

"Me?" Rubião responded, startled. "No, sir." And immediately, in order to soften the effect of his refusal, "I don't deny that she's a fine, perfect girl, but . . . right now . . . I'm not thinking about marriage . . ."

"Nobody's telling you it has to be tomorrow or the next day. Marriage isn't something to be improvised. What I'm saying is that I've got a feeling here. It's just a notion, a feeling. Didn't Sofia ever tell you about my feeling?"

"Never."

"That's strange. She told me she'd mentioned it to you once or twice, I don't remember exactly when."

"It could be. I'm quite absentminded. So the two of you want me to marry the girl?"

"No, I only have a feeling. But let's drop it, let's give time some time."

"Goodbye."

"Goodbye. Come early."

LXXXIV

Well, then, did Sofia want him to get married? Rubião was thinking as he left. It was, of course, the most expeditious way to get rid of him. Get him married, make him her cousin. Rubião tramped along several streets before reaching this other hypothesis: maybe Sofia hadn't forgotten but was purposely lying to her husband in order not to speed the plan along. In that case her feelings would be different. That explanation seemed logical to him. His spirits returned to their former calm.

LXXXV

But there's no moral calm that can trim the sails of time a single inch when the person has no way of making them smaller. On the contrary, his anxiousness to go to Flamengo that evening made the hours drag along all the more. It was too early, too early for anything, to go to the Rua do Ouvidor, to go back to Botafogo. Dr. Camacho was in Vassouras defending a prisoner in court. There was no public diversion of any kind, neither festivity nor sermon. Nothing. Rubião, deeply annoyed, trudged along aimlessly, reading signs or stopping to observe a simple incident like the collision of two carts. He'd never been so bored in Minas, why? He couldn't find an answer to the enigma, given the fact that there was so much more to do in Rio de Janeiro, and things he really enjoyed. But there were hours of deadly tedium here.

Happily, there is a god who looks after people in a bad mood. Rubião suddenly remembered that Freitas—the always jolly Freitas—was gravely ill. Rubião hailed a cab and went to visit him in Praia Formosa, where he lived. He spent close to two hours there chatting with the sick man. The latter dozed off, and Rubião took leave of his mother—an old, old woman—and at the door, before leaving:

"You must have had some tight moments as far as money is concerned," Rubião said and, seeing her bite her lip and lower her eyes, "Don't be ashamed. Need is an affliction, and there's no need to be ashamed of it. What I would like is for you to accept something I'm going to leave you to help with expenses. You may pay it back someday if you can . . ."

He opened his wallet, took out six twenty *mil-réis* notes, rolled them into a lump, and put them in her hand. He opened the door and went out. The old woman, taken by surprise, didn't make a move to thank him. Only when the cab rolled away did she run to the window, but she could no longer see her benefactor.

L X X X V I

All of that had happened so spontaneously with Rubião that he only had time to reflect after the cab had begun to move. It appeared that he did manage to raise the window curtain. The old lady was going back inside. He could still see a bit of her arm. Rubião felt the advantage of not being an invalid. He leaned back, released a deep sigh from his chest, and looked out at the beach. He immediately leaned over. On the way there he had barely seen it.

"Do you like the view, sir?" the cabman asked, happy with the good customer he had.

"I think it's quite pretty."

"Haven't you ever been here?"

"I think I was many years ago when I was in Rio de Janeiro for the first time. I'm from Minas . . . Stop, young man."

The cabman halted his horse. Rubião got out and told him to follow along slowly.

It really was interesting. Great clumps of brush bursting up out of the mud and placed there at the level of Rubião's face made him have a desire to go into them. So close to the street! Rubião didn't even feel the sun. He'd forgotten the sick man and the sick man's mother. Just like that, yes—he said to himself—the sea should be all like that too, an expanse of earth and greenery, then it would be worth navigating. Beyond were more beaches, the Praia dos Lázaros and the Praia São Cristovão. Only a step away.

"Praia Formosa, beautiful beach," he murmured, "a name well chosen."

Meanwhile the beach was changing its aspect. He headed toward the Saco do Alferes and came to houses built along the sea. From time to time they weren't houses but canoes beached on the mud or on dry land with their bottoms up. Next to one of those canoes he saw children in shirtsleeves and barefoot playing around a man lying belly down. They were all laughing. One was laughing more than the others because he couldn't get the man's foot down to the ground. He was a three-year-old toddler. He would grab the leg and pull on it until he got it down to ground level, but the man would make a movement and lift the foot and the boy up into the air.

Rubião stopped for a few minutes, watching. The fellow, seeing that he was an object of attention, redoubled his efforts in the game. It lost its natural aspect. The other, older boys stopped to look in surprise. But Rubião didn't notice anything. He was seeing everything in a confused way. He walked along for a long time. He passed the Saco do Alferes, he passed Gamboa, he stopped by the English Cemetery with its old tombs climbing up the hillside, and he finally reached Saúde. He saw the long, narrow streets, houses crammed together in the distance and on top of the hills, alleyways, lots of ancient houses, some from the time of the king, eaten away, cracked, falling apart, paint covered with grime, but with life inside. And all that gave him a feeling of nostalgia . . . Nostalgia for tatters, for a life of poverty, humble and with no vexations. But it only lasted for a brief moment. The magician he carried inside himself transformed everything. It was so nice not to be poor!

LXXXVII

Rubião reached the end of the Rua da Saúde. He was going along aimlessly with his eyes wandering and unattentive. Flush with him a woman passed, not pretty, not plain, lacking in elegance, more poor than well-off, but with fresh-looking features. She must have been twenty-five and was leading a boy by the hand. He got tangled up in Rubião's legs.

"What are you doing, young man?" the woman said, pulling her son by the arm.

Rubião leaned over to help the little one up.

"Thank you very much, please excuse us," she said, smiling. And she bowed to him.

Rubião tipped his hat and also smiled. The vision of a family came over him again. "Get married, and then tell me if I'm wrong!" He stopped, looked back, saw the young woman clicking along with the boy beside her adjusting his little steps to match his mother's pace. Then, walking slowly, he thought about the several women he might well choose in order to perform the conjugal sonata, four hands around, serious music, regular and classical. He got to thinking of the major's daughter, who only knew a few old mazurkas. Suddenly he was hearing the guitar of sin being plucked by Sofia's fingers as she delighted and dazzled him at the same time. And away went all the chastity of his previous plan. He persevered once more, struggled to change compositions. He thought about the young woman in Saúde, such nice manners, with a small child by the hand.

LXXXVIII

The sight of the cab made him remember the sick man in Praia Formosa.

"Poor Freitas!" he sighed.

Immediately thereupon he thought about the money he'd left with the sick man's mother and felt he'd done a good deed. Perhaps the idea of having given one or two notes too many hovered for a few seconds in our friend's brain, but he quickly shook it off, not without being angry with himself, and, in order to forget about it completely, he exclaimed aloud:

"Fine old lady! Poor old lady!"

L X X X I X

Since the idea kept coming back, Rubião quickly headed for the cab, got in and sat down, fleeing from himself.

"I took a good, long walk. But, yes, sir, it's nice here, it's interesting. These beaches, these streets, it's different from other neighborhoods. I like it here. I've got to come back more."

The cabman smiled to himself in such a particular way that our Rubião became suspicious. He couldn't hit upon the reason for the smile. Maybe he'd let out some word that had a bad meaning in Rio de Janeiro. But he went over them and couldn't find anything. They were all ordinary, everyday words. The cabman was still smiling, however, with the same look as at the beginning, half subservient, half rascally. Rubião was on the verge of questioning him, but he held back in time. It was the other man who picked up the conversation.

"So your worship is quite taken by the neighborhood?" he asked. "You've got to allow me not to believe you, without getting angry, because it's not to offend your worship. I'm not one to upset a good customer. But I don't believe you're taken by the neighborhood."

"Why?" Rubião ventured.

The cabman shook his head and repeated that he didn't believe it—not because the neighborhood wasn't worthy of appreciation, but because his customer naturally knew it quite well already. Rubião corrected that statement. He'd been there many years before when he'd come to Rio de Janeiro at a different time, but he didn't remember anything. And the cabman laughed. And as his customer went on explaining, he got more familiar, made negative signs with his nose, lips, hand.

"I know all about that," he concluded. "I'm not a man who doesn't see things. Your worship thinks that I didn't see the way you looked at that young woman you passed just now? That's enough to show that your worship has a good nose and good taste . . ."

Rubião, flattered, put on a little smile. But he immediately corrected himself.

"What young woman?"

"What did I tell you?" the man retorted. "Your worship is sharp and you do things right, but I'm a person who can keep a secret, and this here cab has been used for lots of these comings and goings. Not too many days ago I carried a handsome young man, very well dressed, a refined person—you know, a skirt-chaser."

"But I . . . ," Rubião interrupted.

But he had trouble holding back in. The supposition pleased him. The cabman thought he was playing innocent.

"Look, I can tell you," he went on, "just like the young man from the Rua dos Inválidos. Your worship can rest easy, I won't say a thing. That's for other people. So, do you expect me to believe that it's for pleasure that a person who has a cab at his disposal goes along from Praia Formosa to here on foot? Your worship got to the meeting place, but the person didn't show up . . ."

"What person? I went to see a sick man, a friend who's at death's door."

"Just like the young man from the Rua dos Inválidos," the man repeated. "That one came to see a lady's seamstress, as if he'd been a married man . . ."

"From the Rua dos Inválidos?" Rubião asked, only now aware of the name of the street.

"That's all I'm saying," the cabman replied. "He was from the Rua dos Inválidos, handsome, a young man with a mustache and big eyes, very big. Oh, if I were a woman I'd be capable of falling in love with him . . . Her, I don't know where she was from and I wouldn't tell if I did. All I know is that she was quite a woman."

And seeing that his customer was listening, wide-eyed:

"Oh, your worship has no idea! She was tall, with a good figure, her face half covered by a veil, a tasty dish. Just because people are poor doesn't mean they can't appreciate fine things."

"But . . . what was it?" Rubião murmured.

"Come, now, what was it? He came the same as your worship, in my cab. He got out and went into a house with a grating. He said he was going to see a lady's seamstress. Since I hadn't asked him anything, and he'd traveled quiet during the whole trip, all wrapped up in himself, I caught onto the game right away. Now, it might just have been true, because there really is a seamstress who lives in a house on the Rua da Harmonia . . ."

"Da Harmonia?" Rubião repeated.

"This is bad! Your worship is pulling the secret out of me. Let's change the subject. I'm not saying anything more."

Rubião looked at the man with astonishment as he really did fall silent for two or three minutes, but immediately after he went on:

"Besides, there isn't very much to say. The young man went in, I stayed waiting. A half hour later I saw the figure of a woman in the distance and I suspected right away that she was headed there. It happened just the way I said. She came, came along slow, sneaking looks on all sides. As she passed in front of the house, I can't say, she didn't even have to knock. It was like magic. The grating opened all by itself and she slipped inside. If I only knew what it was all about. Wouldn't your worship let us earn a few pennies more? The price of the fare barely gives us enough to eat. We've got to do these little extras."

X C

No, it couldn't have been she, Rubião reflected, at home, getting dressed in black.

Ever since he'd arrived, he could think of nothing else but the episode told him by the cabman. He tried to forget about it, putting papers in order or reading or snapping his fingers to watch Quincas Borba leap. But the picture wouldn't go away. His reason told him that there were a lot of women with good figures, and there was no proof that the one on the Rua da Harmonia was she. But the good effect was short-lived. A little while later, sketched in the distance, head down, hesitant, was a person who was none other than Sofia herself, and she was walking and suddenly going through the door of a house, which closed immediately . . . The vision was such on one occasion that our friend remained staring at the wall as if the grating on the Rua da Harmonia were there. In his imagination he followed a series of actions: he knocked, entered, grabbed the seamstress by the throat, and demanded the truth or her life. The poor woman, threatened with death, confessed everything. She took him to see the lady, who was somebody else. It wasn't Sofia. When Rubião came to, he felt annoyed.

"No, it couldn't have been she."

He put on his vest and was buttoning it by one of the windows that opened on the back at the moment when a caravan of ants was crossing the sill. How many of those had he seen pass before? But this time, he never found out why, he picked up a towel and gave the poor ants a couple of swats, killing a good portion of them. Maybe one of them seemed to him to have had "a good figure and a pretty body." He immediately regretted his act and, really, what did the ants have to do with his suspicions? Fortunately a locust began singing so appropriately and so meaningfully that our friend stopped at the fourth button of his vest. *Soooo . . . fia, fia, fia, fia, fia, fia . . . Soooo . . . fia, fia, fia, fia . . . fia . . .*

Oh, sublime and merciful care of nature, to place a living locust alongside twenty dead ants to compensate for them! That reflection is the reader's. It can't be Rubião's. He wasn't capable of getting into things and drawing a conclusion from them—nor would he be doing it now as he reached the last button on his vest, all ears, all locust . . . Poor dead ants! Go now to your Gallic Homer who made you famous. The locust is the one who's laughing now, correcting the text:

> *Vous marchiez? J'en suis fort aisé.*
> *Eh bien! Mourez maintenant.*

X C I

The dinner bell rang. Rubião composed his face so that his regulars (there were always four or five) wouldn't notice anything. He found them in the parlor chatting, waiting. They all arose and went to shake his hand eagerly. Rubião had an inexplicable urge at that moment—to offer them his hand to kiss. He overcame it in time, surprised at himself.

X C I I

At night he hurried to Flamengo. He couldn't speak to Maria Benedita, who was upstairs with two girls from the neighborhood, friends of hers. Sofia came to receive him at the door and took him into the study, where two seamstresses were sewing mourning dresses. Her husband had just come in and hadn't come down yet.

"Sit here," she told him.

She took good care of him. She was divine. Her words came out loving and grave, mingled with friendly, open smiles. She spoke about her aunt, her cousin, the weather, the servants, the theater, the water shortage, a multitude of things, common and uncommon, but as they passed through the young woman's mouth they changed their nature and their aspect. Rubião listened in fascination. She, in order not to be idle, was sewing some ruffles, and when there was a pause in the conversation, Rubião was on the verge of devouring her agile hands as they seemed to be playing with the needle.

"Did you know that they're forming a committee of women?" she asked.

"I didn't know. What for?"

"Didn't you read the news about that epidemic in a town in Alagoas?"

She told him that she'd felt so sorry that she'd immediately resolved to organize a committee of women to seek donations. Her aunt's death interrupted the first steps, but she was going to continue once the seventh-day mass was over. And she asked him what he thought of the idea.

"It sounds fine to me. Aren't there any men on the committee?"

"Only women. The men just give money," she finished, laughing.

Rubião immediately agreed to a large amount in order to obligate those who came after. It was all true. It was also true that the committee was going to make Sofia visible and give her a lift up in society. The women chosen were not from our lady's circle, and she really knew only one of them. But through the intervention of a certain widow who'd dazzled between 1840 and 1850 and was still nostalgic for those times, and through her own efforts, Sofia got everyone to join in that charitable work. For several days she could think about nothing else. Sometimes at night before her tea, she would seem to be asleep in her rocking chair. She wasn't sleeping, she was closing her eyes to think of herself in the midst of her colleagues, people of quality. Understandably, this was the main topic of conversation, but from time to time Sofia would get back to her friend there. Why was he staying away for such long periods, eight, ten, fifteen days and more? Rubião answered for no reason but in such an emotional way that one of the seamstresses tapped the other one on the foot. From then on, even during the long silences cut only by the needles on the woolen cloth, the shears, the ripping, neither one took her eyes off the person of our friend with his eyes fastened on the lady of the house.

A visitor arrived to offer his condolences—a man, a bank director. They immediately went to call Palha, who came down to receive him. Sofia excused herself to Rubião for a few seconds. She was going to look in on Maria Benedita.

XCIII

Rubião, left alone with the two women, began to walk back and forth, muffling his steps so as not to bother anyone. From the parlor an occasional word of Palha's came out. "In any case, you can believe . . ."—"The administration of a bank isn't child's play . . ."—"Absolutely . . ." The director spoke sparsely, dry and softly.

One of the seamstresses folded up her sewing and hurriedly gathered up cuttings, shears, spools of thread, and silk. It was late, she was leaving.

"Wait a bit, Dondon, I'm leaving too."

"No, I can't. Could you please tell me what time it is, sir?"

"It's eight-thirty," Rubião replied.

"Good Lord! It's so late."

Rubião, just to say something, asked her why she wouldn't wait as the other woman had asked.

"I'm only waiting for Dona Sofia," Dondon put in respectfully. "But do you know where this one lives? She lives on the Rua do Passeio. And I've got to drag my boots to the Rua da Harmonia. And you know that the Rua da Harmonia is a fair piece from here."

Sofia came down right after and found Rubião all upset, avoiding her with his eyes. She asked him what was wrong and he said nothing, a headache. Dondon left, and the bank director took his leave. Palha thanked him for his kindness, wished him good health. Where was his hat? He found it. He also gave him his coat, and, as it appeared that he was looking for something else, he asked him if it was his cane.

"No, sir. It's my umbrella. I think this is it. This is it. Goodbye."

"Once more, thank you, thank you very much," Palha said. "Put your hat on, it's damp, don't stand on ceremony. Thank you, thank you very much," he finished, squeezing the man's hand in both of his and bowing.

Returning to the study he found his business partner, who was bent on leaving. He, too, pressed him, telling him to have a cup of tea, that it would soon go away. Rubião refused everything.

"Your hand's cold," the young woman observed to Rubião as she shook it. "Why don't you wait? Lemon-balm water is very good. I'll go get some."

Rubião stopped her. It wasn't necessary. He knew these attacks, they were cured with sleep. Palha wanted to send for a cab, but the other man said that the night air would do him good and that he could find transportation in Catete.

XCV

I'll catch up with her before she reaches Catete, Rubião said, going up the Rua do Príncipe.

He calculated that the seamstress had probably gone that way. In the distance he could make out two shapes on both sides. One of them looked like a woman's. It must be she, he thought, and picked up his pace. It has to be understood, of course, that his head was all dizzy: Rua da Harmonia, seamstress, a lady, and all the open gratings. Don't be surprised that, at wit's end and walking rapidly, he collided with a certain man who was going along slowly with his head down. Nor did he excuse himself, but lengthened his pace, seeing that the woman was also walking fast.

XCVI

And the man who was bumped scarcely felt it. He was walking along absorbed but content, open-spirited, free of cares and annoyances. It was the bank director who'd just paid Palha a visit of condolence. He felt the bump but didn't become angry. He straightened his coat and his spirits and continued along calmly.

It should be mentioned, in order to explain the man's indifference, that within the space of one hour he'd had two contrasting encounters. He'd gone first to the home of a cabinet minister to deal with a brother's petition. The minister, who'd just finished dinner, was smoking, silently and peacefully. The director laid out the matter in a jumbled way, going back, jumping ahead, tying up and untying words. Barely sitting so as not to cross the line of respect, he kept a constant and worshipful smile on his lips. And he bowed, asking to be excused. The minister asked a few questions. He, encouraged, gave long answers, extremely long ones, and ended up handing him a petition. Then he got up, thanked the minister, shook his hand. The latter accompanied him to the veranda. There the director bowed twice—one full one before going down the steps—another useless one already below in the garden. Instead of the minister, he only saw the frosted glass of the door and on the veranda, hanging from the roof, the gas lamp. He put on his hat and left. He went away humiliated, annoyed with himself. It wasn't the matter at hand that bothered him, but the bows he'd made, his begging his pardon, the attitude of a subaltern, a string of unrewarding acts. That was his state of mind when he reached Palha's.

Within ten minutes his spirits had been dusted off and returned to what they'd been before, such were the courtesies of the man of the house, the approving nods of his head and the ray of a perpetual smile, not to mention the offer of tea and cigars. The director then became stern, superior, cold, with few words. He disdainfully tossed aside an idea of Palha's, and the latter immediately retreated, agreeing that it was absurd. He copied the minister's slow gestures. As he left, the bows were coming not from him but from his host.

He was a different man when he reached the street. Therefore his walk was calm and satisfied. The opening up of his spirits devolved to his whole being and led to the indifference with which he received Rubião's bump. Away went the memory of his bowing and scraping. What he was savoring now was Cristiano Palha's bowing and scraping.

X C V I I

When Rubião got to the corner of Catete, the seamstress was chatting with a man who'd been waiting for her and who immediately gave her his arm. He saw them both go off like husband and wife in the direction of Glória. Married? Friends? They disappeared around the first corner of the street while Rubião stood there recalling the words of the cabman, the grating, the young man with a mustache, the lady with a pretty figure, the Rua da Harmonia . . . Rua da Harmonia. She'd said Rua da Harmonia.

He went to bed late. Part of the time he spent by the window, reflecting, cigar lighted, unable to come to any explanation of that business. Dondon had to be the go-between in the affair. She had to be, she had cunning eyes, Rubião was thinking.

"I'm going there tomorrow. I'll leave very early, go and wait for her on the corner. I'll give her a hundred *mil-réis*, two hundred, five hundred. She'll have to confess everything to me."

When he grew tired, he looked at the sky. There was the Southern Cross . . . Oh, if she'd only consented to gaze at the Southern Cross! The life of both of them would have been different. The constellation seemed to confirm that train of thought, gleaming brilliantly. And Rubião stayed there looking at it, composing a thousand beautiful love scenes—living what might have been. When his spirit had had enough of never-revealed love, it came to our friend's thought that the Southern Cross wasn't only a constellation, it was also a medal of honor. From there he went on to a different series of thoughts. He thought that it had been a stroke of genius to get the idea of making the Southern Cross a symbol of national distinction and privilege. He'd already seen the decoration on the chests of a few public servants. It was beautiful, but, best of all, rare.

"So much the better!" he said aloud

It was close to two o'clock when he left the window. He closed it and got into bed, falling asleep immediately. He awoke to the sound of the voice of the Spanish servant who was bringing him a note.

XCVIII

Rubião sat up in bed, bewildered. He didn't notice the hand-writing on the envelope. He opened the note and read:

We were quite concerned last night after you left. Cristiano can't stop by there now because he got up late and has to see the customs inspector. Send us a note saying you're feeling better. Best wishes from Maria Benedita and

Your faithful friend
SOFIA.

"Tell the messenger to wait."

Twenty minutes later the reply reached the hand of the black boy who'd brought the note. It was Rubião himself who gave it to him, asking him how the ladies were. He learned that they were well. He gave him ten *tostões*, telling him that if he ever was in need of money to come by and get some. The boy, startled, opened his eyes wide and promised that he would.

"Goodbye!" Rubião said to him benevolently.

And he stood there while the messenger went down the few steps. When the latter got to the center of the garden, he heard a shout:

"Wait!"

He came back in response to the call. Rubião had already gone down the steps. They approached each other and stopped, not saying anything. Two minutes passed before Rubião opened his mouth. Finally he asked something—if the ladies were well. It was the same question as the one a short time back. The servant confirmed the answer. Then Rubião let his eyes wander over the garden. The roses and the daisies were pretty and fresh, a few carnations were in bloom, other flowers and foliage, begonias and vines, that whole little world seemed to be placing its invisible eyes on Rubião and calling to him:

"You indolent soul, follow your desire for once, pick us, send us . . ."

"Fine," Rubião said finally. "Remember me to the ladies. Don't forget what I told you. If you need me, come here. Have you got the letter?"

"Yes, sir. It's here."

"You'd better put it in your pocket, but be careful not to crumple it."

"I won't crumple it, no, sir," the servant replied, putting the letter away.

The black boy left. Rubião remained there, strolling in the garden, his hands in the pockets of his dressing gown and his eyes on the flowers. Should he have sent some? It was a natural present and even an obligatory one, repaying one courtesy with another. He'd done poorly. He ran to the gate, but the boy was far off. Rubião remembered that mourning excluded happy offerings, and he calmed down.

Except that as he start strolling again he spied a letter next to a flower bed. He leaned over, picked it up, and read the envelope . . . It was in her hand, it could only be hers. He compared it with the note he'd received. It was the same. The name on it was the devil's own: Carlos Maria.

"Yes, that's what happened," he thought after a few minutes. "The fellow who brought my letter was carrying this one and dropped it."

And, looking the letter up and down, he wondered about the contents. Oh, the contents! What could be written there on that homicidal piece of paper? Perversion, lust, the whole language of evil and dementia summed up in two or three lines. He held it up to his eyes to see if he could read some word. The paper was thick, nothing was legible. Remembering that the messenger, when he found the letter missing, would be coming back looking for it, he quickly put it in his pocket and ran inside.

In the house he took it out and looked at it again. His hands hesitated, following the state of his conscience. If he opened the letter, he would know everything. Once read and burned, its contents would never be known to anyone else, while he would be putting an end, once and for all, to that terrible fascination that had been giving him so much pain there on the brink of that pit of infamy . . . I'm not the one who's saying it; he's the one who's putting together those and other horrible names, he's the one who stands in the center of the room with his eyes on the rug, where in the design an indolent Turk figures, pipe in mouth, looking out over the Bosporus . . . It has to be the Bosporus.

"Hellish letter!" he snorted softly, repeating a phrase he'd heard at the theater a few weeks earlier, an odd phrase that was emerging now to express the moral analogy between spectacle and spectator.

He had an urge to open it. It was only a gesture, an act. No one could see him; the pictures on the wall were silent, indifferent; the Turk on the rug continued smoking and looking out at the Bosporus. Nevertheless, he had scruples. The letter, even though found in the garden, didn't belong to him but to the other man. It was the same as if it had been a roll of bills. Wouldn't he return the money to its owner? Annoyed, he put it back in his pocket. Between sending the letter to its addressee and giving it to Sofia, he chose the second solution. It had the advantage of letting him read the truth in the features of the writer herself.

"I'll tell her I found a letter, that's all," Rubião thought. "And before I hand over the letter, I'll take a good look at her face and see if she's frightened or not. Maybe she'll grow pale, then I'll threaten her, talk to her about the Rua da Harmonia. I'll swear to her that I'm prepared to spend three hundred, eight hundred, a thousand *contos*, two thousand, thirty thousand *contos* if necessary to strangle the swine . . ."

C

None of the habitual visitors to the house appeared for lunch. Rubião waited for about ten minutes more and reached the point of sending a servant out to the gate to see if anyone was coming. Nobody. He had to lunch alone.

Usually he couldn't bear solitary meals. He was so accustomed to his friends' talk, their observations, their witticisms, no less than their respect and consideration, that eating alone was the same as not eating at all. Now, however, he was like a Saul in need of some David to expel the malignant spirit that had gotten into him. He was already having evil thoughts about the messenger because he'd dropped the letter. Not knowing would have been a boon. And then his conscience vacillated—it went from delivering the letter to refusing and keeping it indefinitely. Rubião was afraid of finding something out. Now he wanted, now he didn't want to read something on Sofia's face. The desire to know everything was, in short, the hope of discovering that there wasn't anything.

David finally appeared with the coffee and cheese in the person of Dr. Camacho, who'd returned from Vassouras the night before. Like the biblical David he brought an ass laden with loaves of bread, a jug of wine, and a kid. He had left a deputy from Minas gravely ill in Vassouras, and he was preparing Rubião's candidacy, writing to influential people in Minas. That was what he told him after the first sips of coffee.

"Candidate? Me?"

"Who, then?"

Camacho pointed out that there couldn't be a better one. He had connections in Minas, didn't he?

"Some."

"You've got some very important ones here. By backing that organ of principles with me, you've shared the blows I've received as well as the sacrifices we've all made on the monetary side. I tell you, I'm going to do everything I can. Besides, you're the best solution for the split."

"Split?"

"Yes, Dr. Hermenegildo from Catas-Altas and Colonel Romualdo. It's said that they both want to be candidates if there's a vacancy. It's splitting the vote . . ."

"Certainly, but will they insist?"

"I don't think they'll insist when I send them the confirmation of the party leaders here, because that was one of the things they threw in my face, the fact that I had no power. I confessed that in that unforeseen case I didn't, but that I had the confidence of the leaders, who would back me up. You can believe me, it's all set. So what do you think? Do you think that I've been working here sacrificing time and money and a bit of talent if not to be of some use to a friend who's given so many proofs of being faithful to principles? Oh, no! Not that! They'll have to listen to me and accept what I propose."

Rubião, moved, asked a few more questions about the campaign and the victory, whether expenditures would be needed now, or letters of recommendation, petitions, and whether they would get frequent news concerning the sick man, etc. Camacho answered them all. But he advised caution. In politics, he said, the least little thing can derail the campaign and give victory to one's opponent. Nevertheless, as no winner had emerged yet, Rubião had the advantage of having his name put up. And being first is worth something.

"Patience and fortitude," he concluded.

And immediately after:

"Am I not an example of patience and fortitude myself? My province is in the hands of a gang of bandits. There's no other name for the Pinheiros people. And in addition to that (I tell you this with particular pain), I've got friends who are conspiring against me, grasping people who want to see if the party will reject me so they can take my place . . . The scoundrels! Oh, my dear Rubião, this business of politics can only be compared to the passion of Our Lord Jesus Christ. It's all there, the disciple who denies, the disciple who betrays. The crown of thorns, blows, the cross, and, finally, dying on that cross of ideas, held there by the nails of envy, calumny, and ingratitude . . ."

That last phrase, popping out in the heat of the conversation, seemed worthy of an article to him. He stored it away in his memory. Before going to sleep, he wrote it down on a scrap of paper. But on the occasion of the conversation, while Camacho was repeating it to himself to get it down, Rubião said that he should cheer up, that he was a man for great campaigns. And that he shouldn't retreat because of scowling faces.

"Scowling faces? Certainly not. Or from real goblins, if they exist. I'm waiting for them! Let them rue the day we rise up! They'll pay for everything. Take this advice: in politics, never forgive or forget anything. Someone who does something pays for it. You must believe that revenge is sweet," he went on, smiling. "There's a lot of pleasure in it . . . So, adding up the good and the bad in politics, there's more good than bad. There are ingrates, but ingrates are discharged, arrested, prosecuted . . ."

Rubião listened, subdued. Camacho was in charge. His eyes were flashing. Curses poured out of him as from the mouth of Isaiah. The palms of victory were green in his hands. Every gesture was a principle. When he opened his arms, cutting the air, it was as if he were laying out a whole program. He was getting drunk with hope and the wine was heady. All of a sudden he stood still in front of Rubião:

"Let's go, deputy. Rehearse a speech making a motion for the discussion to stop: *Mister President* . . . Come on, say it with me: *Mister President, I ask Your Excellency . . .*"

Rubião interrupted him, standing up. He was in a kind of swoon. He saw himself in the chamber, going in to take the oath, all the deputies standing. And he shivered. It was difficult walking. Nevertheless, he crossed the chamber, went up to the president's rostrum, took the oath in the customary way . . . Maybe his voice would crack on the occasion . . .

C I

That was the state he was in when the news of Freitas's death arrived. He wept a hidden tear. He took on the expense of the burial and accompanied the deceased to the cemetery the following afternoon. The dead man's old mother, when she saw him enter the parlor, tried to kneel at his feet. Rubião embraced her in time to stop her from making that gesture. That act of our friend made a great impression on the invited guests. One of them came over to shake his hand. Later on, in a corner, the man told him about the injustice of the dismissal he'd received days before. A spiteful dismissal, the result of intrigue . . .

"Your Excellency can well imagine that the place (and please excuse the expression) is a den of scoundrels . . ."

The time arrived for the cortege to leave. The mother's farewells were painful: kisses, sobs, cries, all mingled and heartrending. The women were unable to tear her away from there. Two men had to use force. She was shouting and insisting on going back to the corpse: My son! My poor son!

"Scandalous!" the discharged man was insisting. "They say that the minister himself was displeased with the action. But, as Your Excellency knows, in order not to undermine the director . . ."

"Boom . . . boom . . . boom . . ." the hammers rang softly as the coffin was nailed shut.

Rubião acceded to the request that he hold one of the handles and he left the man who'd been dismissed. Outside there were a few people standing, neighbors at their windows leaning over each other with eyes full of the curiosity that death inspires in the living. For the rest, there was Rubião's coupé, which stood out among the old calèches. There'd already been a lot of talk about that friend of the deceased and his presence confirmed it. The dead man was now looked upon with a certain respect.

At the cemetery Rubião was not content with shoveling a spadeful of earth, in which he was first at everyone's request. He waited until the gravediggers filled the pit with their large professional shovels. His eyes were moist. He finished, left, surrounded by the others and at the gate, with just a wave of his hat left and right, he saluted all the uncovered and lowered heads. As he got into his coupé, he could just make out these words spoken in a low voice:

"I think he's a senator or a judge or something."

C I I

Night had fallen. Rubião was going along thinking about the poor devil he'd buried when, on the Rua de São Cristóvão, he passed another coupé with two orderlies following. It was a cabinet minister on his way to imperial business. Rubião stuck his head out, brought it back in, and sat listening to the orderlies' horses, so regular, so clear in spite of the clatter of the other animals. Our friend's spirit was so tense that he could still hear them when they were far out of earshot. Clip-clop . . . clip-clop . . . clip-clop . . .

C I I I

Seven days after the death of Dona Maria Augusta, the customary mass was sung at São Francisco de Paula. Rubião attended, and there he saw Carlos Maria. That was enough to hasten the return of the letter. Three days later he put it in his pocket and hurried to Flamengo. It was two in the afternoon. Maria Benedita had gone out to visit the friends in the neighborhood who had stayed with her during the first days of her sorrow. Sofia was alone, dressed to go out.

"But it doesn't matter," she said, inviting him to have a seat. "I can stay and go out later."

Rubião replied that it wouldn't take long. He'd come to give her a piece of paper.

"In any case, do sit down. You can hand over a piece of paper from a sitting position, too."

She looked so pretty that he hesitated to speak the harsh words he'd brought along all memorized. Mourning was very becoming to her, and her dress fitted her like a glove. When she was seated half of her foot was visible, low shoe, silk stocking, all things that called for pity and pardon. As for the sword in that scabbard—that's what an old-time author calls the soul—it didn't seem to have a sharp edge or deft balance. It was an innocent ivory paper knife. Rubião was on the verge of weakening. Her first word dragged out the others.

"What paper?" Sofia asked.

"A paper that I imagine is important," he replied, holding himself back. "Can't you remember or not whether you lost a letter?"

"No."

"Are you in the custom of writing letters?"

"I've written some, but I can't remember if they were important. Let me see it."

Rubião was wild-eyed. He didn't say or do anything. He got up to leave but didn't. Then, after a few moments of silence and hesitation, he continued, without anger.

"It's no secret for you that I love you. You know that and you neither dismiss nor accept me, you encourage me with your fine manners. I still haven't forgotten Santa Teresa or our train trip, when we were both traveling along with your husband in the middle. Do you remember? That trip was my undoing. Ever since that day you've held me captive. You're wicked, you've got the ways of a snake. What harm did I ever do to you? It's all right if you don't love me, but you might have put an end to my illusions right at the beginning . . ."

"Be quiet, someone's coming," Sofia interrupted, standing up and looking toward the door.

No one was coming. They might hear, however, because Rubião's voice was getting more heated and louder. It grew even louder. He was no longer suing for hope, he was opening up and emptying out his soul.

"I don't care if they hear," he roared. "Let them hear me. I'm going to say everything now, and you can throw me out and it will all be over. No, you can't make a man suffer like this."

"Be quiet, for the love of God!"

"Leave God out of this! Listen to what I have to say, because I'm not prepared to hold anything back . . ."

All confused, really worried that some servant might hear, Sofia raised her hand and covered his mouth. At the contact of that beloved flesh Rubião lost his voice. Sofia took her hand away and made ready to leave the room, but when she reached the door she stopped. Rubião walked over to the window to recover from the outburst.

C I V

Sofia, after listening for a few minutes, came back into the room and with a great rustle of skirts went over to sit down on the blue satin ottoman purchased a few days before. Rubião turned and faced her, shaking his head reprovingly. Before he spoke Sofia put her finger to her lips, asking him to be silent. Then she summoned him with her hand. Rubião obeyed.

"Sit in that chair," she said and after seeing him seated continued: "I have good reason to be angry with you. I'm not because I know that you're a good person, and I believe you're sincere. Be sorry for what you said to me, and everything will be forgiven."

Sofia used her fan to push down the right side of her dress and arrange it properly. Then she raised her arms, shaking her black glass bracelet, finally letting her hands rest on her knees, opening and closing her fan, waiting for an answer. Contrary to what she'd expected, Rubião shook his head negatively,

"I've nothing to be sorry for," he said, "and I prefer not to be forgiven. You will remain inside me here, like it or not. I could lie, but what good does lying do? You're the one who hasn't been sincere with me, because you've deceived me . . ."

Sofia's breast stiffened.

"Don't be angry. I don't want to offend you, but let me say that you're the one who's deceived me, and very much, and with no pity. That you love your husband, all right. I'd forgive you, but . . ."

"But what?" she asked, startled.

Rubião put his hand in his pocket, took out the letter and handed it to her. Sofia, when she read Carlos Maria's name, went pale. He noticed her paleness. Getting control of herself immediately, she asked what it was, what did that letter mean.

"It's your writing."

"It's mine, yes, but what would I be saying inside?" she continued, calm. "Who gave you that?"

Rubião wanted to mention how he'd found it, but he understood that he'd gone far enough. He bowed, as a sign of leaving.

"I'm sorry," she said. "Open the letter yourself."

"I've got nothing more to do here."

"Wait. Open the letter. Here it is. Read all of it," the young woman said, tugging at his sleeve. But Rubião pulled his arm away violently, went to get his hat, and left. Sofia, afraid of the servants, remained in the parlor.

She was so nervous during those first few moments that she forgot about the letter. Finally, she turned it over and over without guessing the contents, but little by little, in control of herself now, she remembered that it must have been the circular about the committee for Alagoas. She opened the envelope: it was the circular. How could such a paper have fallen into his hands? And where did his suspicions come from? From himself or from outside? Was there gossip going around? She went to see the servant who'd taken the circular to Carlos Maria, and she asked him if he'd delivered it. She found out that he hadn't. When the servant had reached the Rua dos Inválidos, he couldn't find the paper in his pocket, and since he was afraid, he didn't say anything to his mistress.

Sofia went back to the parlor, having decided not to go out. She picked up the letter and the envelope in order to show them to Rubião so he could see that it was nothing, but he would no doubt suspect that the paper was a replacement. Damned fellow! she murmured and began to walk about aimlessly.

A surge of memories came into Sofia's mind. The image of Carlos Maria came to plant itself in front of her with his big eyes of a beloved and hated specter. Sofia tried to put it aside, but she couldn't. He followed her from one side to the other, without losing his slender and manly look or his sublime smile. Sometimes she would see him leaning over, pronouncing the same words as on a certain night at a ball, which had cost her hours of insomnia, days of hope, until they were lost in irreality. Sofia never understood the failure of that adventure. The man seemed really to be in love with her, and no one had obliged him to declare it in such a daring way or to pass by her window in the middle of the night as she'd heard him say. She recalled still other encounters, furtive words, big, burning eyes, and she never came to understand why all that passion ended up in nothing. There probably hadn't been any, a simple flirtation—at most a way of sharpening the weapons of attraction . . . The nature of a dandy, a cynic, a coxcomb.

What did she care about the mystery? He was a coxcomb. Her

revulsion and disdain increased. She reached the point of laughing at him. She could face him without any remorse. And she went about having her revenge on the boob—she called him a boob—and staring into space with her virginal eyes. She really was taking up too much time on a matter like that. She began to curse Rubião for having brought a man like that back into her memory because of that damned circular . . . Then she returned to her earlier memories, Carlos Maria's words. If everybody thought she was beautiful, why shouldn't he? Maybe she could have had him at her feet if she hadn't acted so thankful, so humble . . .

Suddenly the maid, who was in the next room and heard something break, ran into the parlor and saw her mistress all alone, standing.

"It's all right," the latter said.

"I thought I heard . . ."

"It was the doll that fell. Pick up the pieces."

"The Chinese one!" the maid exclaimed.

It was, in fact, a porcelain mandarin, a poor devil who'd been resting quite peacefully on top of a bookcase. Sofia found him in her hands, not knowing how he got there or when. As she thought about her voluntary humiliation, she had an impulse—it seemed to be anger with herself—and she threw the doll to the floor. Poor mandarin! It didn't matter that it was made of porcelain, it didn't even matter that it had been a gift from Palha.

"But, ma'am, how did it happen that the Chinaman . . ."

"Get out!"

Sofia remembered her complete behavior with Carlos Maria: her easy acquiescence, excusing herself in anticipation, the eyes with which she sought him out, the strong handclasps . . . That was it. She'd thrown herself at his feet. Then her feelings began to change. In spite of everything, it was natural that he should like her, and the moral conformity of both wouldn't lead to either's giving in. Perhaps something else was to blame. She dug for possible reasons, some cold or harsh act, some lack of attention for him. She remembered that once, for fear of receiving him all alone, she'd had him told that she wasn't at home. Yes, that might have been it. Carlos Maria was proud. The slightest

affront would hurt him. He'd found out that it was a lie . . . That
was to blame.

C V I

. . .   O r, more accurately, a chapter in which the disoriented reader is unable to connect Sofia's sadness
to the cabman's tale. And he asks, confused: "So, is that gabble
in loud,' delinquent rhymes about the meeting on the Rua da
Harmonia, Sofia, Carlos Maria, all slander? Slander for the
reader and Rubião, but not for the poor cabman, who didn't
reveal any names or even get to tell a real tale. That's what you
would have seen had you read slowly. Yes, wretch, take careful
note of how unlikely it was that a man off on that kind of adventure should have his cab stop in front of the designated house.
It would be supplying evidence of the crime. There are more
streets in heaven and earth than are dreamed of in your philosophy—cross streets where the cab could have remained waiting.
"So, the cabman didn't know how to put his facts together.
But what interest did he have in making up the story?"
He'd taken Rubião to a house where our friend spent almost
two hours without sending him away. He saw him come out, get
into the cab, get out shortly after and continue on foot, ordering
him to follow. He drew the conclusion that this was the best
kind of fare, but even so he never thought to invent anything.
A woman with a boy passed, however—the one on the Rua da
Saúde—and Rubião stopped to look after her, showing signs of
love and melancholy. This is where the cabman took him to be
lascivious as well as liberal and complimented his talents. If he
spoke of the Rua da Harmonia, it was suggested by the neighborhood they were coming from. And if he said that he'd carried
a young man from the Rua dos Inválidos, it's quite natural that
he'd taken someone from there the day before—perhaps the very
same Carlos Maria—or because he lived there, or because he

kept his cab there—any circumstance that helped in the invention, the way reminiscences of the day serve as material for the dreams of night. Not all cabmen are imaginative. Mending the tatters of reality is more than enough.

All that's left is the coincidence that one of the seamstresses for the mourning lived on the Rua da Harmonia. That does seem to be the product of chance. The fault lies with the seamstress. She wouldn't have lacked for a house closer to the center of the city if she'd wanted to give up her needles and her husband. On the contrary, she loves them both more than anything in this world. There was no reason for me to cut the episode or interrupt the book.

CVII

As far as Sofia's reflections are concerned, there's nothing to explain. They were all solidly based on the truth. It was certain, ever so certain that Carlos Maria hadn't matched her first expectations—or the second or the third—because they came at different times, even though less fresh or abundant. As for the cause of that, we've seen that Sofia attributed the lack of the first successively to all three. She never got to think that he might have had other loves, or that this one had become just as insipid as they. There must have been a fourth cause, the true one, perhaps.

CVIII

For several months Rubião stopped going to Flamengo. It wasn't an easy resolution to keep. It cost him a lot of indecision, a lot of regret. More than once he reached the point of going out with the intention of visiting Sofia and asking for her forgiveness. For what? He didn't know, but he wanted to be forgiven. In every attempt of this kind the memory of Carlos Maria made him retreat. After a certain point in time it was the lapse itself that prevented him. It would be strange for him to show up there one day like a sad prodigal son simply to beseech the beautiful eyes of the lady of the house. He would go to the warehouse and visit Palha. The latter, after five weeks, scolded him for his absence. And after two months asked him if it was something intentional.

"I've had a lot to do," Rubião replied. "This business of politics takes up a person's time completely. I'll come by on Sunday."

Sofia got all ready to receive him. She would wait for an opportunity to tell him what the letter was, swearing by everything holy so he would see that the truth held nothing against her. Vain plans. Rubião never showed up. Another Sunday came, other Sundays came . . . Nevertheless, Sofia sent him a request for a contribution for Alagoas. He gave five *contos*.

"That's too much," his partner told him at the warehouse when he brought the paper to him.

"I won't give anything less."

"But look, you can give a lot without giving that much. Do you think that this subscription is being circulated among only half a dozen people? It's in the hands of a lot of women and a few men. It's on the counters in shops on the Praça do Comércio and elsewhere. Donate a little less."

"How can I? It's already written down."

"You can easily make a 3 out of this 5. Three *contos* is already a generous donation. There are bigger ones, but they're from people who are obliged by their position or their millions. Bomfim, for example, signed up for ten *contos*."

Rubião couldn't hold back an ironic chuckle. He shook his

head and refused to back down from the five *contos*. He would only change it by writing the number 1 in front—fifteen *contos*—more than Bomfim.

"Of course, you can give five, ten, fifteen *contos*," Palha answered, "but your assets call for caution. You've been digging into them a lot . . . You should be aware that they're not yielding as much now."

Palha was now the custodian of Rubião's holdings (stocks, bonds, deeds) that were locked up in the safe at the warehouse. He was collecting the interest, the dividends, and the rent from three houses that he'd had him buy some time earlier at a ridiculous price and which were bringing in a good return. He was also holding some gold coins because Rubião had the mania of collecting them just to look at. He knew the sum total of Rubião's possessions better than the owner, and he saw the leaks the ship was springing with no storm, on a sea that was milky calm. Three *contos* were enough, he insisted, and he proved his sincerity by the fact that he so happened to be the husband of the one who had organized the committee. But Rubião wouldn't budge from his five. He took advantage of the occasion to ask him for ten more, he needed ten *contos*. Palha shook his head.

"You have to excuse me," he said after a few seconds, "but what do you want them for? Are you sure you're not going to lose them, or risk them at least?"

Rubião laughed at the objection.

"If I were sure I was going to lose them, I wouldn't have come looking for them. I might be taking a risk, but you never gain anything without taking a risk. I need them for a transaction—I mean three transactions. Two are for safe loans that don't go beyond one *conto* five hundred. The eight *contos* five hundred are for an undertaking. Why are you shaking your head if you don't know what it's all about?"

"That's exactly why. If you'd consulted with me, if you'd told me what the undertaking was and who the people were, I'd have seen immediately that there's nothing good about it except the money that's going to be lost. Do you remember the Union of Honest Capital Co. stock? I told you right off that the title was pompous, a way of hoodwinking people, of giving employment to characters in need. You refused to believe me, and you fell for it. The stock went down, and this last quarter there were already no dividends."

"Well, then, just sell those shares. I'll be happy with whatever you get. Or give it to me from the funds of our firm . . . I'll be back in a while if you want—or you can send it to me in Botafogo. Pledge some bonds if you think that's better . . ."

"No, I'm not going to do anything. I'm not giving you the ten *contos*," Palha cut in furiously. "Enough of giving in all the time. It's my duty to resist. Safe loans? What loans are those? Can't you see that they're taking your money and not paying their debts? Characters who reach the point of dining every day with their creditor himself, like a certain Carneiro I've seen there. I don't know if the others owe you anything. They probably do. I can see that it's too much. I'm talking to you as a friend. Don't say someday that I didn't warn you in advance. What are you going to live off if you squander what you have? Our firm could go under."

"It won't go under," Rubião put in.

"It can. Anything can go under. I watched Souto the banker go under in 1864."

Rubião mulled over his partner's advice, not because it was good or probable, but because in it he found an affectionate intent disguised in a rough form. He gave him heartfelt thanks, but rejected it. He needed the ten *contos*. He would be more prudent from then on, and he promised him that he wouldn't be so easygoing. Beyond that, he had more than enough, he had money to sell or give away.

"Only to sell," Palha corrected.

And after a moment:

"All right. It's late now. I'll bring the ten *contos* tomorrow. So why don't you come get them at our place in Flamengo? How have we hurt you? What have the women done to you? Your anger must be with them, because I see you here. What was it, to punish them?" he finished, smiling.

"They haven't done anything to me. I'll come by tomorrow night."

"Come to dinner."

"I can't come to dinner. I've got some friends coming to my

house. I'll come at night." And, trying to laugh, "Don't punish them, they haven't done anything to me."

"Somebody's working on him," Palha reflected as soon as Rubião had left, somebody envious of our relationship . . . It could also be that Sofia did something to him to keep him away from the house . . ."

Rubião appeared in the doorway again. He hadn't had time to get to the corner. He was coming back to say that since he needed the money early, he'd come by the warehouse and get it. Then he'd go visit them at night. He needed the money by two in the afternoon.

C I X

That night Rubião dreamed about Sofia and Maria Benedita. He saw them on a broad terrace, dressed only in skirts, their backs completely bare. Sofia's husband, armed with a cat-o'-nine-tails with iron tips, was lashing them pitilessly. They were shrieking, begging for mercy, twisting, dripping with blood as their flesh fell off in clumps. Why Sofia was the Empress Eugénie and Maria Benedita one of her ladies-in-waiting I can't say for sure. "They're dreams, dreams, Penseroso," a character from our Álvares exclaimed, but I prefer old Polonius's reflection right after hearing some crazy talk from Hamlet, "Though this be madness, yet there is method in 't." There is also method here in that combination of Sofia and Eugénie and even more method still in what followed and which looks even more extravagant.

Yes, Rubião, indignant, immediately ordered the punishment to cease, for Palha to be hanged, and for the victims to be cared for. One of them, Sofia, accepted a place in the open carriage that was waiting for Rubião and off they went at a gallop, she elegant and unharmed, he glorious and dominating. The horses, which were two at the start, were soon eight, four handsome pairs. Streets and windows full of people, flowers raining down on them, cheers . . . Rubião felt that he was the Emperor Louis Napoleon. The dog traveled in the carriage at Sofia's feet . . .

It all finished without any ending or disaster. Rubião opened his eyes. Maybe a flea had bitten him or something: "Dreams, dreams, Penseroso!" Even now I still prefer the words of Polonius: "Though this be madness, yet there is method in 't!"

C X

Rubião took care of the two loans and the undertaking. The undertaking was a Program for Improvement in Embarkation and Disembarkation in the Port of Rio de Janeiro. One of the loans was destined finally to pay a certain overdue bill for paper at the *Atalaia*, an urgent debt. The newspaper was threatened with closure.

"Perfect," Camacho said when Rubião brought the money to his house. "Thank you very much. You can see how our organ could be silenced by a trifle like this. They're the natural thorns along the road. The people aren't educated. They don't recognize, don't support those who are working for them, those who go down into the arena every day in defense of constitutional freedom. Just imagine, that at some given moment, if we didn't have this money, everything would be lost, everyone would go about his own business and principles would be left without their loyal interpreter."

"Never!" Rubião protested.

"You're right. We'll redouble our efforts. *Atalaia* will be like Antaeus in the legend. Every time it falls it will rise up with greater life."

Having said that, Camacho looked at the bundle of banknotes. "One *conto* two hundred, right?" he asked, and he put them in the pocket of his frock coat. He went on to say that things were safe now, the paper was going along at full sail. He had certain material reforms in mind. He went even further.

"We need to develop the program, give a push to our coreligionaries, attack them if necessary . . ."

"How?"

"What do you mean, how? Attacking. Attacking is a way of saying correcting. It's evident that the party's organ is slackening. I say party's organ, because our paper is the organ of the party's ideas, do you understand the difference?"

"I understand."

"It's slackening," Camacho went on, squeezing a cigar between his fingers before lighting it. "We need to stress principles, but frankly and nobly, telling the truth. You have to believe that the leaders need to hear it from their own friends and supporters. I never rejected the conciliation of parties, I fought for it. But conciliation isn't a game. To give you an example, in my province the Pinheiros people got the support of the government just to get rid of me, and my coreligionaries in the capital, instead of fighting, because the government gives them their strength, what do you think they do? They also support the Pinheiros."

"Do the Pinheiros have some influence, then?"

"None at all," Camacho replied, slamming shut the matchbox he was about to open. "One of them's an ex-convict and another was nothing but a barber's apprentice. He studied, it's true, at the Faculty of Law in Recife, in 1855, I think, on the death of his godfather, who left him something, but the man's career has been so scandalous that as soon as he got his diploma he got into the provincial assembly. He's an animal, the man, and as much a lawyer as I'm pope."

They agreed on the political changes in the paper. Camacho reminded Rubião that his candidacy had run onto the rocks precisely because of the opposition of the leaders. Of some of them, he corrected himself immediately. Rubião agreed. That was what his friend had told him at the time, and the memory revived his resentment over the disaster. He could have been, he should have been in the chamber. That bunch hadn't wanted it. But they'd see, Rubião thought, they'd taste the bitterness of what they'd done. Deputy, senator, minister, they'd see him all of those, with twisted and frightened eyes. Our friend's head, even though it was the other man who'd provided the spark, was burning by itself, not out of hate or envy, but with ingenuous ambition, with heartfelt certainty, with the anticipated and dazzling vision of great things. Camacho thought he was in agreement.

"Our people are of the same opinion," he said. "I think a small threat to our friends would be just right."

That same night he read him the article in which he warned the party of the advantage of not giving in to the perfidies of power by supporting certain corrupt and unworthy people in some provinces. Here is the conclusion:

"The parties must be united and disciplined. There are those who claim (*mirabile dictu!*) that this discipline and union cannot reach the point of rejecting the benefits that fall from the hands of their adversaries. *Risum teneatis!* Who can come out with such blasphemy without having his flesh tremble? But let us suppose that this is how it is, that the opposition can, again and again, close its eyes to the irregularities of the government, to contempt for the law, to excesses of authority, to perversion and sophistry. *Quid inde?* Such cases—even though rare—could only be allowed when they favor good elements and not the bad. Every party has its rowdies and sycophants. It is in the interest of our adversaries to see us slacken, which boosts the spirits of the corrupt elements in the party. This is the truth. To deny it is to provoke intestine war among us, that is, the tearing asunder of the national soul . . . But no, ideas do not die. They are the labarum of justice. The vendors will be driven from the temple. Those who believe and are pure will remain, those who place the indefectible triumph of principles ahead of petty local and passing interests. Anything other than this will find us in opposition. *Alea jacta est.*"

C X I

Rubião applauded the article. He found it excellent. Perhaps it wasn't strong enough. *Vendors*, for example, was fine, but *vile vendors* would be better.

"Vile vendors? There's only one problem," Camacho pondered. "It's the repetition of the *v*'s. *Vi-ven-* . . . Vile vendors. Doesn't it sound unpleasant to you?"

"But up above there you've got *ves vis . . .*"

"*Vae victis.* But that's a Latin phrase. We could arrange something else: vile traders."

"*Vile traders* is good."

"Even so, *traders* doesn't have the impact of *vendors.*"

"So why not leave it vile vendors? *Vile vendors* is strong. No one will pay any attention to how it sounds. Look, I was never any good at this. I like strength. Vile vendors."

"Vile vendors, vile vendors," Camacho repeated in a low voice. "It's beginning to sound better to me. Vile vendors. I accept," he concluded, making the change. And he reread it: "The vile vendors will be driven from the temple. Those who believe and are pure will remain, those who place the indefectible triumph of principles ahead of petty local and passing interests. Anything other than this will find us in opposition. *Alea jacta est.*"

"Very good!" Rubião said, feeling himself partial author of the article.

"You think it's all right?" Camacho asked, smiling. "There are people who see the freshness of my student days in my style. I don't know, I can't say. My disposition is the same, yes, I'm going to castigate them. We're going to castigate them."

C X I I

Here's where I would have liked to have followed the method used in so many other books—all of them old—where the subject matter of the chapter is summed up: "How this came about and more to that effect." There's Bernardim Ribeiro, there are other wonderful books. Of those in foreign tongues, without going back to Cervantes or Rabelais, we have enough with Fielding and Smollett, many of whose chapters get read only through their summaries. Pick up *Tom Jones*, Book IV, Chapter I, and read this title: *Containing five pages of paper.* It's clear, it's simple, it deceives no one. They're five sheets of paper, that's all. Anyone who doesn't want to read it doesn't, and for the one who does read it, the author concludes obsequiously: "And now, without any further preface, I proceed to our next chapter."

CXIII

If such were the method of this book, there would be a title here explaining everything: "How Rubião, satisfied with the correction made in the article, composed and pondered so many phrases that he ended up writing all the books he'd ever read."

There is probably some reader for whom this alone is not sufficient. He will naturally want the complete analysis of our man's mental operations, not noticing that Fielding's five pages of paper wouldn't be sufficient for all that. There's a gap between the first phrase saying that Rubião was co-author and the authorship of all books read by him. What certainly would be the most difficult would be going from that phrase to the first book—from there on the course would be rapid. It's not important. Even so, the analysis would be long and tedious. The best thing is to leave it this way: For a few moments Rubião felt he was author of many works by other people.

CXIV

On the other hand, I don't know if all of the next chapter could be contained in a title.

Rubião was keeping to the plan of not seeing Sofia again. At least he wasn't going to Flamengo. He saw her one day as she passed in a carriage with one of the ladies from the Alagoas committee. She nodded with a smile and waved a greeting to him. He returned it, tipping his hat, a bit flustered, but he didn't stand stock still, the way it used to happen to him. He only cast a glance at the carriage as it went on its way. He also went on his way—and as he thought about the episode of the letter, he didn't understand that gesture of a wave, which had no hate or annoyance in it—as if nothing had happened between them. It might have been that her work on the committee and the companion she had with her explained Sofia's gracious benevolence. But Rubião wasn't thinking along those lines.

"Can she have such a lack of self-esteem?" he wondered. "Doesn't she remember the letter I found, which she'd sent to that fop on the Rua dos Inválidos? It's a lot, it's too much. It looks like a challenge, a way of saying it doesn't matter, that she'll write all the letters she wants to. Let her write them, but she should spend some money and send them by registered mail, it's cheap . . ."

He found a touch of malice in himself, and he laughed. That and a man who passed and was excessively polite to him pulled him out of the bitterness of his memories, and he forgot the matter and thought about another, the one that was taking him to the Banco do Brasil.

Entering the bank, he ran into his partner, who was coming out.

"I think I saw Dona Sofia just now," Rubião told him.

"Where?"

"On the Rua dos Ourives. She was in a carriage with another lady I don't know. How have you been?"

"You saw her, and you didn't remember?" Palha observed, not answering the question. "You didn't remember that Wednesday's her birthday, the day after tomorrow? I'm not asking you to come to dinner, I don't dare that much, it would be inviting you to be bored. But a cup of tea doesn't take too long to drink. Will you do me that favor?"

Rubião didn't reply immediately.

"I'll even come to dinner," he said finally. "Wednesday? You can count on me. I'd forgotten, I confess, but I've got so many things on my mind . . . Wait for me a half hour from now, at the warehouse."

Before half an hour was up, he was there, asking him for two *contos*. Palha no longer resisted the crumbling of his assets, and if he'd spoken some weak little word once or twice before, now he gave him the money, unconcerned. Rubião didn't go home before buying a magnificent diamond, which he sent to Sofia on Wednesday, along with a calling card and a few words of good wishes.

Sofia was alone in her boudoir putting on her shoes when the maid gave her the package. It was the third present of the day. The maid waited for her to open it to see what it was. Sofia was dumfounded when she opened the box and came upon the expensive jewel—a beautiful stone in the center of a necklace. She was expecting something pretty, but after the last two events she could scarcely believe that he'd be so generous. Her heart was pounding.

"Is the messenger there?"

"He left already. How pretty, ma'am!"

Sofia closed the box and finished putting her shoes on. She remained sitting there for some time, remembering past things. Then she got up, thinking:

"That man worships me."

She tried to get dressed, but as she passed in front of the mirror, she stopped for a few moments. She enjoyed contemplating herself, her fine figure, her bare arms, up and down, her eyes themselves as she contemplated. She was twenty-nine. She thought that she looked the same as when she was twenty-five and she wasn't mistaken. With her corset tightened and laced, before the mirror she arranged her breasts lovingly and let her magnificent bosom spread out. Then she remembered to see how the diamond would look on her. She took the necklace out and put it around her neck. Perfect. She turned from left to right and back again, went close, moved back, turned the dressing-room light up brighter. Perfect. She closed the jewel case and put it away.

"That man worships me," she repeated.

"He'll probably be there," Rubião thought on his way to dinner in Flamengo. "I doubt that he's given her a better present than I have."

Carlos Maria was indeed there, chatting between one of the Alagoas committeewomen and Maria Benedita. There weren't many guests. The plan had been to limit and to choose. Major Siqueira wasn't there, nor was his daughter, nor the ladies and gentlemen Rubião had met at that other dinner in Santa Teresa. Some ladies from the Alagoas committee could be seen. The bank director was there again—the one who'd visited the cabinet minister—with his wife and daughters, another important banker, an English businessman, a deputy, a judge, a counselor, some capitalists, and not many more people.

Even though obviously in her glory, Sofia forgot about the others in an instant when she saw Rubião enter the room and walk toward her. Either from some change or from not seeing him, to her he seemed to have a different air, a firm step, head held high, the complete opposite, in a word, of his former humbled and reduced appearance. Sofia shook his hand firmly and whispered her thanks. At the table she had him sit next to her, having on her other side the woman who was president of the committee. Rubião was taking in everything with a superior air. The quality of the guests didn't impress him, nor did the ceremonious atmosphere or the lushness of the table. None of that dazzled him. Even Sofia's personal care, although pleasant, didn't stupefy him the way it used to. For her part, her attention was more attentive and her eyes exceptionally tender and friendly. Rubião looked for Carlos Maria. There he was, between the same two women as in the parlor—Maria Benedita and the Alagoas committeewoman. He could see that he was paying attention only to them. He wasn't looking at Sofia nor she at him.

"Maybe they're covering up," he thought.

It seemed to him that as they got up from the table, they exchanged glances—but the general movement of the group might have misled him, and Rubião didn't lend any great importance to the observation. Sofia hastened to take his arm. As they walked she told him:

"I've been waiting for you ever since that day, and you never came back here again. It was my right to demand it of you so I could explain myself. We'll talk later."

A short time after Rubião went to the study where the smokers were. He listened in silence, his eyes wandering. When the others left, Rubião remained behind alone, half-lying on a leather sofa without thinking. His imagination was doing its duty, a little sluggish now—perhaps because he'd eaten too much. Outside, the after-dinner guests were arriving. The house was filling up, the clamor of conversation swelled, but our friend did not come down out of his beautiful dreams. The very sound of the piano, which made everyone fall silent, didn't bring him down to earth. But a rustle of silks coming into the room made him rise up quickly, awake.

"There you are," Sofia said, "hiding in here to get away from the boredom. You don't even want to hear good music. I thought you'd left. I've come to have it out with you."

And without further ado, because she didn't have a minute to spare, she told him what we know about the letter found in the garden in Botafogo. She reminded him that before opening it, she'd asked that he open it himself and read it. What better proof of innocence? The word came out quickly, seriously, properly, and emotional. There was a moment when her eyes grew moist. She wiped them, and they were red. Rubião took her hand and saw a tear still, a small tear, running down to the corner of her mouth. He swore that, yes, he believed everything. What was that crying all about? Sofia wiped her eyes again and held out her thankful hand.

"I'll see you later," she said.

The piano was still playing. Rubião made note of that circumstance. While they were listening to the playing no one would come in on them.

"But I can't be away for so long," Sofia put in. "Besides, I've got to give some instructions. I'll see you later."

"Wait, listen," Rubião insisted.

Sofia stopped.

"Listen. Let me say something to you, and, I don't know, it may be the last time . . ."

"The last time?"

"Who knows? It may be the last time. I couldn't care less if the man lives or dies, but I might find him here sometime, and I don't feel like fighting."

"You're going to meet him every day. Didn't Cristiano tell you what's going on yet? He's going to marry Maria Benedita."

Rubião took a step backward.

"They're getting married," she continued. "It's really startling because it came out when we were least expecting it—or they were very good at hiding it—or it was something that came over them suddenly. They're getting married. Maria Benedita told me a story that was confirmed by somebody else. But the story's always the same in the end. They're in love and that's that. They're going to get married and rather soon. When he spoke to Cristiano, Cristiano replied that it depended on me . . . As if I were her mother! I immediately gave my consent, and I hope that they'll be happy. He seems to be a fine young man. She's an excellent girl. They've got to be happy, it has to be that way. And it's a good bit of business, did you know that? He has his father's and his mother's holdings. Maria Benedita has nothing in terms of money, but she has the education I've given her. You must remember that when she came to live with me she was a shy little thing. She knew practically nothing. I was the one who educated her. My aunt deserved everything, and she does, too. So, it's true, they're getting married very soon. Didn't you see how they've been together all the time tonight? There's been no official notice, but close friends of the family know about it."

For someone in such a hurry it was too long a speech. Sofia realized it a little too late. She repeated to Rubião that she'd see him later, that she had to go back to the parlor. The piano had stopped. A discreet rumble of applause and conversation could be heard.

C X V I

They were going to marry? But how is it, then, that . . . ?
Maria Benedita—it was Maria Benedita who was marrying
Carlos Maria. But then Carlos Maria . . . He was understanding
now; it had all been a mistake, confusion. What seemed to have
been going on with one person was going on with another, and
that's how people can arrive at slander and crime.

That was what Rubião was thinking as he came out into the
dining room where the butlers were clearing the dinner table.
And he continued, walking the whole length of the parlor. "Just
imagine! And Palha wanted me to marry the cousin, not knowing
that fate had a different groom for her. The young man's not
ugly, much better-looking than she. Alongside Sofia, Maria Benedita isn't much or anything at all. But she's pleasant all the
same . . . They're getting married and soon . . . Will the wedding
be sumptuous? It probably will. Palha's a bit better off now . . ."
and Rubião cast his eyes over the furniture, the porcelain, the
crystal, the draperies. "It's got to be sumptuous. And, besides,
the groom is rich . . ." Rubião thought about the coach and the
horses that would pull it. He'd seen a superb team in Engenho
Velho a few days before that was just right. He would order
another pair like them, no matter what the price. He had to give
the bride a present too. As he was thinking about her, he saw
her enter the room.

"Where's Cousin Sofia?" she asked Rubião

"I don't know. She was here a minute ago."

And as he saw her ready to move off, he asked for a word
with her and for her not to get angry. Maria Benedita waited.
Without hesitation he gave her his congratulations. He knew
that she was going to get married . . . Maria Benedita turned
quite red and murmured that he shouldn't tell anybody. There
was no servant around then. Rubião grabbed her hand and
squeezed it between his hands.

"I'm like a member of the family," he said. "You deserve happiness, and I hope that you'll get it."

A bit frightened, Maria Benedita pulled her hand free, but in
order not to upset him, she smiled. None of that was necessary.

He was delighted. We know the girl wasn't pretty, but she looked beautiful from the strength of the good wishes. Nature seemed to have placed its most delicate ideas in her. Smiling too, Rubião went on:

"It was your cousin who told me. She swore me to secrecy. I won't say a word ahead of time. But what can I tell you? You're good and you deserve everything. No need to lower your eyes, there's nothing shameful about marriage. Come, lift up your head and smile."

Maria Benedita cast her radiant eyes on him.

"That's the way!" Rubião applauded. "What's wrong with confessing to a friend? Let me tell you the truth. I think you'll be happy, but I feel that he'll be even happier. No? You just see if I'm not telling the truth. He'll tell you what he feels himself, and if he's sincere, you'll see that I'm only prophesying. I know quite well that there's no scale to weigh feelings on. All I'm trying to say is that you're a beautiful and good young lady . . . Go, get on with you. If not, I'll keep on telling truths, and you'll be blushing all the more . . ."

It was true. Maria Benedita was blushing with pleasure as she listened to Rubião's words. At home she'd found acquiescence, nothing more. Carlos Maria wasn't that tender. He loved her circumspectly. He spoke to her of marital bliss as if it were a tribute he was going to receive from fate—a payment owed, complete and certain. Nor was it necessary to treat her otherwise for her to adore him above all things in this world. Rubião repeated his goodbye and stood looking at her as he would at a daughter. He watched her go off like that, crossing the room, lively and satisfied—so different from the way he'd found her at other times—to disappear through one of the doors. He couldn't hold back these words:

"A beautiful and good young lady!"

The story of Maria Benedita's wedding is brief. And even though Sofia might find it common, it's worth saying so. It has already been admitted that if it hadn't been for the epidemic in Alagoas, there might not have been any wedding, from which it can be concluded that catastrophes are useful, even necessary. There are more than enough examples, but a little story I heard as a child will suffice, and I shall give it to you here in a couple of lines. Once upon a time there was a cottage burning by the side of the road. The owner—a poor ragged wretch of a woman—was weeping over her disaster, sitting on the ground a few steps away. Suddenly, a drunken man happened along. He saw the fire, saw the woman, and asked her if that was her house.

"It's mine, yes, sir, and all I have in this world."

"Do you mind if I light my cigar from it?"

The priest who told me this certainly must have edited the original text. You don't have to be drunk to light your cigar on somebody else's misfortune. Good Father Chagas!—his name was Chagas—a priest who was more than good and who in that way instilled in me for many years the consoling idea that no one in his right mind will profit from the ills of others, not to mention the respect the drunkard had for the principle of property—to the point of not lighting his cigar without first asking permission of the owner of the ruins. All consoling ideas. Good Father Chagas!

Farewell, Father Chagas! I'm getting to the story of the wedding. That Maria Benedita loved Carlos Maria is something that was seen or sensed ever since that ball on the Rua dos Arcos where he and Sofia waltzed so much. We saw her the next morning, all ready to go to the country. Her cousin calmed her down with the promise that she was arranging a fiancé for her. Maria Benedita thought it was to be the waltzer from the night before and stayed on, waiting. She didn't confess anything to Sofia— first out of shame and later so as not to lose the effect of the news when Sofia revealed the person's name. If she were to confess it right away, it might happen that the other woman would slacken in her task, and it would be a lost cause. Let's dismiss all this, a girl's petty calculations.

The epidemic in Alagoas had come about in the meantime. Sofia organized the committee, which brought with it new relationships for the Palha family. Included among the women forming one of the subcommittees, Maria Benedita worked with all of them, but she gained the especial esteem of one of them, Dona Fernanda, the wife of a deputy. Dona Fernanda was a bit over thirty, was jovial, expansive, ruddy, and robust. She'd been born in Porto Alegre, had married a lawyer from Alagoas, the deputy from a different province now, and, according to rumor, about to become a minister of state. Her husband's origins were the reason for her joining the committee. And it was a good move, because she brought in donations like a field commander, not the least bit shy and accepting no refusals. Carlos Maria, who was her cousin, went to call on her the moment she arrived in Rio de Janeiro. He found her even more beautiful than in 1865, the last time he'd seen her, and it could well have been true. He came to the conclusion that the air in the south was made to fortify people, double their charms, and he made the promise to go there to live out his days.

"You must go there because I can arrange a marriage for you," she said. "I know a girl in Pelotas who's a *bijou*, and she'll only marry a man from the capital."

"Me, naturally?"

"From the capital and with big eyes. Look, I'm not fooling. She's a country girl of the highest class. I've got a picture of her here."

Dona Fernanda opened the album and showed him a picture of the person.

"She's not ugly," he agreed.

"Is that all?"

"All right, she's pretty."

"Where can you find something to top that, cousin?"

Carlos Maria smiled without answering. He didn't like the expression. He tried to change the subject, but Dona Fernanda went back to his marrying her friend from Pelotas. She stared at the picture and colored it in with words, saying what her eyes were like, her hair, her skin. And then she gave him a short biography of Sonora. That was her pretty name. The priest who'd baptized her was hesitant about bestowing it in spite of the prestige and influence of the child's father, a wealthy rancher, but he gave in finally, stating that a person's virtues could carry the name to the roster of the saints.

"Do you think she's going to join the roster of the saints?" Carlos Maria asked.

"If she marries you, I do."

"That doesn't explain anything. If she married the devil, the same thing could happen and with even more certainty because of the martyrdom involved. Saint Sonora. It's not a bad name, it sounds nice in that setting. Saint Sonora . . . In any case, cousin . . ."

"You're sounding like a Jew, be quiet," she interrupted. "So, are you refusing my country girl?" she went on, putting the album away.

"I'm not refusing. Just let me go on with my celibacy, which is halfway to heaven."

Dona Fernanda let out a loud laugh.

"Merciful God! Do you really think you're going to heaven?"

"I've been there already for twenty minutes now. Because isn't it this room, peaceful, cool, so far away from the people out there? Here are the two of us, chatting away without hearing any blaspheming, without suffering the presence of any crippled, tubercular, scrofulous, unbearable spirits, hell itself, in a word. This is heaven—or a piece of it. Since we fit into it, it's as good as the infinite. We're talking about Saint Sonora, Saint Carlos Maria, Saint Fernanda, who, in contrast to Saint Gonçalo, has become a matchmaker for young girls. Where can another heaven like this be found?"

"In Pelotas."

"Pelotas is so far away!" he sighed, stretching out his legs and looking at the chandelier.

"All right. This is only the first attack. I'll make others until you end up wanting to."

Carlos Maria smiled and looked at the tassels hanging from the silk sash around her waist, tied with a loose bow, either to observe the tassels or to take note of the elegance of her body. He could easily see, once again, that his cousin was a beautiful creature. Her shape attracted his eyes—respect turned them away. But it wasn't just friendship that made him tarry there a little and that brought him to that house again. Carlos Maria generally loved the conversation of women as much as he detested that of men. He found men declamatory, coarse, tiring, boring, trivial, crude, banal. Women, on the other hand, were neither coarse nor declamatory nor boring. Their vanity was fitting, and a few defects did them no harm. Furthermore, they had the grace and gentleness of their sex. Even from the most insignificant of them, he thought, there was always something to be had. When he found them insipid or stupid, he thought to himself that they were unfinished men.

In the meantime, the relationship between Dona Fernanda and Maria Benedita was becoming closer. The latter, in addition to being bashful, was rather sad at the time. It was precisely the disparity of character and situation that had brought them together. Dona Fernanda possessed the quality of sympathy on a large scale. She loved the weak and the sad from her need to make them happy and courageous. She had many acts of mercy and dedication to her credit.

"What's the matter with you?" she asked her little friend one day. "You almost never laugh, and you always go around with frightened eyes, thinking . . ."

Maria Benedita replied that there was nothing the matter, that it was her manner. And she smiled as she said it out of simple acquiescence. She alluded to the loss of her mother as one of the causes of her melancholy. Dona Fernanda began to take her everywhere, having her to dinner, keeping a seat in her box for her if she went to the theater, and, thanks to that and to her genius for revelry, she shook out of the girl's soul the hateful ravens that had been flapping their wings there. Habit and affection quickly made them intimate friends. Nevertheless, Maria Benedita continued to be silent about her mystery.

"Whatever the mystery is," Dona Fernanda thought one day, "I think the best thing would be to get her married to Carlos Maria. Sonora can wait."

"You need to get married, Maria Benedita," she told her two days later in the morning at her country house in Mata-Cavalos. Maria Benedita had gone to the theater with her and had spent the night there. "I don't want any shuddering. You need to get married, and you're going to get married . . . I've been meaning to tell you that ever since the day before yesterday, but things like that, when they're talked about in the salon or on the street, don't have the force they need. Here in the country place it's different. And if you feel like climbing, come up the hill a bit with me, then it'll be just right. Shall we go?"

"It's getting hot . . ."

"It's more poetic than that, child. Oh, you bloodless Rio people! You've got water in your veins. Let's stay here on this bench, then. Sit down. That's it. I'll stay here next to you, ready for anything. Marry or die. Don't answer me. You're not happy," she went on, changing her tone. "No matter what you do, I can see that you're going through life without any pleasure. Come on, tell me frankly, are you interested in anyone? If you are, confess it, and I'll have that person sent for."

"I'm not."

"No? Well, that's exactly what's needed. You don't have to engrave it on your heart. I know a good candidate . . ."

Maria Benedita turned completely around, facing her, her lips half open and her eyes wide. She seemed fearful of the proposal or anxious for it. Dona Fernanda, without sensing her friend's real state of mind, took her hand first and asked her to tell her everything. She must be in love with someone, it was clear, she saw it in her eyes. She had to get her to confess it, she'd insist, beg—she'd hint at it if that was necessary. Maria Benedita's hand had grown cold, her eyes were piercing the ground, and for a few moments neither said anything.

"Come on, say something," Dona Fernanda repeated.

"I've nothing to say."

Dona Fernanda put on an expression of disbelief. She hugged

her tighter, put her arms around her waist, and drew her close to her. She told her in a very soft voice, into her ear, that it was as if she were her own mother. And she kissed her on the cheek, on the ear, on the back of the neck. She laid the girl's head on her shoulder, stroked it with her other hand. Everything, everything, she wanted to know everything. If her lover was on the moon, she'd send for him on the moon—wherever he was— except in a cemetery, but if he was in a cemetery, she'd give her a much better one who'd make her forget the first in a few days. Maria Benedita listened, all agitated, throbbing, not knowing how to escape—ready to talk and falling silent just in time, as if defending her chastity. She wasn't denying, she wasn't confessing—but she wasn't smiling either and was trembling with emotion. It was easy to guess half the truth at least.

"But I'm your friend, am I not? Don't you trust me? Pretend I'm your mother."

Maria Benedita couldn't resist much longer. She'd used up all her strength and she felt the need to reveal something. Dona Fernanda listened, touched. The sunlight was already beginning to lick the ground around the bench; it wouldn't be long in climbing up their shoes, the hems of their skirts to their knees, but neither noticed it. Love had them absorbed. The revelation of one was like a strange rapture for the other. It was a passion that wasn't known, wasn't shared, wasn't guessed. A passion that was losing its nature and its type and changing into pure adoration. At first, when she saw the beloved person, she would go through two very different states—one that she couldn't define: excitement, foolishness, throbbing of her heart, almost a swoon. The second was one of contemplation. Now it was almost all the last. She'd wept a lot to herself, lost nights and nights of longings. She'd paid dearly for the ambition of her hopes. But she would never lose the certainty that he was superior to all other men, a divine being who, even if he didn't notice her, would always be worthy of adoration.

"Well," said Dona Fernanda when her friend finally fell silent. "Let's get down to the essential thing, which is not idle grieving. No, my dear, this business of adoring a man who doesn't notice you is all poetry. Get rid of the poetry. Just remember that you're the only loser in the matter because he'll marry someone else, the years will pass, passion will ride off in their saddlebags, and one day, when you least suspect, you'll wake up without love and without a husband. So who is this savage?"

"That I won't say," Maria Benedita answered, getting up from the bench.

"Well, don't," Dona Fernanda put in, taking her wrists and making her sit on her lap. "The main thing is to get married. If it can't be to this one, it will be to someone else."

"No, I'm not getting married."

"Only to him?"

"I don't know whether to him," Maria Benedita answered after a few moments. "I love him the way I love God in heaven."

"Holy Virgin! Such blasphemy! Double blasphemy, child. The first is that you mustn't love anyone as much as God, the second is that a husband, even if he's a bad one, is always better than the best of dreams."

C X I X

"A husband, even if he's a bad one, is always better than the best of dreams." The maxim wasn't idealistic. Maria Benedita protested against it, because wasn't it better to dream than to weep? Dreams end or change, while husbands can live a long time. "You said that," Maria Benedita concluded, "because God picked out an angel for you . . . Look, there he comes."

"Let's leave it that there must be an angel for you, too. I know a magnificent one for you. Angels always seek me out."

Teófilo, Dona Fernanda's husband, had seen them from a distance and came over to join them. He was carrying a crumpled newspaper in his hand. He didn't greet their guest, but went straight to his wife.

"Do you know what they've done to me, Nanã?" he said with clenched teeth. "My speech on the fifth came out today. Look at this sentence. I said: *When in doubt, abstain, as the wise man advises*. And they put: *When in debt, abstain* . . . It's intolerable! You should know that it was precisely about an outstanding debt by the navy, and I claimed in my speech that there were too many expenses. So it can look like a crude remark on my part. It's as if I were advising nonpayment. In any case, it's an absurdity."

"But didn't you read the proofs?"

"I read them, but the author's the one least qualified to read them well. *When in debt, abstain*," he continued, with his eyes on the newspaper. And snorting: "That can only . . ."

He was dejected. He was a man of talent, seriousness, and hard work, but at that moment all great acts, the most daunting problems, the most decisive battles, the most profound revolutions, the sun and the moon and the constellations, and all the beasts of the field and all human generations were not as important as the substitution of an *e* for an *ou*. Maria Benedita looked at him, not understanding. She thought she was suffering from the greatest sadness, but here was one just as great as hers and much more painful. In that way the gnawing melancholy of a poor girl was on the same level as a typographical error. Teófilo, who only then noticed her, held out his hand. It was cold. No one can fake cold hands. He must really have been suffering. Moments later he flung the paper to the ground with a violent gesture and started off.

"But Teófilo, you can correct it tomorrow," Dona Fernanda told him, getting up.

Teófilo, without turning around, shrugged his shoulders, hopeless. His wife ran to him. Her friend was still bewildered. She remained alone on the bench, free of them now, receiving the full force of the sun, which didn't make love or speeches. Dona Fernanda took her husband into a study and consoled him for that blow with kisses. At lunch he was already smiling, even though with a pale smile. His wife, to get his mind off his worry, brought up her plan to get Maria Benedita married, and it would have to be a deputy, if there was some bachelor in the chamber, no matter what his politics. He could be in the government, in the opposition, in both, or in nothing—as long as he was a husband. She made a few reflections on that theme, lively, jolly ones, which filled time and were aimed at doing away with the memory of the switched letters. Merciful creature! Teófilo, understanding his wife, was becoming happy, and he agreed to the suitability of getting Maria Benedita married.

"The worst part," his wife put in, looking at her friend, "is that she's in love with someone whose name she refuses to tell."

"She doesn't have to," her husband said, wiping his lips, "it's obvious that she's in love with your cousin."

C X X

The following Sunday Dona Fernanda went to the church of Santo Antônio dos Pobres. When mass was over, amidst the bustle of the faithful greeting each other and bowing to the altar, whom should she see but her cousin rise up, erect, cheerful, somberly garbed, holding out his hand to her.

"Did you come to mass, too?" she asked, surprised.

"I did."

"Do you come regularly?"

"Not regularly, but often."

"Frankly, I didn't expect to see such devotion in you. Men are generally a bunch of heretics. Teófilo never sets foot in a church except to baptize his children. Are you all that religious, then?"

"I can't answer that with certainty, but I have a horror of banality, which is what speaking ill of religion is, that's all. I came to mass, I didn't come to confession. Now I'm going to see you home, and if you invite me to lunch I'll have lunch with you people. Unless you want to have lunch with me. I'm on this street, as you know."

"I'd like to go alone with you, if it's all right, so I can give you a rather long bit of news."

"Let's walk slowly, then," Carlos Maria said at the church door, offering her his arm. And, two steps farther on, "An important piece of news?"

"Important and delightful."

"People want to see God, ever merciful, take our dear Teófilo to his bosom, leaving the most charming of all widows bereft . . . There's no need to put that face on, cousin. Leave your arm where it is. Let's get to the news. The girl from Pelotas has arrived, I'll bet."

"I won't tell you what it is unless you promise to listen seriously."

"I promise."

Dona Fernanda confessed that she was reluctant about getting him married to her countrywoman from Pelotas. She didn't want any regrets. She'd discovered someone here who was deeply in love with her cousin. Carlos Maria smiled, began a witticism, but the news bolstered his spirits. Deeply in love? Deeply in love, a fierce passion, his cousin confirmed, adding that perhaps the definition didn't really fit the person's actual feelings anymore. Now it was a quiet and silent adoration. She'd wept over him night after night while there was still hope . . . And in that way Dona Fernanda went on revealing Maria Benedita's secret. All that was left was the name. Carlos Maria wanted to know it, she refused. She wouldn't say it. Why give him the pleasure of knowing who it was that adored him if he wasn't running off to meet her soul? It was better to leave it a mystery. She wasn't weeping anymore now. Modest and without drive, she'd abandoned all hope of being loved, and, in time, she'd been left as nothing but a devotee, but a devotee without equal, one who didn't expect to be heard or rewarded someday with a kindly look from her beloved god . . .

"Cousin, you . . ."

"I what?"

Carlos Maria ended up saying that the advocate was a match for the cause. Really, if that girl adored him to such a degree, it was proper and natural for his cousin to have such a strong interest in her. But why not tell him her name?

"Right now I'm not saying anything. Maybe someday . . . But, you understand, it would be quite difficult for me to get you married to my countrywoman knowing that another person loves you so much. And it might also be that the one here wouldn't suffer that much if she saw you married. Yes, sir, it seems absurd, but you have to know her. I tell you that once you were happy, she'd be capable of blessing her beautiful rival."

"This isn't romanticism anymore, it's mysticism," Carlos Maria argued after a few steps, his eyes on the ground. "It's not in tune with our times. Have you got some proof of such a state of mind?"

"I have . . . That's your house there, isn't it?" Dona Fernanda asked, stopping.

"It is."

"A nice building. Solid."

"Quite solid."

"One, two, three, four . . . seven windows. Does the salon go from one end to the other? It's just right for a ball."

And, walking:

"If I had a larger house here, I'd give a great ball before going back to Rio Grande. I like parties. My two children don't give me much trouble. By the way, I've been wanting to put Lopo into a good school. Where can I find a good school?"

Carlos Maria was thinking about the unknown devotee. He was far, far away from education and its establishments. How nice it was to feel oneself an adored god, and adored in an evangelical way with the devotee in a room, the door closed, in secret, not in a temple in sight of everyone. "And your father, who sees all that happens secretly, will repay you." Oh, wouldn't he pay if he knew who it was. Married, a proper woman? No, it couldn't be. She wouldn't be confessing it to anyone. A widow or an unmarried woman, more likely unmarried. He sensed that she was unmarried. What room did she shut herself up in to pray, to evoke him, to weep for him, to bless him? He was no longer insistent regarding the name. But the room, at least.

"Where can I find a good school?" Dona Fernanda repeated.

"School? I don't know. I'm thinking about the woman of mystery. You can easily understand that a person who adores me in silence, without hope, is an object of some attention. Is she tall or short?"

"Maria Benedita."

"That girl . . . ? Impossible. I've spoken to her a lot of times, and I never noticed anything. I always found her cold. You must be mistaken. Did she give you my name?"

"No. No matter how many times I asked her. She confessed the miracle without naming the saint, but what a miracle! Be proud to be adored as no one ever has been . . . Whose house is that?"

"You're in the habit of exaggerating things, cousin. It might not be all that much. Adored as no one ever has been? So how did you find out I was the one?"

"Teófilo was the first to spot it. When it was mentioned to her, she turned cherry red. She even denied it afterwards with me, and since that day she hasn't come back to our house."

Such was the beginning of the love affair. Carlos Maria was amused at seeing himself silently loved like that, and all his prejudice was turning into sympathy. He began to see her, savoring the girl's confusion, her fears, her joy, her modesty, her almost imploring expressions, a combination of acts and feelings that was the apotheosis of the man who was loved. Such was the beginning, such was the outcome. That's the way we saw them on that night of the birthday party for Dona Sofia, to whom he'd said such sweet things before. Men are like that. The waters that flow by and the winds that roar past are no different.

C X X I

"Fine, he's getting married, so much the better!" Rubião thought. Between that night and the day of the wedding, Rubião caught a few looks from Sofia in the air that bore a suspicion of temptation. Carlos Maria, if he returned them, did it more out of politeness than anything else. Rubião concluded that the case was fortuitous. He still remembered Sofia's tear on the night of her birthday when she explained the story of the letter to him.

Oh, good, unexpected tear! You, who were enough to persuade a man, might not be explicable to others, but that's how the world goes. What does it matter that her eyes weren't accustomed to weeping or that the night seemed to bring out feelings quite different from melancholy? Rubião saw it drop. Even now, he can see it in his memory. But Rubião's confidence didn't come from the tear alone, it also came from the Sofia who was present there, who had never been so solicitous or so affable toward him. She seemed sorry for all the trouble that had been caused, ready to heal things, either out of delayed affection or because of the very failure of the first adventure. There are virtual sins that lie dormant. There are late-blooming operas in the head of a maestro that await only the first rhythms of inspiration.

C X X I I

" So much the better that he's getting married!" Rubião repeated. The marriage wasn't long in taking place, three weeks. On the morning of the designated day, Carlos Maria opened his eyes with a touch of astonishment. Was he really the one who was getting married? There was no doubt. He looked at himself in the mirror, he was the one. He reviewed the past few days, the quick march of events, the reality of the affection he felt for the bride, and, finally, the sheer happiness she was going to give him. This last idea filled him with great and rare satisfaction. He was still ruminating on it all on horseback during his habitual morning ride. This time he chose the neighborhood of Engenho Velho.

Although he was accustomed to admiring eyes, now in all the people he saw a look that befitted the news that he was to be married. The oaks of a country estate, silent before he passed them, said very strange things that thoughtless people might have attributed to the breeze that was also passing, but which those who knew recognized as nothing less than the nuptial language of oak trees. Birds leaped from one side to the other, trilling a madrigal. A pair of butterflies—which the Japanese consider a symbol of fidelity, observing how they light from flower to flower almost always as couples—a pair of them accompanied the pace of the horse for a long time, going along the hedge of a country house by the side of the road, flitting here and there, sprightly and yellow. Along with this a cool breeze, a blue sky, the merry faces of men riding donkeys, necks stretching out of coaches to look at him in his elegance of a bridegroom. It was difficult, of course, to believe that all those gestures and appearances of people, animals, and trees were expressing any other feeling than the nuptial homage of nature.

The butterflies disappeared into one of the thicker parts of the hedge. Another country house came along, without trees, with an open gate, and in the background, facing the gate, it squinted its eyes in the form of five eaved windows, weary of losing inhabitants. They, too, had seen weddings and festive gatherings. The century found them green still with novelty and hope.

Don't think that this aspect saddened the horseman's spirit. On the contrary, he possessed the singular gift of being able to rejuvenate ruins and to live off the primitive life of things. He even enjoyed looking at the old faded house in contrast to the lively butterflies of a moment before. He stopped his horse, thought of the women who'd entered there, other festive dresses, other faces, other ways. Perchance the very shades of those happy vanished people were coming now to compliment him, too, calling him with their invisible mouths the sublime names they had for him. He could even hear them laughing. But a rasping voice came along to mingle in the concert; a parrot in a cage hanging on the outside wall of the house: *"A royal parrot, give him a carrot. Who goes there? Hop to Papa, Krr . . . Krrr . . ."* The shades fled, the horse continued on. Carlos Maria hated parrots, just as he hated monkeys, two counterfeit humans, he would say.

"Shall the happiness *I give her* be interrupted, too?" he reflected as he went along.

Wrens flew from one side of the street to the other and alighted, singing in their own language. It was redress. That language without words was intelligible. It was saying many clear and beautiful things. Carlos Maria could see a symbol of himself in that. When his wife, bewildered by the parrots of the world, began to fall down with aversion, he would make her rise up to the trilling of the divine flock of birds that he carried in himself, golden ideas spoken in a golden voice! Oh, how he would *make her happy*! He could already foresee her, her elbows on his knees, her head in her hands and her eyes on him, grateful, devoted, loving, all imploring, all nothing.

C X X I I I

So that picture, at the very same moment in which it was appearing in the groom's imagination, was being reproduced in the spirit of the bride, namely, Maria Benedita, by the window, watching the waves breaking in the distance and on the beach, seeing herself kneeling at the feet of her husband, quiet, contrite, as at communion, receiving the host of happiness. And she was saying to herself, "Oh, *he* will make *me* so happy!" The phrase and the thought were different, but the feeling and the moment were the same.

C X X I V

They were married. Three months later they left for Europe. When she saw them off, Dona Fernanda was as happy as if she were greeting them on their return. She didn't cry. The pleasure of seeing them happy was greater than the displeasure of separation.

"Are you going off happy?" she asked Maria Benedita for the last time by the rail of the steamship.

"Oh, very happy!"

Dona Fernanda's spirit came out of her eyes, fresh, ingenuous, singing something in Italian—because the superb woman from Rio Grande do Sul preferred Italian music—perhaps this aria from *Lucia: O bell'alma innamorata.* Or this bit from the *Barber*:

Ecco ridente in cielo
Spunta la bella aurora.

C X X V

Sofia didn't go on board. She was ill and sent her husband. It shouldn't be thought that it was out of grief or sorrow. She managed herself with great discretion on the occasion of the wedding. She took care of the bride's trousseau and took leave of her with many teary kisses. But going on board seemed shameful to her. She became ill, and, so as not to belie the pretext, she stayed in her room. She picked up a recent novel. Rubião had given it to her. Other things there reminded her of the same man, trinkets of all kinds, not to mention the jewels that were put away. Finally, one strange word she'd heard from him on the night of her cousin's wedding, even that, came to join the inventory of memories of our friend.

"You're queen of them all now," he told her in a low voice; "wait till I make you empress."

Sofia didn't understand that enigmatic phrase. She tried to suppose it some grandiloquent enticement to make her his lover, but she dismissed such an intent as too presumptuous. Rubião, though not the same bashful and timid man of other times now, wasn't so sure of himself that one could attribute such high presumption to him. What did the phrase mean, then? Sofia thought anything was possible. There was no lack of flirtatious remarks. She'd come to hear that declaration of Carlos Maria's, she'd probably heard others, which only brought out her vanity. And they all went away. Rubião was the one who persisted. There were pauses, born of suspicions, but the suspicions went away just as they'd come.

"*He deserves to be loved,*" Sofia read on the novel's open page when she continued her reading. She closed the book, closed her eyes, and became lost in herself. The slave girl who came in a short time later to bring her some broth imagined that her mistress was sleeping and tiptoed out.

C X X V I

In the meantime, Rubião and Palha were leaving the ship on the launch returning to the Pharoux docks. They were thoughtful and silent. Palha was the first to open his mouth.

"I've been waiting a long time to tell you something important, Rubião."

C X X V I I

Rubião came to. It was the first time he'd been on board a steamship. He was returning with his spirits all full of the sounds on board, the bustle of the people coming and going, Brazilians, foreigners, the latter of all kinds, French, English, German, Argentine, Italian, a confusion of languages, a hodge-podge of hats, trunks, rigging, couches, binoculars around the neck, men going up and down the gangways inside the ship, women weeping, others curious, others full of laughter, and many who were carrying flowers or fruit from land—all new sights. In the distance the harbor mouth through which the steamship was to sail, the immense sea, the lowering sky, and the solitude. Rubião brought back dreams of an ancient world. He created an Atlantis without knowing anything about the tradition. Not having any notion of geography, he was forming a confused idea of other countries, and his imagination surrounded them with a mysterious mist. Since it didn't cost him anything to travel that way, he sailed in his mind for some time on that tall, long steamer, without any seasickness, waves, winds, or clouds.

C X X V I I I

"Tell me?" Rubião asked after a few seconds.

"Tell you," Palha confirmed. "I should have told you before, but this marriage business, the Alagoas committee, and all that got me caught up, and I didn't have a chance. Now, though, before lunch . . . You'll have lunch with me."

"Yes, but what is it?"

"Something important."

Saying this he took out a cigarette, opened it up, unraveled the tobacco, rolled up the straw casing again, and struck a match, but the wind put the match out. Then he asked Rubião if he would do him the favor of holding his hat so he'd be able to light another. Rubião obeyed impatiently. It could well be that his partner, by extending the wait, wanted in that way to make him believe it was something earthshaking. Reality would prove it to be something beneficial. After two puffs:

"I'm planning to liquidate the business. A banking house has invited me to join them, a directorship, and I think I'll accept."

Rubião breathed easy.

"Of course. Liquidate right now?"

"No, toward the end of next year."

"And is it necessary to liquidate?"

"It is for me. If the bank business wasn't sure, I wouldn't be inclined to give up the certain for the dubious. But it's most sure."

"So that at the end of next year we'll break the ties that bind us . . ."

Palha coughed.

"No, before that. At the end of this year."

Rubião didn't understand, but his partner explained to him

that it was more practical to break up the partnership now so he could liquidate the firm by himself. The bank could be organized sooner or later, but why subject the other man to the demands of the occasion. Besides, Dr. Camacho was sure that Rubião would be in the chamber shortly, and the government was certain to fall.

"Come what may," he concluded, "it's still best to break up the partnership in good time. You're not living off the business, you came in with the necessary capital—you could have given it to someone else or held onto it."

"Of course, I don't doubt it," Rubião agreed.

And after a few moments:

"But tell me one thing, does this proposal carry some hidden reason? Is it a breakup between people, of a friendship? . . . Be frank, tell me everything . . ."

"What kind of a wild idea is that?" Palha retorted. "The breakup of a friendship, between people? . . . You must be crazy. It must be the effect of the rolling of the sea. Because how could I, who've worked so hard for you, who've made you the friend of my friends, who've treated you like a relative, like a brother, break with you for no reason at all? This very marriage of Maria Benedita to Carlos Maria should have been with you. You know quite well that if it hadn't been for her refusal . . . People can break one bond without breaking others. Anything else would be absurd. Are all social or family friends business partners? What about the ones who aren't businessmen?"

Rubião found the argument excellent and wanted to embrace Palha. The latter shook his hand with great satisfaction. He was going to see himself free of a partner whose growing prodigality could bring him trouble. The business was solid. It was easy to turn over to Rubião the part that belonged to him, except for personal and previous debts. A few of those still remained, as Palha had confessed to his wife that night in Santa Teresa, Chapter L. He'd paid very little back. It was generally Rubião who closed his ears to the matter. One day when Palha tried to force some money on him, he repeated the old proverb: "Pay what you have and see what you've got left." But Rubião, joking, said:

"Well, don't pay, and see if you haven't got even more left."

"That's good!" Palha commented, laughing and putting the money into his pocket.

C X X I X

There was no bank, no directorship, no liquidation, but how could Palha have justified the proposal of breaking up by telling the truth? Therefore the invention, all the more handy because Palha had a love for banks and was dying to be part of one. The man's career was getting more and more prosperous and attractive. The business had been quite lucrative for him. One of the reasons for the separation was precisely to avoid having to share any future profits with someone else. Palha, in addition, owned stocks on all sides, gold-backed bonds from the Itaboraí loan, and he'd arranged a couple of deals in war supplies in partnership with an influential man, from which he'd made a tidy profit. He'd already made an oral agreement for an architect to build him a mansion. He was vaguely thinking about the title of baron.

C X X X

"Who would have said that the Palhas would treat us like this? We don't count for anything with them anymore. Stop defending them."

"I'm not defending them, I'm explaining. There must have been some mix-up."

"Celebrating her birthday, marrying off a cousin, and not a single, solitary invitation to the major, to the great major, to the inestimable major, to their old friend the major. Those were the names they called me. I was inestimable, an old friend, great, other names. Now, nothing, not even a sad little invitation, a message by word of mouth by a slave boy at least. 'Missy's having a birthday,' or 'Her cousin's getting married, she says that the house is open to you and for you to come in formal dress.' We wouldn't have gone, formal dress isn't for us. But it would have been something, it would have been a message, a messenger, to the inestimable major . . ."

"Papa!"

Rubião, seeing Dona Tonica's intervention, was brought to defend the Palha family at length. He was in the major's house, no longer on the Rua Dois de Dezembro but on the Rua dos Borbonos, a modest little townhouse. Rubião was passing by, the major was in the window, and he called to him. Dona Tonica didn't have time to leave the parlor and take a look at her eyes in the mirror at least. She was scarcely able to run her hand over her hair, fix the bow in the ribbon around her neck, and pull her dress down to cover her shoes, which weren't new.

"I tell you there must have been a mix-up," Rubião repeated. "Everything over there is in great confusion because of the Alagoas committee."

"Now that you mention it," Major Siqueira interrupted, "why didn't they put my daughter on the Alagoas committee? Ha! I've been noticing this for a long time. In the old days they wouldn't have a party without us. We were at the heart of everything. Beginning at a certain time the change began. They started to greet us coolly, and the husband, if he could, would slip away to avoid saying hello to me. That started quite a while ago, but, before that, nothing went on without us. Are you talking about a mix-up? Well, the day before her birthday, already suspicious that they wouldn't invite us, I went to see him at the warehouse. A few words. He was covering up. Finally, I said this to him: 'At home last night Tonica and I were arguing about the date of Dona Sofia's birthday. I said it had gone by, but she said it hadn't, that it was today or tomorrow.' He didn't answer me, he pretended that he was involved with some figures, he called the bookkeeper and asked for an explanation. I understood the sly fellow, and I repeated the story. He did the same thing. I left.

Come now, Palha, a nobody! I'm ashamed of him. In the old days: major, a toast. I made lots of toasts, there was a certain ease. We played cards together. Now he's on his high horse, going around with fine people. Oh, the vanities of this world! Why, just the other day, didn't I see his wife in a coupé with another woman? Sofia in a coupé? She pretended not to see me, but she set her eyes in such a way that I saw that she was looking to see if I saw her, if I admired her. The vanities of this life! Someone who's never had anything delicate to eat, when she gets it, smears it all over."

"I'm sorry, but the committee work calls for a lot of show."

"Yes," Siqueira put in, "and that's why my daughter wasn't on the committee, so she wouldn't ruin the fine carriages . . ."

"Besides, the coupé could have belonged to the other lady who was with her."

The major took two steps with his hands behind his back and stopped in front of Rubião.

"The other lady . . . or Father Mendes. How is the priest? Living it up, naturally."

"But, Papa, there probably wasn't anything to it," Dona Tonica interrupted. "She's always been nice to me, and when I was ill last month, she asked about me twice through a slave boy . . ."

"Through a slave boy!" her father roared. "Through a slave boy! A great favor! 'Boy, go over to that retired officer's house and see if his daughter is any better. I can't go because I'm polishing my nails!' A great favor! You don't polish your nails! You work! You're a proper daughter of mine! Poor, but honest!"

Here the major wept, but he suddenly suppressed his tears. The daughter, touched, also sat down, upset. The house certainly bespoke the poverty of the family, not many chairs, an old round table, a worn sofa, two lithographs on the wall framed in pine painted black, one a portrait of the major in 1857, the other showing *Veronese in Venice*, purchased on the Rua do Senhor dos Passos. But the daughter's work showed through everywhere: the furniture glowed with polish, the table had a cloth and a mat of her making, the sofa a pillow. And it wasn't true that Dona Tonica didn't polish her nails. She might not have had the powder or the chamois, but she took care of them with a piece of cloth every morning.

Rubião treated them with kindness. He stopped defending the Palhas so as not to make the major lose heart. A short time later he took his leave, promising, without an invitation, that he'd be back to dine "one of these days."

"Poor folks' dinner," the major put in. "If you can let us know, do so."

"I don't want any banquet. I'll come when I get the notion."

He said goodbye. Dona Tonica, after going to the landing, not following to the front because of her shoes, went to the window to watch him leave.

C X X X I I

As soon as Rubião turned the corner of the Rua das Mangueiras, Dona Tonica came in and went to her father, who'd lain down on the sofa to reread the old *Saint-Clair of the Islands, or The Outlaws of Barra*.* It was the first novel he'd known. The copy was over twenty years old. It was the father and daughter's whole library. Siqueira opened the first volume and let his eyes rest on the beginning of Chapter II, which he already knew by heart. He found there now a particular pleasure because of his recent displeasures: "Fill your cups well,' exclaimed Saint-Clair, 'and let us drink right now. Here is the toast I give you. To the health of the good and the valiant in their oppression and to the punishment of the oppressors.' They all went along with Saint-Clair, and the toast made its rounds."

"Do you know something, Papa? Tomorrow you buy some

---

* The Portuguese translation of this 1803 novel by Elizabeth Helme was one of the most widely read books in nineteenth-century Brazil. Machado refers to it frequently. [Ed.]

canned peas, fish, and the rest, and we'll store them away. On the day he comes to dinner we'll put them on the stove, and all we'll have to do is warm them up and we'll have a fine little dinner."

"But I've only got enough money for your dress."

"My dress? Buy it next month, or the one after I can wait."

"But what if we can't find one at the same price?"

"There'll be one. I'll wait, Papa."

CXXXIII

I haven't mentioned it yet—because the chapters scurry along under my pen—but here's one that tells how at that time Rubião's relationships had increased in number. Camacho had put him in touch with many political men, the Alagoas committee with several ladies, the banks and companies with people in business and the exchange, the theater with its frequenters, and the Rua do Ouvidor with everybody. His name was already on everyone's lips. The figure of the man was well known. When he put in an appearance with his beard and long mustache, a well-fitting frock coat, his broad chest, a horn-handled walking stick, and a firm and lordly step, people said right off that it was Rubião—a moneybags from Minas.

They'd made a legend of him. They said he was the disciple of a great philosopher who'd left him an immense fortune— one, three, five thousand *contos*. Some people were surprised that he never talked philosophy, but the legend explained that silence in the philosophical method of his master itself, which consisted in instructing only men of good will. Where were those disciples? They went to his house every day—some of them twice, in the morning and in the afternoon. And that was how the guests at his table were defined. They may not have been disciples, but they were men of good will. They nibbled at their hunger waiting, and they listened to their host's discourse silently and smiling. Between the old and the new there was a touch of rivalry, which the first accentuated by displaying a greater intimacy, giving orders to servants, asking for cigars, going into the interior of the house, whistling, and so forth. But custom made them tolerate one another, and they all ended up in the sweet and common confession of the fine qualities of the master of the house. After a time the new ones also owed him money, either in cash, or in charge accounts with tailors, or in the endorsement of notes that he would pay secretly so as not to upset the debtors.

Quincas Borba was all over their laps. They would clap their hands to see him leap. Some went so far as to kiss him on the head. One of them, more ingenious, found a way to have him at the table at lunch or dinner, on his legs so he could feed him pieces of bread.

"Oh, none of that!" Rubião protested the first time.

"What's wrong?" his guest replied. "There aren't any strangers here."

Rubião reflected for a moment.

"The truth is that there's a great man inside him," he said.

"The philosopher, the other Quincas Borba," the guest went on, looking around at the newer ones to show the intimacy of his relationship with Rubião. But he couldn't keep the advantage to himself because the other friends from the same period repeated in a chorus:

"That's right, the philosopher."

And Rubião would explain to the newcomers the reference to the philosopher and the reason for the dog's name, which they had all attributed to him. Quincas Borba (the deceased) was described and spoken of as one of the greatest men of his time— superior to his fellow countrymen. A great philosopher, a great soul, a great friend. And at the end, after a moment of silence, rapping with his fingers on the edge of the table, Rubião exclaimed:

"I would have made him a minister of state!"

One of the guests, without conviction, out of duty, exclaimed:

"Oh, no doubt about it!"

None of those men, however, knew the sacrifice that Rubião was making for them. He turned down dinner invitations, rides, he interrupted pleasant conversations just so he could hurry home to dine with them. One day he found a way of adjusting everything. If he wasn't home by six o'clock on the dot, the servants were to serve dinner for his friends. There were protests: no, sir, they would wait until seven or eight o'clock. Dinner without him was dull.

"But it's possible I might not be able to come," Rubião explained.

That was the way it was done. The guests set their watches by the clocks in the house in Botafogo. When six o'clock struck, everyone was at table. On the first two days there was a bit of hesitation, but the servants had strict orders. Sometimes Rubião would arrive a little after. Then there was laughter, remarks, jollity. One of them wanted to wait, but the others . . . The others resisted the effort. On the contrary, he was the one who'd pulled the rest of them along, such was his hunger—to the point that if there was anything left, it was only the plates. And Rubião laughed with them all.

C X X X I V

To write a chapter to say only that in the beginning the guests, with Rubião absent, smoked their own cigars after dinner may seem frivolous, but thoughtful people will say that there was some interest in that seemingly minimal circumstance.

It so happened that one night one of the oldest friends thought to go into Rubião's study. He'd been there a few times, where the cigar boxes were kept, not four or five, but twenty or thirty of different makes and sizes, all open. A servant (the Spaniard) lighted the gas. The other guests followed the first, picked out cigars, and those who weren't familiar with the study admired the well-made and well-arranged furniture. The writing desk received general admiration. It was made of ebony, a masterpiece of wood carving, a solid, strong piece. Something new awaited them: two marble busts on it, the two Napoleons, the first and the third.

"When did these come?"

"At noon today," the servant replied.

Two magnificent busts. Next to the eagle-eyed look of the uncle, the pensive look of the nephew was lost in space. The servant said that his master, as soon as the busts had arrived and were in place, had spent a long time admiring them, so oblivious that he, too, was able to look at them, without admiring them. "*No me dicen nada estos dos pícaros,*" the servant concluded, making a broad and noble gesture.

C X X X V

Rubião was a generous patron of letters. Books that were dedicated to him went to press with a guarantee of two or three hundred copies. He had diplomas from literary, choreographic, and religious societies, and he was a member of a Catholic Congregation and a Protestant Fraternity at the same time, not thinking about the one when people mentioned the other to him. What he did was pay his dues regularly to both. He subscribed to newspapers without reading them. One day, when he was paying the bill for one, he discovered from the collector that it supported the government party. He told the collector to go to the devil.

CXXXVI

The collector didn't go to the devil. He collected the price for six months, and, since he possessed the natural observation of bill collectors, he muttered out on the street:

"Now here's a man who hates the paper and pays. How many are there who love it and don't pay?"

CXXXVII

But—Oh, stroke of fortune! Oh, impartiality of nature!—our friend's prodigality, if it had no cure, did have compensation. Time no longer passed for him as for an idler without ideas. Rubião, for lack of them, now had imagination. Formerly he'd lived for others more than for himself, had found no inner equilibrium, and indolence marked hours that never came to an end. Everything was undergoing a change. Now his imagination tended to leap about a little. Sitting in Bernardo's shop, he would spend a whole morning without time's wearying him, nor did the narrowness of the Rua do Ouvidor restrict his space. Delightful visions repeated themselves for him, like that of marriage (Chapter LXXXI) in terms where the grandeur didn't take away from the graciousness. There were those who saw him leap from his chair more than once and go to the door to get a good look at the back of a person passing by. Did he know him? Or could it have been someone who chanced to have the features of the imaginary creature he was looking at? These are too many questions for just one chapter. Suffice it to say that one of those times nobody was passing by. He recognized the illusion himself, went back inside, and bought a bronze geegaw for Camacho's daughter, whose birthday it was and who was going to be married shortly, and then he left.

"What about Sofia?" the lady reader asks impatiently like Orgon: "*Et Tartuffe?*" Alas, my friend, the answer is naturally the same—she, too, was eating well, sleeping soundly and smoothly—things that also don't prevent a person from loving when she wants to love. If this last reflection is the secret motive behind your question, let me say to you that you're most indiscreet, and I want nothing to do with hypocrites.

I repeat, she was eating well, sleeping soundly and smoothly. She'd come to the end of the Alagoas committee with praise in the press. *Atalaia* called her "the consoling angel." And don't think this name made her happy even though it praised her. On the contrary, placing the whole charitable activity in Sofia's hands might mortify her new friends and cause her to lose the work of many months in one day. That was how the article in the next number of the paper explained it, naming individually and glorifying the other committeewomen—"stars of the first magnitude."

Not all the relationships were substantive, but the greater part of them were firm, and our lady was not lacking in the talent for making them lasting. Her husband was the one who sinned for being boisterous, excessive, outgoing, making it obvious that he was collecting favors, that he was receiving unexpected and almost undeserved kindnesses. Sofia, to correct him, bothered him with bits of censure and advice, laughing:

"You were impossible today. You were acting like a servant."

"Cristiano, control yourself when we have people from outside. Don't have your eyes popping out of your face as you bounce from one side to another like a child who's been given some candy . . ."

He would deny it, explain, or justify himself. In the end he concluded that, yes, he mustn't be so obsequious. Courtesy, affability, nothing more . . .

"Exactly, but don't fall into the other extreme," Sofia added, "don't be grumpy . . ."

Palha became both things then, grumpy at first, cold, almost disdainful, but either reflection or unconscious impulse would restore our man to his habitual animation and with it, depending on the moment, excess and clamor. Sofia was the one who really fixed everything. She observed, imitated. Necessity and vocation soon had her acquiring what neither birth nor fortune had given her. Furthermore, she was at that in-between age in which women inspire equal confidence in girls of twenty and matrons of forty. Some had great affection for her, others heaped praise upon her.

That was how our friend gradually cleared the atmosphere. She broke off old familiar relationships, some so intimate that it was hard to dissolve them, but the art of greeting without warmth, listening without interest, and taking leave without regret was not among the least of her gifts. And one by one off they went, poor modest creatures without manners or taste in dress, unimportant friendships of humble merriment, simple, unelevated customs. She did exactly what the major had said with the men when they saw her pass in a carriage—which, parenthetically, was hers. The difference was that she no longer peeked to find out if they'd seen her. The honeymoon with grandeur was over. Now she was casting her eyes firmly in a different direction, avoiding with a definitive action the danger of any hesitation. In that way she was obliging old friends not to tip their hats to her.

CXXXIX

Rubião still tried to stand up for the major, but Sofia's look of annoyance cut him off in such a way that our friend preferred to ask her whether, if it didn't rain the next morning, they were still going riding to Tijuca.

"I just spoke to Cristiano. He told me that he's got some business, that we should put it off till next Sunday."

Rubião, after a moment:

"Let's the two of us go. We'll leave early, ride, have lunch there, and we'll be back by three or four o'clock . . ."

Sofia looked at him with such a desire to accept the invitation that Rubião didn't wait for a verbal response.

"It's all set then, we're going," he said.

"No."

"Why not?"

And he repeated the question because Sofia didn't want to explain her negative response to him, so obvious as well. Obliged to do so, she explained that her husband would be envious and would be capable of putting off his business meeting just to go along. She didn't want to upset his business affairs, and they could wait a week. Sofia's look accompanying that explanation was like a clarion accompanying the Lord's Prayer. Oh, she wanted to! She wanted to go up the road with Rubião the next morning, well mounted on her horse, not idly or poetically musing, but valiant, fire in her face, completely of this world, galloping, trotting, stopping. Up there she would dismount for a while. All alone, the city in the distance and the sky above. Leaning against the horse she would comb its mane with her fingers, listen to Rubião praise her daring and grace . . . She imagined she felt a kiss on the back of her neck . . .

C X L

Since it's a question of horses, it wouldn't be out of place to say that Sofia's imagination was now a lively and willful charger, capable of crossing hills and crashing through forests. A different comparison might be better if the occasion were other, but a charger is the one that fits best. It carries the idea of impetuosity, blood, speed, and at the same time the serenity with which it returns to the straight road and, finally, to the stable.

"It's all set. We're going tomorrow," Rubião repeated as he sought out Sofia's excited face.

But the charger had returned from the race fatigued, and it was left dreaming in the stable. Sofia was a different person now. The madness of the undertaking had passed, the envisioned ardor, the pleasure of going up the Tijuca road with him. When Rubião said he would ask her husband to let her go on the ride, she argued, spiritless.

"You're crazy! Leave it for next Sunday!"

And she fastened her eyes on the piece of linen she was sewing—a trimming, a trifle, it's called—while Rubião cast his eyes over a small stretch of wretched garden alongside the sitting room where he was. Sofia, seated at a corner of the window, was working her fingers. In two ordinary roses Rubião saw an imperial celebration, and he forgot about the room, the woman, and himself. It can't be said for certain how long they were silent like that, alien and remote from one another. It was a maid who woke them up, bringing coffee. When the coffee had been drunk, Rubião stroked his beard, looked at his watch, and took his leave. Sofia, who'd been waiting for him to go, was satisfied, but she covered her pleasure with surprise.

"So soon?"

"I've got to see a fellow before four o'clock," Rubião explained.

"We're all set, then. Tomorrow's ride canceled. I'll tell them not to prepare the horses. But it'll be next Sunday for sure, right?"

"Of course, of course. I can't say for sure, but if it can be worked out with Cristiano, I think so. You know that my husband's a man with a lot on his shoulders."

Sofia saw him to the door, shook hands indifferently, answered some silly remark with a smile, went back to the room where she'd been—to the same spot—at the same window. She didn't go back to her work right off. She crossed her legs, pulling down the skirt of her dress as she habitually did, and she cast a glance over the garden where the two roses had given our friend an imperial vision. Sofia only saw two mute flowers. She stared at them for some time, however. Then she immediately picked up her lacework, busied herself with it a little, stopped for a while, dropping her hands into her lap. And she went back to her work only to abandon it again. Suddenly she got up and tossed the thread and shuttle into the wicker basket where she kept her sewing things. The basket was one more remembrance from Rubião!

"What a bothersome man!"

From there she went over to lean against the window, which opened onto the wretched garden where the two ordinary roses were withering. Roses, when they're fresh, care little or nothing about the anger of others, but if they waste away, everything about them is cause for the vexation of the human soul. I should like to believe that this custom is born of the brevity of life. "For roses," someone wrote, "the gardener is eternal." And what better way to wound eternity than to make fun of its angers? I go, but you stay. But all I did was bloom and give aroma, I served ladies and maidens, I was a symbol of love, I decorated men's buttonholes, or I expired on my own bush, and all hands and all eyes dealt with me and looked upon me with admiration and affection. Not you, oh, eternity! You rant, you suffer, you weep, you flagellate yourself! Your eternity isn't worth one single minute of mine.

So when Sofia got to the window that looked out onto the garden, both roses laughed with unplucked petals. One of them said it was well done! Well done! Well done!

"You're right to get angry, beautiful creature," it added, "but it's got to be over you and not him. What's he worth? A sad man without charm can get to be a good friend and maybe a generous one, but repugnant, right? And you, courted by others, what devil brings you to lend an ear to that intruder in your life? It humiliates you, oh, you superb creature, because you're the very cause of your own trouble. You swore to forget about him and you haven't. But must you forget him? Isn't it enough for you to look at him and listen to him to scorn him? That man hasn't said a single thing, oh, singular creature, and you . . ."

"It's not entirely that way," the other rose interrupted with an ironic and weary voice. "He's been saying something and he's been saying it for a long time, not dropping it, not changing it. He's firm, he ignores pain, he believes in hope. His whole amorous life has been like the ride to Tijuca that you were talking about a while back. 'It's all set for next Sunday!' Come now, some pity at least. Show some pity, my good Sofia! If you've got to love someone outside your marriage, let it be him. He loves you and is discreet. Go on, repent for your action a while back. What harm has he done to you, and what fault is it of his that you're beautiful? And if there's any blame, the basket doesn't have any just because he bought it, even less the thread and the sewing things that you yourself had bought by a servant. You're bad, Sofia, you're unjust . . ."

CXLII

Sofia let herself go on listening, listening . . . She interrogated other plants, and they didn't tell her anything different. There are these miraculous lucky hits. Anyone who knows the soil and the subsoil of life knows quite well that a stretch of wall, a bench, a rug, an umbrella are rich with ideas or feelings when we are, too, and that the reflections of a partnership between men and things constitute one of the most interesting phenomena on earth. The expression "Talking to his buttons," which looks like a simple metaphor for "Talking to himself," is a phrase with a real and direct meaning. The buttons operate synchronically with us, forming a kind of senate, handy and cheap, that always votes in favor of our motions.

CXLIII

The ride to Tijuca took place without incident except for a fall from a horse on the way down. It wasn't Rubião who fell, or Palha, but the latter's wife as she went along thinking about something and whipped the animal in a rage. He reared and dropped her to the ground. Sofia fell gracefully. She was singularly slim, wearing a riding habit, her small, attractive body just right. If he could have seen her, Othello would have exclaimed, "Oh, my beautiful warrior lass!" Rubião limited himself to this as the ride began: "You're an angel!"

CXLIV

"I hurt my knee," she said as she entered the house, limping. "Let me see."

In the drawing room Sofia lifted her foot onto a stool and showed her husband the bruised knee. It had swollen a little, only a little, but touching it made her cry out. Palha, not wishing to hurt her, touched it only with the tip of his lips.

"Did I reveal anything when I fell?"

"No. Because with such a long dress . . . The tip of your foot was barely showing. There was nothing, believe me."

"Do you swear?"

"You're not at all very trusting, Sofia! I swear by everything holy, by the light that guides me, by Our Lord God. Are you satisfied?"

Sofia was covering her knee.

"Let me see it again. I don't think it's anything serious. Put a little something on it. Have someone go ask the druggist."

"It's all right, let me get undressed," she said, struggling to lower her dress.

But Palha lowered his eyes from the knee to the rest of her

leg where it met the top of her boot. It really was a good stretch of nature. The silk stocking enhanced the perfection of its shape. Palha, for the fun of it, kept asking his wife if she'd hurt herself here, and then here, and then here, pointing out the places with his hand as it descended. If just a little piece of this masterpiece were to appear, the sky and the trees would be astounded, he concluded as his wife lowered her dress and took her foot off the stool.

"That might be so, but it wasn't just the sky and the trees," she said. "Rubião's eyes were there, too."

"Come, now, Rubião! But that's right. Did he ever repeat that nonsense from Santa Teresa?"

"Never again, but, really, I wouldn't like it . . . Do you swear, truthfully, Cristiano?"

"What you want me to do is to keep going from one holy thing to the next until I reach the holiest of holies. I swore by God, that wasn't enough. I swear by you, are you satisfied?"

Silly little love plays. He finally left his wife's room and went into his own. That timid and unbelieving modesty of Sofia's had had a good effect on him. It showed that she was his, completely his. For that very reason of possession he felt it was the place of a great lord not to be bothered by some quick, casual glance at a hidden piece of his realm. And he was sorry that the casual glance had stopped at the tip of the boot. It was only the border. The first villages of the territory lying before the city injured by the fall would give the idea of a sublime and perfect civilization. And, soaping and rubbing his face, his neck, and his head in the broad silver basin, scrubbing himself, drying himself, perfuming himself, Palha imagined the surprise and envy of the only witness to the disaster had it been less incomplete.

It was around that time that Rubião gave all his friends a fright.
On the Tuesday following the Sunday of the ride (it was then
January 1870), he told a barber on the Rua do Ouvidor to send
someone to give him a shave at his house the next day at nine
o'clock in the morning. A French journeyman, name of Lucien,
arrived there and went into Rubião's study according to instructions given the servant.

"Grr!" growled Quincas Borba on Rubião's knees.

Lucien greeted the master of the house. The latter, however,
didn't see the bow, just as he hadn't heard Quincas Borba's warning. He was on a chaise longue, bereft of his spirit, which had
broken through the ceiling and had been lost in the air. How
many leagues would it go? Neither a condor nor an eagle would
be able to say. On its way to the moon—all it could see down
here were the perennial bits of happiness that had rained down
upon it, from the cradle, where fairies had swaddled it, to the
Praia de Botafogo, where they had carried it over a bed of roses
and jasmines. No reverses, no misfortune, no poverty—a placid
life, sewn together with pleasure and with an excess of lace. On
its way to the moon!

The barber cast his eyes about the study where the main item
was the desk and on it the busts of Napoleon and Louis Napoleon. Relative to the latter, hanging on the wall there was also
an engraving or lithograph showing the Battle of Solferino and
a portrait of the Empress Eugénie.

Rubião was wearing a pair of damask slippers edged in gold.
On his head, a cap with a black silk tassel. On his mouth, a pale
blue smile.

"Sir..."

"Grr!" Quincas Borba repeated, standing on his master's knees.

Rubião came to and saw the barber. He recognized him from having seen him recently in the shop. He got up from the chair, and Quincas Borba barked, as if defending him against the intruder.

"Quiet! Be still!" Rubião told him, and the dog, ears down, went over behind the wastebasket. During this time Lucien was unwrapping his implements.

"You're going to lose a beautiful beard," he told him in French. "I know people who did the same thing, but to please some lady. I've had the confidence of important men . . ."

"Precisely!" Rubião interrupted.

He hadn't understood a word. Even though he knew some French, he could barely understand the written language—as we know—and he didn't understand the spoken at all. But, a strange phenomenon, he didn't answer as a false pretense. He heard the words as a compliment or praise and, stranger still, answering him in Portuguese, he thought he was speaking French.

"Precisely!" he repeated. "I want to restore my face to its earlier form. Like that."

And as he pointed to the bust of Napoleon III, the barber responded in our language:

"Ah! The emperor. A nice bust, really. A fine piece of work. Did you buy it here or have it sent from Paris? They're magnificent. There's the first, the great one. He was a genius. If it hadn't been for betrayal, oh, the traitors. Do you see, sir? Traitors are worse than Orsini's bombs!"

"Orsini! Poor devil!"

"He paid dearly."

"He paid what he should have. But neither bombs nor Orsini can stand up to a great man," Rubião went on. "When the fate of a nation places the imperial crown on the head of a great man, there's no evil that can do anything . . . Orsini! A fool!"

In just a few minutes the barber began dropping Rubião's

beard to the floor, leaving only the mustache and the goatee of Napoleon III. It was hard work. He stated that it was difficult to make one thing match the other exactly. And as he cut the beard he praised it.—Such fine hair! It was a great and honest sacrifice he was making, really . . .

"Mister barber, you're being presumptuous," Rubião interrupted him. "I already told you what I want. Make my face the way it used to be. You've got a bust there to guide you."

"Yes, sir, I'll do just as you say, and you'll see how close the resemblance will turn out."

And snip, snip, he gave the last cuts to Rubião's beard and began to shave his cheeks and chin. The operation took a long time, and the barber was going along peacefully shaving, comparing, dividing his gaze between the bust and the man. Sometimes, for a better comparison, he would step back two paces, look at them alternatively, lean over, ask the man to turn to one side or the other, and go to take a look at the corresponding side of the bust.

"How's it coming?" Rubião asked.

Lucien made a gesture for him not to talk and went on with his work. He trimmed the goatee, left the mustache, and shaved freely, slowly, in a friendly way, relaxed, his fingers discovering some little, imperceptible hair on the chin or the cheeks. Sometimes Rubião tired of looking at the ceiling while the other man perfected his chin, asked to rest. As he rested, he stroked his face and felt the change through touch.

"The mustache isn't very long," he observed.

"I have to fix the edges. I've got little irons here to make them curve over the lips, and then we'll fix the tips. Oh, I'd rather do ten original pieces of work than just one copy!"

It took ten more minutes before the mustache and goatee were trimmed. Finally, all ready, Rubião jumped up, ran to the mirror in the bedroom next door. He was the other one; in a word, they were the same.

"Just right!" he exclaimed, returning to the study where the barber, having put his implements away, was petting Quincas Borba.

And, going to the desk, Rubião opened a drawer, took out a twenty *mil-réis* note, and gave it to him.

"I don't have any change," the other man said.

"There's no need for change," Rubião hastened to say with a sovereign gesture. "Take out what you have to pay the shop, and the rest is yours."

CXLVII

When he was alone, Rubião dropped into an armchair and watched all sorts of sumptuous things pass by. He was in Biarritz or Compiègne, which one isn't really known. Compiègne, it would seem. He governed a great state, he listened to ministers and ambassadors, he danced, he dined—and performed other acts mentioned in newspaper reports which he had read and which had stuck in his memory. Not even Quincas Borba's whines succeeded in rousing him. He was far away and high up. Compiègne was on the road to the moon. On his way to the moon!

CXLVIII

When he came down from the moon, he heard the whining of the dog, and his chin felt cold. He ran to the mirror and verified that the difference between his bearded face and his smooth face was great but that even smooth like that it didn't look too bad on him. His tablemates reached the same conclusion.

"It's perfectly fine! You should have done it a long time ago. Not that a full beard took away the nobility of your face, but the way it is now, it keeps what it used to have and has a modern look as well . . ."

"Modern," the host repeated.

Outside there was the same surprise. Everybody sincerely found that this changed look became him better than the previous one. Only one person, Dr. Camacho, even though he found that the mustache and goatee looked very good on his friend, argued that it wasn't a good idea to change one's face, a true mirror of the soul, whose stability and constancy should be reproduced.

"I'm not just talking about myself," he concluded, "But I'll never see your face in any other way. It's a moral necessity of my person. My life, sacrificed to principles—because I've never tried to compromise principles, only with men—my life, I say, is a faithful image of my face and vice versa."

Rubião listened seriously and nodded yes, that it must be that way out of necessity. Then he felt he was Emperor of the French, incognito on a stroll. Going down the street he went back to what he was. Dante, who saw so many extraordinary things, states that in Hell he witnessed the punishment of a Florentine who was embraced by a six-footed serpent in such a way that they blended so closely that in the end it was impossible to tell if they were one or two entities. Rubião was still two. There was the mixture in him of his own persona and the Emperor of the French. They took turns. They grew to forget about each other. When he was only Rubião, he was no different from the usual man. When he rose up to emperor, he was only emperor. They were in equal balance, one without the other, both integral.

C X L I X

"What kind of a change is that?" Sofia asked when he appeared at the end of the week.

"I came to find out about your knee. Is it better?"

"Yes, thank you."

It was two in the afternoon. Sofia had just finished dressing to go out when the maid came to tell her that Rubião was there—with his face so changed that he looked like somebody else. Curious, she came down to see him. She found him in the parlor standing, reading the calling cards.

"But what kind of a change is that?" she repeated.

Rubião, without any imperial feelings, replied that he thought he would look better in a mustache and goatee.

"Or do I look uglier?" he concluded.

"You look better, much better."

And Sofia said to herself that perhaps she was the cause of the change. She sat down on the sofa and began to put her fingers into her gloves.

"Are you going out?"

"Yes, but the carriage hasn't come yet."

She dropped one of her gloves. Rubião leaned over to pick it up, and she did the same. Both grabbed the glove, and as they insisted on picking it up, their faces met up above, her nose touching his, and their mouths remained intact, laughing, oh, how they laughed.

"Did I hurt you?"

"No! I'm the one who should ask you . . ."

And they laughed again. Sofia put on her glove, Rubião stared at one of her feet that was moving surreptitiously until the servant came to say that the carriage had arrived. They stood up and laughed once more.

C L

Stiff, his hat off, the footman opened the door of the coupé when Sofia appeared in the doorway. Rubião gave her his hand to help her in. She accepted the offer and got in.

"Well, until . . ."

She couldn't finish the sentence. Rubião had got in after her and sat down beside her. The footman closed the door, climbed up onto his seat, and the carriage left.

C L I

It all happened so fast that Sofia lost her voice and her movement, but after a few seconds:

"What's this? . . . Mr. Rubião, have them stop the carriage."

"Stop? But didn't you tell me that you were going out and were waiting for it?"

"I wasn't going out with you . . . Can't you see that? . . . Have them stop . . ."

At her wit's end, she tried to tell the coachman to stop, but the fear of a possible scandal made her halt halfway. The coupé turned down the Rua Bela da Princesa. Sofia once more asked Rubião to be aware of the impropriety of going like that in the sight of God and everybody. Rubião respected her scruples and suggested they lower the curtains.

"I think it's all right if people see us," Rubião explained, "but if we lower the curtains no one will see us. Shall I?"

Without waiting for an answer, he lowered the curtains on both sides, and the two of them were all alone, because if on the inside they could see one or another person pass, from the outside no one could see them. Alone, completely alone, as on that day when also at two o'clock in the afternoon at her house Rubião had thrown his despair into her face. There, at least, the young woman was free; here, inside the closed carriage, she was unable to calculate the consequences.

Rubião, however, made his legs comfortable and didn't say anything.

C L I I

Sofia huddled in the corner as much as she could. It could have been because of the bizarre situation, it could have been out of fear, but it was mainly out of repugnance. Never had that man had made her feel such aversion, such disgust, or something less harsh if you wish, but which all came down to incompatibility—how shall I put it so as not to injure any ears?—skin-deep incompatibility. Where had the dreams of a few days ago gone? At the simple invitation to a ride to Tijuca by themselves, she'd gone up the mountain with him, dismounted, heard words of adoration, and felt a kiss on the back of her neck. Where had those imagined things gone? Where had the large, staring eyes, the loving, long hands, the restless feet, the bashful words, and the ears filled with pity gone? It was all forgotten, it had all disappeared now that they both found themselves alone, isolated by the carriage and by scandal.

And the horses went along kicking up their hooves, slowly pulling the carriage along over the stones of the Rua Bela da Princesa. What would she do when they got to Catete? Would she ride downtown with him? She thought of going to the house of some friend, leaving him inside, telling the coachman to go on. She would tell her husband everything. In the middle of that agony, some banal memories crossed her mind, or ones strange to that situation, like a jewel theft she'd read about in the morning papers, the wind storm the day before, a hat. Finally, she centered on one concern. What was she going to say to Rubião? She saw that he'd kept on looking straight ahead in silence, with the knob of his cane under his chin. The position didn't look too bad on him, tranquil, serious, almost indifferent, but, then, why had he got into the carriage? Sofia tried to break the silence. Twice she moved her hands nervously. She was almost irritated by the quietness of the man, whose act could only be explained by his old and fervent passion. Later she imagined that he himself was repentant, and she told him so in a pleasant way.

"I don't see that I have to be sorry for anything," he answered, turning. "When you said it wasn't right to travel like this in full view of everyone, I lowered the curtains. I didn't agree, but I obeyed."

"We're coming to Catete," she put in. "Do you want me to tell him to take you home? We can't ride downtown together."

"We can go along drifting."

"What do you mean?"

"Drifting, the horses will go along, and we'll go on chatting, with no one hearing us or guessing what we're talking about."

"Good heavens! Don't talk like that. Leave me, get out of the carriage, or I'll get out right here and you can take it over. What are you trying to say? A few minutes are enough . . . Look, we've already turned toward downtown. Tell him to go to Botafogo, and I'll drop you at the door of your house . . ."

"But I only left my house a little while back. I'm going downtown. What's wrong with taking me there? If it's because we shouldn't be seen together, I'll get out anywhere—on the Praia de Santa Luzia, for example—on the side by the shore . . ."

"The best thing would be for you to get out right here."

"But why can't we go downtown?"

"No, it can't be. I ask you by everything you hold most sacred. Don't make a scandal. Come, tell me what it takes to get something so simple from you. Do you want me to go down on my knees right here?"

In spite of the narrowness of the space, she started bending her knees, but Rubião quickly made her sit again.

"You don't have to kneel," he said softly.

"Thank you. Then I ask you in God's name, for your mother in heaven . . ."

"She must be in heaven," Rubião confirmed. "She was a holy woman! All mothers are good, but everyone who knew that one could only say that she was a saint. And skilled like few others. What a housekeeper! When it came to guests, whether five or fifty, it was all the same to her, she took care of everything at the right time and in the right place and was famous for it. The slaves gave her the name of *Missy Mother* because she really was a mother to them all. She has to be in heaven!"

"Fine, fine," Sofia put in, "so do this for me out of love for your mother. Will you?"

"Do what?"

"Get out right here."

"And go downtown on foot? I can't. It's a notion of yours. Nobody's going to see us. And, besides, these horses of yours are magnificent. You've seen how they pick up their hooves, slowly, clip . . . clop . . . clip . . . clop . . ."

Tired of asking, Sofia fell silent, folded her arms, and withdrew even more, if possible, into the corner of the carriage.

"Now I remember," she thought, "I told the driver to stop at the door of Cristiano's warehouse. I'll tell him how this man got into the coupé, how I begged him, and the answers he gave me. That's better than having him get out mysteriously on just any street."

In the meantime Rubião was quiet. Every so often he would twirl the diamond ring on his finger—a splendid solitaire. He wasn't looking at her, wasn't saying anything or asking her for anything. They went along like a bored married couple. Sofia had begun not to understand what motive could have made him get into the carriage. It couldn't have been a need for transportation. Nor vanity; he'd drawn the curtains at her first complaint of being seen in public. No word of love, as remote an allusion as it might have been out of fear, full of veneration and beseeching. He was an inexplicable man, a monster.

C L I I I

"Sofia . . .," Rubião said suddenly and continued without a pause. "Sofia, the days pass, but no man can forget the woman who truly loves him and deserve the name of man. Our love will never be forgotten—by me, that's for certain, and I'm sure not by you either. You gave me everything, Sofia. Your very life was in danger. It's true that I would have avenged you, my lovely. If vengeance can bring happiness to the dead, you would have had the greatest possible pleasure. Luckily, my fate protected us, and we could love without blood or bounds . . ."

The young woman looked at him with astonishment.

"Don't be frightened," he went on. "We're not going to separate. No, I'm not talking about separation. Don't tell me that you would die. I know that you would shed many tears. Not I—I didn't come into the world to weep—but my grief would be no less because of it. On the contrary, sorrows kept in the heart are more painful than others. Tears are good because a person can open up. My dear friend, I'm talking to you like this because we have to be careful. Our insatiable passion might make us forget that need. We've run a lot of risks, Sofia. Since we were born for each other, we think we're married, and we run risks. Listen, my dear, listen, soul of my soul . . . Life is beautiful! Life is great! Life is sublime! With you, however, what can I call it? Do you remember our first meeting?"

As Rubião said those last words, he tried to take her hand. Sofia drew back in time. She was disoriented, she didn't understand, she was afraid. His voice grew louder, the coachman might hear something . . . And here a suspicion shook her: maybe Rubião's intent was precisely to let himself be heard, to oblige her through fright—or so that people would slander her then. She had an urge to throw herself against him, shout for help, and save herself by the clamor.

He, very softly, after a short pause:

"I remember as if it were yesterday. You came in a carriage. It wasn't this one, it was a public cab, a calèche. You stepped out, fearful, with a veil over your face. You were trembling like a green reed. But my arms protected you . . . The sun must have come to a halt that day the way it had for Joshua . . . And still and all, my lovely flower, those hours were devilishly long, I don't know why. They really must have been short. Perhaps it was because our passion had no ending, never ended, would never end . . . On our return, we didn't see the sun again. It was sinking behind the mountains when my Sofia, still fearful, went out onto the street and took another calèche. Another or the same one? I think it was the same one. You can't imagine the state I was left in. I looked foolish, I kissed everything you'd touched. I went so far as to kiss the doorsill. I think I already told you that. The doorsill. And I was on the verge of crawling down the stairs and kissing every step . . . I didn't. I held back. I closed the door so that the smell of you wouldn't be lost. Violets, if I remember well . . ."

No, it was impossible that Rubião's intent was to make the coachman believe some lying adventure. His voice was so muffled that Sofia could barely hear it. But if it was difficult for her to understand the words, she never got to understand their meaning. What was the purpose of that story that had never happened? Anyone who heard it would have accepted everything as the truth, so sincere was the tone, the sweetness of the terms, and the likelihood of the details. And he went on sighing over the beautiful reminiscences . . .

"But what kind of a joke is this?" Sofia finally cut in.

Our friend didn't answer her. He had the image before his eyes, he didn't hear the question, and he went right on. He mentioned a concert by Gottschalk. The divine pianist was making the piano sing. They were listening, but the demon of the music lifted their eyes to each other, and they both forgot the rest. When the music stopped the applause broke out and they woke up. Oh, unfortunate ones! They woke up with Palha's eyes on them, the look of a fierce jaguar. That night he thought he would kill her.

"Mr. Rubião . . ."

"Not Napoleon, call me Louis. I am your Louis, isn't that so, you charming creature? Yours, yours . . . Call me yours. Your Louis. Oh, if you only knew the pleasure you give me when I hear those two words: 'My Louis!' You're my Sofia—the sweet, loving Sofia of my soul. Let's not lose these moments. Let's call each other tender names. But softly, very softly, so that the scoundrel on the driver's seat won't hear us. Why must there be coachmen in this world? If the carriage could only go along by itself, people could say whatever they wanted, and it would go on to the ends of the earth."

They were now passing the Passeio Público. Sofia wasn't aware of it. She was staring at Rubião. It couldn't be the scheme of an evil man, or did she think he was making fun of her? . . . Delirium, yes, that's what it was. His words had the sincerity of a person who really sees or has seen the things he's telling.

"I've got to get him out of here," the young woman thought. And, gathering up courage, "Where can we be now?" she asked him. "It's time we went our separate ways. Look out that side. Where are we? It looks like the convent. We're on the Largo da Ajuda. Tell the coachman to stop. Or, if you want, you can get out on the Largo da Carioca. My husband . . ."

"I'm going to make him an ambassador," Rubião said. "Or a senator, if he wants. Senator is better. The two of you will stay here. If it were ambassador, I wouldn't allow you to go with him, and the malicious tongues . . . You know the opposition I have, the gossip . . . Oh, rotten people! The Ajuda convent, you said? What do you have to do with that? Do you want to be a nun?"

"No. I said we've already passed the Ajuda convent. I'm going to drop you on the Largo da Carioca. Or shall we go on to my husband's warehouse?"

Sofia went back to the second option. The coachman wouldn't be suspicious, she could prove her innocence to Palha better, telling him everything, from the unexpected entry into the carriage down to the delirium. And what delirium might that be? Sofia thought that she herself could have been the reason, and that conjecture made her smile with pity.

"What for?" Rubião asked. "I'm getting off right here. It's safer. Why make him suspect us and mistreat you? I could punish him, but I would always be left with the remorse of the harm he might do you. No, my lovely flower, my friend. If the wind dared touch your person, believe me, I would order it off as a wicked wind. You're still not aware of my power, Sofia. Go on, confess."

Since Sofia didn't confess anything, Rubião called her beautiful and offered her the diamond solitaire he wore on his finger. She, however, while she loved jewels and had a special liking for single diamonds, fearfully turned down the offer.

"I understand your scruples," he said, "but you're not losing anything by them because you're going to receive an even more beautiful stone and from the hand of your husband. I'm going to make you a duchess. Did you hear? The title is given to him, but you're the cause. Duke . . . Duke of what? I'm going to look for a pretty title. Or I'll let you choose it yourself, because it's for you, it's not for him, it's for you, my sweet. You don't have to pick it now, go home and think about it. Don't worry over it. Send me word which one you think is the prettiest, and I'll have the decree drawn up immediately. You can also do something else. Pick it and tell me at our first meeting, in the usual place. I want to be the first to call you duchess. My darling duchess ... The decree will come later. Duchess of my soul!"

"Yes, yes," she said, bewildered, "but let's tell the coachman to take us to Cristiano's place."

"No, I'm getting off here ... Stop! Stop!"

Rubião raised the curtains, and the footman got down to open the door. Sofia, to remove any suspicions on his part, once more asked Rubião to go with her to her husband's place. She told him he had to talk to him, urgently. Rubião looked a little surprised at her, at the footman, and at the street and answered no, he would come by later.

C L I V

No sooner had they separated than a contrast came over them both.

Rubião, on the street, turned his head all about. Reality took hold of him, and the delirium vanished. He walked, lingered in front of a shop, crossed the street, stopped an acquaintance, asked him for news and opinions. An unconscious effort to shake himself free of the borrowed personality.

Sofia, on the other hand, with the surprise and the shock over, sank into a reverie. All the references and stories of Rubião's seemed to be giving her longings—longings for what?—"longings for heaven," which is what Father Bernardes said of the feelings of a good Christian. Different names flashed in the blue of that possibility. So many interesting details! Sofia reconstructed the old calèche where she'd entered rapidly, from which she'd got out trembling to slip into the hallway, go up the steps, and find a man—who told her the most delightfully sweet things in the world, and he repeated them now, next to her in the carriage, but it wasn't, it couldn't be Rubião. Who could it have been? Different names flashed in the blue of that possibility.

C L V

The news of Rubião's mania spread. Some, not encountering him at the moment of his delirium, did experiments to see if the rumors were true, turning the conversation to French affairs and the emperor. Rubião slid into the pit and convinced them.

C L V I

A few months passed, the Franco-Prussian War came, and Rubião's attacks become more acute and more frequent. When the mail from Europe arrived early, Rubião would leave Botafogo before breakfast and run to wait for the newspapers. He would buy the *Correspondência de Portugal* and read it right there under the street light. Whatever the news was, it felt like victory to him. He kept track of the dead and wounded and always came out with a large figure in his favor. The fall of Napoleon III was the capture of King Wilhelm for him, the September 4th revolution a banquet of Bonapartists.

At home, his old dinner friends didn't get involved in dissuading him, nor did they confirm anything, to their collective shame. They would smile and change the subject. All, however, had their military ranks, Marshal Torres, Marshal Pio, Marshal Ribeiro, and they would answer to the title. Rubião saw them in uniform. He would order a reconnaissance, an attack, and it wasn't necessary for them to go out to obey. Their host's mind would take care of everything. When Rubião left the field of battle to return to the table, it was something else. Without silverware now, almost without china or crystal, even like that it appeared regally splendid to Rubião's eyes. Poor scrawny hens were promoted to pheasants, humble hash and pitiful roasts bore the taste of the finest delicacies on earth. His tablemates would make some comment among themselves—or to the cook—but Lucullus always dined with Lucullus. All the rest of the house, worn by time and neglect, faded rugs, shabby, broken furniture, soiled curtains, had nothing of its actual look but a glowing and magnificent one, and language was different too, rotund and copious, the same as thoughts, some of them extraordinary, like those of his late friend Quincas Borba—theories that he hadn't understood when he'd heard them in Barbacena in times gone by and which he repeated now with lucidity and spirit—sometimes using the same phrases as the philosopher. What explanation was there for that repetition of the obscure, that knowledge of the inextricable, when the thoughts and the words seemed to have gone with the wind of other days? And why did all those reminiscences disappear with the return of his reason?

CLVII

Sofia's compassion—with Rubião's illness explained by the love he had for her—was a mixed feeling, neither pure sympathy nor hard egotism, but partaking of both. As long as she could avoid any situation identical to the one in the coupé, everything went well. At times, when Rubião was lucid, she would listen to him and talk to him with interest—simply because his illness, which brought on audacity during an attack, redoubled his timidity under normal circumstances. She didn't smile, like Palha, when Rubião would ascend the throne or take command of an army. Believing herself the author of the illness, she forgave him for it. The idea of having been loved to the point of madness sanctified the man for her.

"Why doesn't he get some treatment?" Dona Fernanda asked one night. She'd met him the year before. "He might be cured."

"It doesn't seem to be anything serious," Palha put in. "He has those attacks, but they're mild like that, the way you saw, delusions of grandeur that pass quickly. And you can see that, except for them, he converses perfectly. However, it's possible . . . What does Your Excellency think?"

Teófilo, Dona Fernanda's husband, answered yes, it was possible.

"What did he do, or what does he do now?" the deputy went on.

"Nothing, neither now nor before. He was rich—but a spend-thrift. We met him when he was coming from Minas, and we were, in a manner of speaking, his guides to Rio de Janeiro, where he hadn't been for many years. A good man. Always living in luxury, remember? But no wealth lasts forever when you start to touch the principal. That's what he did. I don't think he's got too much left today . . ."

"You could save that little for him by having yourself named guardian while he gets treatment. I'm not a doctor, but it's possible that this friend of yours could recover."

"I don't say that he couldn't. It's really a shame . . . He gets along with everybody and is always helpful. Did you know that he almost got to be a relative of ours? Yes. He wanted to marry Maria Benedita."

"Speaking of Maria Benedita," Dona Fernanda interrupted, "I almost forgot. I've got a letter from her to show you. It came yesterday. You probably know already that they'll be returning soon, don't you? Here it is."

She handed the letter to Sofia, who opened it without enthu-siasm and read it with boredom. It was more than an ordinary trans-Atlantic letter, it was a moral repository, an intimate and complete confession from a happy and thankful person. She spoke of the most recent episodes of the trip in a mixed-up fashion because the travelers themselves dominated everything, and the most beautiful works of man or nature weren't worth as much as the eyes that beheld them. Sometimes an incident in a hostelry or on the street would gobble up more paper and carry more interest than others in order to put her husband's fine qualities in relief. Maria Benedita was as much in love or even more so than on the first day. At the end, timidly, in a postscript, asking that she not tell anyone, she confessed that she was going to be a mother.

Sofia folded the piece of paper, no longer with boredom but with resentment, and for two reasons that contradicted each other. But contradiction is part of this world. When that letter was compared to the ones she had received from Maria Benedita, it could have been said that she was nothing but an acquaintance with no ties of blood or affection. And yet she wouldn't have cared to be the confidante of that joy whispered from across the ocean, full of minutiae, adjectives, exclamations, the name of Carlos Maria, the eyes of Carlos Maria, the remarks of Carlos Maria, finally the child of Carlos Maria. It looked like spite, and it almost made her believe in the complicity of Dona Fernanda.

Skillful, knowing enough to control herself in time, Sofia hid her spite and returned her cousin's letter with a smile. She wanted to say that according to the contents Maria Benedita's happiness must have been just the same as when she carried it off from here, but her voice never left her throat. Dona Fernanda was the one who took the task of a conclusion upon herself:

"It's obvious that she's happy!"

"It would seem so."

C L I X

If the following morning hadn't been rainy, Sofia's mood would have been different. The sun isn't always the craftsman of good ideas, but at least it comes out and, in exchange for the spectacle, it alters feelings. When Sofia awoke, the rain was already coming down heavily and without letup, and the sky and the sea were all one, the clouds so low, the haze so thick.

Tedium inside and out. There was nothing to broaden one's view or give the soul some rest. Sofia put her soul into a cedar casket, closed the cedar one up in the lead casket of the day, and left it there, sincerely deceased. She didn't know that the deceased think, that a swarm of new notions comes to take the place of the old, and that they emerge criticizing the world the way spectators come out of the theater criticizing the play and the actors. Her deceased soul felt that a few notions and feelings kept life going. They came out of a mixture but they had a common starting point—the letter of the day before and the memories it brought of Carlos Maria.

She really thought she'd left that hateful figure far behind, and there he was reappearing, smiling, staring at her, whispering in her ear the same words of a selfish and conceited loafer who had invited her once to do the waltz of adultery and had left her all alone in the middle of the ballroom. Around that figure came others, Maria Benedita, for example, a joke of a person that she'd gone to the country to bring out and give the luster of the city to and who'd forgotten all those benefits only to remember her ambitions. And Dona Fernanda, too, the sponsor of their love, who'd purposely brought Maria Benedita's letter the day before with its confidential postscript. She wasn't aware that her friend's pleasure was enough to explain her forgetting the private part of the letter. Even less did she consider whether Dona Fernanda's moral nature supported that supposition. Other thoughts and images came like that, and the first ones returned and they all went off, coming together and breaking apart. Among them was one remembrance of the night before. Dona Fernanda's husband had wrapped Sofia in a great look of admiration. She really was in one of her best days. Her dress admirably enhanced the grace of her bustline, her narrow waist, and the delicate curve of her hips. It was foulard, straw-colored.

"The color of straw, *palha*," Sofia stressed, laughing, when Dona Fernanda praised it soon after coming in. "Straw, *palha*, to make me think of this gentleman."

It's not easy to hide the pleasure of praise. Her husband smiled, puffing up with vanity, trying to read the effect of that tiny proof of love in the eyes of the others. Teófilo also praised the dress, but it was difficult to look at it without also looking at the body of the lady, and that gave rise to the long looks he cast on her, without lust, of course, and almost without insistence. So that memory of the day before, an uninvited gesture, an undesired admiration, came to counteract what Sofia was now thinking about the other woman's wickedness.

Carlos Maria, Teófilo . . . Other names flashed in the sky of that possibility, as was made clear in Chapter CLIV. And they all came now because the rain, still falling, and the sky and the sea were all joined together in one closed atmosphere. All those names came along with their own respective people, and people without names even came—strangers and unknown people— who'd passed by once, sung the hymn of admiration, and received her donation of good will. Why hadn't she retained one of so many to hear him sing and to enrich him? It wasn't that the donations enriched anyone, but there are different coins of greater value. Why hadn't she retained one of so many elegant ones? That question without words ran through her like that, in her veins, her nerves, her brain, with no reply but agitation and curiosity.

C L X

At that point the rain let up for a bit, and a ray of sunshine managed to break through the mist—one of those damp rays that seem to be coming from weeping eyes. Sofia thought she could still go out. She was anxious to see things, to have a ride, to shake off that torpor, and she hoped the sun would sweep away the rain and take charge of earth and sky. But the great star perceived that her intention was to turn it into the lantern of Diogenes and it told the damp ray: "Come back, come back to my bosom, chaste and virtuous ray. You're not going to lead her where her desire wants to take her. Let her love if she feels like it. Let her answer love notes—if she receives them and doesn't burn them—don't you be a torch for her, light of my bosom, child of my entrails, ray, brother of my rays . . ."

And the ray obeyed, retreating into the central focus, a bit startled at the fear of the sun, who has seen so many ordinary and extraordinary things. Then the veil of clouds grew thick and dark again, and the rain began to fall in buckets once more.

C L X I

Sofia resigned herself to reclusion. Her soul was now as confused and diffused as the spectacle outside. All images and names were being lost in a desire for love. It's proper to say that she, when she came out of those vague and obscure states of consciousness, would try to flee them and lead her spirit into a different matter. But what happened to her was the same as what happens to those who are sleepy and struggle to stay awake: her eyes would close every time she awoke, and she would awaken again only to have them close once more. Finally, she stopped looking at the rain and the mist. She was tired and she went to open the pages of the latest number of the *Revue des Deux Mondes*. One day, during the best times of the Alagoas committee, one of the elegant ladies of that time, married to a senator, had asked her:

"Have you been reading Feuillet's novel in the *Revue des Deux Mondes*?"

"I have," Sofia answered. "It's very interesting."

She wasn't reading nor did she know the *Revue*, but the next day she asked her husband to subscribe to it. She read the novel, she read the ones that followed, and she talked about all the ones she'd read or was reading. After she'd opened the pages of that number and read a novella, Sofia retired to her room and dropped onto the bed. She'd spent a bad night, and it didn't take her long to fall asleep—a deep, long sleep without dreams—

except toward the end, when she had a nightmare. She was facing the same wall of mist as during that day, but at sea, in the prow of a launch, lying face down, writing a name in the water—Carlos Maria. And the letters were engraved on it and making themselves even clearer, they filled up with foam. Up to that point, there was nothing to bewilder her unless it was the mystery. But it's common knowledge that the mysteries in dreams resemble natural events. That's when the wall of mist splits apart, and no one else but the owner of the name himself appears to Sofia's eyes, walks toward her, takes her in his arms, and speaks many tender words to her, similar to the ones she'd heard from Rubião's mouth a few months before. And they didn't annoy her like the latter's. On the contrary, she listened to them with pleasure, half falling back, as if fainting. It was no longer a launch but a carriage where she was riding with her cousin-in-law, holding hands, saying loving things with words of gold and sandalwood. Here, too, there was nothing to terrify her. The terror came when the carriage stopped, several masked figures surrounded it, killed the coachman, pulled open the doors, stabbed Carlos Maria, and left his corpse on the ground. Then one of them who seemed to be the leader took off his mask and told Sofia not to be frightened, that he loved her a thousand times more than the other man. Immediately after that he grabbed her by the wrists and gave her a kiss, but a kiss damp with blood, smelling of blood. Sofia let out a scream of horror and woke up. There was her husband, standing by the bed.

"What's the matter?" he asked.

"Oh!" Sofia took a deep breath. "I screamed, didn't I?"

Palha didn't say anything in reply. He was looking off, thinking about business. Then an apprehension took hold of the woman that she'd really spoken, murmuring some word, some name—the same one she'd written on the water. And immediately stretching her arms into the air, she dropped them onto her husband's shoulders, touched the tips of her fingers around his neck, and murmured, half jolly, half sad:

"I dreamt they were killing you."

Palha was moved. Having made her suffer for him, even in dreams, filled him with pity, but with a pleasant pity, a personal, intimate, deep feeling—which would make him wish for other nightmares so they could murder him before her eyes, and so she would scream in anguish, shaking, full of grief and terror.

C L X I I

The next day the sun came out bright and warm, the sky was limpid, the air was cool. Sofia got into the carriage and went visiting and for a ride in order to make up for her reclusion. The day itself was already good for her. She hummed as she dressed. The manners of the ladies who received her in their homes— and those whom she met on the Rua do Ouvidor, the continuous activity, the news of society, the fine appearance of so many elegant and friendly people were enough to chase the cares of the day before out of her soul.

C L X I I I

In that way, then, what had seemed like a pressing urge was reduced to pure fancy, and with the interval of a few hours all bad thoughts withdrew to their chambers. If you were to ask me about any remorse on Sofia's part, I wouldn't know what to tell you. There's a balance between resentment and reproval. It isn't only in actions where consciousness passes gradually from novelty to habit and from fear to indifference. The simple sins of thought are subject to that same alteration, and the custom of thinking about things shapes them to such a degree that in the end the spirit neither finds them strange nor rejects them. And in those cases there is always a moral refuge in external immunity, which is, in other more explicit terms, the unblemished body.

C L X I V

Only one incident afflicted Sofia on that pure, bright day—it was an encounter with Rubião. She'd gone into a bookstore on the Rua do Ouvidor to buy a novel. While she was waiting for her change, she saw her friend come in. She quickly turned her face away and ran her eyes over the books on a shelf—some books on anatomy and statistics—got her money, put it away, and with her head down, swift as an arrow, went out onto the street and headed up it. Her blood calmed down only when she left the Rua dos Ourives behind.

Days later, going into Dona Fernanda's house, she ran into him in the entranceway. She thought he was going up, and she was ready to go up also, although a touch fearful. But Rubião was coming down. They shook hands in a friendly way and said goodbye, until later.

"Does he come here often?" Sofia asked Dona Fernanda, after telling her about meeting him at the entrance.

"This is the fourth time, the fourth or fifth. But he was in a delirium only on the second time. The other times he was the way you saw him now, calm and even talkative. There's always something about him that shows he's not completely well. Didn't you notice that his eyes were a little vague? That's it. Otherwise, he chats quite normally. Believe me, Dona Sofia, that man can be cured. Why don't you get your husband to work on it?"

"Cristiano is planning to have him examined and treated. But let me hurry him up a bit."

"Why, yes. He seems to be a good friend of yours and Mr. Palha's."

"Could he have said anything inopportune regarding me to

her in his delirium?" Sofia thought. "Would it be proper to reveal the truth to her?"

She concluded that it wouldn't. Rubião's illness itself would explain anything inopportune. She promised that she'd get her husband to hurry things along, and that same afternoon she laid the matter before Palha. It's a great bother, he replied. And he asked what business it was of Dona Fernanda's to bring it up. Let her take care of it herself! It was a muddle, having to look after the other man, accompany him, and, probably, gather together and manage any remains of the money that still might be left, making himself guardian as Dr. Teófilo had said. A devilish annoyance.

"I've already got enough responsibilities on my shoulders, Sofia. And then what's it to be? Will we have to bring him to our house? I don't think so. Where can he be placed? In some nursing home . . . Yes, but what if they can't take him? I'm not going to send him to Praia Vermelha . . . And what about responsibilities? Did you promise that you'd talk to me?"

"I promised and I said you'd do it," Sofia answered, smiling. "Maybe it won't be as difficult as it looks."

Sofia still insisted. Dona Fernanda's compassion had impressed her a great deal. She found it to be a distinguished and noble thing in her, and she felt that if the other woman, with no close or long-standing relationship to Rubião, showed herself interested to such a degree, it would be fashionable not to be any less generous.

C L X V

Everything was done calmly. Palha rented a small house on the Rua do Príncipe, near the sea, where he installed our Rubião, a few pieces of furniture, and his dog friend. Rubião adjusted to the move without any displeasure and, whenever his delirium returned, with enthusiasm. He was on his estate in Saint-Cloud.

That wasn't how it was with his household friends, who received the news of the move as a decree of exile. Everything in the old dwelling had been part of them, the garden, the grill-work, the flower beds, the stone steps, the cove. They knew everything by heart. It was a matter of entering, hanging up their hats, and going to wait in the parlor. They'd lost all notion of its being someone else's home and of the favor they were receiving. After that, the neighborhood. Every one of Rubião's friends was accustomed to seeing the people in the area, the morning faces and the afternoon ones; some of them went so far as to greet them as they would their own neighbors. Patience! They would now go to Babylon like the exiles from Zion. Wherever the Euphrates might be, they would find the willows on which to hang their nostalgic harps—or, more exactly, hooks on which to put their hats. The difference between them and the prophets was that at the end of a week they would pick up their instruments again and pluck them with the same charm and strength. They would sing the old hymns, as fresh as on the first day, and Babel would end up being Zion itself, lost and recovered.

"Our friend needs rest for a while," Palha told them in Botafogo on the eve of the move. "You must have noticed that he hasn't been well. He has his moments of forgetfulness, upset, confusion. He's going to receive treatment, and, in the meantime he needs rest. I've arranged a small house for him, but it could be that he'll have to go into a rest home even so."

They listened in astonishment. One of them, Pio, recovering more quickly than the rest, replied that it should have been done a long time ago. But in order to do it one would have had to exert a decisive influence on Rubião's spirit.

"I told him many times in a nice way that he had to see a doctor because it looked as if he had something wrong with his stomach . . . It was a way of avoiding the real meaning, you understand, but he always said no, that his digestion was fine . . . 'But you're eating less,' I told him, 'there are days when you eat practically nothing. You're thinner, a bit sallow . . .' You understand that I couldn't tell him the truth. I even got to consult a doctor, a friend of mine, but our good Rubião refused to see him."

The other four confirmed all of that invention with their heads. It was the most they could ask for and the only thing that would soften the stunning blow. They ended up asking for the address of the new house so they could check up on him. Poor friend! When they left there and took leave of one another, a phenomenon they'd hadn't foreseen took place. They themselves had trouble separating. Not that they were joined together by friendship or esteem, their very self-interest made them dislike each other. But the habit of seeing themselves together every day at lunch and dinner—around the same table as if it had joined them to each other—made them necessarily tolerant, and time had made them mutually necessary. In short, it was the eyes of each that would suffer with the absence of the customary faces, the gestures, the sideburns, the mustaches, the bald spots, the individual faults, the way of eating, speaking, and being of their companions. It was more than a separation, it was a disjointing.

C L X V I

Rubião noticed that they hadn't accompanied him to the new house, and he had them called. None came, and their absence filled our friend with sadness—during the first weeks. It was his family who'd abandoned him. Rubião tried to recall if he'd done them some hurt, either by word or deed, but he could find none.

"I talked to the man. I thought he had some crazy ideas. Even though I'm not a psychiatrist I think he can get well ... But do you want to know an interesting discovery?"

"Do you think he'll get well?" Dona Fernanda asked, paying no attention to Dr. Falcão's question.

Dr. Falcão was a deputy and a physician, a friend of the family, a wise, skeptical, and cold man. Dona Fernanda had asked him to do her the favor of examining Rubião shortly after the latter had been moved to the house on the Rua do Príncipe.

"Yes, I think he'll get well as long as he receives regular treatment. It could be that the illness has no antecedents in his family. Have him go see a specialist. But don't you want to know what my interesting discovery was?"

"What was it?"

"His illness might be related to a person of your acquaintance," he answered, smiling.

"Who?"

"Dona Sofia."

"How's that?"

"He spoke about her with great enthusiasm, told me that she was the most splendid woman in the world and that he was going to make her a duchess, since he couldn't make her empress. But they shouldn't fool with him, that he was capable of doing what his uncle did, get divorced and marry her. I gathered that he had a passion for the young lady. And then the intimacy, Sofia here, Sofia there ... You have to excuse me, but I think the two of them had been lovers ..."

"Oh, no!"

"Dona Fernanda, I think they were lovers. What's so strange? I scarcely know her. You don't seem to have known her for a long time or to have been intimate friends with her. It could be that they were lovers and that some violent passion ... Let's suppose that she threw him out of the house ... It's true that he has delusions of grandeur, but everything might be connected ..."

Dona Fernanda wasn't looking at him, annoyed at hearing that supposition on his part. She avoided discussing it because of the delicacy of the matter. She found the suspicion baseless, absurd, unlikely. She wouldn't have believed that spurious love even if she'd heard it from Rubião himself. A crackbrain, in short. Even if he weren't, it was still probable that she wouldn't believe him. She couldn't believe that Sofia could have been in love with that man, not because of him, but because of her, so correct and pure. It was impossible. She wanted to defend her. But in spite of her close relationship with Dr. Falcão, she changed the subject a second time and repeated the question of a while back.

"Do you think he'll get well, then?"

"He might, but my examination's not enough. You know that in these matters a specialist is best."

A while later, as he left, Falcão smiled at Dona Fernanda's resistance in accepting the hypothesis. "There surely must have been something," he said to himself. "A good appearance and if he's not a dandy, he's good-looking, and he's got fire in his eyes. Surely . . ." And he repeated some of Rubião's comments, recalled his expression and the tender tone of his voice, and the suspicion kept growing. "Surely . . ." Now it was impossible for them not to have been lovers. Dona Fernanda's opposition seemed ingenuous to him—unless it was really a way to change the subject and not touch on the matter. It must have been that . . .

At that point, without meaning to, the deputy stood still. A new suspicion attacked his mind. After a few quick moments, he shook his head voluntarily as if to deny himself, as if to find himself absurd, and he continued walking. But the suspicion was insistent, and one that really occupies a man's inner part doesn't pay any attention to his head or gestures. "Who knows, maybe Dona Fernanda herself was sighing over him. Couldn't that dedication be a prolongation of love and the rest?" And that was how questions were taking shape that ended up in Dr. Falcão's most intimate part with an affirmative answer. He still resisted. He was a friend of the family, he respected Dona Fernanda, he knew her to be virtuous, but—he went on thinking—it could well be that a hidden, discreet feeling—who knows, maybe even brought on by the other woman's passion . . . There are those temptations. The contagion of leprosy can corrupt the purest blood. A sad little germ can destroy the most robust organism.

Little by little, his faint wish for resistance was giving way to the notion of the possibility, the probability, and the certainty. In truth, he'd heard of certain works of charity by Dona Fernanda, but this case was new. That special dedication to a man who wasn't a frequenter of the house or an old friend or a relative, a follower, a colleague of her husband, anything that would make him a participant in their domestic life by relationship, by blood, or by custom couldn't be explained except for some secret reason. Love, most certainly. The curiosity of a virtuous woman, which can descend into sin and remorse. She probably withdrew in time. She was left with her morbid sympathy . . . And, therefore, who knows?

CLXVIII

"And, therefore, who knows?" Dr. Falcão repeated the next morning. Night hadn't snuffed out the man's mistrust. And, therefore, who knows? Yes, it might not be just morbid sympathy. Without knowing Shakespeare, he improved on Hamlet: "There are more things in heaven and earth, Horatio, than are dreamt of in your *philanthropy*." The finger of love was at work there. And he wasn't mocking or tarnishing anything. I've already said that he was a skeptic, but since he was also discreet, he didn't pass his conclusion on to anyone.

The return of Carlos Maria and his wife interrupted Dona Fernanda's concern regarding Rubião. She went on board to greet them and took them to Tijuca, where an old friend of Carlos Maria's family had rented and furnished a house on his instructions. Sofia didn't go on board. She sent her coupé to wait for them on the Pharoux docks, but Dona Fernanda was already there with a calèche that took them along with herself and Palha. Sofia went to visit the new arrivals in the afternoon.

Dona Fernanda was bursting with contentment. The letters from Maria Benedita had said they were happy. She couldn't read the confirmation of what had been written immediately in the eyes and manners of the couple, but they seemed satisfied. Maria Benedita couldn't hold back her tears when she embraced her friend, nor could the latter hers, and they hugged each other like blood sisters. The next day Dona Fernanda asked Maria Benedita if she and her husband were happy, and, finding out that they were, she grasped her hands and stared at her for a long time, unable to find anything to say. All she could manage was to repeat the question.

"Are you two happy?"

"We are," Maria Benedita answered.

"You don't know how good your answer makes me feel. It's not just that I would have felt remorse if you didn't have the happiness I imagined I'd given you both, but also because it's so nice to see other people happy. Does he love you as much as on the first day?"

"More, I think, because I adore him."

Dona Fernanda didn't understand those words. *More, I think, because I adore him!* In truth, the conclusion didn't seem to match the premise, but it was a case of improving on Hamlet again: "There are more things in heaven and earth, Horatio, than are dreamt of in your *dialectics.*" Maria Benedita began to tell her about the trip, unwinding her impressions and reminiscences. And since her husband came to join them a short while after, she had recourse to his memory to fill in the gaps.

"How was it, Carlos Maria?"

Carlos Maria remembered, explained, or rectified, but without interest, almost impatiently. He'd guessed that Maria Benedita had just confided her good fortune to the other woman, and he had trouble covering the unpleasant effect it had on him. Why say that she was happy with him since it couldn't be any other way? And why divulge the caresses and loving words, the charity of a great and friendly god?

The return to Rio de Janeiro had been a concession on his part. Maria Benedita wanted to have her child here. Her husband gave in—with difficulty, but he gave in. Why with difficulty? It's hard to explain, even harder to understand. Carlos Maria had personal and peculiar ideas regarding motherhood, hidden, not confided to anyone. He found nature to be shameless in making a public phenomenon of human gestation, in full view, growing into physical deformity, suggestive to the point of disrespect. That was what brought on his desire for solitude, mystery, and absence. They would live the final moments with pleasure inside a solitary house on the top of a hill, shut off from the world, and the woman would go down from there one day with her child in her arms and divinity in her eyes.

He made no such proposal to his wife. He would have had to argue, and he didn't like arguing. He preferred giving in. Maria Benedita, naturally, had just the opposite feeling. She considered herself a divine and reserved temple in which a god was living, the child of another god. Her gestation went along filled with tedium, pain, discomfort, which she tried to hide from her husband as best she could. But all of it gave a greater value to the future little creature. She accepted her troubles with resignation—if not accepting them with joy—since it was a condition of the coming of the fruit. She fulfilled the duty of her species cordially. And she would repeat without words the reply of Mary of Nazareth: "I am the servant of the Lord; let His will be done in me."

"What's the matter with you?" Maria Benedita asked as soon as they were alone.

"Me? Nothing. Why?"

"You seemed annoyed."

"No, I wasn't annoyed."

"Yes you were," she insisted.

Carlos Maria smiled without answering. Maria Benedita already knew that special smile of his, inexpressive, without tenderness or censure, superficial and wan. She didn't persist in wanting to know. She bit her lip and withdrew.

In her room she thought for some time of nothing else but that wan, mute smile, the sign of some annoyance, the cause of which could only have been she. And she went over the whole conversation, all the gestures she'd made, and she found nothing that could explain the coldness or whatever it was with Carlos Maria. Maybe she'd been excessive in her talk. She was accustomed, if she was happy, to opening up her heart to friends and strangers. Carlos Maria disapproved of that generosity because it gave an air of great happiness to their moral and domestic status and because he considered that banal and inferior. Maria Benedita remembered that in Paris, with the Brazilian colony, she'd felt more than once that effect of her expansiveness and had repressed herself. But could Dona Fernanda be in the same situation? Wasn't she the author of the happiness of them both? She rejected that hypothesis and tried to look for another. Not finding it, she returned to the first one, and, as always happened, she found her husband right. Really, no matter how intimate and pleasing it might be, she hadn't ought to tell her good friend the minute details of their life, it was thoughtless of her . . .

Nausea came along to interrupt her at that point in her reflections. Nature was reminding her of a reason of state—the reason of the species—more immediate and superior to her husband's annoyances. She gave in to necessity, but a few minutes later she was beside Carlos Maria, curving her right arm around his neck. He, seated, was reading an English magazine. He took the hand hanging over his chest and finished the page.

"Do you forgive me?" his wife asked when she saw him close the magazine. "From now on I'll be less of a chatterbox."

Carlos Maria took both her hands, smiling and answering yes with his head. It was as if he'd thrown a beam of light over her. The joy penetrated her soul. It might be said that the fetus itself reacted to the feeling and blessed its father.

C L X X I

"Perfect! That's the way I want to see you!" a voice shouted from the window side.

Maria Benedita moved rapidly away from her husband. The veranda, which was accessible from the living room by three doors, had one of them open. The voice had come from there.

Rubião's head was peeping in and smiling. It was the first time they'd seen him. Carlos Maria, without getting up, looked at him, stern, waiting. And the head smiled with its thick mustache and pointed tips, looking from one to the other and repeating:

"Perfect! That's the way I want to see you!"

Rubião came in, held out his hand to them, which they took without warmth, said some words of admiration and praise to Maria Benedita, she so elegant, he so handsome. He noted that they both bore the name Maria, a kind of predestination, and he ended up by giving them the news of the fall of the government.

"The cabinet fell?" Carlos Maria asked involuntarily.

"That's all they're talking about in the city. I'm going to sit down without asking permission since you haven't offered me a chair yet," he went on, sitting down, taking the cane he carried under his arm and placing his hands on it. "Well, it's true, the government has resigned. I'm going to organize another. Palha will be in it, our Palha—your cousin Palha and you, too, sir, if it should so please you, will be a minister. I need a good cabinet, all strong friends, ready to lay down their lives for me. I'm going to call on Morny, Pio, Camacho, Rouher, Major Siqueira. You remember the major, don't you, ma'am? I think I'll give him War. I don't know any man more apt for military matters."

Maria Benedita, annoyed and impatient, walked about the room waiting for her husband to tell her to do something. The latter told her to leave with his eyes. She didn't wait for a second gesture, excused herself to their guest, and withdrew. Rubião, after she'd left, praised her again—a flower, he said, and corrected himself, laughing, "Two flowers, I think there are two flowers there. May the Lord bless them both!" Carlos Maria held out his hand as a sign of saying goodbye.

"My dear sir . . ."

"May I include you in the cabinet?" Rubião asked.

Not hearing a reply, he assumed the answer was yes, and he promised him a good portfolio. The major would go to War and Camacho to Justice. Did he know them by chance? "Two great men, Camacho even greater than the other." And obeying Carlos Maria, who was heading toward the door, Rubião was leaving without being aware of it. But he wasn't all that ready. On the veranda, before going down the steps, he mentioned several facts about the war. For example, he'd given Germany back to the Germans. It was a nice thing to do and good politics. He'd already given Venice to the Italians. He didn't need any more territory. The Rhineland provinces, yes, but there was time to go after them . . .

"My dear sir . . . ," Carlos Maria repeated, holding out his hand.

He said goodbye to him and closed the door. Rubião came up with a few more words and went down the steps. Maria Benedita, who was spying on them from inside, came over to her husband, took his hand, and stayed looking at Rubião as he crossed the garden. He wasn't walking straight, or hurriedly, or silently. He would stop, gesticulate, pick up a dry twig, seeing a thousand things in the air, more elegant than the lady of the house, more handsome than the man. They were watching our friend from the window, and after one grotesque action Maria Benedita couldn't hold back a laugh. Carlos Maria, however, looked on placidly.

CLXXII

"But if the fall of the government is true," she said, "do you know who's going to be a minister?"

"Who?" Carlos Maria asked with his eyes.

"Your cousin Teófilo. Nanã told me that he's got his hopes up, and that's why he stayed in the capital this year. He suspected, or there was already talk of the government's falling. He must have suspected. I don't remember exactly what she told me, but it seems he'll be joining in."

"It could be."

"Look, there goes Rubião. He stopped, he's looking up, maybe he's waiting for the public coach or his carriage. He had a carriage. There he goes, walking . . ."

CLXXIII

"So Teófilo's a minister!" Carlos Maria exclaimed. And after a moment:

"I think he'll make a good minister. Would you like to see me a minister, too?"

"If you'd like to be, why not?"

"So I have your vote then, right?" Carlos Maria asked.

"What am I supposed to answer?" she thought scrutinizing her husband's face.

He, laughing:

"Confess that you'd adore me even if I were only a minister's errand boy."

"Exactly!" the young lady exclaimed, throwing her arms around his neck.

Carlos Maria stroked her hair and murmured seriously: "Bernadotte was a king and Bonaparte an emperor. Would you like to be the queen mother of Sweden?"

Maria Benedita didn't understand the question nor did he explain it to her. In order to explain it to her it would be necessary to say that possibly she was carrying a Bernadotte in her womb. But that supposition meant a desire and the desire a confession of inferiority. Carlos Maria ran his hands over his wife's head again with a gesture that seemed to be saying: "Maria, you chose the best there was . . ." And she seemed to understand the meaning of that gesture.

"Yes! Yes!"

Her husband smiled and went back to the English magazine. She, leaning on the armchair, ran her fingers through his hair, ever so lightly and silently so as not to disturb him. He went on reading, reading, reading. Maria Benedita was limiting her caresses, withdrawing her fingers little by little until she left the room, where Carlos Maria continued reading a study by Sir Charles Little, M.P., on the famous statuette of Narcissus in the Naples Museum.

C L X X I V

When Rubião got to Dona Fernanda's in the late afternoon, he heard from the servant that he couldn't come in. The lady wasn't feeling well. Her husband was with her. It seems that they were waiting for the doctor. Our friend didn't insist, and he went away.

It was just the opposite. It was the husband who was ill, and his wife was with him. But the servant couldn't change the message they'd given him. Another servant was suspicious, it's true, that he was the ill one and not she, because he'd seen him come in in low spirits. Upstairs in their bedroom there was the sound of voices, sometimes loud, sometimes low, with intervals of silence. A servant girl who'd tiptoed up came down saying that she'd heard the master complaining. The mistress was probably in trouble. Downstairs soft words back and forth, sharp ears, conjectures. They noted that there was no request from upstairs for water, medicine, a broth at least. The table was set, the butler in uniform, the cook proud and anxious . . . Surely one of his finest dinners!

What was it? Teófilo had the same downcast expression as when he came in. He was on a settee, his vest off, staring. Next to him, also sitting, grasping one of his hands, Dona Fernanda was asking him to calm down, that it wasn't worth it. And, leaning over to look into his face, she pulled him over, wanting him to lay his head on her shoulder . . .

"Let it go, let it go," her husband murmured.

"It's not worth it, Teófilo! Is it a ministry now . . . ? Is a short-term position full of annoyances, insults, and hard work worth all that? What for? Isn't a peaceful life much better? Of course it's unfair. I do think you've got the capacity, but is it that great a loss? Come, my dear, relax. Let's go down to dinner."

Teófilo bit his lip, pulling on one of his sideburns. He hadn't heard anything his wife had said, neither exhortations nor consolations. He'd heard the conversations of the night before and that morning, the political combinations, the remembered names, the refusals and the acceptances. No combination included him, even though he'd spoken to a lot of people concerning the real aspect of the situation. He was listened to with attention by some, impatience by others. Once the eyeglasses of the organizer seemed to be interrogating him—but it was a quick and illusory gesture. Teófilo was reconstructing the agitation of so many hours and places now—he remembered the ones who looked askance, the ones who smiled, the ones who had the same expression as he. Finally, he was no longer speaking. His last hopes had been blown out in his face like a night-light at dawn. He'd heard the names of the ministers, was obliged to find them good. But what strength it took for him to articulate a single word! He was afraid they would discover his disappointment or resentment, and all his efforts ended up accentuating them even more. He grew pale, his hands trembled.

"Come, let's go down to dinner," Dona Fernanda repeated. Teófilo slapped his knee and stood up, speaking disjointed, angry words, walking back and forth, stamping his foot, threatening. Dona Fernanda was unable to overcome the violence of that new attack, she hoped it was brief, and it was brief. Teófilo went to an armchair, shook his head, dropped into it again, prostrate. Dona Fernanda took a chair and sat down beside him.

"You're right, Teófilo, but you've got to be a man. You're young and strong, you've still got a future, and maybe a great future. Who knows, getting into the cabinet now might mean a loss later. You'll get into another one. Sometimes what looks like misfortune is good luck."

Teófilo squeezed her hand with thanks.

"It's treachery, it's intrigue," he murmured, looking at her. "I know all of those swine. If I were to tell you everything, everything . . . But what's the use? I'd rather forget . . . It isn't because of a miserable cabinet position that I'm upset," he went on after a few moments. "Ministries aren't worth anything. A person who knows how to work and has talent can laugh at a cabinet position and show that it's beneath him. Most of those people can't hold a candle to me, Nanã. I'm sure of that and so are they. Dirty bunch of schemers! Where can they find more sincerity, more loyalty, more readiness for a fight? Who worked more with the press during our time out of power? They excuse themselves, say that cabinets come all set up from São Cristóvão . . . Oh, if I could only speak to the Emperor!"

"Teófilo!"

"I'd tell the Emperor: 'Sire, Your Majesty is unaware of these lobby politicians, these arrangements of cliques. Your Majesty wants the best people to work in your councils, but the mediocre ones arrange them . . . Merit is put aside.' That's what I'll tell him someday. It might even be tomorrow . . ."

He fell silent. After a long pause he arose and went to his study, which was next door to the bedroom. His wife went with him. It was already dark. He lighted the gas jet and ran his eyes veiled with melancholy about the room. There were four wide bookcases full of books, reports, budgets, Treasury ledgers. The desk was orderly. Three tall cabinets without doors held manuscripts, notes, memoranda, calculations, appointments, all stacked methodically and labeled—*Extraordinary Credits—Supplementary Credits—Army Credits—Navy Credits—1868 Loan—Railroads—Internal Debt—Budget for 61–62, for 62–63, for 63–64*, etc. That was where he worked in the morning and at night, adding, calculating, gathering together the material for his speeches and reports, because he was a member of three parliamentary committees and generally worked for himself and six colleagues. The latter listened and approved. One of them, when the reports were extensive, would approve them without hearing them.

"You're the expert, old man, and that's enough for me," he would tell Teófilo. "Hand me the pen."

Everything there breathed attention, care: assiduous, meticulous, and useful work. From hooks on the wall hung the week's newspapers, which were later taken down, put away, and finally bound in six-month batches for future consultation. The deputy's speeches, printed and bound in quartos, were lined up on a shelf. No picture or bust, decoration, nothing for recreation, nothing to admire—everything dry, exact, administrative.

"What's this all worth?" Teófilo asked his wife after a few moments of silent contemplation. "Weary hours, long hours, from night into dawn sometimes . . . It can't be said that this is the study of an idle man. Work gets done here. You're witness to the fact that I work. All for what?"

"You get consolation out of your work," she murmured.

He, bitingly:

"Fine consolation! No, no, I'm through with this. I'm going to forget about everything. Look, in the chamber they all ask for my advice, even the ministers—because I really apply myself to administrative things. What's the reward? To come here in May and applaud the new masters?"

"So don't applaud anything," his wife said softly. "Do you really want to give me a present? Let's go to Europe, in March or April, and we'll come back a year from now. Ask for a leave from the chamber, from wherever we might be—from Warsaw, for example, I've always wanted to see Warsaw," she continued, smiling and holding his face lovingly between her hands. "Say yes. Answer me so I can write to Rio Grande today, the steamer sails tomorrow. It's all said and done. Shall we go to Warsaw?"

"Stop joking, Nanã, this is no joking matter."

"I'm serious. I've been thinking a long time about proposing a trip to you to see if you can have a rest from this infernal paperwork. It's too much, Teófilo! You can barely find time for a visit. A ride is rare. We almost never chat. Our children hardly see their father because no one can come in here when you're working . . . You've got to take a rest. I beg of you, take a year off. Look, I'm serious. We're going to Europe in March."

"It can't be," he stammered.

"Why not?"

It couldn't be. It was inviting him to get out of his own skin. Politics was everything. There was politics out there, but what did he have to do with it? Teófilo didn't know anything about what went on outside Brazil except for our debt to London and a half dozen economists. Nevertheless, he thanked his wife for the intention behind her proposal.

"You're very good."

And a vague feeling of hope restored the deputy's voice to the softness it had lost during that moral crisis. The papers blew encouragement at him. That whole mass of studies appeared to him like fertilized and seeded land to the eyes of the farmer. It wouldn't be long in sprouting. Work had its recompense. Some-day, sooner or later, the sprout would bloom, and the tree would bear fruit. It was precisely what his wife had said with other direct and apt words. But only now was he seeing the possibility of a harvest. He remembered his explosions of rage, indignation, despair, the complaints of a while ago; he was annoyed. He tried to smile and he made a poor job of it. At dinner and over coffee he amused himself with the children, who went to bed later that evening. Nuno, who was in secondary school now, where he'd heard mention of the change in government, told his father that he wanted to be a minister. Teófilo became serious.

"My son," he said, "choose anything else but a minister."

"They say it's nice, Papa. They say you go around in a carriage with soldiers behind."

"Well, I'll get you a carriage."

"Were you a minister already, Papa?"

Teófilo tried to smile and he looked at his wife, who took advantage of the occasion to send the children off to bed.

"Yes, I was a minister already," his father answered, kissing Nuno on the forehead. "But I don't want to be anymore. It's a rotten job, lots of work. You'll be a chaplain."

"What's a chaplain?"

"A chaplain is bed," Dona Fernanda answered. "Go to bed, Nuno."

C L X X V I

At lunch the next day Teófilo received a letter by an orderly. "Orderly?"

"Yes, sir. He says it's from the president of the council."

Teófilo opened the letter with a trembling hand. What could it be? He'd read the list of the new ministers in the newspaper. The cabinet was complete. There was no change of names. What could it be? Dona Fernanda, across from her husband, was trying to read the contents of the letter on his face. She saw a clearing. She perceived that his mouth was experiencing a smile of satisfaction—of hope, at least.

"Tell him to wait," Teófilo ordered the servant.

He went to the study and returned minutes later with his reply. He sat down at the table, silent, giving the servant time to hand the letter over to the orderly. This time, expecting it, he heard the horse's hooves and then its gallop out on the street, and he felt good.

"Read it," he said.

Dona Fernanda read the letter from the president of the council. It was a request to speak with him at two in the afternoon.

"But the cabinet then . . . ?"

"It's complete," the deputy hastened to say. "The ministers have been appointed."

She didn't completely believe what he was saying. She imagined some last-minute vacancy and the urgent necessity to fill it.

"It must be some political matter, or maybe he wants to talk about the budget—or assign me some study."

Saying that in order to put off his wife, he felt the probability of the hypotheses, and he was downcast again. But three minutes later the butterflies of hope were fluttering in front of him, not two, not four, but a swarm that was darkening the sky.

C L X X V I I

Dona Fernanda waited, full of anxiety, as if the cabinet post were for her and that it would give her some pleasure as long as it wasn't bitter and complicated. Once her husband was satisfied, however, everything would be much better. Teófilo was back at five-thirty. From his look she could see that he was satisfied. She ran to grasp his hands.

"What was it?"

"Poor Nanã! Here we are, always on the move. The marquis asked me right off to accept a provincial presidency of the first order. Unable to put me in the cabinet—where he'd had a place all marked out for me—he wished, wanted, asked me to participate in the political and administrative responsibilities of the government by taking on a presidency. He couldn't, in any case, do without my prestige (those are his words), and he hopes that in the Chamber I'll take on the position of majority leader. What do you say to that?"

"That we get ready for the move," Dona Fernanda answered.

"Do you think I could have refused?"

"No."

"I couldn't. You know that you can't refuse a service of that kind to a friendly government. Or else you should get out of politics. The marquis treated me well. I already knew that he was a superior man, but how smiling and affable! You can't imagine. He also wants me to attend a meeting, the ministers and a few friends, not many, half a dozen. He confided to me that he's holding the cabinet program in reserve . . ."

"When do we leave?"

"I don't know. I have to see him tomorrow night. The meeting is tomorrow at eight o'clock . . . But do you think I did the right thing in accepting?"

"Of course."

"Yes. If I'd refused, I would have been criticized, and rightfully so. In politics the first thing you lose is your freedom. You can stay behind for now if you want. Five months from now—or four—the chambers open. I'll barely have time to get there and take a look."

CLXXVIII

Dona Fernanda approved of the proposal. It wouldn't interrupt their son's education. It was a separation of four months. Teófilo left in a matter of days. On the morning of his sailing, quite early, he went to take leave of his study. He took a last look at his books, reports, budgets, manuscripts, that whole part of the household that only spoke his language and was of interest for him. He'd tied up the papers and folders so they wouldn't get lost and gave long instructions to his wife. Standing in the middle of the room, he ran his eyes around the shelves and spread his soul over all of them. In that way he took leave of his saints and his friends with genuine regret. Dona Fernanda, who was next to him, hadn't lived there more than the ten minutes of his farewell. Teófilo had lived there for many years.

"Don't worry, I'll take care of things. I'll dust them every day myself."

Teófilo gave her a kiss . . . Any other wife would have taken it sadly, seeing that he loved his books so much that he seemed to love them more than her. But Dona Fernanda felt herself lucky.

C L X X I X

Rubião, ever since the day of the ministerial crisis, never returned to Dona Fernanda's house. He knew nothing of the presidency or of Teófilo's leaving. He lived with the dog and a servant, without any great attacks or long rest periods. The servant carried out his duties in an irregular way, gobbling up gratuities and frequently receiving the title of marquis. Otherwise he would amuse himself. When his master took it upon himself to converse with the four walls, the servant would run to spy on him, listen to the dialogue, because Rubião paid attention to their words, answering as if they had asked some question. At night the servant would go to chat with friends in the neighborhood.

"How's the nut?"

"The nut's fine. Today he invited the dog to sing. The dog did a lot of barking and carrying on. He liked it a lot and acted like a bigshot. When he's got one of his spells, it's like he was the ruler of the world. Just yesterday at lunch he said to me: 'Marquis Raimundo . . . I want you . . .' and he got the rest of it so mixed up I couldn't understand a thing. At the end he gave me ten *tostões*."

"You put them away . . ."

"Come on!"

When Rubião would come out of his delirium, that whole wordy phantasmagoria became a silent sadness for a moment. His consciousness, where traces of his previous state remained, forced him to get rid of them. It was like the painful ascent a man was making from the pit, climbing up the walls, tearing his skin, leaving his nails behind in order to reach the top and not fall back down again and be lost. Then he would go visit friends, some new, others old, like the major's people and Camacho's, for example.

The latter, for some time, had been less talkative. Politics wasn't giving him as much material for speeches as formerly. In his office, when he saw Rubião appear in the door, he would put on an impatient look that he immediately corrected. The other man noticed it and was lost in conjectures, whether he'd committed some offense out of carelessness—or whether Camacho was beginning to dislike him. And in order to break the tedium or the resentment he would speak strongly, merrily, opening long respectful pauses, waiting for him to say something. He turned in vain to the Marquis of Paraná whose picture still hung on the wall. He repeated the names he'd heard—the great marquis! the consummate statesman! Camacho continued holding his head and writing without cease, consulting his briefs and attorneys, Lobão, Coelho da Rocha, quoting, scratching out, excusing himself. He had a libel case that day. He stopped to go to the bookcase.

"Excuse me . . ."

Rubião pulled back his legs to let him pass. He took down a volume of *Ordinances of the Realm* and leafed through it, jumping ahead, going back, idly, without finding anything, simply to get rid of the unwelcome visitor. But the unwelcome visitor stayed right there for that very reason, and they cast concealed glances at each other. Camacho went back to his libel suit. In order to read, sitting down, he leaned way over to the left, where the light was coming from, turning his back to Rubião.

"It's dark in here," Rubião ventured one day.

And he didn't hear any answer, so intent did the lawyer seem on reading his briefs. Really, it might be inconvenient, our friend thought. He looked at the stern and serious face, the gesture with which he picked up his pen in order to go on with the endless libel suit. Twenty more minutes of absolute silence. At the end of that time, Rubião saw him lay down the pen, tighten his chest, stretch out his arms, and pass his hands over his eyes. He said to him, interested:

"Tired, eh?"

Camacho made an affirmative gesture and made ready to continue. Then our man got up and took advantage of the interval to say goodbye.

"I'll come back when you're less tied up."

He held out his hand. Camacho shook it weakly and went back to his papers. Rubião went down the stairs puzzled, heartsick at the coldness of his illustrious friend. What could he have done?

C L X X X

L eaving there he happened to run into Major Siqueira.
"I was just on my way to your place," he said. "Are you going there?"

"I am, but we're not in the same place anymore. We moved to Cajueiros, Rua da Princesa . . ."

"Wherever it is, let's go."

Rubião needed a piece of string to tie him to reality because his mind felt overcome by madness once more. He spoke so reasonably and properly, however, that the major found him completely in control of his senses, and he told him:

"Do you know that I've got a great piece of news to give you?"

"Let's have it."

"It'll have to wait till we get there."

They got there. It was a two-story house. Dona Tonica came to open the grating for them. She was wearing a new dress and earrings.

"Take a good look at her," the major said, holding his daughter by the chin.

Dona Tonica drew back in embarrassment.

"I'm looking," Rubião answered.

"Can't you see right away that she's a person who's going to be married?"

"Oh! Congratulations!"

"It's true. She's going to be married. It took a bit of doing, but she made it. She found a fiancé who adores her, as they all do. Me, when I was a fiancé, I adored my late wife who was something never seen before . . . She's getting married. She found a fiancé. It took a bit of doing, but she made it. A serious person, middle-aged. He comes here and spends the evening. In the morning on his way to work I think he raps on the window, or she's already waiting for him. I pretend not to notice . . ."

Dona Tonica was saying it wasn't so with her head, but she was smiling in a way that seemed to say it was. She was so excited! She didn't even remember that she'd courted Rubião, that he'd been one of the last and, finally, the very last of her hopes. They went into the living room. Dona Tonica went to the window, came back, head held high, walking about, reconciled with life.

"A good fellow," the major repeated, "a good chap . . . Tonica, go get the picture . . . Go on, go get your fiancé . . ."

Dona Tonica went to fetch the picture. It was a photograph showing a man of middle age, short, sparse hair, looking startled, hollow cheeks, thin neck, with his jacket buttoned.

"What do you think?"

"Very nice."

Dona Tonica took the picture back and looked at it for a few seconds, but she turned her eyes away and remained seated as her imagination went out to wait for Rodrigues. His name was Rodrigues. He was shorter than she—something that didn't show in the picture—and he worked in a bureau of the war ministry. A widower with two sons, one of whom was a cadet, the other a victim of tuberculosis—twelve years old—a sentence of death. What difference did that make? He was her fiancé. Every night when she retired, Dona Tonica would kneel before the image of Our Lady, her patroness, thank her for the favor, and ask her to make her happy. She was already dreaming of a son. His name would be Álvaro.

Rubião listened to the major's discourse in silence. The marriage was set for a month and a half from then. The groom had to get his house fixed up. He wasn't a wealthy man, but lived off his salary and had recourse to loans. The house would be the same one and there was no need for new or fine furniture, but there were always certain necessities . . . In short, a month and a half from then, or five weeks at most, they would be joined in the holy bonds of matrimony.

"And I'll be free of the burden," the major concluded.

"Oh!" Rubião protested.

The daughter laughed. She was used to her father's joking and was so given to joy that nothing bothered her. Even if her father referred to the forty years that were behind her, it was no great blow for her. All brides are fifteen years of age.

"You'll see. He'll come looking for you out of loneliness," Rubião said to Dona Tonica.

"Ha! I might just get married myself!"

Rubião stood up suddenly and took a few steps. The major didn't see the expression on his face, didn't perceive that the man's mind was getting unhinged and that he himself sensed it. He told him to sit down, and he went on about his days as a married man and a campaigner. When he came to the narration of the Battle of Monte-Caseros with the attacks and counterattacks that were part of his discourse, he had Napoleon III before him. Silent at first, Rubião offered a few words of congratulation, mentioned Solferino and Magenta, and promised Siqueira a decoration. Father and daughter exchanged looks. The major said that it was getting ready to rain heavily. Indeed, it had grown a bit dark. It would be better if Rubião left before the rain started. He was carrying no umbrella, and they only had an old one, the only one in the house.

"My coach will be coming for me," Rubião argued calmly.

"It's not coming. It went over to wait for you on the Campo. Can you see the coach from there, Tonica?"

Dona Tonica made a vague, unwilling gesture. She didn't like lying, but she was afraid and wanted Rubião to leave. From the house it was impossible to see the Campo da Aclamação. Her father was already taking Rubião by the arm and leading him to the door.

"Come back tomorrow, later on, whenever you want."

"But why can't I wait until my coach comes?" Rubião asked. "The Empress can't get caught in the rain . . ."

"The Empress has already left."

"That was a mistake. That was a great mistake on Eugénie's part. General . . . Why are you still a major? General, I saw the picture of your son-in-law. I want to give you one of mine. Send for it to the Tuileries. Where's the coach?"

"It's on the Campo, waiting."

"Have it sent for."

Dona Tonica, who was at the window, turned and said:

"There comes Rodrigues."

And she looked out at the street again, leaning over and smiling while her father continued guiding Rubião to the door, not roughly, but firmly. The latter stopped, scolding him:

"General, I am your emperor!"

"Of course, but come along with me, Your Majesty . . ."

They'd reached the door. The major opened the grating just as Rodrigues crossed the threshold. Dona Tonica went out to receive her fiancé, but the door was blocked by her father and Rubião. Rodrigues took off his hat, showing his coarse gray hair. On his sunken cheeks he had a touch of freckles, but his smile was pleasant and humble—more humble than pleasant, though— and, not withstanding the triviality of the expression and the person, he was agreeable. His eyes didn't show the fright in the photograph. That effect had been due to the stress he was giving to his whole body so that the picture *would come out nice.*

"This gentleman is my future son-in-law," the major said to Rubião. "Didn't you see a coach and a squadron of cavalry on the Campo?" he asked Rodrigues, winking.

"I think so, sir."

"So, then," Siqueira continued, turning to Rubião. "Go on, go on, head down the Rua de São Lourenço and go straight to the Campo. Goodbye, until tomorrow,"

Rubião went down three steps—there were five—and stopped in front of the newcomer, stared at him for a few seconds, and declared that he was very pleased to meet him, that he would make a good husband and son-in-law. What was his name?

"João José Rodrigues."

"Rodrigues. I'm going to send you a ribbon for your tunic. It's my wedding present. Remind me, Siqueira."

Siqueira took him by the arm so he could go down the last two steps to the street.

"On the Campo, you say?"

"On the Campo."

"Goodbye."

From the street Rubião took another look up at the windows with his fingers to his hat as a way of saluting Dona Tonica, but Dona Tonica was in the living room, which Rodrigues had just entered, fresh and delightful, like the first rose of summer.

C L X X X I I

Rubião wasn't thinking about the coach or the cavalry squadron anymore. He went along by himself down several streets until he turned up São José. From the imperial palace he went along gesticulating and talking to someone he imagined holding by the arm. Was it the Empress Eugénie or Sofia? Both in a single person—or, rather, the second with the name of the first. Men who were passing would stop. People ran to the door from inside their shops. Some laughed, others were indifferent. Some, after seeing what it was, turned their eyes away to spare themselves the sorrow that the sight of his delirium gave them. A mob of urchins was accompanying Rubião, some so close that they could hear his words. Children of all sorts came to join the group. When they caught sight of the general curiosity, they decided to give voice to the mob, and the jeering began.

"Hey, loony! Hey, loony!"

That shouting drew the attention of other people, many house windows began to open, curious people of both sexes and all ages appeared, a photographer, an upholsterer, three or four figures together, some heads over others, all leaning out, watching, following the man who was talking to the wall, his gestures full of grandeur and courtesy.

"Hey, loony! Hey, loony!" the ragamuffins were bellowing.

One of them, much younger than the rest, clung to the pants of another lanky one. They were on the Rua da Ajuda now. Rubião still heard nothing, but when he did hear something, he imagined it was cheering, and he bowed in thanks. The jeers grew louder. In the midst of the noise the voice of a woman in the door of a mattress shop could be distinguished:

"Deolindo! Come home here, Deolindo!"

Deolindo, the child who was clinging to the pants of an older one, didn't obey. It could have been that he didn't hear, the shouting was so loud and the little fellow's joy was such that he was shouting in his own tiny voice:

"Hey, loony! Hey, loony!"

"Deolindo!"

Deolindo tried to hide among the others to get out of the sight of his mother, who was calling him. She ran to the group, however, and dragged him out. He was really too small to get involved in street tumults.

"Mama, I want to see . . ."

"See, hah! Come on!"

She put him inside the building and stood in the doorway looking at the street. Rubião was picking up his pace. She could see him clearly with his gestures and his words, his chest out, waving his hat all around.

"Crazy people are funny sometimes," she said to a neighbor woman, smiling.

The boys continued shouting and laughing, and Rubião kept on walking with the same chorus behind him. Deolindo, at the door, watching the group go off, tearfully begged his mother to let him go too or to take him along. When he'd lost all hope he put all of his energy into one little shrieking shout:

"Hey, loony!"

The neighbor woman laughed. The mother laughed too. She confessed that her son was a little pest, a devil who was never still. She couldn't let him out of her sight. With the least distraction he was out on the street. And that was ever since he was little. He was only two when he almost got killed under a wagon right there. He missed by a hair. If it hadn't been for a man who was passing, a well-dressed gentleman, who jumped in quickly, even at the risk of his life, he would have been dead, stone dead. At that point her husband, who was coming from across the street, interrupted the conversation. He was frowning, barely greeted the neighbor woman, and went inside. The wife went in to see him. What was wrong? The husband told her about the jeering.

"He passed by here," she said.

"Didn't you recognize the man?"

"No."

The husband crossed his arms and stood staring, silent. The wife asked him who it was.

"It was that man who saved our Deolindo's life."

The woman shuddered.

"Did you get a good look?" she asked.

"Good and clear. I've come across him other times, but he wasn't that way then. Poor devil! And the urchins hollering after him. Damn! Aren't there any police in this country?"

What pained the woman wasn't so much the man's illness or the jeering but the part her son had had in it—the same child whose life the man had saved. Really, how could the boy have recognized him or known that he owed his life to him? She was pained by the encounter, by the coincidence. In the end she contented herself with taking on all the blame. If she'd been more careful, the little one wouldn't have gone out, and he wouldn't have got mixed up in the mockery. She shuddered from time to time and was restless. The husband took his son's head in his hand and gave it two kisses.

"Did you see that scene today?" he asked his wife.

"I did."

"I kept wanting to take the man's arm and lead him away from here, but I was embarrassed. The hoodlums could have come after me. I turned my head away because he might have recognized me. Poor devil! Did you notice that he didn't seem to hear anything and that he went happily on his way. I think he was even smiling . . . It's a sad thing to lose your mind!"

The woman was thinking about her son's mischief. She didn't say anything about it to her husband. She asked her neighbor not to mention it, and at night it took her a long time before she could close her eyes. She'd got it into her head that years later her son would go crazy as punishment for that same mockery and that she would be spitting at heaven, indignant, cursing.

C L X X X I V

Two hours after the scene on the Rua da Ajuda, Rubião reached Dona Fernanda's house. The urchins were dispersing little by little, and their places weren't being taken. The last three put their farewells together in one single and formidable roar. Rubião went on alone, unnoticed by the dwellers in the houses because his gesticulating had lessened or changed pattern. He was no longer talking to the wall, to the imagined empress, but he was still emperor. He would walk, stop, murmur something without any grand gestures, still dreaming, still wrapped in that veil through which all things were something else, opposite and better. Every lamppost had the look of a chamberlain, on every corner there was the figure of a groom. Rubião was going straight to the throne room in order to receive some ambassadors or such, but the palace was interminable. He had to pass through so many rooms and galleries, over carpets—and between tall, robust halberdiers.

Of the people who saw him and stopped on the street or leaned out of windows, many suspended their sad or bothersome thoughts and worries of the day for a moment, the tedium, the resentments, a debt for this one, an illness for that one, slighted in love, betrayed by a friend. Every misery was forgotten, which was better than bemoaning oneself. But the forgetting lasted only as long as a flash of lightning. When the sick man had passed, reality took hold of them again, the streets became streets because the sumptuous palaces went off with Rubião. And more than one felt sorry for the poor devil, comparing their two fates; more than one thanked heaven for the lot that had befallen him— bitter, but conscious. They preferred their real hovels to that phantasmagoric castle.

C L X X X V

Rubião was placed in a hospital. Palha had forgotten the duty Sofia had imposed on him, and Sofia didn't remember the promise made to the woman from Rio Grande. They were both involved with a new house, a mansion in Botafogo, whose renovation was about to be completed and which they wanted to inaugurate in winter when Parliament was in session and everyone had come down from Petrópolis.* But now the promise was fulfilled. Rubião was accepted into the establishment, where he had a living room and a bedroom, especially arranged through Dr. Falcão and Palha. He offered no resistance. He went along gladly and went into his quarters as if they'd been long familiar to him. When they took their leave, saying they would return later, Rubião invited them to a military review on Saturday.

"Of course, Saturday," Falcão nodded.

"Saturday's a good day," Rubião commented. "Don't fail to come, Duke of Palha."

"I won't," Palha said, walking out.

"Look, I'm going to send one of my coaches for you, a brand new one. Your wife can't rest her beautiful body where someone

---

* The summer residence of the Brazilian court. [Ed.]

else dared sit. Damask and velvet cushions, silver harness and wheels of gold. The horses are descended from the very horse my uncle rode at Marengo. Goodbye, Duke of Palha."

CLXXXVI

"It's clear to me," Dr. Falcão was thinking on the way out. "That man was the lover of this fellow's wife."

CLXXXVII

The man was left there. Quincas Borba tried to get into the carriage that took his friend away and struggled to accompany him by running alongside. The servant had to use all his strength to grab him, hold him, and lock him in the house. It was the same situation as in Barbacena, but life, my fine friend, is made up strictly of four or five situations, which circumstances vary and multiply in people's eyes. Rubião immediately requested that the dog be sent to him. Dona Fernanda, obtaining the director's permission, took it upon herself to satisfy the patient's wishes. She wanted to write a note to Sofia but went to Flamengo in person.

"I'll send someone to see him, it's close by," Sofia proposed. "Let's go ourselves. What's wrong? I've already thought about something. Is it worth keeping the house ready and rented since the cure might take a long time? It would be better to let it go, sell the furniture, and settle accounts."

The walked from Flamengo to the Rua do Príncipe, three or four minutes away. Raimundo was on the street, but when he saw people at the door, he came over to open it. The inside of the house had a look of abandonment, with no permanence or regularity of things that seemed to hold a remnant of an interrupted life. It was the abandonment of negligence. But, on the other hand, the disorder of the furniture in the parlor expressed quite well the delirium of the one who lived there, his twisted and confused ideas.

"Was he very rich?" Dona Fernanda asked Sofia.

"He had something when he arrived from Minas," the latter replied, "but it seems that he squandered everything. Careful, lift up your skirt. It doesn't look as if the floor's been swept in a hundred years."

It wasn't just the floor. The furniture had the crust of neglect. Nor did the servant have anything to say about it. He watched, listened, and softly whistled a popular polka. Sofia didn't ask him about cleanliness. She was dying to get away from "that filth," as she said to herself, and she wanted to find out about the dog, which was the main reason for the visit, but she didn't want to show any great interest in him or anything else. The triviality of it all said nothing to her mind or her heart. The memory of the madman didn't help her any in tolerating the moment. To herself she thought her companion either singularly romantic or affected. "Such foolishness!" she was thinking without changing the approving smile with which she followed all of Dona Fernanda's observations.

"Open that window," the latter said to the servant, "everything smells musty in here."

"Oh, it's unbearable!" Sofia agreed, snorting with distaste.

But in spite of the exclamation, Dona Fernanda wasn't ready

to leave. With no personal memory of those miserable quarters in her mind, she felt taken by a particular and deep upset, but not the kind that the ruination of things gives off. That spectacle didn't bring her any generalized reflections, it didn't point out the fragility of the times or the sad state of the world. It only bespoke the illness of a man, a man whom she scarcely knew, to whom she'd spoken only a few times. And she stayed there looking, not thinking, not deducing anything, withdrawn into herself, pained and mute. Sofia didn't dare speak a word, fearful of its being disagreeable to such a distinguished lady. They were both lifting their skirts so as to avoid getting them dirty. But Sofia added a continuous lively and impatient agitation of her fan to that precaution, like a person who was suffocating in that atmosphere. She got to coughing a few times.

"What about the dog?" Dona Fernanda asked the servant.

"He's locked up in the bedroom back there."

"Go get him."

Quincas Borba appeared. Thin, downcast, he stopped in the parlor door, wondering about the two ladies but without barking. He barely raised his dim eyes. He was about to turn around toward the interior of the house when Dona Fernanda snapped her fingers. He stopped, wagging his tail.

"What's his name?" Dona Fernanda asked.

"Quincas Borba," the servant answered, laughing with a weary voice. "He's got a human name. Hey, Quincas Borba! Go over there, the lady's calling you."

"Quincas Borba, come here! Quincas Borba!" Dona Fernanda repeated.

Quincas Borba answered the call, not leaping or happy. Dona Fernanda leaned over and asked him about his friend, if he was far away, if he wanted to see him. Leaning over like that she questioned the servant about the dog's treatment.

"He's eating now, yes, ma'am. As soon as my master went away he wouldn't eat or drink—I even thought he was done for."

"Does he eat well?"

"Not much."

"Does he look for his master?"

"He seems to be looking for him," Raimundo replied, covering a smile with his hand, "but I locked him in the bedroom so he wouldn't run away. He doesn't whine anymore. At first he whined a lot, he even woke me up . . . I had to pound on the door with a stick and holler at him to make him quiet down . . ."

Dona Fernanda scratched the animal's head. It was his first petting after long days of solitude and neglect. When Dona Fernanda stopped petting him and raised her body up, he stayed looking at her and she at him, so steadily and deeply that they seemed to be penetrating each other's intimacy. Universal sympathy, which was the soul of that lady, forgot all human consideration as she faced that obscure, prosaic misery, and she gave a part of herself to the animal, which enveloped him, fascinated him, and attached him to her feet. In that way the pity she'd had for the master's delirium was now extended to the dog himself, as if they both represented the same species. And, sensing that her presence was giving the animal a good feeling, she didn't want to deprive him of the benefit.

"You're getting full of fleas," Sofia observed.

Dona Fernanda didn't hear her. She continued looking at the animal's sad and gentle eyes until he dropped his head and began sniffing about the room. He'd caught his master's scent. The street door was open. He would have fled through it if Raimundo hadn't run to grab him. Dona Fernanda gave the servant some money so he could wash him and take him to the hospital, recommending the greatest care, that he carry him or take him on a leash. Sofia became involved at that point, ordering him to come see her first, at her home.

C L X X X I X

They left. Sofia, before she set foot on the street, took a look around to see if anyone was coming. Luckily the street was deserted. On seeing herself free of that pigsty, Sofia recovered the use of fine words, the suave and delicate art of captivating others, and she lovingly took Dona Fernanda's arms. She spoke to her of Rubião, of the great misfortune of his madness, and, in the same way, about the mansion in Botafogo. Why didn't she come and see how the work was coming? It was only a question of taking a peek, and they'd leave right after.

C X C

An event took place that distracted Dona Fernanda from Rubião. It was the birth of a daughter to Maria Benedita. She hurried to Tijuca, covered mother and child with kisses, gave Carlos Maria her hand to kiss.

"Always exuberant!" the young father exclaimed, obeying.

"Always dry!" she retorted.

In spite of her cousin's resistance, Dona Fernanda stayed on for Maria Benedita's convalescence, so cordial, so good, so merry that it was a delight to have her in the house. The happiness of this place made her forget the unhappiness of the other, but when the new mother was fully recovered, Dona Fernanda turned her attention to the sick man.

C X C I

"I'm counting on his recovering his sanity at the end of six or eight months. He's coming along very nicely."

Dona Fernanda sent Sofia that reply from the director of the hospital and invited her to go with her to see the patient if she thought it wouldn't be bad for him. "What harm could there be?" Sofia replied in a note. "But I don't feel up to seeing him. He was such a good friend of ours, and I don't know if I could bear the sight and the conversation of the poor man. I showed the letter to Cristiano, who told me he'd liquidated Mr. Rubião's holdings. It amounted to three *contos* two hundred."

C X C I I

"Six months, eight months pass quickly," Dona Fernanda reflected.

And they went along, leaving events behind—the fall of the government, the accession of a new one in March, her husband's return, the debate over the law freeing the children born to slaves, the death of Dona Tonica's fiancé, three days before the wedding. Dona Tonica shed her last tears, some out of love, others out of despair, and she was left with eyes so red that they looked ill.

Teófilo, who enjoyed the same confidence of the new cabinet that he'd had from the old, took a major part in parliamentary debates. Camacho declared in his paper that the law of freeborn children made up for the government's sterility and crimes. In October Sofia inaugurated her salons in Botafogo with a ball that was the one most talked about that season. She was dazzling. She displayed all of her arms and shoulders without any show of pride. Fine jewelry. The necklace, which was one of Rubião's earliest presents, showed that in the case of this type of adornment, style stays the same for long periods. Everybody admired that fresh-looking, robust lady in her thirties. Some men spoke (sorrowfully) of her conjugal virtue, of the deep adoration she had for her husband.

CXCIII

The day after the ball Dona Fernanda woke up late. She went to her husband's study. He'd already gone through five or six newspapers, written ten letters, and put some of the books on the shelves in order.

"I got this letter a while ago," he said.

Dona Fernanda read it. It was from the director of the hospital. It notified them that Rubião had been missing for three days, and they'd been unable to find him in spite of all the efforts on his part and that of the police. "I am all the more startled by this flight," the letter concluded, "since there had been great improvement, and I was sure that he would be entirely well within two months."

Dona Fernanda was aghast. She pressed her husband to write the chief of police and the minister of justice asking them to order the most thorough investigation. Teófilo didn't have the slightest interest in finding Rubião or in his cure, but he wanted to serve his wife, whose charity was well known to him, and, perhaps, he was pleased to be in correspondence with people high in the administration.

CXCIV

How could they find our Rubião or the dog, however, if they'd both left for Barbacena? Rubião had written to Palha to come see him. The latter went to the hospital and saw that his reason was clear, without the slightest shadow of delirium.

"I had a mental breakdown," Rubião told him. "I'm well now, perfectly well. I'm asking you to get me out of here. I don't think the director will be against it. In the meantime, since I want to give some remembrances to the people who've taken care of me, and Quincas Borba, too, I'd like you to advance me a hundred *mil-réis*."

Palha opened his wallet and gave him the money without hesitation.

"I'm going to see about getting you out," he said, "but it may take a few days [it was just before the ball]. Don't worry about it. You'll be out of here within a week."

Before leaving, he consulted the director, who gave him some good news concerning the patient. A week isn't much time, he said, in order to get him well, completely well, I still need two months. Palha confessed that he found him sane. In any case, the person who knew was in charge, and if six or seven months more were needed, there was no reason to hurry his discharge along.

C X C V

Rubião, as soon as he reached Barbacena and began to go up the street that's now called Tiradentes, exclaimed, stopping: "To the victor, the potatoes!"

He'd forgotten the formula and the allegory completely. Suddenly, as if the syllables had remained intact in the air, waiting for someone who could understand them, he brought them together, recomposed the formula, and brought it forth with the same emphasis as on that day when he took it for the law of life and truth. He didn't remember the allegory completely, but the words gave him a vague feeling of struggle and victory.

He went along accompanied by the dog and stopped in front of the church. No one opened the door for him. He didn't see any sign of the sexton. Quincas Borba, who hadn't eaten for several hours, stayed close to his legs, downcast, expectant. Rubião turned and from the top of the street cast his eyes down and into the distance. There it was, it was Barbacena, his old home town was becoming familiar out of the deep reaches of his memory. There it was. Here was the church, there was the jail, beyond it the pharmacy from which the medicines for the other

Quincas Borba had come. He knew that this was it when he arrived, but, as his eyes looked all about, reminiscences kept coming along, more and more, in droves. He didn't see anyone. A window on the left seemed to have someone there peeping out. Everything else was deserted.

"Maybe they don't know I've come," Rubião thought.

C X C V I

Suddenly there was a flash of lightning, clouds were piling up fast. A stronger lightning flash and a peal of thunder. It began to rain heavily, more heavily still, until the storm broke. Rubião, who had left the church with the first drops, was walking down the street, always followed by the dog, famished and faithful, both dazed, in the cloudburst, with no place to go, with no hope of rest or food . . . The rain was beating down on them mercilessly. They couldn't run because Rubião was afraid of slipping and falling, and the dog didn't want to leave him. Halfway down the street the pharmacy returned to Rubião's memory. He turned back, going against the wind, which was hitting him in the face, but within twenty paces the idea was swept out of his head. Goodbye pharmacy! Goodbye shelter! He no longer remembered the reason for changing direction and he went on down again with the dog behind, neither understanding nor running off, both of them soaked, confused, to the sound of the strong, continuous thunder.

They wandered without any direction. Rubião's stomach questioned, exclaimed, hinted. Luckily, delirium came on to deceive necessity with its banquets in the Tuileries. Quincas Borba was the one who didn't have any recourse like that. And he began to walk back and forth. Rubião, from time to time, would sit down on the flagstones, and the dog would climb onto his legs to sleep away his hunger. He found the trousers wet and dropped back down, but he would climb up again. The night air was so cold, late night now, dead night now. Rubião ran his hands over him, muttering some sparse words.

If, in spite of everything, Quincas Borba did manage to fall asleep, he would wake up immediately and start going up and down the hill again. A sad wind that was like a knife was blowing and made the two vagabonds shiver. Rubião walked slowly. His very weariness wouldn't allow him the great strides he'd made at the start when the rain was falling in buckets. The halts were more frequent now. The dog, dead with hunger and fatigue, couldn't understand that odyssey, was ignorant of its reasons, had forgotten the place, didn't hear anything except his master's dull words. He couldn't see the stars that were twinkling now, free of clouds. Rubião discovered them. He'd come to the door of the church, as when he'd arrived in the town. He'd just sat down when he discovered them. They were so beautiful. He recognized them as the chandeliers in the main salon and he ordered them to be extinguished. He was unable to see his order carried out. He fell asleep right there with the dog at his feet. When they awoke in the morning they were so close together that they seemed glued to one another.

CXCVIII

"To the victor, the potatoes!" Rubião exclaimed when his eyes hit the street, without night, without water, kissed by the sun.

CXCIX

It was Rubião's old friend Angélica who took him in along with the dog when she saw them pass by her door. Rubião recognized her and accepted her shelter and breakfast.

"But what's this all about, old friend? How did you get this way? Your clothes are soaked. I'm going to give you a pair of my nephew's pants."

Rubião had a fever. He ate little and without any relish. His friend asked him questions about the life he'd led in the capital, to which he replied that it would take a long time and only posterity could finish it. Your nephew's nephews, he concluded magnificently, are the ones who will see me in all my glory. He began a brief account, however. At the end of ten minutes his old friend didn't understand a thing, the facts and ideas were so confused. Five minutes later she began to feel afraid. When twenty minutes had passed, she excused herself and went to tell a neighbor woman that Rubião seemed to have lost his mind. She came back with her and a brother, who only stayed for a short time and went out to spread the news. Other people came by in twos and fours, and before an hour had passed a great crowd of people was there looking on from the street.

"To the victor, the potatoes!" Rubião shouted to the onlookers. "Here I am, the emperor! To the victor, the potatoes!"

That obscure and incomplete expression was repeated in the street, examined, without anyone's making any sense out of it. A few of Rubião's old enemies were going in, uninvited, the better to enjoy it. And they told his old friend that it wasn't good for her to have a crazy man in her house, it was dangerous. She should have him put in jail until the authorities could send him away. A more compassionate person suggested the recourse of sending for the doctor.

"Doctor? What for?" one of the first put in. "This man's crazy."

"It could be delirirum from a fever. You can see he's running a temperature."

Angélica, at the urging of so many people, took his pulse and found him feverish. She sent for the doctor—the same one who'd treated the late Quincas Borba. Rubião recognized him, too, and answered that it was nothing. He'd captured the King of Prussia and didn't know as yet whether to have him shot or not. It was certain, however, that he would demand an enormous monetary indemnification—five billion francs.

"To the victor the potatoes!" he concluded, laughing.

C C

A few days later he died . . . He didn't die vanquished or defeated.

Before the start of his death agony, which was short, he put the crown on his head—a crown that wasn't even an old hat or a basin, where the spectators could touch the illusion. No, sir. He took hold of nothing, lifted up nothing, and put nothing on his head. Only he saw the imperial insignia, heavy with gold, sparkling with diamonds and other precious stones. The effort he made to lift his body up halfway didn't last long and his body fell back again. His face maintained a glorious expression, however.

"Take care of my crown," he murmured. "To the victor . . ."

His face grew serious, because death is serious. Two minutes of agony, a horrible grimace, and his abdication was signed.

C C I

I should like to speak here of the end of Quincas Borba, who also fell ill, whined ceaselessly, ran off unhinged in search of his master, and was found dead on the street one morning three days later. But on seeing the death of the dog told in a separate chapter, it's possible that you will ask me whether it is he or his late namesake who gives the book its title and why one instead of the other—a question pregnant with questions that would take us far along . . . Come now! Weep for the two recent deaths if you have tears. If you only have laughter, laugh! It's the same thing. The Southern Cross that the beautiful Sofia refused to behold as Rubião had asked her is so high up that it can't discern the laughter or the tears of men.

The Misadventures of Unity:
An Afterword

Heir to a great fortune and, perforce, to a dog, Rubião moves from Barbacena to Rio de Janeiro toward the end of the Empire. He had previously tried his hand, unsuccessfully, at business and had been a school teacher before he dedicated himself entirely to caring for the eccentric philosopher Quincas Borba; the latter had returned, sick and delirious, from the Court in Rio de Janeiro to the interior city of Barbacena, in the province of Minas Gerais. Rubião is credulous and a believer in moral principles; easily offended and without any opinions of his own, he aspires to all the advantages wealth can confer. When he is named the sole heir of Quincas Borba, who had himself unexpectedly inherited a fortune, Rubião sees a chance to fulfill his dreams and aspirations for greatness in the capital city of the Brazilian Empire; he is convinced that the mere possession of wealth will afford him luxury, power, glory—in short, all of the progress of modern life. It is also his chance for revenge, "to get one up on the people who'd paid scant attention to him," those who laughed at his friendship for the mad philosopher and for the philosopher's homonymous dog (Chapter XV).

Rubião is unfamiliar with the complexities of the flourishing bourgeois lifestyle of the elite in Rio de Janeiro, unaware of stratagems for upward social mobility, of Court intrigues, of all the nuances of modern behavior and the wiles of power. He is, therefore, easy prey for social climbers who pretend to be eager to introduce him to business and to politics, but who exploit his trust. Filled with romantic fantasies, Rubião falls madly in love with Sofia, who seduces and abandons him; unfamiliar with business, he delegates the management of his capital to Cristiano Palha, Sofia's husband; aspiring to political power, he is deceived by Camacho. Confused and disillusioned, unprepared for the pretense and selfishness that are the rule in the elite circles he has so suddenly entered, Rubião slowly loses his way and breaks apart. He loses his moral bearings, his unity, his identity. Fragmented, the victim of "diverse and contrary sensations" (Chapter XLIX), he is stripped of his money, of his dreams of greatness, of his fantasies of love and power; he oscillates between bedazzlement and disenchantment, between excitement and boredom, between lust for power and delirious megalomania. He wanders joylessly through salons, down avenues, through the Chamber of Deputies; he takes refuge in dreams and seeks spiritual repose in the "glow of luxury" of his house, reading novels that describe "a noble and royal society" (Chapter LXXX). Bereft of ideas, like Madame Bovary he compensates by using imagination to escape reality and to reconstitute his lost unity of consciousness. Split in two, existing at the "extremes of heart and spirit" (Chapter XL), he shifts back and forth between madness and a certain lucidity. Abandoned by those who once besieged him with protests of friendship, Rubião is now reborn as the image of Quincas Borba, with all the philosopher's eccentricity and his inheritance of madness—confirming the theory of Humanitism the philosopher devised. Finally, Rubião disappears from Rio de Janeiro and returns to Barbacena; sick and in rags, his only companion is the dog. There he dies insane, crowning himself like the Napoleon of his delusions: "He took hold of nothing, lifted up nothing, and put nothing on his head." Going from nothingness to nothingness, Rubião brings the pitiful illusion of human destiny full circle, showing us "the laughter or the tears of men" (Chapters CC and CCI).

Such, in brief, are the plot and themes of *Quincas Borba*, a novel which is also a continuation of an earlier novel by Machado de Assis, *The Posthumous Memoirs of Brás Cubas*, in which the philosopher Quincas Borba also appears. It is a social, political, and philosophical satire; more precisely, it is an allegory of bourgeois modernization in late nineteenth-century Brazil. Superficially, it is a typical novel of the period, dealing with the topics of love, family, social life, and politics with all the usual plot lines. Its method of composition, however, displaces the clichés that appear in fictional narratives, a displacement that implies a critique of literature, of mimetic Naturalism, of the novels then in fashion. And, as allegory, it is a terrifying compendium of the asynchronisms inherent in nineteenth-century Brazilian efforts to adopt modern European mores and mechanisms.

Quincas Borba, like life itself, "is made up strictly of four or five situations, which circumstances vary and multiply in people's eyes" (Chapter CLXXXVII). The plot itself is simple; what matters is the nuancing of specific situations, of circumstances created by the "gulf . . . between the spirit and the heart" (Chapter II), by individual self-interest, by social competition, by politics and business. These circumstances create the so-called inner life, the alliance between love and money, the vicissitudes of power. Profit, the supreme value of "modern life," however disguised as friendship, love, progress, social solidarity, nonetheless exposes the emptiness of imported and supposedly universal values, the falsity of modernity, and the illusory nature of the new bourgeois ideal of private life.

Quincas Borba dramatizes the inadequacy of the historical novel, the naturalist novel, and the bildungsroman in the face of the loss of existential unity which is so obvious in the modern experience. Endorsing diversity, it proposes that compromise is the only way to deal with the loss of individual unity, the impossibility of mimesis, and the inviability of all organic systems, whether ethical, political, or artistic. This is the modern effect of the novel; going far beyond its portrait of the elites of the Brazilian Second Empire, it dramatizes the limitations of the human condition through the crisis of the novel itself as a genre.

Determined to remain an open, discontinuous and nonfinite narrative, this novel by Machado—like his other works—sets out to create an inventory of the forces set in action by imposed modernization, contrasting those forces with the still-active remnants of a previous world in which life was in harmony. Rubião's illness—in contrast to Palha's impassive single-mindedness, Sofia's wiles, and Camacho's guile—reveals the uncritical positivism of the modern era. In Rubião's condition, we cannot discern the boundaries between the real and the ideal, between sanity and madness, between appearance and true value, between stagnation and progress.

Machado pushes language, our "poor human tongue" (Chapter XXVIII), to its limits, intensifying and transforming both symbolic structures and the fixed discourse of social life, playing language like an instrument. He explores the outer boundaries of language; he explodes the use of language as a mere representation of reality. He thus displaces both plot elements and metaphors, emphasizing their articulation; by creating a gap between sign and significance, he produces a vacuum of meaning which must be filled in by the reader, who is thereby brought into the text as an active participant. Machado thus redefines realism through a new balance between content and expression; this redefinition is alien to the Naturalist tradition.

As the narrator addresses the reader with feigned benevolence and describes the harshness of this new, modern world—a specific reference, in the Brazilian context, to the rise of capitalism—the narrator suggests that nothing changes in the reality he describes but that, rather, the change lies in how that reality is portrayed, a change that affects the reader's perception. Sententiously enunciated maxims implying transcendent values are simultaneously displaced and devalued by the form in which they are enunciated. Irony and humor are precisely the tactics Machado uses to invert high moral principles, to emphasize the particular rather than the universal, to encourage the reader to laugh at the pomposity of dogmatic ideas and opinions.

Modernity is central to *Quincas Borba*. Through allegorical representation, the novel reveals the process which had created a "modern" reality; beneath the surface of that reality, nonetheless, the old Brazil—its economy based on large landholding, its society embracing the values of nineteenth-century liberalism—can still be seen in the structures of mutual obligation and compromise which have replaced patriarchal authority.[1] Brazil's rush to adopt the ideals of the Enlightenment, while producing the charm of an ornamental culture like that of Europe, nonetheless somehow magically ignored an ideology still based upon personal favor and upon slavery. An uncritical, Positivist belief in progress, which translated into a mercantilist view of the production of ideas, of patterns of behavior, and of emotions, disguised the fact that social inequality and the profit motive were the driving forces behind the new social order. None of this escapes Machado, however. In love, friendship, and family relationships, compromise in fact simply disguises domination, imposes equilibrium, and promotes social status and its privileges. Machado skewers the formal representation of egalitarianism, both in the actions of his characters and in the parody of Positivism and of Darwinian Evolutionism that is found in the theory of Humanitism—expounded by Quincas Borba and made flesh in Rubião's experiences.

Equally central to the text is Machado's narrative strategy. Here, the novelist's technical solution is unique in Brazilian literature, but is linked to other challenges to the bourgeoisie from Sterne to Flaubert. Machado's novel is crafted with intellectual rigor as an open text. His search for exactly the right word and his use of calculated effects go hand in hand with his exploration of ways to pare down his narrative and to muddle its form, mixing and subverting such standard styles and forms of representation as classical elegance, romantic sentimentality, and naturalistic description.[2] Irony, humor, the grotesque, parody, and allegory combine to distance the reader from content and form alike. Moreover, that reader is also required to participate in deciphering the narrative—not as a spectator-receiver and reader-consumer of romances, but as a producer. In this sense, the openness of Machado's narrative implies the sort of open-endedness typical of the twentieth-century novel.

Quincas Borba's double modernity, then, is fundamentally structural in nature. Machado's skeptical and ironic portrayal of an enlightened elite's integration into modernity—whether in business, in politics, in the press, or in fashion—represents the optimistic faith in progress of a bourgeoisie which nonetheless still enjoyed the privileges, status, and honors which proximity to the Imperial Court could provide. Machado violently reduces this to a personal level, using several characters as emblems of the appeal of modernization's promises and, simultaneously, of the imitative character of changes in Brazilian society and the anachronistic nature of that society's disorder. One of the central themes of the novel, therefore, is moral and political compromise as a means, in formal terms, of creating unity in the face of inequality. But this reductionism is also functional,[3] in that it is also manifest in the text's intertextuality and visible in the creative process of reading.

Rejecting both the pessimism of Naturalism and the sensibility of the Romantics, Machado articulates a very personal realism that resists easy interpretations based on psychological projection and identification with characters or on the establishment of pathologies and predetermined traits—elements typical of the novels of his time. Cleverly and with great irony, Machado exploits his contemporaries' taste for intrigue and cultural ornamentation, turning that taste against the reader. He demands from the reader a different sort of reading, a reading of what is hidden in the narrative—a narrative in which his characters' lack of consistency is the objective correlative of his critique of verisimilitude.[4] Interrupting the narrative flow, reshuffling the chronology, and changing the focus of the text from one character to another, he makes it impossible for the reader simply to follow the plot: reading, as a result, is no longer an automatic process.

The double discourse of Machado's novel implies a negation of the legitimacy of systems and fixed values, of social territories and identities. Given that "the landscape depends upon the point of view" (Chapter XVIII), the narrative denies the universality of enlightened reason, a central value of the nascent urban and commercial bourgeoisie and one which was expressed in individualism, in the belief in progress typical of liberal political speeches about slavery and republicanism, and, above all, in the concept of bourgeois individualism.

Machado forces us into uncharted territory, but he does not merely use the falsity of his characters as a device to demonstrate the duplicity of intention and action, of consciousness and imagination, of class divisions and formal egalitarianism. Nor does he directly criticize power (in this, moreover, he is ambiguous, since he never offers any support for Republicanism or any criticism of the monarchy). His aim, rather, is a critique of all representations of reality in which systems, ideas, and emotions become dependent upon power and wealth. His strategy is modern; it is indirect. He uses technique to point out the inconsistencies of society and of art, forcing the reader down a slippery path that leads from the transcendent level of the symbol (which allows the sublimation of tension) towards a perception of the symptoms which indicate disorder. Machado's use of diverse perspectives provides evidence of his efforts to reconstitute ideas which modern science—Positivism and Darwinism—and liberal ideology had declared obsolete, but which he viewed, in essentially conservative terms, as fundamental to the reconstruction of identity.

Making the fulcrum of his narrative the contrast between Rubião's loss of personal unity and the effective reunification of Palha and Sofia, Machado sets up an outline of modernization which exemplifies the negative consequences of his characters' rationalizations. There are legitimizing motives and hidden interests in both the Palhas' calculations and Rubião's confusion. The couple's lack of scruples and Rubião's regrets both presuppose, albeit with very different expectations, the common basis of enlightened reason—individualism. There is method in his madness, insists the narrator, commenting on Rubião's dream linking Sofia to the Empress Eugénie (Chapter CIX). There is logic in Rubião's delusions and delirium, but reason succumbs in the face of the destruction of its categories: harmony, perfection, beauty, plenitude. His delirium and madness are counterweights to the imbalance between mind and heart, between nature and society, between consciousness and imagination. In Palha and Sofia, on the other hand, the equilibrium of life is restored, in moments of weakness, by pretense; their conflicts are sublimated in their mutual desire to get ahead in society. Antithesis merely serves to convey different attitudes toward a single fact; it dramatizes the coexistence, within modernity, of the eternal and the conditional. And the narrative itself is that drama—a stage filled with ruins.

Thus a representational narrative designed for the reader of fashionable novels and a nonrepresentational narrative designed for an ideal reader are not mutually exclusive; both readers exist and coexist. These are the dimensions of Machado's novels beginning with *The Posthumous Memoirs of Brás Cubas.* That which cannot be represented is the true subject of *Quincas Borba*; it is the presence and presentation of a "reality" that is still under construction. Machado depicts a landscape which is at once determinate and indeterminate, depending upon the point of view from which that landscape is viewed. The narrowly focused eye of the reader of fashionable novels, a participant in the contemporary historical situation of nineteenth-century Brazil, views the events in the novel as a tableau of inequalities which form part of the melancholy spectacle of human existence. The cynical eye of the ideal reader, skeptical and perverse, sees what is happening from another angle entirely, forming associations among the signs that pass, however disguised, before it. The narrator indicates that certain states of being cannot be represented; those states make alternative interpretations possible and can only be described with an "I know not what," a "How can I say?"— expressions that do not refer to something presumably ineffable and sublime, nor to the limitations of language; they refer, rather, to the insufficiency of any point of view which seeks universality. For Machado, the "necessary variety" that creates the "balance of life" and explains the "nature of human actions" excludes the total representation of experience.

Through the allusive brilliance of his images Machado nonetheless creates for the reader a fictional totality that is constantly variable and deceptive. As a representation of reality, an allegory of power, the book is structured by reason; at the same time, it catalogues and critiques precisely the sort of rational, moral, and artistic categories that are distilled into propositions such as: "The best way to appreciate a whip is to have its handle in your hand," or "To the victor, the potatoes" (Chapter XVIII). These categories are encoded as "symmetry and regularity" in terms of the "spiritual unity" of the individual and of the formal unity of the narrative.

The action of *Quincas Borba* takes place from 1867 to 1871, a period marked by the institutional crisis of the Second Empire, by overwhelming enthusiasm for the idea of progress, and by the rise and fall of ministries and the regular rotation, in power, of Liberals and Conservatives (though the difference between these groups was far from clear). During the debates about abolition, about the Paraguayan War (1864–1870), and about republicanism, there was a search for political unity through the compromise of party interests; in this process, conflicts over issues were dampened by the personal and imperial prestige of Pedro II. The modernization that was under way was conservative in nature; the rural upper classes had weakened, and new leadership had emerged among the increasingly powerful commercial bourgeoisie, but in ideological terms the goals of these two groups were not in conflict. Power was primarily based on personal prestige, a prestige reinforced by the distribution of favors, rather than on accomplishment. Despite a series of crises that were the result of the power struggle between the provinces of the north and south, of the discontent of the armed forces, of spats between Church and State, of the shift in the focus of economic power from Northeastern sugar to the coffee plantations in the Paraíba Valley, institutional changes were reformist rather than revolutionary. The law ending the importation of slaves (1850) and the Law of the Free Womb (1871) met resistance in rural areas, already facing economic difficulties; one result was the start of efforts to replace slave labor with that of immigrants.

The situation was complex. Modernization, propelled by currents of liberal ideas and policies from Europe and North America, brought about changes in the country's physiognomy—there were railroads, and capital that had been tied up in the slave trade was now free to be invested in speculation and in business—but it did not fundamentally alter power relationships. The ideology of personal favor, the privileges of proximity to the Court, and social inequality were still very much in evidence. Nonetheless, something was happening, and abolition and the Proclamation of the Republic were just over the horizon. Two power centers were clearly visible: the army, strengthened by the Paraguayan War, and the press, the focus of liberal ideas.

Playing with duality and incompleteness, Machado sketches the landscape of morality and history in terms of power relationships, picturing a world that is dissolving just as another is being formed. It is a landscape of ruins. As Freitas says of himself, although he wears a "smiling mask," he is melancholy—"an architect of ruins" (Chapter XXX). *Quincas Borba* depicts the difficulties inherent in a moment of crisis, a moment in which the still active ruins of the past coexist with the ruins of an as yet incomplete present characterized by Brazil's predatory modernization. The implacable process which leads to Rubião's destruction is a portrait of this convergence of a dying age and an age that is still being born. This is also what happens in the narrative. The narrative pace begins to accelerate as madness takes control of Rubião. The character's ruination is quickly accomplished with sudden cuts from one scene to the next, creating the allegory of the potatoes that Rubião's downward trajectory is designed to demonstrate.

Machado scatters representations of all of this throughout his text, capturing the interplay of ambition, vanity, self-interest, and, no less, the horrors of slavery, the pettiness of political solutions, and the abstract rationalizations that validated those solutions. The congruence between what happened within the family and in public salons, in political conversations and business deals, derived from a general inability to distinguish between appearance and ideals. Individuals moved from one sphere to the other without any trace of conflict; conflicts that did occur were simply repressed or were accepted implicitly. In either case, conflict was relegated to the small tyrannies of private life.

Thus the tableau Machado paints denies any positive effects of enlightened reason, which should have found expression in the separate spheres of religion, of science, of morality, and of art, but which, in Brazil, failed to produce any truly modern break with the past. The elites constructed, through compromise, an image of happy tranquillity. Belief in science and enthusiasm for progress—both of which were supposed to lead to control over nature and to the creation of just institutions—are denounced by Machado as illusions. The elite's optimism is satirized because the concrete results of its actions belie its abstract ideals. Economic relationships based on slave labor make ludicrous the lovely ideas which serve to assuage the consciences of his self-deluding and social-climbing characters. In the tradition of the moralists, Machado reveals the outlines of a human nature that is monstrous, distilling a "poisoned" wisdom.[5]

In his construction of *Quincas Borba*, Machado makes the anachronism of Brazilian modernization concrete by juxtaposing its fragments. Characters and situations are articulated through antithesis, more specifically through duality. Meaning does not flow directly from the description of characters, landscapes, and situations. The reader is frequently warned not to expect, in this narrative, what the avid consumption of other novels has led him or her to expect: "the analysis of our man's mental operations" of the characters, since that would be "long and tedious" (Chapter CXIII). In Machado's pairings—Quincas Borba as philosopher and dog, Quincas Borba and Rubião, Rubião and Sofia/Palha, Rubião and Camacho, Carlos Maria and Sofia, Carlos Maria and Maria Benedita, etc.—the gaps left by the novelist's narrative leaps can only be filled in by the reader. The reader is not working to analyze characters and situations that are missing, but to find meaning in a constellation of scattered signs, like a hunter who has leapt back in time, like an investigating eye which, viewing everything anew, tries to put together fragments. The representation the reader confronts is one ordered not by reason, but by delirium, by madness, by the imagination.

If the narrator cuts short the episode or interrupts the book, it is because the reality he seeks to describe cannot be narrated—

or, at least, cannot be narrated using the techniques of the time. However, if the reader winds up confused and lost, it is because he or she did not read slowly and carefully. Even such a reading, however, will not lead to an understanding of "reality." At best, the reader will be able to stitch together "the tatters of reality." In this way, however, the reader may discover "a fourth cause, the true one, perhaps," which will explain the characters' motivations; that cause, however, is indeterminate, outside the order of causality: it is no more than chance (Chapters CVI-CVII).

This novel is written for those who "know how to read," for those who seek not verisimilitude but a mental shock, a liberation of the imagination, the surprise and laughter that derive from unconscious motivations. Machado toys with the expectations of readers who desire, out of habit, to follow plot lines; he leads those readers to presume that facts, feelings, and situations are linked together in ways that appear logical and probable but that are, in fact, the product of a sickly imagination, of a guilty conscience, of jealousy. In this sense, the book uses Rubião as symbolic of the misadventures of desire—the fire that occasionally burns, out of control, within him.

A writer of the implicit and the inverted, Machado symbolizes the lost unity of life through his dualities. The desire to reconstitute that unity consumes Rubião; his attempts to use action and reason to do so lead to disaster. Unable to understand what is happening within himself or—because he has never mastered the art of deceit—within others, Rubião becomes enmeshed in thoughts that are not "the product of his spirit or his legs but . . . caused by something else, which, like a spider, he couldn't tell if it was good or bad." Moreover, "what does a spider know about Mozart? Nothing. But it listens with pleasure to a sonata by the master. The cat, who has never read Kant, could still be a metaphysical animal . . . Rubião felt scattered. Transitory friends . . . gave life the feeling aspect of a journey to him, a trip where language changed with the cities, Spanish here, Turkish there" (Chapter LXXX).

The reference to the spider is not, obviously, accidental. It is an image of Rubião's entrapment, of his duality, of his confusion—foreshadowing the fragmentation that will follow. It is also a metaphor for the process through which the narrative is constructed, and a critique of reason. In the Greek myth, Arachne challenges Athena, the goddess of reason, to a weaving contest and, as punishment, in transformed into a spider. Arachne, here, is a metaphor for writing and, by extension, for all art. The apparently arbitrary association of the spider with Mozart and of the cat with Kant would seem to derive from the unconscious rather than the conscious, despite Machado's feigned rationalism. Mozart and Kant are emblems of regularity, in art and in philosophy. But Mozart also refers to leaps, to his capering musical phrases, and Kant to the inversion of classical metaphysics. These are interwoven signs that suggest the diversity and the power struggles that lie beneath the representation of harmony. But there remains the cat, a "metaphysical animal." The spider is in the myth; it is crafty, arrogant, and competitive. The cat is clever and wary, always watching but never understanding; its reactions are immediate and precise. If the spider, in its eternal weaving, is the image of remembrance, like that of Rubião, then the cat is a metaphor for displacement and adaptation, abilities Rubião lacks. And remembrance clearly presupposes rumination on a presumptive original sin, a sin always ready to be reborn in remorse and in guilt. But the cat has no origin; it exists solely in the extended present of events.

Thus Machado speaks to the reader, saying: do not seek the truth in my plot; it is hard enough to "mend the tatters of reality"; nor should you seek an easy ending to the spectacle of humanity, since the only finality is that of nature. The most to which one can aspire, given that the soul is a "patchwork quilt," is "for the colors not to contradict each other—when they are unable to follow symmetry and regularity." Rubião represents the impossibility of even this precarious agreement. Palha, on the other hand, "had a mixed-up look at first sight, but with close attention, as opposite as the tones might be, the man's moral unity could be found there" (Chapter LV). If the unity to which Rubião aspires is transcendent, Palha's unity is transcendental, the unity inherent in the profit motive.

Machado's novel is already a fully modern text in which the characters are not constructed as symbols of a totality; his theme is the fragmented, dispersed individual in all of his loneliness. The novel deals with a structural change in human experience, with individuals whose lives are ruled by chance rather than by eternal verities. The text is no longer a narrative of man's spiritual adventure in the world; rather, it represents the ridiculous consequences of man's loss of unity, which makes him a stranger to himself. The fragmentation of the individual is replicated in the fragmentation of the narrative, in the use of techniques of deceptive distancing. One of Machado's tactics here is the displacement of the reader—the "serious" and "frivolous" reader alike—through the dissolution of our expectations of totality. Allegorical in structure, *Quincas Borba* sets up the "four or five situations" in the very first chapters; the novel catches Rubião in his delusions of greatness and in his disunity ("what a gulf there is between the spirit and the heart!"); in the flashback, the text introduces the theory of Humanitism which the novel objectifies; it sketches Rubião's personality—weak, without opinions, easily wounded—and contrasts that weakness with Sofia's guile and Palha's calculation. Finally, the novel sets up the historical background upon which his narrative strategies will function.

If Machado addresses the reader constantly, as frequently happens in *Quincas Borba*, it is because the reader seeks, by reading novels, to in some way repair his or her loss of moral unity—a loss visible in the increasingly powerful presence of the newspaper. Machado not only used the periodical press to transmit his writings to readers; his novels are also contaminated by journalism. He explores the form of the news item in order to satirize readers of serialized novels in newspapers, using the press as symbolic of the "corruption" of traditional narrative.[6] Look, for example, at the news item which informs Rubião of the philosopher's death:

"Mr. Joaquim Borba dos Santos has died after enduring his illness philosophically. He was a man of great learning and he wore himself out doing battle against that yellow, withered pessimism that will yet reach us here one day. It is the *mal du siècle*.

His last words were that pain was an illusion and that Pangloss was not as dotty as Voltaire indicated . . . He was already delirious. He leaves many possessions. His will is in Barbacena. (Chapter XI)

Machado mixes references to banal death notices with references which have come, through constant reuse, to identify grand moral principles and cultural values. He alludes to the explanation of the philosophy of Humanitism in *The Posthumous Memoirs of Brás Cubas*, especially in chapter CXVII, quoting but deforming the final phrase of that allusion ("Pangloss was not as dotty as Voltaire indicated"). Machado parodies the moralizing tone of reactionary Brazilian conservatism ("that yellow, withered pessimism that will yet reach us here one day"), that Quincas Borba "wore himself out doing battle against"; it is one of the consequences of modernization that the social "crisis" is defined in terms of traditional ethics. He validates the figure of Quincas Borba by inserting him in the tradition of impassivity and of the consolations of philosophy. A man of great knowledge, Quincas Borba was nonetheless "already delirious" and, finally, left "many possessions." Madness deconstructs the philosophy and the values attributed to Quincas Borba, while the statement about the size of his estate restores his social position.

The emphatic tone of the item parodies newspaper death notices but also Humanitism—which is itself, it should be remembered, a parody of Positivism. As is well known, Pangloss, a character in *Candide*, postulates an unshakable optimism. The quote of the principle that "pain was an illusion" in turn stands in contrast to Machado's statement that "various forms of illness" exist.

Quincas Borba, then, as a demonstration of the allegory of the potatoes, is also a critique of Brazilian Positivism. The latter, an amalgam of fashionable ideas—from Comte, from Spencer, from Darwin, from naturalist rationalism, from monism and skepticism—is a "philosophy" only in the sense of an accumulation of doctrines.[7] Humanitas is the principle of life, existing everywhere: "All things have a certain hidden and identical substance in them, a principle that's singular, universal, eternal, common, indivisible and indestructible, . . ." The equilibrium of life is guaranteed by the "necessary variety" of events, of individual, social and natural phenomena. Evil does not exist, pain is an illusion, and "man only commemorates and loves what he finds pleasant and advantageous." Thus, competition and war are fundamental to the preservation of the species: "To the conquered, hate or compassion; to the victor, the potatoes" (Chapter VI). And individuals are no more than "transitory bubbles."

The author brings the book to a close, but the narrative does not end like a romance. Machado leads Rubião, sick and in rags, back to Barbacena; he gives him the dog as companion, recreating the philosopher's situation. Delirious, Rubião understands the allegory of the potatoes—at least, he gets from it "a vague feeling of struggle and victory" (Chapter CXCV). Thus the philosophy of Humanitism is objectified in the character's fate, sending the reader back to the beginning of the text. The last chapter, in which the dog's death is recounted, opens with the question of the book's title, "a question pregnant with questions that would take us far"—a question and questions related to the validity of fiction and the novel's ability to represent reality. More precisely, by confusing the reader about the book's title, a title which refers to allegorical characters in the text rather than to events in the narrative, Machado throws doubt on the forms of narration as they were structured in his time—as efforts to distinguish between human laughter and tears to describe and decipher the human condition though the epic construct of experience. Machado here indicates the crisis of narrative, the crisis of the novel as a genre characterized by ideas of unity and totality. *Quincas Borba*, on the contrary, only pretends to be a novel. Remember the warning to the reader at the beginning of *The Posthumous Memoirs of Brás Cubas*: "I might add that serious people will find some semblance of a normal novel, while frivolous people won't find their usual one here. There it stands, deprived of the esteem of the serious and the love of the frivolous, the two main pillars of opinion."[8]

Machado delineates ambition, vanity, and passion as "the different forms of a single disease." The effect of his moralizing—

"unreasonable, timeless, unexpected, untimely"—gives concrete form to "the truth of his age," esthetically internalized.[9] In contrast, Rubião's ineptitude in this society based upon pretense makes him a stereotypical symbol, a grotesque monument to imitative modernization. In Rubião, purely conspicuous consumption of all that is fashionable coexists with the morality of a sensitive conscience, brimming with regret and desires to make amends. If the other emblematic characters, Palha, Sofia, and Camacho, are stereotypical, historically based representations of indifference, Rubião is a figure out of time and out of place. On the one hand, indifference or pleasure; on the other, pain—but all indicate the illusory nature of modernity. Within the narrative, everything depends on the fickleness of desire—and on the self-interest and the willfulness that creates desire. Beyond lies the fickleness of the stars, of the moon, of the Southern Cross, all of which, impassive, neither laugh nor cry at the spectacle of human life—skepticism.

—*Celso Favaretto*
Translated by David T. Haberly

NOTES

1. See John Gledson, *Machado de Assis: Impostura e Realismo* (São Paulo: Companhia das Letras, 1991), p. 102.

2. See "Machado de Assis: Um debate. Conversa com Roberto Schwarz," *Novos Estudos CEBRAP* (São Paulo), 29 (March 1991), 68–69. (This is a discussion of Schwarz's *Um Mestre na Periferia do Capitalismo: Machado de Assis* [São Paulo: Duas Cidades, 1990]).

3. *Ibid.*, pp. 67, 71.

4. See John Gledson, *Machado de Assis: Ficção e História* (Rio de Janeiro: Paz e Terra, 1986), p. 113.

5. "Conversa com Roberto Schwarz," p. 66.

6. Kátia Muricy, "Machado de Assis, um Intempestivo?," *Gávea* (Rio de Janeiro), 10 (March 1993), 13–15.

7. "Conversa com Roberto Schwarz," p. 66.

8. Joaquim Maria Machado de Assis, *The Posthumous Memoirs of*

Brás Cubas, trans. Gregory Rabassa (New York and Oxford: Oxford University Press, 1997), p. 5.

9. See Kátia Muricy, *A Razão Cética: Machado de Assis e as Questões de seu Tempo* (São Paulo: Companhia das Letras, 1988), p. 35; and Paulo Eduardo Arantes, "O Positivismo no Brasil," *Novos Estudos CEBRAP* (São Paulo), 21 (July 1988), 186.